Most Wanted

· · · · · · · · · · ·

LISA SCOTTOLINE

 ST. MARTIN'S GRIFFIN ☒ NEW YORK

MOST WANTED. Copyright © 2016 by Smart Blonde, LLC. All rights reserved. Printed in the United States of America. For information, address St. Martin's Press, 175 Fifth Avenue, New York, N.Y. 10010.

www.stmartins.com

Excerpt from *One Perfect Lie* copyright © 2017 by Smart Blonde, LLC.

The Library of Congress has cataloged the hardcover edition as follows:

Names: Scottoline, Lisa, author.
Title: Most wanted / Lisa Scottoline.
Description: First edition. | New York : St. Martin's Press, 2016.
Identifiers: LCCN 2015045858 | ISBN 9781250010131 (hardcover) | ISBN
    9781250088123 (e-book)
Subjects: LCSH: Pregnant women—Fiction. | Murder—Investigation—Fiction. |
    BISAC: FICTION / Thrillers. | FICTION / Suspense. | GSAFD: Suspense
    fiction. | Mystery fiction.
Classification: LCC PS3569.C725 M65 2016 | DDC 813/.54—dc23
LC record available at http://lccn.loc.gov/2015045858

ISBN 978-1-250-01014-8 (trade paperback)

Our books may be purchased in bulk for promotional, educational, or business use. Please contact your local bookseller or the Macmillan Corporate and Premium Sales Department at 1-800-221-7945, extension 5442, or by e-mail at MacmillanSpecial Markets@macmillan.com.

First St. Martin's Griffin Edition: February 2017

10 9 8 7 6 5 4 3 2

Praise for *Most Wanted*

"My favorite of Scottoline's novels so far, this twisting tale should be 'Most Wanted' on your to-read list."   —Elin Hilderbrand

"In novel after novel, Lisa Scottoline has proven herself a master of stories that combine familial love—especially that of mothers for their children—with nail-biting stories of spirited every-women bent on finding the truth. Her new novel, *Most Wanted,* demonstrates again her skill with this kind of domestic suspense tale."   —*The Washington Post*

"Scottoline's most inventive plot to date . . . *Most Wanted* is Scottoline at her best, once again. You will want to read this novel not only for its plot, but for its warmth and humane appeal. She deals with some serious subject matter but makes it easy to read and impossible not to like."   —*The Huffington Post*

"This is a potboiler of a book, crammed full of agonizing choices confronting appealing, relatable characters. Scottoline has penned more hardboiled tales, but never one as heartfelt and emotionally raw, raising her craft to the level of Judith Guest and Alice Hoffman. *Most Wanted* is a great thriller and a gut-wrenching foray into visceral angst that is not to be missed."   —*The Providence Journal*

"A suburban crime tale told with Scottoline's penchant for humor and soul-baring characterization."   —*Booklist*

"A page-turner that will satisfy."   —*Library Journal*

"A Connecticut teacher's long-sought and hard-fought pregnancy turns into a nightmare when Scottoline unleashes one of her irresistible hooks on her."   —*Kirkus Reviews*

"A page-turner filled with unpredictable twists . . . A must-read book for anyone looking for a thrilling ride from a master storyteller!"   —*RT Book Reviews* (4 ½ stars)

Also by Lisa Scottoline

For my amazing daughter, Francesca

The cradle rocks above an abyss . . .
—Vladimir Nabokov, *Speak, Memory*

Chapter One

Christine Nilsson walked to the closed door with anticipation. She knew everyone was waiting for her inside the teachers' lounge, ready to surprise her. She'd guessed what they were up to, leaving their classrooms after the dismissal bell, then her principal summoning her for a "quick meeting," even though there was no such thing at Nutmeg Hill Elementary. It was sweet of them to throw her a good-bye party, especially on the last week of school when everybody was crazy busy. She felt grateful and loved all of her fellow teachers, except Melissa Rue, Resident Blabbermouth.

Christine reached the lounge door and plastered on a smile, then stopped herself before she turned the knob. She could manufacture enthusiasm like a professionally cheery machine, but that wouldn't do. Her friends knew the difference between Teacher Enthusiasm and Real Enthusiasm, and she didn't want to fake anything. She was going to truly enjoy every minute of her party, which was the end of her teaching career, at least for now. She had finally gotten pregnant and she was going to stay home with the baby, embracing her New Mom status like an immigrant to the United States of Parenthood.

The notion flooded her with a hormonal wave of happiness,

plus residual Clomid. Pregnancy may have been a breeze for other couples, but it had been a three-year struggle for Christine and her husband Marcus. Thank God it was over, and she was looking forward to painting a nursery, buying a crib, and fetishizing motherhood in general. She'd read the baby books and visualized her baby at its current stage, two months old and curled like the most adorable shrimp ever. She couldn't even wait for her baby bump, so she could wear ugly maternity clothes. A smile spread naturally across her face, and she knew it would remain in place throughout the party, if not forever. She opened the lounge door.

"Surprise!" everybody shouted, a gaggle of female teachers with end-of-the-day grins, their makeup worn off and their hair slipping from ponytail holders. There were only two men, Jim Paulsen, who was rail-thin and taught gym, so he was obviously called Slim Gym, and bearded Al Miroz, who taught sixth-grade math and was the faculty trivia expert, whom they called Trivi-Al. Bowls of pretzels and potato chips sat atop the counter next to paper plates, Solo cups, and liter-size jugs of Diet Coke. The damp aroma of brewing coffee permeated the air, and the bulletin board held notices from the district, under a sign: **The best way for students not to act like the school year is over is for teachers not to act like the school year is over.** Under that, someone had written, **GET OVER YOURSELF!**

Everyone hugged Christine, filling the small windowless lounge, which had a few fake-wood tables and chairs, a donated coffeemaker, an old microwave, and a brand-new TV playing cable news on mute. They'd won the TV as a consolation prize in a contest for Teachers' Lounge Makeover, but they'd deserved first place. Burn in hell, Dunstan Elementary.

"Thanks, everyone!" Christine said, overwhelmed by their kindness, and she felt how much she would miss them, after eight years at Nutmeg Hill. She was the reading specialist on the Instructional Support Team, helping students who had reading issues, and she'd grown closer to her friends on the faculty since her fertility drama. They all knew bits and pieces of her story and they'd been kind enough to ignore her premature hot flashes from Pergonal or to schedule meetings around her doctors' appointments. Christine was grateful to all of them except Melissa Rue, who'd caught her throwing up in the ladies' room and blabbed about her pregnancy. Everyone had assumed that one of Christine's fertility procedures had been successful, but only her best friend, Lauren Weingarten, knew the whole truth.

"Girl!" Lauren shouted, her big arms outstretched, in a loose white blouse and black cropped pants, enveloping Christine in an embrace that smelled of fruit-scented Sharpies. Lauren was the Academic Coach at school, so she taught the faculty whichever new curriculum came down from Common Core, which they all called Common Enemy. Lauren's oversized personality made her the most popular member of the faculty: their Pinterest Queen, Ed-camp Organizer, and Head Energizer Bunny. This, even though Magic Marker covered her arms like defensive wounds.

"Thanks so much, honey," Christine said, touched, when Lauren finally let her go.

"Were you really surprised?" Lauren's dark eyes narrowed, a skeptical brown. She barely had crow's-feet, but she had beginner laugh lines because she loved to joke around. Her dark brown hair was pulled back, trailing in loose curls down her back.

"Totally," Christine answered, smiling.

"Yeah, right." Lauren snorted, her full lips curving into a grin, and just then there was a knock on the door.

"What's that?" Christine asked, turning.

"Aha! Now you *will* be surprised!" Lauren crossed the room and opened the door with a flourish. "Ta-da!"

"Hey, everybody!" Christine's husband Marcus entered to applause and laughter, ducking slightly as he came through the doorway, more by habit than necessity. Marcus was six-foot-two and 215 pounds, built like the college pitcher he had once been.

4 | LISA SCOTTOLINE

He must have come straight from the airport because he still had on his lightweight gray suit, though his tie was loosened.

"Babe!" Christine burst into startled laughter.

"Surprise!" Marcus gave Christine a big hug, wrapping his long arms around her, and Christine buried herself against his wilted oxford shirt, its light starch long gone.

"I thought you were in Raleigh."

"It was all a ruse." Marcus let her go, meeting her eye in a meaningful way. "Your boss gets the credit. I just do what I'm told."

"Well, thanks." Christine smiled back at him, reading between the lines, that the party was the principal's idea and he had gone along with it. She turned to Pam, who was coming forward holding a flat box.

"We'll miss you, Christine, but a baby is the only acceptable reason to leave us." Pam beamed as she set the box down on the table. "I brought this from a bakery near me. No grocery-store sheet cake for *this* occasion."

"Aw, how nice." Christine went over to the table, with Marcus following, and everybody gathered around. She lifted the lid, and inside was a vanilla frosted cake that read in purple script, *Goodbye and Good luck, Christine!* Underneath was a drawing of an old-school stork in a hat, carrying a baby in a diaper.

"This is too cute!" Christine laughed, though she felt Marcus stiffen beside her. She knew this couldn't have been easy for him, but he was putting on a brave face.

Pam looked over at Christine and Marcus. "The stork is okay, right? I know this isn't your baby shower, but I couldn't resist."

"Of course it's okay," Christine answered for them both.

Pam smiled, relieved. "Great!" She looked up at Marcus. "Marcus, so, do you want a boy or a girl?"

"I want a golfer," Marcus shot back, and everybody laughed.

Lauren handed over the cake knife. "Christine, will you do the honors?"

"Grab your plates, kids!" Christine eyeballed the cake, then started cutting pieces.

"Isn't somebody going to make a toast?" Melissa called out from the back of the crowd. "Marcus, how about you?"

"Sure, right, of course. Yes, I'll propose the toast." Marcus flashed a broad smile, his blue eyes shining, but Christine knew what he was really thinking.

"Go for it, honey!" she said, to encourage him. "They hear enough from me."

Lauren snorted. "Ain't *that* the truth."

Everybody chuckled, holding their plates and looking at Marcus expectantly. They didn't know him as well as the other husbands because he traveled so much, and Christine could tell they were curious about him from the interest in their expressions. Lauren used to joke that Christine had the Faculty Alpha Husband, since Marcus was an architectural engineer who owned his own firm in Hartford and probably made a better living than many of the faculty spouses, most of whom were also educators. The running joke was that it took two teachers' salaries to make one living wage. But Lauren had stopped making her alpha-husband joke when it turned out that Marcus was completely infertile.

He'd been devastated by the diagnosis of azoospermia, which meant, literally, that he produced no sperm. It had come as a shock after they had been trying for a year and couldn't get pregnant, so Christine's OB-GYN referred her to Dr. Davidow, an RE, or reproductive endocrinologist. Christine had automatically assumed that she was the problem, since she was thirty-three years old and her periods had never been super regular, but tests revealed that she was perfectly healthy. Dr. Davidow had broken the news to them, choosing his words carefully, cautioning that male infertility was "a couple's joint problem" and neither husband nor wife was "to blame."

Marcus had taken the diagnosis as a blow to his ego, as well as his manhood, and it was a revelation for them both that a handsome, masculine college All-American could be completely infertile. Marcus attacked the problem with characteristic goal-mindedness; he ate enough kale to start a farm, since vitamin A was supposed to raise sperm counts, and he avoided tighty whiteys, bicycling, and hot tubs, the last not proving a problem since he thought they were disgusting. As a last resort, he even underwent the TESA procedure he'd dreaded, whereby Dr. Davidow had operated on his testicles in an attempt to find viable sperm, but it didn't succeed.

I'm really shooting blanks? Marcus had said when it was all over, still in stunned disbelief.

They'd entered therapy with Michelle LeGrange, a psychologist employed by their fertility clinic Families First, and she had taught them that the key word was "acceptance." Christine and Marcus had come to accept that they had a choice, either to adopt or to use a sperm donor. Christine would've gone with adoption so that Marcus wouldn't have felt left out, which Michelle told them was common among infertile men, who didn't make a "genetic contribution." But Marcus knew that Christine wanted the experience of being pregnant, and he'd said in one session that he wanted a child to be "at least half-ours." Michelle had suggested that wasn't the best way to think about the decision, but there it was. After more therapy and tears, one night, they'd been sitting at the kitchen island, having take-out Chinese for dinner.

Marcus looked over, chopsticks poised. *I made a decision. I think we should go with a donor.*

You sure? Christine hid her emotions. It was what she wanted, too, but she didn't want to pressure him.

Yes. We tried everything else. Marcus set down his chopsticks, moved his plate aside, and pulled his laptop toward him. *Let's find this kid a father.*

Not a father, a donor.

Whatever. Let's do it. Let's make a baby.

So they'd gone on the websites of sperm banks, which had the profiles of their donors online, so you could search the physical characteristics of each donor before you chose, and in the beginning, Christine and Marcus felt uncomfortably like they were on Zappo's, shopping for people. They wanted a donor who matched their blood type and phenotype, their *physical traits*, so the child would look like them. Marcus was an ash blonde with a squarish face, heavy cheekbones, and a strong jawline, and his parents were of Swedish ancestry. Christine was petite, five-three, with an oval face, fine cheekbones, a small, upturned nose, and long, straight, brown hair; her father was Irish-American and her mother Italian-American. Christine and Marcus both had blue eyes, his rounder in shape and hers more squinty but wide-set, and they both had decent teeth, never having worn braces.

Christine got used to the idea of shopping for a donor online, admittedly sooner than Marcus did, and she became obsessed with checking the bank websites, like Facebook for the infertile. She could "Like" and "Favorite" donors, and the banks refreshed their pages throughout the day—**New Donors Daily!**—although the tall blond donors were often **Sorry, Temporarily Unavailable! Try Again Soon!** Finally, Christine narrowed it down to three choices, the way she had when they'd bought their first house.

Donor 3319, Marcus had said, which was Christine's first choice as well. Donor 3319 was on the Homestead Bank and had kept his name and identity anonymous, but he had nevertheless, like many of the donors, provided two photos of himself, one as a child and one as an adult. Donor 3319 had round blue eyes like Marcus's, lemony-blond hair a shade darker than Marcus's but more like her highlights, and a medium build, like a combination of them both. He reportedly had an outgoing and friendly personality, plus he had been accepted to medical school, which had been the clincher for Marcus. What had made the decision for Christine was that she'd loved the expression in his eyes, an intelligent and engaged aspect that showed interest in the world around him.

So they had phoned Dr. Davidow, who ordered Donor 3319's sample, and when Christine was ovulating, she returned to Families First, where Dr. Davidow performed IUI, or intrauterine insemination, injecting the pipette of sperm inside her while she held hands with the nurse. Unfortunately, Marcus had been called back to a job site in Raleigh the night before and so was out of town when their child was conceived, but that was form over substance. He was back for the home pregnancy test, which they weren't supposed to take but did anyway, its happy result confirmed later by the doctor. And in the end, Christine had gotten pregnant and Marcus was going to be a father, a fact he was still trying to wrap his mind around as he stood before the teachers in the lounge, about to make a toast.

"Everybody, let's raise a glass, or a paper cup, or what have you." Marcus grabbed a Solo cup of Diet Coke from the counter and hoisted it high. "To all of you, for being such good friends to my wonderful wife. Nutmeg Hill is a great school, and she will miss all of you, I know."

"Aw," Christine said, feeling a rush of love for him.

"Hear, hear," Pam said, nodding.

Marcus turned to Christine, smiled at her with love, and raised his cup to her. "And to my amazing wife, whom I love more than life, and who truly deserves the happiness and joy to come."

"Thank you, honey." Christine felt her throat catch at the glistening that came suddenly to his blue eyes, and she put her arms around him while he set the cup down and hugged her back, emitting a tiny groan that only she heard.

"Love you, babe."

"I love you, too."

"Get a room!" Lauren called out, and everybody chuckled. The party swung into gear, and Christine circulated with Marcus, introducing him to those who hadn't met him and saying good-bye to all of her colleagues, whom she would miss. They exchanged teary hugs, and the party wound down until only a handful of people were left: Christine, Marcus, Lauren, Pam, and Trivi-Al, who turned on the TV while they cleaned up.

Suddenly Trivi-Al gestured to the TV screen. "Oh look, they caught that serial killer."

"What serial killer?" Christine asked idly, gathering her good-bye gifts.

"That serial killer they've been looking for, they caught him in Pennsylvania." Trivi-Al pressed the button on the television to raise the volume, and the voiceover said, "Zachary Jeffcoat, here being transferred, remains in custody outside of Philadelphia for the stabbing murder of nurse Gail Robinbrecht of West Chester, which took place on June 15. The FBI and Pennsylvania, Maryland, and Virginia authorities also link him to the murders of two other nurses . . ."

"Al, really?" Lauren said, annoyed, as she picked up dirty cake plates. "Don't be so weird."

The voiceover continued, "The first alleged murder took place January 12, of Lynn McLeane, a nurse at Newport News Hospital in Virginia, and the second alleged murder was of Susan Allen-Bogen, a nurse at Bethesda General Hospital in Maryland and took place on April 13—"

"Al, please turn it off," Pam chimed in.

Trivi-Al ignored them, glued to the TV. "Oh this guy's a freak, let me tell you. They call him the Nurse Murderer. I've been following this guy."

Christine finished her task and glanced at the TV, then did a double-take at the screen. It showed a young blond man in a rumpled jacket, his hands handcuffed behind his back as he was escorted to a police cruiser. A cop put a hand on the man's head to press him into the backseat, then the man glanced up with round blue eyes.

Christine felt her heart stop.
She recognized those eyes.
She would know that face anywhere.
The serial killer was their donor, Donor 3319.

Chapter Two

"Did you see that?" Christine asked, almost breathless, as soon as they left through the exit doors, alone outside the building. All she had been able to think about during the cleanup was Donor 3319, inwardly freaking out while everybody gathered the presents, and then finally turned out the lights.

"See what?" Marcus asked, squinting to read his smartphone in the bright sun, as they headed down the walkway to the parking lot. He'd slowed his usual lengthy stride to account for her since she had shorter legs.

"On TV, the prisoner, the serial killer?" Christine glanced over her shoulder, to check if anyone was within earshot, but nobody was around. The scene was calm and idyllic, in contrast with the tumult inside her. Nutmeg Hill Elementary was in a rural pocket of Glastonbury, Connecticut, and though it was a Title I school, meaning it had an underprivileged segment, the building was relatively new, two stories of yellow limestone with modern windows, surrounded by acres of open pasture and cornfields.

"No, I didn't see him." Marcus pulled his car keys from his pants pocket. "You drove in with Lauren, right? My car is right over here. We can load the presents into my car."

"Okay, but Marcus, the serial killer—" Christine couldn't finish her sentence, suddenly feeling that to say it aloud would make it real, and Marcus was barely listening anyway, scrolling through his email. They passed the playground with its new red, yellow, and cobalt plastic chutes and weather-treated timber, set on a square of perfect mulch. In front was an asphalt play area with bright yellow lines for the walking track and foursquare games.

"That was a nice party," Marcus said idly, still checking his email.

"Right, yes, they really went over the top," Christine heard herself saying. She couldn't stop thinking about their donor and the serial killer. She couldn't believe that something could go so horribly awry. Her heart fluttered like a panicked bird in her chest. She telescoped away from the playground with its newly planted trees, their slender trunks protected by white plastic sleeves. She wished she had a plastic sleeve of her own, one that would encircle her body, protecting her and the baby from harm, from threat, from everything, forever and ever.

"Babe, are you okay?" Marcus asked, pocketing his phone. They crossed to the visitor parking lot and reached his black Audi sedan.

"I'm fine," Christine forced herself to answer.

"But your face is red." Marcus opened the car door for her. "Is it the heat? Are you gonna faint?"

"No, I'm okay."

"Get in, and I'll turn on the air-conditioning." Marcus gestured at the passenger seat.

"Okay, great." Christine let him guide her into the seat, then she put her quilted purse on her lap.

"Okay, hold on." Marcus closed her door, hustled around the front of the car, climbed in the driver's side, and started the engine, which blasted the air conditioner. He aimed the vents at her, which blew initially hot, but cooled surprisingly fast. "Better?"

"Yes, thanks." Christine felt the chilly blast as a relief on her cheeks, which were burning. It had to be her blood pressure. She felt as if she were bursting, as if the news had an explosive force of its own.

"What's up? Is it the heat?"

"No." Christine had to tell him. She couldn't keep it to herself. "Marcus, the serial killer on that TV report looked like our donor. He looks like Donor 3319."

"What?" Marcus blinked.

"Did you see him? I swear, I think I recognized him."

"What are you talking about?" Marcus frowned in confusion, but Christine was already reaching for her phone, tucked in the side pocket of her purse.

"He looks like our donor. Let me check that video—"

"Of course he's not our donor." Marcus snorted, then faced front, shrugging it off.

"But he looked a lot like him."

"Don't be silly." Marcus put the car in reverse, still shaking his head.

"I know what I saw. Did you see the video?"

"No, and what's up with Al? What kind of guy follows serial killers?" Marcus backed out of the space, then drove toward the side entrance of the school, where they had left the gifts and left-over cake, because teachers never wasted anything.

"Hold on." Christine tried to log onto the Internet, but couldn't. Cell reception was spotty around the school, which drove her crazy.

"What are you doing?" Marcus pulled up at the side entrance and parked.

"Going on CNN. They probably have the video on their website."

"You're not serious, are you?" Marcus looked at Christine like she was crazy or hormonal, which was an expression she'd seen on him in the past, not completely unjustified.

"I don't know, it was just weird."

"What was weird?" Marcus let the car idle, readjusting the lattice vent so that it blew on Christine.

"I just took a look at the TV, and it struck me all of a sudden—that's him. It was like I recognized him."

"You think that guy was our donor?" Marcus's lips parted in puzzlement. "He's just a guy on a news story."

"But he was blond and tall, and he had those eyes, his blue eyes—"

"A lot of guys look like that. My dad does. I do." Marcus opened the car door, and the hot air blew in. "Stay here. Try to relax. I'll load the trunk and drive you home. I don't want you driving like this. We'll get your car later."

"I can drive, I'm fine."

"No, sit tight." Marcus got out and shut the car door, and Christine returned her attention to her iPhone. She tried again to get online but there was no service. She knew she'd have better luck near the office, so she opened the door and got out of the car. She walked down the sidewalk until she saw a bar pop onto the top of her iPhone screen, then logged onto the Internet. She typed CNN into the search function and tapped through to the news of the day until she got to the third story, with the heading SUSPECTED SERIAL KILLER APPREHENDED.

"Christine, I thought you had left!" Pam emerged from the front doors with a surprised smile, carrying three tote bags.

"Marcus is just packing up. Thanks so much again." Christine tried to put on a happy face, but she was dying to look at the CNN video. She slipped the phone into her pocket as Marcus returned to the car with the bags and started loading the trunk, which caught Pam's attention.

"Oh, I could've given him a hand," Pam said, waving to Marcus, who shut the trunk.

"Thanks. He's got it, and you're carrying enough."

"When are we ever *not* carrying enough? Did you see my new

bag, by the way? My daughter gave it to me." Pam held out her largest tote bag, a floral Vera Bradley pattern, which was the real version of Christine's knockoff purse.

"Gorgeous. Teacher porn."

"Hey ladies!" Marcus called out, striding toward them, his hand in his pocket. "Pam, you sure know how to throw a party, thanks again."

"Happy to do it."

"Honey?" Marcus took Christine's arm and they walked as a threesome toward his car, which was in the same direction as the parking lot. They said good-bye to Pam again, and Marcus opened the door for Christine, then went to the driver's side of the car and got inside. "Why did you get out of the car?" he asked, putting the car in gear.

"To see the video."

"You're being silly." Marcus pulled out of the drive and headed for the exit.

"Maybe, probably. Let's just head home. In three blocks I'll be able to get better reception, on Glastonbury Road."

"Silly." Marcus reached on the console for the wraparound Maui Jims that he used for golf, and slipped them on his face. "Honey, he's not our donor."

"He could be. I mean, it's possible."

"No, it's not possible. It's out of the question. I can't even believe you're serious. They screen these donors."

"I'm sure they do some, but how much? And what?" Christine thought about it. She had never asked anyone the question about what kind of screening they did for donors. She remembered reading some boilerplate on the site and wished she had paid more attention.

"These are reputable banks. We were referred to them by Dr. Davidow. It's not like some fly-by-night operation."

"But still, it's not impossible. Someone committing a murder, or really any kind of crime, how do you screen for that?"

"Our donor must be a medical student by now. That guy they arrested wasn't a medical student."

"Maybe he was, we didn't hear the story." Christine thought that sounded improbable, even to herself, which made her feel a little better. They drove down the winding road toward the stone bridge. She checked her phone but there was still no reception. They'd be at Glastonbury Road in minutes. Sunlight dappled the asphalt from tall oaks lining the street, and the cornfield was a solid block of leafy green, fairly high for mid-June.

"Anyway, you only have one day left of school. Amazing, huh?"

"Yes, but I want to get this video up. Then I want you to look at it and see if I'm crazy."

"You're crazy." Marcus chuckled, his eyes hidden behind his sunglasses. He steered the car onto Shire Road, and Christine logged onto Safari, then navigated to the CNN site, tapping the heading of the news story on her iPhone screen, then enlarged it with her fingers to read it better.

"It says, 'Zachary Jeffcoat, a Pennsylvania man, was arrested today—'"

"See, already. It's not our guy. Our guy's from Nevada."

"Right, good, but let me read the story." Christine tried to focus in the jostling car. "'. . . was arrested today for the murder of Gail Robinbrecht, a thirty-one-year-old nurse from West Chester, PA. The murder is the third of three murders of nurses in Newport News, Virginia, and Bethesda, Maryland. Nurse Lynn McLeane, a pediatric nurse, was stabbed to death on January 12, and Susan Allen-Bogen, an operating-room nurse, was also stabbed to death using the same MO, on April 13—'"

Marcus clucked. "The guy kills nurses? What's the matter with people? Nurses are great."

"Right, but it's weird that Donor 3319 was a medical student and the victims were nurses."

"The guy they arrested isn't a medical student."

"Right, I know." Christine was confusing herself. Her face

still burned, despite the air-conditioning. She returned her attention to the iPhone screen. "It says, 'The murders gained national attention as the Nurse Murders.'"

"Does it say the killer is a medical student?"

"No, it doesn't." Christine skimmed the last two lines of the story. "'The police commissioner is gratified that the suspect is in custody and thanks federal and state law enforcement for their hard work.' Hmmm. It doesn't say any more about him, like where he went to school. Even his age."

"There. It's not him. If he was a medical student, it would say so. That's a relevant detail."

"True," Christine said, but her heart was still racing. She scrolled down to the end of the story and tapped a camera icon for the video. A freeze-frame showing the group of police officers came onto the screen, and she hit PLAY. The video showed the police walking and behind them, a thatch of blond hair bobbing up and down. She couldn't see the prisoner's face because the police blocked the view, and sunlight coming through the car window made it hard to see her screen. She hit PAUSE. "Can we pull over so I can see this?"

"Do we have to? We'll be home in twenty minutes." Marcus kept driving, his expression opaque behind the sport sunglasses.

"I don't want to wait. Just pull over, it'll take a minute. We can watch it together."

"Fine." Marcus peeled off the road onto a gravel service road that traveled uphill into the woods, ending in a tall mound of discarded logs and tree limbs, then he put the car in PARK and shifted over toward her in the seat. "Let me see what you're talking about."

"Thanks." Christine hit PLAY, and they both watched the video, which showed the police walking below the frame and then in the next instant, the tall blond prisoner walking with them, his hands behind his back.

"It doesn't look like him. Our guy's taller."

Christine pressed STOP. "You can't tell how tall he is from this."

"Yes, you can. Look at him in relation to the cops."

"But you don't know how tall the cops are."

"The cops look like they're just under six feet, which makes sense. They're not staties. Staties tend to be taller. Besides, you know I have eagle eyes."

Christine knew that was true. A lifetime of playing golf had made Marcus almost preternaturally skilled at guessing distances, and he had an engineer's sense of spatial relationships, which she lacked completely.

"Besides, he looks older than our donor. Our guy should be about twenty-five, I think. That guy looks over thirty."

"I can't tell how old the guy is from this picture. Anyway, a twenty-five-year-old doesn't look a lot different from a thirty-year-old." Christine squinted at the video image, which was still hard to see in the car.

"Yes they do. Our guy is young. A kid, a med student. This prisoner is not young."

"But we don't know when our donor entered med school. We only know that he was accepted." Christine gestured at the video. "Think about it. He's tired, not old. He's been on the run from the police."

"It doesn't say that."

"I'm assuming." Christine hit PLAY, and the video continued, the cops coming forward and the prisoner coming into view, from the waist up. He had on a rumpled navy Windbreaker and a white T-shirt underneath, but she couldn't see his face because his head was tilted down. His blond hair caught the sunlight at the crown, showing its darker caramel tones. Christine pressed PAUSE. "That looks like our donor's hair color, doesn't it?"

"I don't know, I don't remember."

"I do." Christine scrutinized the man's hair, thinking that she remembered his hair color, only because she always spent time noticing variations of blonde, so she could tell her colorist what she wanted. She'd been highlighting her hair for a long time, but she was always looking in magazines to get new color ideas, so she had the blond vocabulary. "His hair color was tawny. Not ashy like you, but a warm golden, like caramel, not cool Scandinavian—"

Marcus rolled his eyes. "Are you *trying* to make yourself crazy?"

"Let's keep watching." Christine hit PLAY and watched the video as a fine spray of the prisoner's bangs blew off his face. She remembered that she had noted the fineness of their donor's hair in the photo of him. She remembered she had even talked about it with Lauren.

· *Best. Hair. Ever,* Lauren had said, eyeing the photo in Christine's phone. *Do they charge extra?*

It said in the profile that his hair is fine.

Oh, it's fine, all right. He's fine, too. Meow mix.

Please don't lust after my donor.

Christine pressed the memory from her mind, and she and Marcus watched in silence as the video played. In the next few frames, the prisoner was led to the police cruiser and put in the backseat. Marcus stiffened beside her, which told her that he wasn't completely dismissing her worries, and she held her breath, waiting for the telltale shot of the prisoner looking up, just before he was closed inside the squad car.

"Here!" Christine blurted out, experiencing the same flash of recognition that she had in the teachers' lounge. She hit PAUSE, freezing the prisoner, who was looking up. His eyes were round and blue. He had that same look about him, an aspect that regarded the world with curiosity and intelligence. She had thought the same thing when she first saw his photo online. She was a visual learner, she knew that about herself. This image, it was fixed in her brain. "I swear, that's—"

"*Not* him," Marcus interrupted, his tone dead certain. "That's not him."

"What makes you say that? I think I recognize him. I think it is him. It looks like him."

"No, it doesn't." Marcus frowned.

"How is it different?" Christine looked over, her heart in her throat, begging him to say words that would convince her. He *had* to convince her. She *couldn't* be right. She *had* to be wrong.

"Our guy had like a wider face, here, across his cheekbones." Marcus drew a line under his eyes, with his fingers. "I remember thinking, pick him. My dad has broad cheekbones like that and I have my dad's cheekbones, the Nilsson cheekbones. Remember when you first met me, you said something about my cheekbones? I remember thinking, what is it with women and cheekbones?"

"What's your point?"

"I'm saying, look at the cheekbones of this guy in the video. They're not as broad as my dad's. My dad's a heavy-boned Swede, and I have the same cheekbones. That's what I liked about our donor, one of the things. There was Swedish in his background, the bio said it. You can check it." Marcus waved airily at the video. "He's not our guy."

"But what about the eyes?" Christine pointed, unconvinced. "They're big and round, like our donor's."

"A lot of people have big, round eyes. I do."

"But don't they look like the ones in the donor photo to you?"

"No, not at all." Marcus tapped her phone screen with his index finger, and the video ended, showing the prisoner shut inside the police cruiser. "Now can we go home?"

"Hold on a second." Christine tapped her phone, navigated out of Safari, and found her photos, then started swiping backwards through the pictures of her cat, dog, and garden.

"What now? What are you doing?"

"Finding his picture."

"You have a picture of our *donor* in your phone?" Marcus peered over his sunglasses in surprise. "Why?"

Christine kept swiping. "I wanted to show Lauren."

"You could have showed her online. They sent it to us by email."

"Maybe, but I had it in my phone. I saved it." Christine felt vaguely busted. "I save pictures of everything, you know that. Everybody does."

"Okay, whatever."

"Wait. Look." Christine swiped back through the photos of the nurses and techs at Families First, girl selfies with everybody hugging or making duck faces, and then she finally reached the picture of their donor as a little boy. She tried to look at it with new eyes, but she couldn't fight the feeling that he looked like the man in the video.

"Pssh." Marcus shook his head. "It's a little blond boy."

"You don't think that looks like the guy in the video?"

"No, and I don't think it's him."

Christine swiped to the next picture, which was their donor as an adult, and her heart stopped. She didn't know if she could say it out loud, but her brain was telling her something. She recognized that face.

"Nope." Marcus moved away and put the car in gear. "Granted, it looks a *little* like him, but it's obviously not him."

"How is it obvious?"

"I'm telling you, our guy has a wider face than the guy in the video." Marcus hit the gas, steering the car onto the main road. "The coloring is similar, I'll give you that, but blond people have basically the same coloring. Blond hair, blue eyes, light skin. My dad always said we glowed in the dark."

"But what about the way he looks around the eyes, his aspect?"

"What about his aspect?" Marcus drove without glancing over.

"It's his attitude, the way he looks out at the world."

"I know what a person's aspect means. I just don't see what you see in his aspect. In any event, what difference does *aspect* make?"

"I feel like the guy in the video has the same aspect as our guy. Alert. Engaged. Intellectually curious." Christine's stomach clenched. Trees whizzed by, and cars were coming in the opposite direction. She thought Marcus was driving too fast but didn't say anything.

"So he looks curiously and intelligently at the world." Marcus snorted. "It's not our guy."

"I feel like it might be." Christine began to feel sick to her stomach, but she prayed it was only her hormones. Her first two months had been rocky, and she threw up every morning. The only time she felt good was after she had thrown up, which was a sorry state of affairs.

"Worry, worry, worry. You worry too much. Don't worry."

"It's worrisome."

"Tell you what, honey. When we get home, look at the video on the laptop. You'll be able to see it better on a bigger screen. If you want, call Lauren." Marcus looked over, but Christine couldn't see his eyes behind his wraparound sunglasses. All she saw was a reflection of her own frown, distorted in their dark curve.

"What if she agrees with me?"

"If Lauren agrees with you, then you're both nuts."

Chapter Three

Christine followed Marcus inside the house, slid her laptop from her quilted tote, left her purse on the chair, and kicked off her flats. Her nausea had abated slightly, and the cool of the house came as a relief. They kept the central air on during the day since she'd gotten pregnant, and it was worth the money. Marcus went ahead of her into the kitchen, and she padded after him across the hardwood floor, patting their dog Murphy on the head when he came to greet them, wagging his thick comma of a tail. Murphy was a chubby yellow Lab, still hyperactive at six years old, so they'd finally given up waiting for him to mellow. His nature was gentle enough to ignore their cranky orange tabby Marmalade, nicknamed Lady, which they had rescued back in the days when they were practicing for the kids they couldn't have.

"You want some ice water?" Marcus asked, from the refrigerator. He took out the Brita pitcher with his right hand and with his left, scratched Murphy behind the ears.

"Yes, thanks." Christine made a beeline for her makeshift home office, a large pantry off the kitchen that had a granite counter, a built-in desk and old-school cubbyholes to sort bills, junk mail, and the endless memos that came home from school, handed out in hardcopy despite the district's green initiative. She set her laptop on the counter, fired it up, logged on CNN's website, and navigated to the video again, then hit PLAY. The same voiceover started, but she muted it to concentrate on the visual, watching as the police escort filled the screen, walked forward, then got out of the way, so that she could see the prisoner, his head tilted down.

Christine pressed the icon to enlarge the video to full screen, and as soon as the photo expanded, she found herself swallowing hard. Once again, something about the prisoner's hair struck her as their donor's. Nevertheless, she waited, stomach clenched, as she watched the prisoner duck to get into the back of the police cruiser, then he looked up one last time. Christine hit STOP, but her hand was shaking. She couldn't believe what she was seeing. The man's blue eyes. The look around his face. His aspect in general, all of it struck her the same way it had before. He looked like their donor.

Marcus came over, setting the glass of ice water on the counter, the ice tinkling. "Why don't you sit down?"

"I can see better this way. Marcus, I can't help it. This guy looks like our donor."

"It's not, honey." Marcus put an arm around her and gave her a gentle squeeze. "You're worrying for nothing, really."

"Watch it with me again, full screen, would you?"

"Okay." Marcus leaned over, frowning. "Start the video."

"It's easier to see on the bigger screen." Christine started the video and played it until the frame when the prisoner looked up from the backseat. "Doesn't that look like him?"

"It looks a little *like* him. But it doesn't look like it *is* him." Marcus shook his head. "As I said in the car, this guy has a narrower face, especially around the cheekbones."

"So you see him as more gaunt than our donor?"

"Exactly, he has a longer face." Marcus raked his bangs from his forehead, which was whiter than the rest of his face, a golfer's tan. "Really, believe me. You're worrying over nothing."

"But I am worrying." Christine couldn't let it go. She could never let anything go.

"Why don't you call Lauren?"

"I texted her from the car. She's going to come over after the kids are asleep."

Marcus blinked. "Why didn't you just send her a link to the video?"

"I wanted to see her reaction. Hold on a sec. I have another idea."

"What?" Marcus asked, beginning to lose patience. He withdrew his arm from her shoulder.

"Bear with me." Christine was already pulling the accordion file that held their medical information. There had been so many bills related to the infertility procedures, forms upon forms to fill out to get what they could covered, and the files took up five accordions. The last accordion was the one that held their donor profiles, probably a hundred pages of bios that they had printed out from the banks.

"What's the point?" Marcus sighed.

"Hang in one more minute." Christine rummaged through the donor profiles, passing the Sperm Bank of California with its characteristic green banners, the smaller old-fashioned font of Fairfax Cryobank, and coming finally to the bright red borders of their bank, Homestead, with its cute logo of a house and a heart inside. Dr. Davidow used banks all over the country, but had sent them to these three because he rotated the banks among his patient base, explaining his reason with characteristic candor.

I do it so donor-conceived children aren't concentrated in the same geographic area. You don't want to have a Gymboree class full of 3319 offspring, do you?

Marcus shifted his feet. "Babe, I have things to do. The dog wants to go out, and I need to return some phone calls."

"Here we go." Christine found the Donor 3319 profile, stapled together at the corner, then pointed to the first page of the form.

"Under Physical Characteristics, it says 'Hair Color—Blond,' 'Hair Type—straight, fine.' Our donor has fine hair, like the guy in the video."

Marcus eyed her with disbelief. "You can't tell if somebody has fine hair on a *video*."

"Well, not absolutely accurately, but I had the idea." Christine read to the next entry, Complexion. "Plus the skin is the same. It says, 'fair, rosy, creamy.' "

"Donor 3319 has 'creamy' skin?" Marcus chuckled. "The interviewer had a crush on him."

"The guy in the video was also fair-skinned."

"But was he *creamy*?" Marcus lifted an eyebrow, his crow's-feet wrinkling with irony.

"Look, I don't know what 'creamy' means either, but—"

"I do. The interviewer was creamy. Good luck." Marcus pulled open the top drawer and grabbed an old tennis ball from among the rubber Kong Balls and raggedy canvas pull toys, which set Murphy trotting over, his tail wagging and his toenails clicking on the tile floor.

"Marcus, please look at this bio with me."

Marcus closed the drawer. "No, you do it. Knock yourself out. I said my piece. I'm done." He bounced the tennis ball once, as if punctuating his sentence, then turned and left the kitchen with the dog dancing around his heels.

Christine swallowed hard, returning her attention to the profile of Donor 3319. After Height, Weight, Hair Color, Hair Type, Complexion, and Eye Color, was a typically breezy profile from an interview with him, which was written by the interviewer. Christine had memorized the interviews, but Marcus thought they were ridiculous.

Are you kidding me? he had said, reading the interview notes from Donor 3319's profile. *"At 6 foot 3 inches with conventional good looks and a masculine build, Donor 3319 could be a tennis professional. He came to the interview wearing a white polo shirt from Ralph Lauren, khaki pants, and Teva sandals, and though his clothes fit comfortably, they did not hide his musculature."* Marcus had looked up, laughing. *What the hell?*

She has to give her impression. It says at the top of the form, "Interview notes are intended to give a subjective idea of how the donor appears to an experienced interviewer and are not intended as medical information."

I know, but it has to be factual to be useful.

It tells you how he relates, and that she liked him. That's useful to know.

Why? Who cares who she likes?

We want a donor who's likable.

We want likable sperm? Marcus had laughed. *If I had sperm, would it be likable?*

It would be lovable.

Marcus had smiled and resumed reading the form, but then started shaking his head. *"Donor 3319 has shiny blond hair, so much so that I found myself asking him what conditioner he uses."* *Are you freaking kidding me?*

She's a girl.

Clearly. Marcus had rolled his eyes. *"He has an easy smile and one I would say is confident, and he comes off as reliable, well-spoken, and serious-minded, with a hint of humor. The movie star he looks most like is Bradley Cooper."* *Why did they have to compare him to a movie star? Of what relevance is that?*

It's a shorthand.

I can't believe these profiles. *"This one looks like Justin Timberlake, that one looks like Colin Farrell."* *It's Hollywood sperm, everybody!*

Christine put the memory out of her mind, skimming through Donor 3319's profile. After the interview was the form that included Personal Information: year of birth, 1990; Education, Bachelor of Arts in Chemistry; Current Occupation, Student, Accepted to Medical School; Ethnic Origin, Dutch, Swedish, English; and Religion, Agnostic/Atheist.

Christine read on to the family medical history of Donor 3319, his parents, and paternal and maternal grandparents. There were also his lab results, showing that he tested negative for chlamydia, hepatitis B, HIV I and 2, gonorrhea, CMV total antibody, and syphilis. After that was genetic screening for cystic fibrosis, spinal muscular atrophy, and then a boldfaced warning: **Genetic screening tests can significantly reduce but never completely eliminate the chance that a person is a carrier for a particular disorder.**

Christine remembered that Marcus had been most interested in the medical history.

Christine, it says his father had asthma and the age of onset was two. He says it's "managed," but that's not a good thing. I don't know if asthma is hereditary.

I'll make a note to ask. Christine always had a list of questions before they went to the doctor. She wrote down, asthma.

The mother has "uterine fibroids." She had a hysterectomy. Does that matter?

No idea. I'll make a note to ask, too.

It says it was resolved.

Then it's resolved. Christine crossed out the entry. *I don't want to waste his time with dumb questions.*

It's not dumb, it's important. Anything about the DNA matters. For example, it says here, "maternal grandmother had skin cancer, basal cell, on the arm. Age at onset was forty, surgical removal, outcome—resolved." We should ask about that, too.

Will do. Christine made a note on her list. *But I don't think skin cancer is hereditary.*

Marcus frowned, in thought. *I do. The predisposition is inherited, I think. He has fair skin. He'll fit right in. The Nilssons burn like bacon.*

Christine returned her attention to the profile, flipping through until she came to the questions and answers that Donor 3319 had filled out himself. The first one made her stop short:

Q: Are you going to enter Homestead's Open Identity
Disclosure program?
A: No.
Q: If no, why?
A: As I understand the Open Identity Disclosure
program, the sperm donor would be willing to meet
the child conceived using his sperm when the child is
18 years old. I expressly *do not want* to do that
because I do not consider myself the father of the
child. I consider myself as providing genetic material
that would help make a family, but it is not my family, it
is theirs. Also, I know that my parents, given their
strict religious beliefs, would not approve of what I am
doing. I am certain about keeping my information
private and my identity anonymous, except for the one
adult and one child photo I have provided.

Christine felt her stomach drop. She set the profile aside, went
back to her laptop, and hit the mouse pad to wake it up. The CNN
website came to life and the video was still there, but the news story
had grown longer, with two new paragraphs added. She read the
first one:

> Pennsylvania authorities seized Jeffcoat's automobile, a 2013 white
> Nissan Sentra, and reportedly discovered the contents of his trunk: a
> shovel, a roll of garbage bags, a large hunting knife, and a bone
> saw, of medical grade.

Christine's mouth went dry. The shovel and the garbage bag
sent shivers down her spine, and the medical saw left her dizzy with
questions. Who would have access to a medical saw but a medical
student? Was that a link to Donor 3319? Who would know how to
use a medical saw but a medical student? Did he steal it from the
hospital? Did he buy one on his own? Who else could it belong

to? Somebody, anybody in the medical profession. Then again, how hard could it be to use a medical saw? And how skilled a job did it have to be if the person was already dead? She read the second paragraph:

The Nurse Murderer is known for having a distinct modus operandi, or MO. His three victims, all female nurses between the ages of 30 and 40, were found in their beds in their home, fully clothed, with their hands tied in a praying position, using a tourniquet. They were also bound at the ankles, using a tourniquet. Each woman was murdered in the same manner, stabbed through the heart by a bone saw, in a precise location with only a single stab wound. Police authorities and FBI profilers report that the method suggests the killer has medical knowledge. The fact that his victims are nurses suggests an animus or a revenge motive against the nursing profession. Unlike many serial killers, however, The Nurse Murderer does not sexually molest his victims.

Christine felt queasy, shaken. She picked up her glass of water, took a sip, then set it down, her gorge rising with an unmistakable sensation she experienced every morning though never before in the afternoon.

She reached for the wastecan.

Chapter Four

Christine hurried to the front door and flung it open like the cavalry had arrived. "Lauren, great to see you!"

"Really?" Lauren grinned as she stepped inside. Her dark, curly hair had been twisted up into a tortoiseshell clip, and she had on a faded gray Columbia University T-shirt and light blue nylon shorts. "What did I do right?"

"Everything." Christine gave her a big hug, then closed the door as Marcus came up behind her.

"Lauren, hey. Thanks again for helping with the party. It was awesome."

"It was, wasn't it? You're welcome."

Arf! Murphy came up wagging his tail to sniff Lauren.

"Hiya, Murph. How's my big boy today?" Lauren ruffled up the dog's fur around his neck. She didn't have any pets because her husband Josh was allergic, and she always joked that she'd trade her husband for a dog. Josh was an accountant in Rocky Hill, which was why she'd moved to Connecticut from her beloved Manhattan.

"You want a soda or anything?"

"No thanks. You were so mysterious in the text." Lauren looked from Christine to Marcus and back again. "What's going on?"

Marcus smiled. "I'll let my lovely wife explain it to you. I'm going out to hit some balls."

Christine looked at him in surprise. He hadn't mentioned he was going to the driving range. They'd had a quiet dinner, with her trying to keep down some light vegetable soup and him having a tuna fish sandwich and leftover cake.

Christine touched his arm. "Don't you want to stick around? You can make your case."

"No, I'll leave you two to it." Marcus kissed her on the cheek and opened the door. "Lauren, take care. Give my best to Josh and the kids."

"I will, bye."

"See you, honey." Marcus shot her a final smile, then closed the door, and Lauren flared her eyes as soon as the latch had engaged. "What is going on? Are you pregnant? Oh right, yes. What *else* is going on?"

Christine wished she could smile, but she felt wetness come to her eyes. "I'm worried about something."

Lauren frowned, instantly concerned. "Oh no, are you serious? Is something the matter? Are you spotting? Should we call the doctor?"

"Oh, nothing like that, God no. Sorry. Come with me, upstairs." Christine headed for the stairwell, getting back in control.

"Are you sure you're all right?"

"I'm fine."

"No, you're not." Lauren fell into step beside her, and they climbed the stairwell together, Christine running her hand along the banister. She didn't feel so nauseous anymore, but she was suddenly exhausted, which happened every night. She'd read that fatigue was typical during the first trimester, and there had been many nights when she couldn't keep her eyes open as she did the paperwork required by her job. Tonight she was pretty sure she could keep her eyes open.

"Why are we going upstairs?"

"I want to show you something and ask you your opinion."

"What is it?"

"Wait and see. I don't want to say."

"Why not?"

"I don't want to prejudice you. Come in." Christine turned on the light in Marcus's home office, which he rarely used. One of the benefits to being an infertile couple was that they had a lot of spare rooms, having moved into their four-bedroom in Cornwell expecting to fill it with children.

"Why are we in Daddy's office? I can't remember the last time I was in here."

"Because he has the biggest computer in the house."

"Wow, it's so ritzy. Did Greenwich explode in this room?" Lauren glanced around, taking in the neat bookshelves filled with engineering textbooks, job files from work, hardcover biographies, copies of *Golf Digest,* and an entire shelf of golf books. The window on the right side of the room had green plaid window treatments, and underneath was a strip of artificial turf with a white plastic cup at one end, his Callaway putting green.

"Sit down at his desk." Christine gestured her into the mesh ergonomic chair at the sleek walnut desk, which boasted the latest-and-greatest iMac, with a twenty-seven-inch screen and retina display. Marcus used it for Excel spreadsheets from work and Madden golf video games, but tonight it was going to serve a more important function.

"Are you guys in a fight?" Lauren sat down, swiveling around like a kid in the chair.

"No." Christine leaned over, palmed the mouse, and woke up the computer, which showed the landing page of SportsIllustrated.com. She navigated to the CNN website and clicked on the story, which she noted hadn't changed since the addition of the medical saw. She clicked on the video and enlarged it, without playing it. "I would like to show you a video. It's the one they played in the teachers' lounge today, of that serial killer they arrested in

Pennsylvania." Christine could barely bring herself to say the words. "Take a good look at the guy they arrested, a young blond man. Then I want to show you something else."

"Okay." Lauren turned her attention to the computer as Christine clicked PLAY. The video began the way it always did, with the police walking forward and out of frame, then came the prisoner.

Christine tried not to react as the blond man ducked into the police cruiser and looked up, which was when she reached over and clicked STOP to freeze the video. "You see that face?"

"Sure, yes." Lauren nodded.

"Now I want to show you something else." Christine slid her iPhone from the pocket of her jeans, swiped to the photo of Donor 3319 as an adult, and set it down on the desk. "Now, look at this. This is a picture of our donor."

Lauren looked down at the phone, but said nothing, her expression impassive and her lips pursed.

"What's your first impression?" Christine asked, holding her breath.

Lauren looked over at the screen, then back down at the photo, apparently double-checking.

"Well?"

"Well." Lauren looked up, her forehead creased. "They look alike. I mean, they look a little like each other."

"Right? I mean, it's weird, you have to admit." Christine had to force herself to say the words out loud. "Our donor looks like that serial killer."

"Yeah, I see that." Lauren swallowed visibly and palmed the mouse. The computer woke up, with the freeze-frame of the prisoner looking up.

"Let's compare." Christine picked up her phone, unlocked it, and held Donor 3319's photo right next to the prisoner's face on the monitor. "Please tell me they're not the same guy."

"No, they're not." Lauren shook her head, then threw up her

hands. "I mean, obviously, your donor is not a serial killer. It's just not possible."

"That's what Marcus says, and I know they screen these donors." Christine's words raced out, as if they were escaping pressurization. "Our donor is a medical student, and it doesn't say this guy's a medical student, but they did find a medical saw in his trunk."

Lauren kept shaking her head. "It does look a little like him, I know why you're saying this. But it's not him. I mean, they could be brothers, for God's sake. It could be anything. They don't look *exactly* alike, for what that's worth."

"What difference do you see?"

"I think the guy they arrested has a narrower face. Like his face is thinner. The eyes look a lot alike, but blue-eyed people have those eyes. Round, pretty, blue. Like a doll. *Goyische* eyes."

"What?"

"Gentile eyes, WASPY. But, wow, this is scary. You must've been scared." Lauren looked up, her forehead buckling, and Christine could read the sympathy in her expression.

"I'm worried it's the same person. Marcus doesn't think so."

Lauren palmed the mouse. "Wait, hold on. What's the name of the serial killer?"

"Zachary Jeffcoat."

"Okay." Lauren navigated to Google, plugged in Zachary Jeffcoat, and searched under Images. A mosaic of the prisoner's face flooded the screen, and Christine tried to take in all the faces, photographed from different angles. Most of the photos had been taken after his arrest, shot in the same sunlight, with him wearing the same clothes. Some of the other photographs were of dark-haired men who weren't him, and there were two black men. But the overwhelming number were the blond prisoner. Something about seeing them all together was nightmarish, as if the parts all added up to the same place, Christine's worst fear.

"Hold on," Lauren said, on task. "Let's look him up on Facebook."

"Really? A serial killer, on Facebook?"

"Why not? Everybody's on Facebook." Lauren logged out of Google and navigated to Facebook, typing in her name and password, then she plugged in Zachary Jeffcoat, and a full page of Zachary Jeffcoats popped onto the screen. Some showed men with families who looked older, some were African-American, but there were plenty of shadowy faces from pages that were kept private.

"All I know about him is he's from Nevada and that he's in medical school. I don't know his hometown or where he goes to school, they don't tell you that."

"Hmmmm." Lauren scrolled down through the thumbnails. "I don't see anybody from Nevada. Or anybody from a medical school. He's got to be on Facebook. He's young and good-looking and a medical student."

"He might be keeping his settings private."

"Right." Lauren logged out of Facebook and navigated to Instagram, plugging in her username and password. "You never know, right? It's certainly worth checking."

"Right." Christine watched, her stomach still tense.

"Okay, so he's not on Instagram, at least under his name. Let me check Twitter." Lauren's fingers flew across the keyboard, and Christine felt a wave of gratitude for her best friend.

"What would I do without you?"

"Without me, you would've ended up with a coconut sheet cake, which I know you hate." Lauren shook her head, eyeing the Instagram search. "I'm not seeing him. Is it odd that he is not on social media? I mean everybody is, especially his generation."

"Not necessarily. Some people boycott. Not everybody's a teacher." Christine wanted to laugh it off. It was a running joke that teachers were more obsessed with social media than teenagers, but they used it for exchanging lesson plans, telling each other new ways to engage students, and sending links to the latest mole in district headquarters, who leaked them confidential info about what was coming from Common Enemy.

"That's true." Lauren half-smiled.

"I don't think it means anything. We know teachers who hide their identities online. They don't want the administration to know. He might go under ScooterGuy, or Reds fan, or something like that." Christine was starting to convince herself. "Like, Marcus's firm has a professional page on Facebook, but he also has a personal page under Golden Bear Posse, for his golf buddies."

"I never knew that."

"You know he loves Jack Nicklaus." Christine gestured at Marcus's treasured piece of sports memorabilia, a framed U.S. Open poster that Jack Nicklaus had autographed, with a color photograph of the golfer with his nickname, Golden Bear.

"Cute. Why do they have the Facebook page?"

"They post videos of their swings and critique each other."

"Whatever." Lauren chuckled. "Anyway, as far as your donor, I don't think it means anything that he's not on social media. I take it back."

"Unless he gave an alias to the bank," Christine said, the thought coming out of nowhere "But I'm sure they verify who somebody says he is when he donates. If a donor is trying to hide something, he can do that."

"But it's not like they give them a lie detector test."

"No, right. Here, look at his bio." Christine pulled over the Donor 3319 profile.

"I remember looking at this," Lauren said, frowning as she read, then looked up. "You know, you could call the bank and just tell them what you're worrying about."

"Homestead? That's not how it works. I never dealt with them. Dr. Davidow orders it, I never dealt with them at all."

"Then I think you should call him."

"You do?" Christine glanced at the clock on the computer, which read 7:45. "It's after hours."

"So leave a message. It doesn't have to be an emergency. Just say you have a question about your donor." Lauren reached for her arm and gave it a soft squeeze. "Honey. I know it's going to bother you, that's why I'm telling you to call. But if you ask me, they're not the same person."

"Okay, I will. Hold on a sec." Christine picked up her phone, scrolled through CONTACTS, and called Dr. Davidow's cell. The call rang twice then was picked up.

"Hello?" Dr. Davidow answered warmly. "Christine, hi!"

"Hi, Dr. Davidow." Christine felt her heart leap at the sound of his voice. He had been so good to her, through everything. "Sorry to bother you."

"No worries. How are you? How can I help you?"

"Do you mind if I put you on speaker? My friend Lauren is here, and I want her to listen in."

"Sure, no problem."

"Great, thanks." Lauren pressed the button to put the call on speaker. "Can you hear me?"

"Sure," Dr. Davidow answered, his voice echoing in the quiet room. "So what's the problem, how are you feeling?"

"I'm fine, but I happened to see a news report on television today about a serial killer being arrested, and when I looked at the video, it looked a lot like our donor." Christine felt silly, but she wasn't stopping now. "I know that sounds strange, but I think I recognize him from the two pictures we have, one baby and one adult. Is that even possible?"

Dr. Davidow paused. "You're saying you identified him from his adult photo?"

"Not positively, but yes. It looks like him."

"Which bank did you use?" Dr. Davidow's voice changed slightly, losing its casual tone.

"Homestead."

"Did your donor join their Open Identity Disclosure program?"

"No, it was an anonymous donation, and he's not willing to be known either. Can you look him up and check if the name is the same? The name of the man they arrested is Zachary Jeffcoat."

"We don't have the name of your donor. If a donation is anonymous, it's anonymous to Families First, too. The bank gives us only the information that you get."

"Oh, I didn't realize that." Christine glanced at Lauren, who puckered her lower lip in disappointment. "I thought you would have some record."

"No, that's completely out of our control. We place the order for you and take receipt of the vials, which are shipped in a cryogenically frozen state. But the donation, retrieval, and transport is handled by the bank. Still, Homestead is extremely reputable. I'm at liberty to say that my own sister used them with two successful pregnancies, using the same donor twice so the children could be biological siblings."

"Really?" Christine hadn't known that.

"Yes, I sent her there, as my first choice. Homestead's one of the most selective banks in the country. They get about twenty-five thousand donor applicants a year and accept fewer than one percent. To give you a reference point, Harvard University gets thirty-five thousand applicants and accepts six percent. In other words, it's easier to get into Harvard than Homestead."

"Oh." Christine listened, still not comforted. She had noticed that Homestead had offices in Cambridge, New Haven, Chicago, Philadelphia, and Palo Alto, and had assumed it wasn't a coincidence that they were near Ivy League and other prestigious schools.

Lauren leaned over the iPhone speaker. "Dr. Davidow, I'm Lauren. So are you saying that you're basically the broker for the donation?"

"Yes, but I wouldn't put it that way." Dr. Davidow chuckled. "Christine, tell me your donor number."

"3319." Christine and Lauren exchanged tense glances.

"Hold on, I'm in front of my computer." Dr. Davidow fell silent a moment, then continued, "Okay, so I just logged into Homestead and I see that Donor 3319 sperm is available. Are you near a computer?"

"Sure. Hold on a second." Christine leaned over the keyboard, went on to the Homestead website, and logged in under her username and password. She plugged Donor 3319 into the search engine, and his bio popped onto the screen. Next to **Anonymous Donor**, it read **Sperm Available! Order Now!**

"Do you see that it's still available? Homestead would've taken it off the shelves if Donor 3319 were arrested."

Christine thought a moment. "But that assumes they saw the same report I did, which they might not have. It just happened this afternoon. What do you mean by 'take it off the shelves'? Does that ever happen, that banks take donations 'off the shelves'?"

"Yes, but rarely, and generally for physical abnormalities that appear in the offspring of a particular donor, such as a lazy eye. A few years ago, one of my patients had a baby that was born with a clubfoot. I notified the bank, and they took that donation off the shelves."

"Was it Homestead?"

"No. Christine, I don't think you have to worry about this, but I'll call Homestead and let them know your concern."

"That would be great."

Lauren leaned over the phone. "Doctor, can she call them herself?"

"No, it's better coming from me. I have reporting requirements if there's a defect found in offspring, so it should properly come from our office." Dr. Davidow paused. "Christine, I'll get back to you as soon as I speak with them."

"Thanks, but Dr. Davidow, can I ask you, what screening do they do for donors?"

"They do significant screening, mainly blood tests. I understand that you're concerned, but I don't think this is something that should worry you overmuch. As I say, these are the top banks in the country. It's the same thing when we use egg donors. Our egg donors undergo blood tests for HIV, STDs, screening for Tay-Sachs and the like, and they get interviewed by Michelle to make sure that they're good candidates psychologically."

"So Michelle sees them in a session, like she saw Marcus and me?"

"Exactly, and I rely on her evaluation. You know what an ace she is. If she doesn't give them an A+, they're not eligible to be egg donors."

"What's the kind of thing that eliminates them?"

"Hmm, let me think." Dr. Davidow paused, clucking his tongue. "If the putative egg donor says something like she really wants to be a mother, Michelle eliminates her. We don't want someone who wants to be a mother. We want someone who wants to donate an egg so that someone else can become a mother. You follow?"

"Yes." Christine wanted to be reassured, but she couldn't quite, yet. "Do you know if the banks have a psychologist do an evaluation on the sperm donors?"

"No, I don't know if they do that."

Lauren frowned. "Dr. Davidow, it sounds like the egg donors are tested more rigorously than sperm donors. Is that true?"

"There may be some asymmetry, but I don't want to speculate. I can only control the procedures that happen in my office. I harvest eggs in my office so I am intimately involved and responsible for the egg donors that we select and the methods by which eggs are stored and transferred. We don't collect sperm in our offices. But as I say, Homestead is one of the most reputable banks in the country."

"Have you ever had a problem with them?" Christine asked.

"No, not at all." Dr. Davidow cleared his throat. "I'll call Homestead as soon as we hang up. I might not reach them tonight because they're closed, but I'll call you back as soon as I speak with them."

"Great, thank you so much."

"How are you otherwise? Feeling okay?"

"Yes. Nauseated but okay."

Dr. Davidow chuckled. "When you're pregnant, nauseated is good. Okay, let me get back to you."

"I will, thanks. Bye now."

"Good night." Christine pressed END to hang up, then met Lauren's eye. "He's taking it seriously."

"He should."

"I wish he'd told me it was silly." Christine was only half-joking, and Lauren patted her hand.

"I don't think anything that worries you is silly. But you've done all you can do, and I think you should try to rest easy tonight."

"I will," Christine told her, wondering if that was possible.

Chapter Five

Christine woke up in her bedroom, stretched out on top of the comforter in her sweatclothes. Her laptop was open, and around her lay the last of her unfinished Data Summary Sheets, the paperwork that went into each student's file, detailing their progress and their meetings with the Instructional Support team and their parents. Murphy snored at the foot of the bed, and she heard water running in their bathroom. Marcus must've come home and was showering. She propped herself up on her elbow, realizing that she had fallen asleep while she was working, even though the bedside clock read only 9:45. She used to be a night owl, staying up to watch Jimmy Fallon, but the exhaustion of her first trimester had thrown her for a loop.

Christine's hand went automatically to her tummy, and she wondered when she'd be able to feel the baby moving. The thought suffused her with happiness, and she leaned back on the soft pillow, feeling the smile spread across her face. The bedroom was so pretty, with a sky-blue color scheme that made her feel restful, and the comforter was a blue hydrangea pattern that matched the curtains on the far wall, three mullioned panes that overlooked their street, with white sheers for privacy. The ceiling was a soft cumulus white, and Christine felt as if she were in girl heaven, for which she sent up a silent prayer of thanks.

Her gaze fell on the laptop, and its dark screen told her that it had fallen asleep, too. Suddenly she remembered. Donor 3319. Zachary Jeffcoat. Her stomach clenched all over again, and she picked up her phone from the night table and checked the screen. Dr. Davidow hadn't called her, and she checked her phone to make sure that the ringer was on, which it was. She lay back on the pillow, holding the phone. She was close to her mother and wished she could call her to talk it over or maybe go visit them, since her parents lived in nearby Middletown, where she had grown up. But Christine didn't want to worry her mother any more; her hands were full taking care of Christine's father, who had Alzheimer's.

She reminded herself of Dr. Davidow's sensible words, that Homestead is one of the best banks in the country, that they had procedures in place to ensure only the highest-quality donors, that his own sister had used them, with two successful pregnancies, using the same donor twice. Christine remembered being weirded out when she first heard that was possible, as well as the other icky facts about infertility procedures, but that was when she was a rookie in the infertility world. She'd gotten over the ick factor, like with any other medical malady, and in no time found herself talking with other women in the waiting room about sperm motility or vaginal secretions, the lingo of a club that no one wanted to join. She had come to understand that they were a random group of people linked by a heartbreaking predicament, trying to attain what the rest of the world took for granted, a baby. A family.

So much about the fertility process had opened Christine's eyes, and some was the exact opposite of what she'd expected; for example, she had expected the doctor's office to be full of bulletin boards of photos from babies conceived through the various procedures offered by the clinic. But there had been nothing in the decor of Families First that related to babies at all. The art was watercolor landscapes, and the magazines mainstream, unrelated to parenting or pregnancy. A small sign on the door read: **Out of consideration for our other patients, we ask that you not bring any babies or children with you to your appointments at our practice**.

As Christine went through month after month without becoming pregnant, she came to appreciate the wisdom of the rule, and its mercy. It would've killed her to see a new baby in the waiting room; she'd had a hard enough time when she saw babies in the store, smiling and kicking their chubby legs in shopping carts. Christine had never in her life wanted something so badly as she wanted a baby, experiencing her wish as the most fundamental of desires, the primal yearning of an organism to reproduce, obeying an imperative embedded in the DNA of every living creature. She had never given up faith that she would somehow be pregnant, and now she finally was. And she had been the happiest woman on earth until she saw the CNN video.

"Hey," Marcus said, coming out of the bathroom, a light blue bath towel wrapped around his waist. His body looked pumped, his shoulders broad with strong caps, his biceps full, and his torso tapered to the towel. His hair was wet, which made it look almost brown, and water droplets dotted his chest.

"Oh, hi." Christine managed a smile as she shifted up against the headboard, upholstered with the hydrangea fabric. "Have fun at the driving range?"

"Not really."

"Why not?" Christine asked, surprised. Usually Marcus felt terrific after he'd been to the driving range. It reduced his stress level, relaxing him, and they'd had some of the best times in bed after he'd come home from hitting a bucket.

"You're not interested in golf."

"No, but I'm interested in you." Christine patted the bed beside her, and Marcus sat down, showing her his palm, which was pink and large, but callused at the pads under each finger.

"See how that's red? I'm squeezing too hard. It's like a death grip. It's an easy fix. I have to chill out. It's just a bad night. Everybody has a bad night."

"Sure, of course." Christine could see he didn't want to dwell on it, so she let it go. Marcus was a sensitive man despite his jocky appearance, and it was best to say less when he was out of sorts. His late mother Barbara "Beebee" Nilsson, a lovely woman and an accomplished equestrian, used to refer to Marcus as a "draft horse," explaining that he had a big, strong body but was a softy inside. Christine wouldn't have put it that way, but understood that it was meant with love, and she had known Beebee only a year when she passed suddenly, from an aneurism. Christine was less a fan of her egotistical father-in-law Frederik, who hadn't waited long to start dating before he eventually remarried.

"You fell asleep early."

"I know, I'm beat."

"You hungry? Do you want anything from downstairs?"

"No, did you eat? I feel terrible there's nothing in there. I was going to go food shopping after school, but then we had the party."

"Don't worry about it. I had more cake. I'm having a cake baby." Marcus patted his waist, which was still trim enough to qualify as a four-pack. She had met him her freshman year of college, when he was a hunky junior in her Government class. She'd done a double-take when she saw him pick up his backpack and his forearm rippled with not only two muscles, but three. It was lust at first sight, though love came later and happily, stuck around for the duration. They had been married for seven years, happy as fried clams.

"So what did Lauren think? About our donor?"

"She didn't think it was the same person, either. For what it's worth, we called Dr. Davidow and told him."

"Really?" Marcus pursed his lips. "What did he say?"

"He said he would call Homestead and get back to us. They're the only ones who know the donor's identity. The doctor's only the broker."

"I knew that."

"I didn't." Christine blinked, feeling vaguely dumb. It wasn't a feeling she liked, which was why she had so much empathy with her reading students. Most of them had tracking problems or problems identifying words, the kind of challenges that left them feeling stupid or excluded even though they fell short of dyslexia or other diagnosed reading disorders.

"Did Dr. Davidow tell you about the screening they do for donors?"

"Not really." Christine saw the pain crossing Marcus's face, and she felt guilty even having the discussion. "Truly, I'm not worried about it as much as I was before. I think it's probably just a fear. I felt better after I talked to him."

"Good." Marcus lifted an eyebrow. "I was worried Lauren would rile you up."

"No, she didn't. She listened, but she didn't get me crazier than I already am."

"Good. I like you just the level of crazy you are."

"Me, too." Christine touched his arm, stroking the curve of his bicep, still damp.

"God, I'm beat, too," Marcus said, unsmiling, and Christine knew it was code that he wasn't in the mood to make love. She hadn't been either, so she didn't press the point. Their sex life hadn't been a problem until their infertility issues. The fun had gone out of their lovemaking back when they still thought Christine was the one with the problem; instead of a loving expression, sex acquired a single-minded purpose, to get pregnant. The situation had gotten worse after their problem was diagnosed as Marcus's. He had lost all interest in sex, and one or two times, hadn't been able to perform. They had only recently gotten their sex life back on track, but Christine worried that today's focus on Donor 3319 wouldn't help.

"I really like Dr. Davidow," she said. "He took me seriously, but he didn't become alarmed."

"There's no reason for alarm."

"He told me that if there were any problem with our donor, they would take the sperm off the shelves."

"Really." Marcus lifted an eyebrow, and Christine leaned over, pulled her laptop into her lap, and pressed ENTER to wake it up.

"Yes, they take the donation off the shelf if the kids are born with a clubfoot or a lazy eye, stuff like that."

"Interesting."

"Agree." Christine felt she had redeemed herself, knowing something he didn't. She navigated out of the Nutmeg Hill website and back to Homestead's, plugging in Donor 3319 into the search function. She had checked it every fifteen minutes until she had fallen asleep. "He said that it probably wasn't a problem if his sperm was still available."

"That makes sense."

"He and I checked together, and it was still available." Christine clicked the link for Donor 3319, but froze when she read the screen. The entry for Donor 3319 had been changed. Now it read: **Sperm Temporarily Unavailable! Sorry!**

"Oh my God, no," Christine said, stricken.

Chapter Six

W ho are you calling?" Christine asked, as Marcus pressed a number into his cell phone. Still in his towel, he had gone for his phone as soon as he'd seen that the sperm was unavailable. He didn't seem upset, only determined, but Christine was panicking. Her mouth was dry, her heart was pounding. She kept refreshing the laptop screen, thinking there must have been some mistake with the website.

"I'm calling Homestead."

"But they work through Davidow."

"Homestead sold us the sperm and they're going to answer to us." Marcus brought the phone to his ear.

"Don't you think we should call him first?" Christine couldn't think clearly. Her emotions tumbled one over the other: fear, disbelief, agony, shock. She didn't know if she was making too much of it, or too little. She felt sick to her stomach again, not knowing if it was from her pregnancy, the turn of events, or both.

"I'm not going to ask anybody for permission to find out what I need to know."

"Not for his permission, just to see if he talked to them." Christine didn't even know why she was fussing at him. Marcus was great in an emergency, a logical thinker with an innate mechanical sense. He was tailor-made to be an architectural engineer, working every day to make buildings functional and structurally sound, and he had endless patience for calculating stresses and loads, as well as hammering out the details of electrical, heating, plumbing, and energy efficiency systems, which had become a growing specialty of his firm.

"Davidow must have called Homestead. It's too coincidental that our donor comes off the shelves after you phoned him."

Christine couldn't deny that Marcus might be right. Still, she couldn't collect her thoughts.

Marcus said into the phone, "Hello, my name is Marcus Nilsson, and my wife conceived about two months ago using Donor 3319. I would like to speak with someone in charge about him. Yes, I'll hold for the assistant director."

Christine sat straighter in bed, trying to get her act together. "Can you put it on speaker?"

"Yes." Marcus hit the SPEAKER button, then a woman's voice came on the line.

"Mr. Nilsson, this is Lee Ann Demipetto. How may I help you?"

"My wife conceived using sperm from Donor 3319 and she is almost two months pregnant. We saw a news report today that a man named Zachary Jeffcoat was arrested for serial murder in Pennsylvania, and my wife is concerned that he is our donor. Now we see that Donor 3319's sperm has been taken off the shelves. We'd like to know if Donor 3319 is Zachary Jeffcoat."

"Mr. Nilsson, we usually deal with your healthcare provider—"

"I understand that, but I'd like you to deal with me." Marcus kept his tone firm and controlled. "Is Donor 3319 Zachary Jeffcoat?"

"Mr. Nilsson, I did have a phone conversation tonight with Dr. Davidow, and he told me of your concerns. We are going to investigate this matter, and we agreed that in an abundance of caution, we would remove 3319 from our general inventory of available donors."

"You didn't answer my question. Is Donor 3319 Zachary Jeff-coat or not?"

Christine tried to stay calm while she listened. Her panic was giving way to stone cold fear. If Marcus was worried, then she was really worried.

"Mr. Nilsson, I'm sorry, but we cannot disclose that information. If you review the contract you signed with Homestead—"

"I didn't sign any contract."

"I have the file in front of me, and you did sign a contract. I'm looking at a scanned copy of your signature and your wife's signature. It would've been given to you by Dr. Davidow or one of his associates."

Christine remembered their signing the contract, four pages of fine print, probably in her file. She didn't remember reading it, but she would've signed anything to get a baby.

"Mr. Nilsson, do you recall that contract now? Paragraph 27 of your agreement clearly states, 'Homestead will not under any circumstances release identifying information on our donors to any other party, including the parents of individuals conceived using Homestead donor sperm.'"

"So you're not going to answer my question?"

"No, I can't. The terms of our contract with you are clear. In addition, we have a contractual relationship with 3319, which states explicitly that we promise to keep his identity anonymous, under any and all circumstances."

"So you really won't tell me?" Marcus raised his voice.

"I'm legally bound to 3319 not to."

"Legally bound to a serial killer, over a paying customer? Over *us*?"

"In any event, Mr. Nilsson."

Christine's heart hammered. Demipetto sounded so final, her voice rich with authority, as if she had been ready for the call.

"Mr. Nilsson, our legal requirement that we keep confidential the identity of our sperm and egg donors is the cornerstone of Homestead and every other bank in the country. In addition, 3319 stated explicitly in his interview that he did not want his identity revealed because of his parents' religious beliefs, which conflicted with his own."

Marcus scoffed. "What kind of religious beliefs does a serial killer have?"

"I understand your concern, and we hope that you will understand our concern. Homestead helps over twelve thousand women a year to conceive, and the integrity of our process is of paramount importance to us. The keystone of our system is the anonymity of our donors—"

"Can you at least tell me his birth date?"

"No."

"Place of birth?"

"No."

"When did he make the donation?"

"I can't disclose that."

"Can you verify that he's in medical school? He had been accepted when he filled out the form."

"The information we are given by our donors is verified, to the extent possible, at the time of donation. We do not keep ongoing tabs on our donors, and you can understand how updating this information would be beyond our means."

Christine felt herself slump backwards against the headboard, suddenly weak. She tried to wrap her mind around what she was hearing, the shock settling into her very bones.

"No, I *don't* understand that," Marcus shot back, irate. "I think that's your responsibility. I own a business, and I stand behind my relationships to my clients."

"Homestead is not a business, *per se*—"

"Of course it is. You charged me for the sperm. What screening do you do for your sperm donors, specifically?"

"We screen for chlamydia, HIV one and two, hepatitis B, gonorrhea, hepatitis C, syphilis. We do genetic screening for cystic fibrosis, spinal muscular atrophy, and various hemoglobins for thalassemia. We do a standard CBC and chem panel. Our sperm samples meet current FDA and Tissue Bank licensing protocol at the time of release, which you will see at paragraph 17 of your contract and—"

"I'm not talking about blood panels. This is a situation where someone is arrested for serial killing. Do you do criminal-background checks?"

"Yes."

"You checked our donor's criminal record?"

"Yes, or he would not have been approved for donation."

"So Donor 3319 had no criminal record?"

"As I said, no one is approved with a criminal record."

Marcus shook his head. "That doesn't answer my question, but okay."

Suddenly a text alert sounded on Christine's phone, and she glanced at the screen. The banner showed it was Lauren, and the text read, **Call Me. The website is changed**. Christine picked up the phone and texted back, **On it**.

Marcus was asking Demipetto, "Do you do psychological checks?"

"We screen for immediate family with a mental illness, such as schizophrenia or bipolar disorder. You can see that in the online donor profiles."

"But that relies on the donor's say-so."

"Yes, and we note that in every donor profile, including 3319's. It reads, 'The above family and medical history, and all other information, has been self-reported by the donor. We work with each donor to obtain as complete and accurate information as possible, but we are unable to completely rule out the existence of health or other information that is not known or that remains unreported to us.'"

"You're missing my point. This isn't health information."

"True, but this falls within 'other' information, such as a subsequent arrest or even any other adverse occurrence, such as a donor who developed alcoholism or a substance-abuse problem, as well as late-onset cancer or any other illness. This is not something we warrant against, nor could we be expected to—"

"But a serial killer is somebody with major psychological problems. A *sociopath*." Marcus raised his voice, but only slightly. "How could you *not* pick that up? What testing do you do for psychological problems?"

"Homestead uses Myers-Briggs—"

"Myers-Briggs is an employment test."

"It's used in a variety of applications to classify temperament, which is something that many of our sperm and egg recipients are interested in—"

"But any idiot can see which is the right answer to yield the right result. If I answer yes to the questions about liking people and making friends easily, I'm an extrovert. Anybody smart enough to be a serial killer knows how to manipulate that test."

"We can't be expected to account for intentional deception—"

"Then how are we protected? How can we have confidence in your product?" Marcus raked his wet hair back with his hand. "Is Donor 3319 even a medical student? Did you check that out, or did you just take his word for it?"

"We ascertained, at the time of his application and interview, that 3319 was accepted as a medical student to an accredited medical school. I can assure you, we will begin our investigation of this matter tomorrow—"

"How long does it take you to *investigate*?" Marcus threw up his free hand. "You have a file, a list somewhere that tells you exactly the identity of Donor 3319. It will take you three minutes to look that up. You probably know the answer to this question right now. Tell me if it's him or not."

"I can't do that, Mr. Nilsson."

"Is that why you took him off the shelves? Because you looked up the file and you saw that Donor 3319 is Zachary Jeffcoat?"

Christine didn't want to think about what Marcus was saying, about the implications. He was acting like it was true. Like they wouldn't have taken it off the shelves if it wasn't true. Like they wouldn't tell the truth because they wanted to keep it secret. And the only way they'd want to keep it secret was if Donor 3319 really was Zachary Jeffcoat. Murphy lifted his head from his paws, watching her.

"Mr. Nilsson, we removed 3319 from general inventory out of an abundance of caution. That same is true, I might add, of the other samples you purchased, which are stored in our tanks and reserved for you."

"What other samples?" Marcus frowned, confused, but Christine knew what Ms. Demipetto was talking about. When they had picked Donor 3319, they'd bought the standard set of three vials, in case the pregnancy didn't take the first time. They were paying storage fees on the two remaining vials; Christine had just written the check.

"Mr. Nilsson, I will direct you to paragraph 15 of your agreement, where it states, 'I understand that Homestead reserves the right to retain any samples that I have purchased if an unforeseen situation arises where, at the complete discretion of Homestead, it is necessary to do so. In such an event, Homestead shall not reveal the reason for retaining the samples, if issues of confidentiality or other privacy issues are involved. In the event that Homestead retains any samples that I have purchased, Homestead shall refund the cost of the samples but will not refund any storage fees I may have paid.' "

"So this is an 'unforeseen circumstance'?"

"Certainly, it would fall easily within an 'unforeseen circumstance.' We share your concerns."

"No you don't. You can't. You're protecting your donor. My wife is pregnant. We're the ones left holding the bag, so to speak."

Christine cringed, hearing the way Marcus talked. She never thought about the baby that way. She didn't know he thought about it that way.

"Let me ask you this," Marcus was saying. "How long have you been using Donor 3319's sperm?"

"We don't disclose that information."

"What about other women who use his sperm? There have to be others."

"We don't disclose that information, either. I will tell you that we are generally conservative in the number of vials we sell from a given donor."

"Does Homestead have to notify those women if Donor 3319 is Jeffcoat? Will you notify *us*?"

Demipetto hesitated. "This is beyond my bailiwick, Mr. Nilsson. I doubt that we have a notification requirement with respect to a situation like this, where a donor is arrested for a crime."

"Not just a crime, the serial killing of three women. Nurses, and he said he was going to be a medical student. Don't you think we have a right to know that? Don't you think we have a right to be informed?"

"Your rights are outlined by contract—"

"I'm not talking about law, I'm talking about what's the right thing to do. How do you feel about yourself, knowing that you're withholding an answer I have a moral right to know? That I deserve to know? It's the truth, and you don't own it!"

"Mr. Nilsson, please hold a moment."

Marcus held on as the phone went dead, seeming not to remember Christine was in the bedroom. The phone clicked, signaling that Ms. Demipetto had come back on the line.

"Mr. Nilsson, I have to terminate this conversation. As you may know, Homestead is owned and operated by Fertility Assurance Associates, Inc., and I can have a representative call you tomorrow during office—"

"Don't hang up. I want to talk about this now. I don't want—"

"I'm sorry. I've been instructed to refer this to our corporate headquarters. I can assure you that we are following up on your concerns, and we will have someone contact you."

"Did they tell you not to talk to me?"

"I'm sorry, Mr. Nilsson. I must go. Thank you for your call, and I'll have someone get back to you tomorrow. Good-bye."

Marcus hung up, pursing his lips. "I'm calling the doctor. I'm going to get to the bottom of this, once and for all."

Christine nodded, numbly, her heart sinking, but Marcus was already scrolling through the contacts, finding a number, and pressing CALL.

"Hi, Dr. Davidow, this is Marcus Nilsson, with Christine on speaker."

"Hi, Marcus, hi, Christine."

"Hi," Christine said, noting the difference in Dr. Davidow's voice from earlier this evening. Before, he had sounded warm, lively, and interested, but now he sounded tense, worried.

"Dr. Davidow, I know you spoke with Christine today about Donor 3319. I see his sample has been taken off the shelves. Do you know why?"

"I did speak with Lee Ann at Homestead tonight. I was just about to call you—"

"And what did she tell you?"

"She said they would take 3319 off the shelves, pending investigation. I told her that was the most prudent course of action, and they agreed, out of an abundance of caution."

"So is our donor Zachary Jeffcoat?"

"I don't know, but the fact that 3319 was taken off the shelves does not mean that he's Jeffcoat. Homestead took it off pending their investigation—"

"Doc, is it him or not?" Marcus raised his voice, still controlled.

"They won't confirm or deny."

"Level with me. They won't tell *you*? They're your subcontractor, for God's sake!"

Dr. Davidow cleared his throat. "I know this is hard to understand, but they can't disclose that information to me. They have a legal relationship to the donors and it's sacred to them."

"Do you really not know, or you don't want to know?"

"I *don't* know. I did ask them, but they wouldn't confirm or deny."

Christine slumped against the headboard, noticing that Murphy had crawled over to her, resting his head on her thigh. She put her hand on his soft, furry head, not knowing who was comforting whom.

"Dr. Davidow, did they do an investigation after they spoke with you but before they took him off the shelves?"

"I don't know that."

"Did they take him off the shelf while you were speaking with them?"

"No. 3319 was available when we were on the phone, and we spoke for maybe fifteen minutes, about a half hour or so ago. I don't know when 3319 was taken off the shelves, but it was still available when I was speaking with them, so I'm sure it was in response to my call."

"Doesn't that mean it's him?"

"No, it doesn't. It means they're going to investigate."

"But how much investigation can it take? They have the guy's name on file. It takes three minutes to look at a file."

"No, Marcus, I'm sure the files concerning the identity of the donors are protected, if not encrypted. Not everyone in the Homestead office may have access. The assistant director may not even have access. We don't know."

"Okay, *that* I'll buy." Marcus stopped pacing, then nodded.

"Look, I've never had this situation before, or anything like it. I care about you and Christine, and I think you should come in tomorrow and we can talk this over."

"Are they going to call you back and tell you the results of their investigation?"

"No they're not. I asked them to and they declined."

"But I have a right to know that information." Marcus started pacing again. The dog swiveled his head around, watching him, too.

"It's not a question of whether you have that right. It's a question of what Homestead is obligated legally to tell you. Look, I just got off the phone with Michelle. I think you both should come have a session with her, at four o'clock."

"I don't need a therapy session, I need an answer. My wife could be carrying the baby of a serial killer."

Christine felt the words like a blow. Hearing Marcus say it aloud made it so real. Tears sprang to her eyes. It *was* real. It was *true*. And she was lost, all was lost. Her dream of motherhood, of parenthood, of their new family, was over. Her thoughts raced. She knew Marcus would never think of the baby as his, would never see himself as the father, and the baby's father was a killer, a murderer. But she was carrying the baby, it was still *her* baby, and she and the baby were all alone, on their own. She was *holding the bag*.

Marcus and Dr. Davidow kept talking on the phone, but their voices grew far away. Christine couldn't hear anything they were saying, she couldn't feel the dog's head under her palm. Marcus was turning toward her, his forehead buckling in alarm, but she couldn't speak. The bedroom fell away, the heavenly blue walls and soft lamplights vanished, and she felt herself slipping into blackness.

She didn't have another thought before she fainted dead away.

Chapter Seven

The entrance hall buzzed with last-day activity as Christine entered the school building. Teachers' aides hustled back and forth to the office with forms, workmen rolled handcarts of taped boxes toward trucks idling outside, and two kindergarten teachers, Linda Cohen and Melissa DiMarco, hurried to the office, looking over, grinning, when they spotted Christine.

"Christine," Linda called out. "Your party was so fun! Stay in touch, okay?"

"Sure, thanks!" Christine kept up her smile, still trying to wrap her mind around what was going on. She had vomited this morning, but had told herself it was morning sickness. She only had to keep it together for one more day.

Melissa chimed in, "Best of luck! We'll miss you!"

"I'll miss you, too!" Christine beelined for her office door, but she had to pass the administrative office, where Pam and the staff were boxing files and taping bookshelves. Pam motioned to her to come in, but Christine pointed to her watch and kept walking. She reached her office, opened the door, and went inside.

"That you?" Lauren called out from the adjacent office, rising from her desk.

"Yes!" Christine called back, letting her tote bags, backpack, and purse drop onto the blue carpet. She glanced around, but she'd already packed up her office, so the place didn't look familiar at all, much less somewhere she'd worked for almost ten years. Her desk, of brown indeterminate wood, was generic without her photos of Marcus, Lady, and Murphy, and her white walls looked so empty without her American Library Association poster of Elvis Presley reading a book, captioned READ. Her bookshelves were covered with brown paper, and her bulletin board stripped to original cork, covered with thumbtack holes like public-school constellations. Christine had left posted only her Fountas & Pinnell Literacy Scale and her favorite inspirational poster, from Maya Angelou: **If you are always trying to be normal, you will never know how amazing you can be**.

"Honey, how *are* you?" Lauren rushed over and enveloped her in a morning hug fresh enough to smell like citrusy hair conditioner.

"I can't believe this is happening." Christine let herself be held for a moment. "I just can't believe it."

"Tell me. I was worried when you didn't call back." Lauren let her go, her expression full of love and concern. Her curly hair was still wet from the shower, twisted up into a topknot, and she had on a gauzy smock with a bright pink T-shirt underneath.

"I'm sorry, I should have called. Believe it or not, I fainted."

"Oh my God." Lauren's hand flew to her mouth.

"I know, what a drama queen." Christine brushed dirt off her seersucker shirtdress, which she knew would get filthy in five minutes, but she'd been too distracted this morning to find the right clothes. She'd showered but hadn't even bothered to blow-dry the back of her head.

"No, not at all! Here, sit down." Lauren pulled out a blue plastic chair, which was undersized for students, but Christine sat down anyway, squeezing.

"Then I cried, then we talked and I cried some more, I was so exhausted I slept . . . the whole night." Christine had been about to say *like a baby*, but caught herself.

"So why did they take it off the shelves? Is it really him?" Lauren's eyes flared with alarm.

"They took it off the shelves pending their investigation, whatever that means. We don't know anything more than you do. We're going to meet with Michelle and Davidow today, after school."

"Good."

"But Homestead won't tell Davidow, or us, if our donor is Jeffcoat, because it has contracts for confidentiality with our donor, and we signed a contract saying that we understood that."

"Oh boy." Lauren leaned against the desk, folding her arms. "So they don't have to tell you?"

"Right; legally nobody has to tell us anything."

"Let's see what the investigation yields. We shouldn't freak until we know the results. How's Marcus? How is he handling this?"

"I conked out last night, but I don't think he slept at all. He was on the computer in his office when I woke up." Christine glanced at the clock and realized she had an appointment with a student in fifteen minutes, the first in a day full of appointments, before the end of the year.

"Doing what?"

"I don't know, we didn't get time to talk about it this morning. I just noticed he was printing a lot of things, which he never does, and he was running late this morning, which he never is."

"The poor guy." Lauren's lower lip puckered, with sympathy.

"I know." Christine leaned over, unzipped the first tote bag, and started unpacking the gift bags. She was giving each of her students a book, a squiggle pen, and a self-addressed postcard, so they could tell her their impressions of the book. It was lucky that she had bought the gifts and packed the bags last week, because she never would've had the energy last night.

"Is there anything I can do?"

"No, I'll let you know what happens tonight." Christine pulled out the gift bags and set them on the desk. She'd customized the gifts for each of her students, so Cal Watson, a second-grader with tracking problems who loved dogs, got a puppy-themed gift bag with a copy of *Fun Dog, Sun Dog.* Talieeta Choudhoury, a sixth-grader who had reading comprehension problems but was obsessed with pirates, got a copy of *Treasure Island* in a black gift bag; the book was a reach for Talieeta, but Christine had put an encouraging note inside, telling her to give it a shot. Gemma Oglethorpe, a first-grader who struggled with her sight words, got *Hot Rod Hamster* in a floral gift bag, because it was impossible to find a hamster-themed gift bag.

Lauren helped her unpack. "You are so sweet to do this. You must have spent a fortune."

"It wasn't that bad." Christine flashed back to her early teaching career, when she first realized how much of their own money teachers spent on their students. It had come as a surprise, but she never begrudged it and didn't know any teacher who did.

"So what are you thinking? How are you dealing?"

"Until yesterday, I was super happy. I thought I was carrying this adorable baby, and the truth is, I wasn't really focused on the donor. I forgot all about him. I think of this baby as our baby, Marcus's and mine." Christine unpacked the bags, on autopilot. "Or at least, as my baby, but not because I made a 'genetic contribution,' as they say. But just because it's *in* me."

"Of course, that makes total sense." Lauren gestured at Christine's belly. "I mean, you're pregnant. Duh."

"But now all of a sudden, we're back where we were two months ago, talking about sperm donors and 'genetic contributions,' and now it feels so strange, like everything is ruined." Christine felt her eyes film but blinked them clear as she loaded the gift bags onto her empty desk.

"But it's not ruined, it's not ruined yet."

"Honestly, yes it is. You don't even know what Marcus said to the doctor last night." Christine stopped short, knowing that if she told Lauren what Marcus had said, Lauren would permanently hate him, in the way of all true BFFs.

"What did he say?"

"It doesn't matter, he didn't mean it. Well, he did mean it, but he didn't mean it to hurt me." Christine kept unpacking the gift bags. "I mean, if I go back two months ago, when I was still thinking about the stupid donor, I thought I was carrying the baby of a medical student. Now I could be carrying the baby of a serial killer."

"What are you saying?" Lauren frowned deeply, still helping her unpack.

"I'm saying I don't know what's *inside* me." Christine shuddered. "Is it a bad-seed baby? Is it 'Rosemary's Baby'? Is it 'Alien'?"

"Oh honey, no." Lauren squeezed her arm. "It's none of those things. It's your baby."

"And who else's? Who's the father? The biological father, that is."

"Who *cares* who the biological father is?" Lauren touched her arm. "It doesn't matter who the biological father is. You are the mother, and you're going to be a great mother, and it's going to be a great baby—"

"I don't know if that's true." Christine checked the clock and she only had three minutes before Gemma showed up. "You know what I was thinking about on the drive in? I used to feel great about the baby, *connected* to the baby, but now I feel distant. I get that it's a part of me, but it's not a part of me that I'm so happy with right now." Christine stopped unpacking for a moment. "If I had known that Donor 3319 was capable of murder, much less *serial murder*, I never would've picked him. Homestead never would've taken him as a donor. Right?"

"Okay," Lauren said slowly.

"So, we can't pretend it doesn't matter just because that's the way it turned out."

Lauren blinked. "Okay, I get that."

"Good." Christine resumed unpacking. "Can you imagine when it comes time to tell him who his father is? First, your dad isn't your biological dad. Second, your biological dad is a serial killer."

"You're getting ahead of yourself."

"I have to. That day will come. We talk in therapy about disclosure, how to tell our friends we used a donor, how to tell our child." Christine kept unpacking. "That's the kind of news that can destroy a child. And if we don't tell him, can you imagine if he finds out on his own?"

"You're getting carried away—"

"No, I'm not. By the time he grows up, there'll be major advances in technology. You read about facial recognition software, he'll use it. It'll be an app on his damn phone. It's not a secret we can keep."

"Okay, here's what I think." Lauren's dark eyes flashed with intensity. "You wouldn't have picked him if you had known, but now you have what you have. It's not what you expected, isn't it like a kid with special needs or reading problems? You adore your students. It doesn't matter to you that they're not what their parents expected."

"This isn't that." Christine had thought it over. "A child with special needs is just a child who needs more help than someone else. A child of a serial killer, or whatever mental illness that makes someone a serial killer, may be a child who has a lifetime of no connections with other people. Of anger, of pain. Of isolation, of *violence*. He could grow up to harm others, to kill others, even to kill *us*."

Lauren gasped. "What?"

"Lauren, be real. You've heard the stories about parents who have to lock their kid in his room so he doesn't come out and kill them at night. You think I'll sleep easy, knowing that my child has half the genes of a *serial killer*?"

"You can't inherit being a serial killer."

"Let's not get technical, okay? I'll be waiting for the other shoe to drop, won't I?" Christine felt her throat tighten. "And even if I can deal with it, do you really think Marcus can?"

"That *does* worry me. He has to buy in."

"Look, maybe I can love this baby, raise this baby, no matter who his biological father is. Marcus was almost there. But all that's changed." Christine felt it was true as soon as she said it aloud, like when Marcus had, last night. "He's acting different. Colder. We'd come so far, but now it's undone."

"Do you think he's blaming you that you even went with the donor instead of adopting? Or if you picked the wrong one?"

"Please, that's what *I'm* thinking. I'm the queen of second-guessing. I'm asking myself a million what-ifs." Christine unpacked the last gift bag. "If I know him, he's blaming himself because if he hadn't been infertile, we wouldn't have this problem in the first place."

"Oh boy."

"It's just going to bring everything back for him, all his feelings of inadequacy, and his reaction when he feels bad about himself is to withdraw." Christine looked over, feeling ragged and sad. "Remember when he first got diagnosed? It was like living with the turtle who kept sticking his head inside his shell. We'll probably have to go back into counseling."

"If that's what you have to do, that's what you have to do. You guys love each other and you will get through this."

"All I know is, I don't feel like he's in it with me. I feel like I'm in it alone."

"Honey, you're not alone. You got me." Lauren looped an arm around her shoulder.

"Aw, thanks." Christine scanned the desk, blanketed with festive bags, and it looked like she was having a party, which was the effect she had wanted for her students, even if it clashed with her current state of mind. Just then there was a knock on the door, meaning Gemma had arrived. Lauren left to meet with teachers, and Christine started her day, though Gemma was too distracted by her hamster book to concentrate on her drills, but allowed that she was "over hamsters" and moving on to guinea pigs.

Christine saw one student after the other, working with them when she could, dispensing their gift bags, listening to their last stories and little worries, giving them her final words of encouragement, hugging them all good-bye, and reminding them to keep up with summer reading. She knew that even the younger grades would be given summer homework by their other teachers, but her reading students had made so much progress during the year, she didn't want them to lose it in just two months. She didn't care *what* they read, just that they read, even if she wasn't going to be their teacher anymore.

Christine accepted small gifts from the moms who stopped in, because Nutmeg Hill allowed it, and she was happy to see the moms and grateful for their kindness, whether their gifts were gift-wrapped boxes from a department store or tin-foiled loaves of home-baked banana bread. She truly believed it was a privilege to teach their children, and she told them so, with tears in her eyes.

Last, she said good-bye to Pam, the office staff, and her fellow teachers, holding back more tears though she felt an undercurrent of sadness and profound loss. There was no emptier-feeling day than the last day of school, when the desks are pushed together and the chairs turned upside down on top, and she'd felt that way even when she had been a student herself. Both of her parents were high-school educators, so she'd never doubted that her work had meaning, especially teaching children to read, because reading was the cornerstone of self-esteem, success, and even a simple pleasure that was lifelong. She had expected that her last day of school would be bittersweet, knowing she'd be leaving teaching behind, as well as students she loved, but she'd been willing to give everything up for a baby of her own and a happy new family.

My wife could be carrying the baby of a serial killer.

At the end of the day, Christine left the building alone, deep in thought, her head down. She didn't know what to think or expect. The rug had been pulled out from under her, and she felt hopeless, rudderless. She knew what she was leaving behind, but she didn't know where she was heading.

Except to see a therapist, with her husband.

Chapter Eight

"Hi, Coach." Christine entered the office with Marcus, finding a heartfelt smile for their therapist, Michelle LeGrange. Michelle was in her late fifties, but looked younger; though her bright blue eyes were hooded behind her preppy tortoiseshell glasses, she had on a cheery, almost child-like turtle-print shift from Lilly Pulitzer. She rose quickly and gave Christine a warm hug.

"Honey, come in. I'm so sorry about what happened, or may have happened." Michelle's touch was soothing and familiar, and Christine almost didn't want to let her go. Marcus had been distant in the waiting room, and she could tell that he was completely preoccupied. She had driven separately from him since she had come from school and he from the office. He even looked out of sorts, his dark silk tie just slightly askew against his cutaway collar, which he had on with a lightweight tan suit.

"So you heard."

"Of course. I can only imagine how hard this is for you both, to have such a cloud over happiness you worked so hard for."

"Exactly." Christine sat down in a cozy conference area, with several sea-foam club chairs opposite Michelle's sleek walnut desk. Her framed diplomas and awards lined the walls, and medical binders and textbooks stocked her bookshelves. Christine and Marcus usually had sessions in Michelle's home office at her lovely Tudor in Rowayton, which Christine preferred. She couldn't forget that she had been inseminated one office down, and the techs had shown her the gray cryotanks under their counter across the hall, where they fertilized eggs in petri dishes, for IVF. One of the techs had told her that there were four thousand fertilized embryos in their tanks, and that the techs had two fears; one was mixing up the embryos, and the other was dropping them.

"Thanks for coming in. I'm glad we can talk this over." Michelle turned to Marcus, extending a hand, but he was already heading for the other chair.

"Michelle, I don't know what good 'talking it over' will do."

"How so?" Michelle took her seat opposite them, crossing her legs, which were trim and muscled. Late-day sunlight filtered into the office through blinds on the window behind her.

Marcus asked, "Aren't you the one who talks about the 'elephant in the room'?"

"Yes," Michelle answered, pleasantly.

"So, there's a question that has to be answered before we discuss our feelings. Is the serial killer Donor 3319 or not?"

"I understand how you feel, and unfortunately, I don't know the answer to that question."

"How typical is this that Homestead won't confirm or deny something so basic?"

"Nothing about the situation is typical. I've never seen anything like it before."

Christine sighed. "I'm sure."

Marcus was shaking his head. "Really? It seems like it's exactly the kind of thing that can happen. These aren't gods who donate sperm, they're just guys, mostly college kids or graduate students, whatever. They're young guys. Things are going to happen as they grow up, criminal or not, that have to impact this process."

Michelle nodded. "You would think that's true, but the fact is this hasn't happened to us before. Our task is to try to bring some perspective to the situation, even in the absence of facts we wish we had known."

"I don't think that's possible," Marcus shot back.

"Thank God," Christine said, at almost the same moment, but she could see that Michelle wanted to finish a thought.

"Marcus, I understand where you're coming from. Like most of my patients, you're used to setting goals and arriving at them. You run a multimillion-dollar company, you're a CEO. You're used to a degree of control. You've been very successful in life, setting goals and meeting them. Is that a fair statement?"

"Yes," Marcus answered, but he pursed his lips, and Christine knew what he was thinking. He always felt that Michelle stroked him too much, overly sensitive to the fact that his male ego was bruised by his infertility. Christine didn't buy into the criticism because she did the same thing. She walked on eggshells when the subject of his infertility came up, a classic no-win position.

"So this situation is going to challenge you in new ways, both of you."

"Oh it's *challenging* me all right," Marcus said, with a smirk.

Michelle glanced at Christine. "Christine, how are you feeling?"

"I'm really upset. I'm upset for me, for the baby, and obviously for Marcus."

"And what upsets you the most?"

"It's hard to say. Everything."

Marcus interjected, "That nobody will answer a simple question."

Michelle kept her eyes on Christine. "You were saying?"

"Well, I guess, first, it does bother me that Homestead won't tell us the truth." Christine didn't want to begin there, but she wanted to back Marcus up. "We don't know what to do. I don't know what to do. There's nothing to do."

"I understand how you could feel that way." Michelle's voice remained soothing. "None of us here knows the identity of 3319. We are not withholding information from you. We simply don't have the information, though we wish—"

"You could get it," Marcus interrupted.

"What makes you say that, Marcus?" Michelle asked, tilting her head.

"You deal with Homestead all the time. You probably send lots of your patients there. You're familiar with them. Dr. Davidow called Demipetto by her first name. Lee Ann."

"And what follows from that, in your view?"

"I think you can put pressure on them to give us the information." Marcus stabbed the air with an index finger. "I think you could say, 'we're not going to send you any other patients, and we're not going to spend a single dollar at Homestead unless you give the Nilssons the information they need.'"

"You think *I* could do that?"

"Why not? Or if not you, then Dr. Davidow, or his boss, or whoever owns this place."

"Dr. Davidow is the owner."

"Fine, him then. I'd go the extra mile for one of my clients. I wouldn't take no for an answer. But no one's doing that for us, or even offering to do that."

Christine cringed at the accusatory tone in Marcus's voice, which though it was controlled, was plainly resentful.

Michelle leaned back in her chair. "Marcus, how do you feel about that?"

"How do you think I feel? What difference does it make how I feel?"

Christine felt torn, understanding his frustration but not wanting to alienate Michelle. She turned to Marcus. "Babe, this is a discussion we should have with Dr. Davidow, don't you think?"

Michelle smiled at Christine, in a pat way. "Christine, thank you, but you needn't come to my aid." Then she turned to Marcus. "However, I do think we're getting off track—"

"No, we're finally on track, if you ask me. As for how I feel, I would say I feel angry. Angry enough to do something about it."

Christine swallowed hard, but having been signaled not to interrupt, stayed quiet.

"Marcus, we've talked before about how infertility issues have been a challenge for you as a couple, and you, in particular, because you tend to assume the role of fixer, as many men do. This may be a situation which you can't fix."

"That's what *you* think. I'm not going to let my wife go through what she's going through. I'm not going to put myself through this either. I *will* fix the situation."

Michelle sighed, her tanned shoulders going up and down, once. "Please, let's start over. I feel as if we've gotten off on the wrong foot. Fair enough?"

"Suit yourself." Marcus sat back in his chair. "It's your bus. You drive it."

"Marcus, I'm here as your therapist and Christine's. I'm on your side."

Christine felt tears come to her eyes, knowing it was true. Michelle was always on their side, even through the hardest times, and she'd helped both of them. Families First had made her a mother, but she wouldn't say that aloud, right now.

Michelle continued, "If you remember in our earliest sessions, we talked about the importance of acceptance in dealing with infertility. That you accept the situation you find yourself in and try to find solutions from there."

Marcus snorted. "Doesn't 'find solutions' mean fix it?"

Michelle shook her head. "No. It means, accept what there is and move forward. My job is to help you understand, both as individuals and as a couple, what will make you feel better and most comfortable, going forward. That's how you arrived at your wonderful solution, which was to use a donor, so that you both could experience the joys of pregnancy."

Marcus rolled his eyes. "And it's turned out to be *such* a joy."

Christine looked over, stung. "It has, honey. I'm excited, at least I was before this happened." She turned to Michelle in bewilderment. "But now, I have to admit, I'm confused. I can't sort out my feelings. I'm bollixed up."

Michelle nodded. "Yes, and part of this process is that you and Marcus are not always in the same place at the same time. Christine, you're going to experience this pregnancy more directly than Marcus. That's also true of whatever bad or good news may come. You're carrying the child, and you made a genetic contribution to the child. Right now, this is happening to you in a way it isn't to him."

Christine swallowed hard. It was exactly how she felt.

Michelle turned to Marcus. "In the past, Marcus, you have felt, and understandably so, more removed. Our work in therapy has been to help you see how involved you can be, *equally* involved, and that will come more easily as the pregnancy progresses and you two go to doctor's appointments, see the ultrasound, and hear the heartbeat. You will experience all of that together." Michelle sat back, gesturing to them both as a couple. "You are not yet in the same position, but you will get there. I'm here to help you both accept what is happening, cope with it, and move on."

"But how do we move on from *this*?" Christine blurted out, her heart speaking out of turn.

"When we don't even know the truth?" Marcus added.

Michelle eyed them both. "We put this in perspective. Granted, we don't know if 3319 is the man who was arrested. But let's assume for the purposes of discussion that he is."

"Oh no." Christine moaned.

Marcus grimaced, looked away, saying nothing.

Michelle held up a manicured index finger. "But wait. I have help. I've arranged for a wonderful genetics counselor to join us, if you wish. Her name is Lucy McCabe. She came in today at our request, but I did not want to invite her into our session unless you agreed. How do you feel about that?"

"Bring her in." Marcus shifted forward in the soft chair. "I think it makes more sense to talk about facts rather than feelings, right now. I'd love to talk to a geneticist. I did some research of my own."

Christine looked over, surprised. "What do you mean?"

"I read some things online, last night."

Michelle nodded. "Okay, but Lucy is not a geneticist. A geneticist is an M.D. Lucy is a genetics counselor, she has a master's degree. She conducts risk assessments for hereditary conditions, whether the child is conceived via a third-party or not."

Christine translated the jargon. A third-party conception was one involving either an egg donor, a sperm donor, or a gestational surrogate, which was a woman who carried a couple's child to term though she made no genetic contribution. "So why do you want us to talk to her?"

"We ask her to consult from time to time, and I think the world of her. She's full of useful information." Michelle turned to Christine. "Would you like her to join us? Or would you rather we talked alone, then you can meet with her at another time? Christine?"

"I'd like that, and now is fine."

"Why wait, right?" Marcus answered, motioning at the door. "Send her in."

"Terrific." Michelle half-rose, reached for a landline on the desk, and pressed an intercom button. Silence fell, and Christine tried to not let it bother her. Normally their sessions with Michelle were so chatty, they'd often run beyond their allotted hour, but the air in the room felt newly charged, so that it came as a relief when someone knocked.

"That must be Lucy." Michelle rose and opened the door, admitting a petite, wiry woman in her sixties, with fluffy gray hair, silver hoop earrings, and steely, wire-rimmed glasses, which she had on with a beige pantsuit, giving her a clinical appearance that was mitigated by a flowery silk scarf.

"Hello, Christine, Marcus," Lucy said, smiling tightly as she shook both of their hands, then sat down in the last chair next to Michelle.

"Thank you for inviting me into your session. I'm always happy to consult with Michelle, whom I've known for twenty years."

"We walk together," Michelle added. "Lucy got me into her walking club, and I can barely keep up with them."

Christine smiled. "I find that hard to believe."

"Don't," Lucy said simply, and the three women laughed.

Marcus shifted impatiently.

Lucy's smile faded. "Now, I've been given your case background, so let's jump right in, shall we?"

"Fine." Marcus nodded.

"Yes, please," Christine said, liking Lucy's demeanor. The genetics counselor linked her slim fingers in her lap and spoke deliberately, which seemed somehow reliable and comforting.

"I understand that Homestead can't confirm or deny the donor's identity for an anonymous donation, so we'll have to work with the hypothetical, if we can. Can we?"

Marcus frowned. "We have no other choice. Our question is, if our donor has a predilection for violence, is that an inherited trait? Also, our donor could be a sociopath. I read that a lot of serial killers are sociopaths. Or thrill seekers. Is that inherited?"

"First, some background is in order." Lucy held up a hand. "I don't get a lot of psychological issues, and I've been a genetics counselor for twenty-nine years. The problem with psychological disorders is that there's no test, such as a blood test or tissue test, that I can perform for them."

"Really?"

"Unfortunately, yes. So, there is no psychological test or clinically available testing I can perform that can answer your questions. However, I collected and reviewed the current population data and studies, at Dr. Davidow's request. I would be happy to send them to you, by email, and I can summarize my conclusion from these articles, right now."

"Please do."

"The question with psychological disorders is one of nature vs. nurture. The answer is that it depends on the disorder. For example, the data shows that bipolarity is inherited, as is schizophrenia and clinical depression. Likewise, with substance-abuse issues and alcoholism, maternal genes play a role, as in the case of egg donors."

"We used a sperm donor, not an egg donor."

"Understood." Lucy nodded, still deliberate. "With respect to sociopathy, the weight of authority and data is that it's a matter of environmental factors. In other words, a sociopath isn't born but made. That's my conclusion."

Christine breathed a relieved sigh. She was thinking back to her conversation with Lauren. "So you're saying that even if our donor is Jeffcoat, this serial killer, that our baby may not have inherited his—well, whatever he has. His psychological disorder."

"Yes. That's my conclusion with respect to sociopathy." Lucy nodded, satisfied. "I have reached the same conclusion with respect to a propensity for violence. I pulled the articles and studies, and the weight of authority is that such a propensity is not inheritable. Environmental factors are determinative, so that children who grow up in families with violence will tend to resort to violence. We see this, anecdotally, in domestic abuse. It's not hereditary. It's learned behavior."

Michelle smiled. "I thought that would put your mind at ease, Christine."

"It does." Christine felt her heart lift. "I mean, it's still a little strange, but it is reassuring."

"Not to me," Marcus said, frowning. "Lucy, from what I read online, there are studies that go the other way."

"Which way?"

"They say a propensity for violence is inherited. I was reading about the 'warrior gene,' and it said that people who are thrill seekers or seek high-risk activities inherit that predilection, through their genes. They can become violent adults."

Christine recoiled. "How do you know?"

"I read it, I can show you the articles," Marcus answered, his mouth a grim line. "Not all the geneticists think it's nurture. Some think it's nature. Thrill seekers have different MAO levels and different levels of hormones like testosterone, which is inherited. The studies show that those people tend to commit crime more often than other people. In other words, a serial killer *could* be born, not made."

Lucy frowned, her lined forehead buckling. "Marcus, Christine, I based my opinion on my research and experience. I think you can rely upon that."

"But there are those who don't agree with you, isn't that right?" Marcus asked, coolly.

Lucy opened her palms. "Can you find people on the Internet who have different opinions from mine? Of course. But that's the nature of the Internet. I wouldn't rely on the Internet over *my* opinion."

Marcus shifted forward. "But there are no guarantees, correct? You're not about to guarantee that these factors aren't inherited, are you?"

"Of course not," Lucy answered, firmly. "There are never guarantees. But I evaluate statistical risk, and it is very low in this case."

"Okay, thank you," Christine said, hiding her discomfort. She was willing to go with Lucy's opinion and she hated that Marcus seemed to be alienating both women. She didn't know where he was coming from.

"You are free, of course, to seek a second opinion," Lucy added, glancing at Michelle. "Both Michelle and I know other genetics counselors. We would be happy to supply you with their names."

"Do they work for Families First, like you?"

"Yes," Lucy and Michelle answered in unison.

"Do you know any genetics counselors who don't work for Families First?"

Christine cringed, embarrassed at the implication. "Marcus, seriously? That's uncalled for."

Marcus looked over, his blue eyes cold. "It's a legitimate question."

"Understood," Lucy was saying. "I'll be happy to email you some names of my colleagues not employed by us."

"Thanks." Marcus folded his arms. "So, what would a couple do in our position? What should we do?"

"It's completely individual. It's up to you both. I've said that I think the risk in this case is low to baseline. I counsel couples who can't tolerate a risk level above baseline, and others do much better with risk." Lucy paused. "For example, I currently counsel a couple whose testing shows that their baby is anencephalic, which means that he'll certainly die. They want to continue the pregnancy."

"Wait, what?" Christine asked, confused. "What are you talking about?"

"The decision to terminate the pregnancy," Marcus answered matter-of-factly.

"What?" Christine asked him, incredulous. "You mean abortion? Who's talking about that? I don't want an abortion."

"It's just a possibility. We're talking about possibilities."

"It's not a possibility," Christine shot back, finding her bearings. "I don't want an abortion. Do *you* want an abortion?"

"No, but we're exploring it."

"I don't want to explore it." Christine noticed that both Lucy and Michelle had fallen abruptly silent. "Is that what this is about? You think we want an abortion?"

"No." Michelle shook her head, her eyebrows sloping unhappily down. "Christine, on the contrary, my point in bringing Lucy into our session is to show you that your risk of a hereditary issue with your baby is low."

Lucy nodded. "That's correct. That's my sole purpose in being here. I would never dream of directing you, one way or the other.

I'm non-directive by training as well as by nature. I view myself as someone who can offer you the best available information with which to make your decision. You make your own decision, as a couple."

"Do people abort for something like this?" Christine asked, surprised.

Lucy nodded. "We have had patients terminate for less than this, and we don't judge them. Some patients terminate pregnancies for reasons relating to the health of the child. Others terminate pregnancies of healthy babies for a variety of reasons. It's well within the parameters of the law, in the first trimester."

"I'm not talking about whether it's legal." Christine didn't want to get into a political debate, but she couldn't hold her tongue. "I mean, I believe it's a personal choice, but I don't want to abort this baby."

"Fine," Marcus said abruptly.

"Good, it's settled," Christine said, but she felt shaken to her core. She realized that Marcus must have been thinking about their getting an abortion, but it hadn't even occurred to her.

Michelle checked her watch. "Okay, folks, I believe Dr. Davidow is free, and he wants to touch base with you both."

"I'd like that." Marcus jumped to his feet. He went to the door, and Christine felt the distance between them growing, with her on one side and him on the other, as if the tectonic plates beneath their feet were suddenly shifting, destabilizing their marriage.

"Me, too," Christine said, rising on shaky knees.

Chapter Nine

I'm so happy to see you," Christine said, surprised to find herself tearing up when she gave Dr. Davidow a hug as soon as she'd entered his office.

"I'm happy to see you, too, Christine." Dr. Davidow released her with a broad, sympathetic smile. His eyes were large, round, and warmly brown, and they were his best feature, mainly because he looked everyone right in the eye, connecting with confidence. His crow's-feet were well established, since he was in his late forties, and his bulbous nose was an unfortunate echo of his round, bald head. Still, he had always had a big smile for her, even through the toughest times.

"This has *not* been easy," Christine blurted out, relieved to release the pressure that had been building up inside. She couldn't shake off what Marcus had said in the counseling session. She hoped he didn't mention an abortion to Dr. Davidow.

"I'm sure. I can imagine. As my daughter says, I feel you." Dr. Davidow turned to Marcus, extending a hand. "I'm sorry this has been so difficult."

"So am I." Marcus shook his hand, more stiffly than Christine would have liked, then sat down. She sat down in the leather chair next to him, feeling almost at home in Dr. Davidow's office. She had gotten some of the worst news of her life here, but more recently had gotten the absolute best, and even in the circumstances, she still trusted their doctor. His office reflected his personality: friendly, unstuffy, but still furnished in a classy way, with a polished glass desk that was remarkably uncluttered except for a new desktop and photos of his family, in matching glass frames. His framed diplomas, certifications, and various awards lined the walls, attesting to the fact that he was one of the top reproductive endocrinologists in Connecticut, and his bookshelf held medical books, more family photographs, and his adored, built-in tropical fish tank. A bluish light glowed faintly from the surface of its water, and a bright yellow fish swam by, wiggling its filmy tail fins.

"So, how did your meeting go with Lucy and Michelle?" Dr. Davidow went around the side of his desk, pulled out his black leather chair, and sat down, patting the knot of his tie, which he had on with a blue shirt and khaki slacks under his long white lab coat.

"I thought it went well," Christine answered, taking the lead. She didn't want this meeting to go south, like the previous session. "I feel reassured knowing that the mental illnesses that could cause somebody to be a serial killer aren't inherited. I thought that was really helpful."

"I knew you would." Dr. Davidow smiled again, his forehead relaxing all the way back to the top of his pate. There was a pinkish indenture where his hairline had been, and Christine tried not to look at it, because she sensed it made him self-conscious.

"But it's still a strange sensation, that our donor could be a killer. I mean, that's horrifying to me."

"Of course, I get that." Dr. Davidow frowned. "I wish I could give you peace of mind as to your donor's identity, but that's not possible. I'll keep lobbying on your behalf with Homestead, but to be realistic, I don't think I'll be successful."

Marcus cleared his throat. "Doctor, I'm not as satisfied with Lucy as my lovely wife is—"

"I didn't say I was satisfied, Marcus." Christine bristled. "I said I was reassured. You said you wanted facts, and Lucy gave us facts."

"And those facts are in dispute." Marcus pursed his lips, turning to Dr. Davidow. "Lucy feels confident that the psychological disorders that make someone turn into a serial killer aren't inherited, but my research is to the contrary. I'm going to seek a second opinion."

Dr. Davidow blinked. "If that's what you want to do, then you should feel free."

Christine interjected, "Doctor, do you have an opinion about whether things like that are inherited or not?"

"I know some genetics, but Lucy is a trained and qualified genetics counselor, a true expert. She has absolutely top-shelf credentials and decades of experience. That's why I have her on staff, and I have complete confidence in her." Dr. Davidow met Christine's eye. "I did discuss this with her, and she told me that she believes the risk of heritability of any traits or disorders was slim to none. I think you can credit her opinion completely."

"Good." Christine eased back into the chair. "I do."

"I don't, but that's neither here nor there." Marcus set his jaw. "Dr. Davidow, I'm not satisfied having hypothetical discussions about the genetic makeup of this child. I refuse to accept that you can't find out from Homestead whether Donor 3319 is Zachary Jeffcoat."

Christine interjected, "Marcus, they're not going to tell him. They signed the contracts. There's nothing he can do."

Marcus held up a hand to her. "Honey, let him tell me that. I believe that there's plenty he can do."

"No, there isn't," Christine shot back, defensive.

"Marcus, what would you have me do?" Dr. Davidow asked, his tone reasonable. "Believe me, if there was a way I could get that information from Homestead, I would."

Christine felt her frustration boil over. "Dr. Davidow, he thinks you can pressure them. He thinks if you threaten not to send them any more patients, they'll tell you. Is that true?"

"No." Dr. Davidow hesitated, looking from Christine to Marcus. "That won't make any difference. They're the best in the country, and all the best practices use them. In fact, they have a waiting list. If I stop sending Homestead my patients, it won't matter to them. They have legalities to think of, and they're not about to breach their contract of confidentiality with your donor, or any donor. They have a reputation to protect."

"Okay, well, I've been investigating the legalities, too." Marcus slipped a hand inside his suitjacket and pulled out a folded piece of paper. "I spoke with a lawyer, and he came up with an idea. He said—"

"What lawyer?" Christine interrupted, in surprise. They didn't have a family lawyer, nor did Marcus's engineering firm. Some of his golf buddies were lawyers, but she couldn't read the piece of paper, which appeared to have letterhead embossed on the top.

"His name is Gary Leonardo. He has a law firm in New Haven. His own firm."

Dr. Davidow cleared his throat. "I know who he is. He's a medical malpractice lawyer."

"Medical malpractice?" Christine felt dumbfounded. "Marcus, what are you doing? Why didn't you talk to me about this? Are you going to sue Homestead?"

"Relax, and let me explain," Marcus answered, handing the letter to Dr. Davidow. "Doctor, this is a letter that Gary wrote and wants to send to Homestead. Bottom line, it says that they were negligent in screening donated sperm in our case. It outlines a lawsuit that we could file against them, and Gary says he could have it filed by the end of next week."

"What's the point of that?" Christine was trying to come up to speed, and Dr. Davidow's expression was changing. His face fell, and he ran a tongue over his lips. He set the letter aside, then folded his hands on his desk in front of him. His gold wedding band gleamed in the soft recessed lighting.

"So Marcus," Dr. Davidow said, "let me get this straight. Gary Leonardo advised you to sue Homestead, which by the way, is a massive undertaking, because it has eighteen separate offices across the country and is headquartered in Wilmington, Delaware."

"Yes, he said we have to sue under Delaware law, according to our contracts. He's not afraid to take on the big guys."

"Marcus!" Christine couldn't contain herself, then tried to dial it back. "I know you're trying to help us, but you should've talked to me about this. You think you're going to *sue* them into telling us?"

"Yes." Marcus turned to Christine, his expression still cold. "If our donor really is a serial killer, then I think Homestead was negligent in their screening. So does Gary. We both think Homestead should do more psychological screening of their donors, instead of worrying about whether they look like Bradley Cooper or Colin Farrell. Don't you agree?"

"I wish they had known, but I don't know if they could have done better—"

"Gary said that if he sends them a lawyer's letter"—Marcus gestured at the letter on Dr. Davidow's desk—"saying that we will file a negligence complaint and go public about their negligent practices, then they will tell us."

"How will that make them tell us?"

"You can negotiate anything. It would be the negotiated settlement to the lawsuit. All they have to do is disclose to us whether or not our donor is Zachary Jeffcoat, and we will agree to keep confidential the lawsuit *and* the settlement." Marcus drew himself up, inhaling. "Nobody will know that they disclosed, and their reputation for confidentiality is unharmed. And we have our answer."

"But *suing*?" Christine asked, trying to process the information. "We never sued anybody."

"Christine, whose side are you on?" Marcus frowned.

"Oh my God, Marcus." Christine felt herself flush with embarrassment. She couldn't believe they were having this conversation in front of Dr. Davidow.

"You want to know, don't you?" Marcus persisted. "You're the one who started this."

"But I don't know if I want to *sue* people, and you should have discussed—"

"Guys, time-out." Dr. Davidow signaled a football time-out, but he wasn't smiling, and both Christine and Marcus fell silent. "Marcus, this is a major step, if you're serious."

"I am."

Dr. Davidow frowned. "I find it very hard to believe that a lawyer like Gary Leonardo would advise you to file a suit against Homestead and not against Families First." He sucked his cheeks in slightly, his gaze hardening. "Are you going to sue us, too?"

"I hadn't decided that yet," Marcus answered, his tone equally firm.

"*What?*" Christine swallowed, mortified. "Don't I have a say in this? Marcus, we're *not* suing Families First. I won't let you do that, not in my name."

Marcus snapped his head around to her. "Honey, you're not thinking about this the right way. It's not like we'd be suing Homestead or Families First. It's only a way of formally asking them to tell us something that we have every right to know."

Dr. Davidow stood up behind his desk. "Beg to differ, Marcus. It's suing us. I know about Gary Leonardo and how he operates. If you're suing Homestead, then you'll be joining Families First as a codefendant. You might even end up suing me, personally."

"No, never," Christine rushed to say. "You didn't do anything wrong!"

Dr. Davidow seemed not to hear her, walking around his desk and opening his office door. "I'm sure my lawyer would advise me to call my malpractice carrier, right now. I'm sorry, folks, but this conversation is over."

"So be it." Marcus rose quickly, walking out the open door.

"Marcus? No!" Christine jumped to her feet, heartsick. She had just lost Michelle and she didn't want to lose Dr. Davidow, too. She stopped in the threshold, where Dr. Davidow was standing. "We're not going to sue you, Dr. Davidow."

"I'm sorry, Christine." Dr. Davidow edged backwards, and a tech in the hall spotted Christine and started to wave to her, then stopped.

"Dr. Davidow, please. Don't worry. I'll talk to him."

"It's best for you to go, Christine. And I don't think you and Marcus should come back."

Chapter Ten

Christine followed Marcus through the clinic's waiting room, feeling the curious stares of the staff behind the counter. They must have figured out that something was wrong, especially because Christine always made a point to say good-bye before she left. A young couple waiting to be seen glanced up from their smartphones but quickly averted their eyes. It wasn't uncommon that couples left Families First unhappy, angry, or even teary, but Christine knew they couldn't have guessed what was going on. She followed Marcus to the exit door, which he held open for her because he had excellent manners, even if he could be a total jerk.

"My car is closer than yours," Marcus said, closing the door behind her. "Let's go to mine. I'll drive you to yours."

"Fine." Christine barely looked at him as she went through the door, which led to a vast, glass-walled entrance hall of the east wing of Pilgrim Point General Hospital, which was the new addition, built only last year. Families and visitors crisscrossed the modern lobby, some carrying balloons and others using walkers or pushing wheelchairs. Christine and Marcus passed the circular reception desk and walked to the exit together, and she could barely wait until they were alone to start the conversation.

"What the hell?" Christine said under her breath. "What were you thinking?"

"I'd ask you the same question. What were *you* thinking?" Marcus looked down at her stiffly as they walked through the automatic doors, stepping outside into the warm, humid air.

A couple whom Christine recognized from the clinic passed them, and she and Marcus fell silent. The sun was turning a coppery color, low in a cloudless June sky, and out front was a fancy courtyard of Belgian block, where people stood talking in groups or waiting to be picked up. Beyond that was a large outdoor parking lot that had an area designated for Families First, and they both walked in that direction. Usually they held hands, but not today. Christine ignored an acrid cloud of cigarette smoke that wafted their way from someone lighting up on the way to his car. She was much more sensitive to smells since her pregnancy, but she was too angry to let it bother her right now.

"Marcus, *you're* the one. You've lost your damn mind. I'm so mad at you, I don't know where to begin." Christine didn't raise her voice because she wasn't a big yeller, even when they fought. They had two ground rules: no yelling and no name-calling. That was why whenever she called Marcus a jerk or a total asshole, she had to do it in her mind.

"How? Why?" Marcus walked along, his pace quicker than usual. "Because I'm trying to get an answer to a question we have every right to know? Because I'm trying to do what's best for us?"

"How is it best for us if you antagonize all those people who are our friends—or *were* our friends?"

"They're not our *friends,* honey. They're professionals we hired."

"They're more than that. Dr. Davidow is, for sure. So's Michelle." Christine felt a wrench in her chest, thinking of how Dr. Davidow's face had fallen in his office.

"No, they're not." Marcus took the lead between the parked cars. "If they were our friends, they'd tell us what we have a right to know. If they were our friends, they wouldn't withhold information that's *our information.*"

"They don't know it. Homestead knows it."

"Then they'd find it out. They'd move mountains to find it out. That's what a *friend* would do." Marcus shook his head, as they walked. "*Lauren* is a friend. Lauren would pick up the phone and call Homestead. Lauren would read them the riot act. She would be outside their building, *picketing,* until they told you. *That's* what a friend would do. They're not acting like friends, so they're not friends."

"Dr. Davidow tried to get the information." Christine spotted Marcus's Audi two cars away. He did have a better space. He always got the best space. It drove her crazy. Today, it made her want to kill him.

"He's not trying hard enough. I'm going to make him try harder." Marcus's eyes glittered with suppressed anger.

"I'm not going to sue him, Marcus."

"Why not? Don't you want to know who our donor is?"

"Of course I do, but not that way. My God, he practically threw us out of his office. You offended him, Marcus. You *hurt* him!"

"He hurt me! He hurt us. He's hurting my family."

"He *made* us a family!" Christine blurted out, but she knew it was the wrong thing to say as soon as she'd said it.

"Thanks for the reminder." Marcus looked away, raising his chin. His jaw clenched.

"Marcus, you know I didn't mean it that way." Christine felt suddenly exhausted and raw, unwilling to shore up his ego any longer, not the way he was acting. "We wouldn't be pregnant without his intervention. I'm grateful to him for that. We owe him."

"We paid him. That's all we owe him. You heard him, it's his practice. He owns it. He does it for the money."

"No he doesn't." Christine knew how much joy Dr. Davidow

took in helping couples have children. He'd told her himself, and she had seen the sincerity shining in his eyes. Maybe she identified with him because she did her job for love, too. It was why it had hurt so much today, to walk away from the school building for the last time.

"Oh please. Davidow has more leverage with Homestead than he's letting on. He's one of the top REs in the country. If he stops using Homestead, word will get around."

"You don't know that."

"Yes I do. Gary told me. This is his expertise, his field."

"Who's this Gary, by the way? How did you find Gary?"

"I asked Bruce. He knows the top lawyers in town, and he got me in today. Gary's famous, you heard Davidow." Marcus arched a light eyebrow, in a newly knowing way. "Sometimes you have to get tough, honey. We'd be suing Davidow for leverage, to force Homestead's hand. I'm glad we have a lawyer."

"Now we have a lawyer?" Christine rolled her eyes, and they stopped walking when they reached the Audi.

"Yes, and we need one. You know what your problem is?" Marcus chirped his car unlocked, aiming his fob like a weapon. "You want everybody to like you, and everybody does like you. You're *nice*. That's what makes you a great teacher. But this isn't elementary school, this is big business."

"Please don't condescend to me," Christine snapped, fuming.

"I'm not. But this is about dollars and cents. We have to sue and we have to sue them both. You have to hit them where it hurts, in their pockets. It's the only way to get an answer." Marcus opened the passenger-side door for her, but Christine didn't move to get inside.

"I don't want to sue Dr. Davidow."

"It's not really Davidow, it's his insurance company. You heard him. He's going to call his malpractice carrier. It's not him we'd be suing."

"He said it was, and I don't want to do that to him. It's his liveli-hood. He has a family—"

"Why are you loyal to his family and not ours?"

"It's not right."

"Yes, it is. Why are you tying my hands? We're not power-less. We don't have to sit on our thumbs. Why don't you want to sue?"

"It's mean, and it's expensive—" Christine stopped herself, because she didn't know what else was involved with a lawsuit, but she knew enough to know it was terrible. "I'm not going to, I'm just not."

"Look, we'll meet with Gary. He'll explain it to you. He al-ready told me he'd squeeze me in. Tomorrow, okay?"

"Why don't you just give it a few days? Homestead is investigat-ing, let's see what they turn up."

Marcus scoffed. "Why wait? We could have an answer by next week if they settle."

"We don't need to jump the gun and start suing people. What's the rush?"

Marcus hesitated, blinking, and suddenly, Christine realized why.

"Oh, is it because you want me to get an *abortion*? I can't be-lieve you said that. I can't believe you're even *thinking* that!"

"Babe, we have to be able to talk about it." Marcus met her eye evenly, gesturing at the hospital. "You heard what they said. People abort for less than that."

"I don't, and I won't! How dare you suggest such a thing?" Christine remembered in a flash that her first ultrasound was to-morrow. Marcus was supposed to come with her. Now she didn't want to remind him. She didn't want him there now.

"If it were a really sick baby, we'd abort it."

"That's different."

"No it isn't. It's a baby who's psychologically sick, who's inheriting serious mental issues." Marcus threw up his hands. "Look at the upside. The pregnancy isn't that far along. We can pick another donor. We can start over."

"No, it's out of the question."

"You could be pregnant again in no time. You're Fertile Myrtle! I'm the one with the problem!"

"We already have our child!" Christine gestured at her belly.

"It's the child of a serial killer. Is that what you want?" Marcus's eyes flared an incredulous blue. "I can show you the articles in medical journals. They talk about how psychological disorders like that are inherited. Lucy's only giving you her opinion. There are lots of contrary opinions, you'll see."

"Even if they told us it was inherited, I wouldn't get an abortion, not now."

"It's not even two months! Women miscarry in two months."

"Here's hoping!" Christine shot back, sarcastically.

"That's not funny."

"I know. I *want* this baby!"

"Well I *don't*!"

Christine gasped, shocked. Marcus's eyes flared, and his lips parted slightly. She could tell that he had surprised even himself. They faced each other in the parking lot, in a sort of marital suspended animation. Marcus had said the unsayable, the *unthinkable*, and there was no going back. She was carrying a child that he did not want. Christine turned on her heel and walked away.

"Babe, don't go, get in the car!" Marcus called after her.

"No!" Christine felt tears come to her eyes.

"Let me give you a ride!"

"I'll walk!"

"Fine! See you at home then!"

Christine didn't reply. She didn't know if she was going home. She didn't know where she was going. She felt untethered, unmoored. Disconnected. She had lost everything. She had left a job she loved, for nothing. She had lost Michelle and Dr. Davidow. And she had no hope of a happy family anymore.

Tears streamed down her cheeks, and she found herself picking up the pace toward her car.

And then, she ran.

Chapter Eleven

Christine left the hospital via the back roads, since Marcus always took the Parkway. She kept her face front and her hands on the steering wheel, but the last of her tears were running down her cheeks behind her sunglasses, in the time-honored tradition of women everywhere, who drive-while-crying. She had done it once in high school after she got dumped by Michael Rotenberg, and she had done it again in college, after she got an undeserved C in American Civilization. She knew Lauren had done it when she didn't get into Penn, and she'd seen other women on the road, driving-while-crying, probably enough to make it its own acronym, DWC.

Christine felt the lowest she had ever felt in her life, but she still had her sense of humor, and it kept hysteria at bay to know that she was a cliché on wheels. The rush-hour traffic was stop-and-go, and she braked behind a tall truck. She avoided looking at the other drivers, who were texting or talking on the phone; she never texted while she drove, and she talked only hands-free, so she could be forgiven a crying jag after her husband had just told her he didn't want their child. A serial killer's child. *Her* child. Or all of the above.

Christine sniffled, reached in the console for the umpteenth Starbucks napkin, and blew her juicy nose into its recycled brown scratchiness. She tossed it used onto the passenger seat, where it joined a soggy pile of other used napkins, evidence that she was the ugliest crier of all ugly criers. She thought about calling Lauren, but the dashboard clock read 6:15, and she remembered that Lauren was going out to dinner with Josh and the kids, celebrating the last day of school. The thought made Christine reach for another napkin, since leaving teaching might've been the dumbest thing she ever did, after using a serial killer as a sperm donor.

The truck finally moved, the traffic got going, and she gave the car gas, noticing that at the exit ahead was a cluster of box stores, including her favorite food store, Timson's. Her stomach growled in response, and she realized that she was starving, which was probably her favorite symptom of pregnancy so far. She'd always wondered if she'd have food cravings while she was pregnant, and it turned out that she did—she craved food. All food, any food, at any time.

She dried her eyes and headed for Timson's, and in no time, pulled into the parking lot in front of the massive grocery store, with its characteristic façade of indeterminate beige stone, which, though it wasn't her Timson's, looked exactly the same as her Timson's, and gave her comfort. She kept her sunglasses on, grabbed her purse and phone, and went inside the store, letting the air-conditioning soothe her jangled nerves. She glanced around in the artificial darkness, and the layout was the same, so the prepared foods were straight ahead.

She made a beeline for the glistening stainless-steel counters bubbling with cooked food, then grabbed the large-sized plastic clamshell from an upside-down stack and followed her nose to the spicy Indian food. She felt her mood improve as she shoveled goopy orange glop into her clamshell, then added a pile of

French fries and a square of eggplant parmesan, wondering in which universe these foods went together. Answer: Pregnancy World.

She got a bottle of water, checked out, and carried her tray to one of the dining areas for grown-ups; she had learned to avoid the kid-friendly dining area, with the undersized chairs and tables and the television that showed *The Lego Movie* on a continuous loop, because she used to wonder if she would ever be lucky enough to be one of those mothers. Now that she was, it didn't feel so lucky.

She sat down at a circular wooden table in the sunny eating area, which was filled with adults and children, but no matter. She'd realized long ago that the suburbs were about children, and it was part of the reason she felt so odd being childless; she didn't fit in in their neighborhood without a kid to take to school, soccer practice, or the pediatrician. Between the children at home and the children at school, Christine lived a life surrounded by children, and she'd be damned if she was ending this pregnancy, no matter what Marcus had said.

Christine picked up her little plastic fork and dug into her Indian food, glancing up at a flat-screen TV on the wall, which was showing CNN on mute. She flashed on Trivi-Al at her good-bye party, but noticed that the TV program was showing political coverage, with the presidential election around the corner, in November. She wolfed down a forkful of food, which tasted hot and delicious, as she picked up her phone, logged on to Google, and typed in Zachary Jeffcoat, wondering if there had been any new developments. She clicked on the first link that popped onto the screen, which took her to the CNN article from yesterday. She scanned it quickly, but it hadn't been changed. She navigated back to the Google page and clicked on the second link, which was from the *Philadelphia Inquirer.* There was no photo, and the story was only a paragraph long:

NURSE MURDERER CHARGED

By William Magni

Zachary Jeffcoat, 24, was arraigned today for the murder of Gail Robinbrecht, 31, a nurse at Chesterbrook Hospital. Federal and state authorities believe that Jeffcoat may be responsible for serial killings of other nurses in Maryland and Virginia. Jeffcoat is awaiting trial at SCI Graterford Prison in Collegeville, Pennsylvania, on a special hold to the prison, a maximum-security penitentiary.

Christine navigated back to the Google page and clicked on the third link, which was another Philadelphia-area newspaper that ran the same story verbatim. She kept researching, reading as she ate, but there was no further information about Jeffcoat. She clicked back to the front page of the *Inquirer*, and the lead stories were about the presidential election. She glanced back at the television, which was showing another set of talking heads, with closed captioning about the election. She watched TV as she ate, and there was a news story about a bombing in the Middle East, then another one in Kabul, and by the time she had finished her meal, the political commentators were back on, talking about the election. It looked like the news cycle had pushed the Jeffcoat story to the background.

Suddenly her phone rang, and the screen said it was Marcus calling. She thought about letting it go, but answered it. "Hello?"

"Hi, are you on your way home?" Marcus asked, but his tone was still too cool for Christine's liking. It told her that he wasn't about to apologize or back down, nor was he having any second thoughts. She should have expected as much, he wasn't that kind of man. Her mouth went dry, so she picked up her water and took a sip.

"No, I'm grabbing something to eat."

"Oh, okay. Well, I just got a call that I have to go back to Raleigh. There's a problem at the site."

"Oh." Christine knew he meant the office complex his firm was building in North Carolina.

"I have to be there tomorrow morning, so I'm going to leave tonight. They got me on the last flight out. That okay with you?"

"Fine." Christine heard herself sounding angry, but it couldn't be helped.

"We both need to cool off."

Christine snorted. "I don't think I'll be cooling off, Marcus."

"We can talk about it when I come back."

"I'll look forward to that." Christine took another sip of water. She could be sarcastic, too, when circumstances required. She knew it wasn't a good thing, necessarily.

"I thought about what you said about the lawsuit."

"And you decided I'm right?"

"No." Marcus paused. "I called Gary. He agreed to meet with you tomorrow morning at ten o'clock."

"I don't want to meet with Gary."

"I was going to go with you, but then I got the call. You can go alone, and I think you should. He can answer any questions you have."

"I don't have any questions."

"Look, I spoke with him. He said that we don't necessarily have to sue the clinic. He said he could explain it to you if you went in." Marcus's voice softened slightly. "I really wish you could go. Then, if you really don't want to file a lawsuit against Families First, we won't. Okay? We won't sue Davidow for leverage against Homestead. But the least you can do is get the facts before you make your decision."

Christine set down her water bottle. "Okay, I'll go, but no promises."

"Fine." Marcus sighed, exasperated. "I'll text you the address and let him know to expect you."

"When are you leaving for Raleigh?" Christine decided not to remind him about the ultrasound. She didn't want him there.

"I'm going to leave for the airport any minute. I let the dog out and fed the cat."

"Thanks." Christine swallowed hard. She knew Marcus had a soft heart, and she always thought he'd be a great father. Tears came to her eyes, and she was glad she'd kept her sunglasses on. People around her probably thought she was blind.

"Okay. Sleep tight. I'll land too late to call you. I'd wake you up."

"No worries, travel safe."

"Love you," Marcus said, after a moment, but it didn't sound that way.

"Love you, too," Christine said back, matching his tone. She hung up and pushed her tray away, her thoughts racing. She wanted to know if Jeffcoat was their donor as much as Marcus did, and she wondered what the lawyer would say about it tomorrow. She didn't relish the meeting, but her thoughts strayed to Homestead and their donor, and she found herself thumbing through her phone to his profile. She had saved it to Dropbox, and she could access it through her phone. There had to be something, *anything,* in it, that would be a clue to his identity or suggest that he was somehow Zachary Jeffcoat.

She opened the file and skimmed through the interview notes, and after that was the self-reported section of the profile, where Donor 3319 had answered questions on a form. She read the first one:

Q: Describe your personality: funny, timid, brave,
bold, serious, goal-oriented, curious, impulsive, etc.
A: I think of myself as a serious person, but that
doesn't mean I'm not fun to be with. I find fun in
different places. I genuinely enjoy reading and learning
new things. I love learning about different civilizations,
their architecture, the government, and how they set
up a system of laws.

Christine thought he didn't sound like a person capable of killing anyone, much less more than one person. But then again, he could have been an excellent liar. She read the next question and answer:

Q: What are your interests and talents?
A: I love reading and research. I intend to become a research physician for that reason. I'm not crazy or boastful enough to say that I could cure cancer, but I do feel that I could best utilize my talents in advancing the cause of medicine and making people's lives better. I know the medical world is fraught with political and insurance issues, but doctors heal, and I actually want to try to cure something in my lifetime. I want to make a difference.
Q: Where do you see yourself in five years?
A: Answer above. Except to add that I would like to have a family of my own someday. I have a girlfriend of one year, but she isn't ready to start a family soon.

Christine paused a moment. She hadn't seen any mention of a girlfriend in the articles about Zachary Jeffcoat, nor had they mentioned any family, but then again, the articles had been so short. She remembered she thought it showed maturity, but now she wondered if that was a lie. She doubted Homestead followed up on facts like that. She went back to the profile and resumed reading.

Q: Tell us how skilled you are in the following subjects:
Math:
A: I love math and am excellent at it. I considered being a math major.
Q: Mechanical:
A: My manual dexterity is excellent and I'm good at engineering tasks like repairing things around my apartment. I consider myself handy.

Q: Athletic:
A: I am not athletic, I must admit. Because I'm tall,
basketball coaches always used to approach me, but
I am not interested. I don't think I really like team
play and am much more a loner. I'm an only child, and
I like chess very much. I'm good at it because I think
I am a strategic thinker. I noticed that the question-
naire doesn't even ask about games like that, which
I think is a deficiency with the questionnaire.

Christine remembered that Marcus had liked that answer
because it sounded like his younger self. He'd played chess in college. She read the answers again and thought about them differently, trying to view them with a critical eye, but their donor didn't
sound like some kind of vicious criminal. He just sounded like a
thoughtful, smart young man, with just a touch of superiority. She
didn't know if that sounded like a serial killer, but she knew it
sounded like Marcus. She read on:

Q: Creative writing:
A: This is not something that interests me.
Q: Literature:
A: As above, I read to learn, so fiction and poetry do
not interest me.
Q: Science:
A: Obviously this is my strong suit, and the memoriza-
tion that will be required by medical school comes
easily to me.
Q: Favorite book, movie, or album:
A: My favorite book is *Cosmos* by Carl Sagan. My
favorite movie is *Awakenings* because it showed what
good doctors can do in society, even though it had a
sad ending. I'm not a big music person.

Christine reached for her water and downed the last of it. Her thoughts were all over the map, thinking of what Lucy had told them about the traits that made someone a serial killer, Marcus talking about the warrior gene, then what their donor had said in these answers. There was only one question left, and Christine used to think it was the most important question:

Q: Why do you want to become a donor?
A: As I said above, I really want to help people in this world, in any way I can. I want to help people who are infertile, or have illnesses, and that's why I want to become a donor. This is an easy way to help people, and I don't know if it's okay to say this, but I could also use the money. I need money for med-school tuition and my parents are not in a position to help me financially.

Christine scrolled back to the Internet and clicked the link for the *Philadelphia Inquirer.* She glanced again at the reporter's by-line, one William Magni, and beside his name was an email address, a Twitter handle, and a phone number. On impulse, she navigated to her phone and pressed the reporter's number in.

"Newsroom," a woman answered.

Christine swallowed, nervous. "I'd like to speak to William Magni."

"Who's calling?"

Christine's gaze fell on her cup. "Timson. Christine Timson."

"Please hold." There was a click on the line, and Christine felt her heart begin to pound. "Can I help you?"

"William Magni?"

"Yes."

"I saw your story about Zachary Jeffcoat, that man who murdered the nurses?"

"Oh yes. What is it?" Magni sounded impatient.

"I think I was a neighbor of his and I'm trying to figure out if it's the same person. Do you know where he's from?"

"No, I got the story off the wire."

Christine had no idea what that meant. "So who reported it originally?"

"A stringer for AP, probably."

Christine knew that AP meant Associated Press. "What's a stringer?"

"A freelancer. Anybody who wants to report a story. No journalistic credentials. A *citizen* journalist." Magni snorted, enjoying his own inside joke. "In other words, somebody who thinks he can make a living from this job. Anybody can be anything these days. It's not a coincidence that the Information Age is full of misinformation."

Christine let it go. "Was Jeffcoat in medical school?"

"I don't know. Like I said, I didn't report the story."

"Do you know if he had a girlfriend? The guy I know was in med school and had a girlfriend."

"Sorry, I got nothin'." Magni rustled some papers.

"Did Jeffcoat have a lawyer?"

"Again, don't know. Try the public defender's office."

"How about a family? Do you know if they were at the arraignment?"

"No idea. I need to go."

"One last question. Are you going to be following the story?"

"The guy's in Graterford. There won't be anything worth covering until trial, which will be right before the election. It won't be me. It's not my beat."

"I know, sorry. Thank you for your time. Bye."

Magni hung up, and so did Christine, lost in thought. She got her purse, rose, and bused her tray, trying to figure out what to do next.

But part of her already knew.

Chapter Twelve

Christine didn't get to talk to Lauren until later, when she'd gone up to bed early, teary and exhausted. She lay on top of the comforter in her T-shirt and sweatsuit, with Murphy sleeping with his head on her left arm and Lady curled under her right. She'd had to pee for the past hour but didn't want to wake either of them up.

"I can't believe he really said that." Lauren's tone was hushed.

"I can. He doesn't want the baby." Christine blew her nose, finishing her last ugly cry of the day. She tossed her Kleenex into the wastecan, which she kept next to the bed for morning sickness.

"He doesn't mean it."

"Yes he does."

"Look, maybe we need to relax." Lauren sighed. "You're not the first couple in the world to be in different places when they get pregnant. You remember, the first time we got pregnant, Josh wasn't ready."

"But he came around. You both wanted the child. Marcus is not going to come around."

"He has to."

"No, he doesn't. He can't have a feeling he doesn't have." Christine reached for another Kleenex and dried her eyes, bucking up. She didn't want to cry anymore. She was sick of feeling sorry for herself. She was working on a plan in the back of her mind.

"I hate that this happened to you guys."

"Me, too." Christine felt relieved that Marcus was out of town tonight. She needed the house to herself, and it was quiet, still, and dark except for the bedroom. A light summer rain fell outside, tapping at the roof and blowing the sheers from time to time.

"He gets that you're not having an abortion?"

"Oh, he gets *that* all right." Christine swallowed bitterly. She dropped her Kleenex into the wastecan.

"He didn't really mean it. He was just exploring his options."

"That's what he said, but still." Christine's gaze found the TV across the room, playing CNN on mute, with closed captioning. The words ran across the screen in a red banner, SENATE DEMOCRATS ANNOUNCE A NEW EDUCATION INITIATIVE. She'd turned on the TV in hopes of seeing something about Zachary Jeffcoat, but so far, no luck. She realized that she had forgotten to tell Lauren about calling the reporter, there had been so much to tell to bring her up to speed.

"So what do you do now?"

"I decided to go see his lawyer. I don't really have another choice. I want to know if our donor is Jeffcoat, and I have to work with Marcus." Christine hesitated, then confided her deepest fear. "I don't know what happens with him and me, going forward. I mean, Lauren, is my marriage in trouble?"

"No! Don't get crazy. You guys love each other. You don't even fight. Josh and I have couple-envy."

Christine couldn't smile. "The thing is, we're not fighting, even now. We just have really different views, and that's a lot worse. How can I ask him to parent a child he can't love? How can a marriage sustain that? And no child deserves to be born into a family like that. I went through hell to have this child. So did he."

"Right, he had that TESA operation, where they opened up his balls." Lauren groaned.

"We wanted a baby. This was the most wanted child in the world. But not to him, anymore. He already believes that a tendency to violence is hereditary, and he's going to find a doctor to tell him that." Christine knew that Marcus was so proactive, he was probably making the phone calls in the airport, trying to find another genetics counselor. "Even so, let's say he comes around. Do I really want a husband who's half-interested? Half-loving our baby?"

Lauren moaned.

"I want to be on the same page with him. I want us to be in this together, completely. That's why I'm going to the lawyer. I mean, remember, there's still a possibility that our donor isn't Jeffcoat."

"You want me to go with you to the lawyer? I want to. I'm free tomorrow. My kids are still in school, remember?"

"Okay, and I have my OB-GYN appointment tomorrow, too. I hear the heartbeat." Christine had been looking forward to her first ultrasound, but that was tainted now. Marcus wouldn't even be there, and she could hear the heartbeat of a baby he didn't want.

"Oh, can I please go with you, too? You can't hear the heartbeat for the first time all by yourself."

"Aw, thanks, yes, come," Christine answered, touched. "I still can't believe this. It's all happening so fast, it's like everything went to hell in a handbasket in just one day."

"Everything's going to be okay, honey."

"You think?" Christine wanted to believe her, but didn't. She checked CNN, where political pundits were arguing, and the closed captioning read REPUBLICANS BACK NEW JOBS BILL.

"Yes, I do. You guys are too good together."

"We used to be. I don't want to sue Davidow, but I feel like it's the only way I can make Marcus happy. The way I look at it, I'm trying to save my marriage." Christine swallowed hard, feeling a wrench in her chest.

"This is not going to break up your marriage."

"I don't want a divorce. I love my husband. I do."

"I know you do," Lauren said, warmly.

"But I'm not giving up on this baby," Christine said, meaning it, too.

"Hang in. Let's see what the lawyer says."

"Right, because lawyers are always so helpful."

And they both laughed.

Chapter Thirteen

Christine and Lauren exchanged glances as they sat down in the waiting room of Leonardo & Associates, with its unique decor. According to a wall of laminated news articles, Gary Leonardo was known as "The Lion" of the Medical Malpractice Division of the Connecticut Bar Association, and his firm name was engraved into a gleaming bronze plaque in the shape of a lion's head. Two gold-toned lion statues held up glass end tables, and the lamp bases were black statues of roaring lions. They flanked the black leather wing chairs on which the women found themselves.

Lauren leaned over. "He likes lions. We *get* it."

"Bingo." Christine forced a smile, knowing her best friend was trying to cheer her up.

"He inspires fear. He's the king of Connecticut." Lauren snorted, quietly. "It can be very dangerous here. Those hedge funders, they bite. Plus, he's very manly."

"Obviously."

"He has plenty of sperm. Sperm to spare." Lauren clammed up as the pretty, dark-haired receptionist rose, with a pleasant smile.

"Gary will see you now," she said, motioning them forward.

"Thank you," Christine and Lauren said in unison, rising. They followed the slim twenty-something as she sashayed down the hallway in a flashy red jersey dress, with Christine and Lauren distinctly unfashionable by comparison. Christine had on a blue-checked shirt, blue cotton skirt, and her good sandals, and Lauren had on a navy blazer over a tan muslin smock with her best Danskos, so they both looked like it was Parents' Night.

"Ladies, welcome!" boomed Gary Leonardo, who pumped Christine's hand, practically pulling her into his office. "Now I know the whole family! Come in! Siddown, take a seat!"

"Well, thanks." Christine smiled, off-balance, since Gary struck her as completely caffeinated. His dark eyes danced with animation, and he flashed a broad smile with lightened teeth. He was tan for early summer, and his shiny hair was suspiciously jet-black. He was trim in a European-fit dark suit, crisp white shirt, and a jungle-print silk tie, and though he was on the short side, it did nothing to diminish his power, which seemed to emanate from his life force, like Al Pacino with a law degree.

"I have to win you over!" Gary's eyes narrowed, with a mischievous glint. "I haven't yet! But I will. I will *win you over.*" Gary turned to Lauren. "And you are—"

"Lauren Weingarten, her best friend."

"The best friend! Happy to have you! Welcome!" Gary beamed, pumping Lauren's hand. "Believe me, I know how important the best friend is. My wife Denise has a best friend. Together, they run my life. They rule my world. They are my sun and moon. Here, sit down. Make yourself comfortable."

"Thanks." Christine sat down in another black leather chair, and so did Lauren.

"Ladies, you want a coffee? You want a Diet Coke? I know you do." Gary gestured at the receptionist. "Theresa, get 'em some Diet Cokes?"

"Thank you, but can I have a water instead?" Christine said, turning to the receptionist, who smiled back before she left.

"Christine, don't get the wrong idea. Theresa's my niece. My wife Denise is my paralegal. She's at a client's or I'd introduce you. Nothing funny's going on here. I'm a faithful guy."

"Good to know." Christine and Lauren both smiled, as Gary scampered around the side of his massive desk, of antique mahogany with carved curlicues. Matching built-in bookshelves lined the office, bursting with lawbooks, notebooks, files, family photographs, pictures of lions, toy lions, rubber lions, and even a Pez dispenser with a lion top, which Christine recognized as being from *The Lion King.*

"Welcome to my den!" Gary threw open his hands and plopped into his chair, also of black leather, but the tallest chair in the room. He looked over as Theresa returned with two drinks on a gold-toned tray, which she set down in front of Christine and Lauren, with ice in a glass and napkins for each.

"Thank you," they both said.

"You're welcome," Theresa answered, then sashayed to the door and shut it behind her, which was when Gary's expression changed, growing instantly serious, and his manner became strictly business.

"Christine, your husband says you're not on board with this litigation. Tell me why." Gary opened his palms. "I'm all ears."

"I don't think Dr. Davidow did anything wrong. He referred us to the best bank in the country, one that his sister has used." Christine thought a moment. "Plus, I like him, personally. I don't want to sue him."

"Okay, you win." Gary shrugged. "I only wanted him for leverage anyway. You convinced me."

"I did?"

"Yes." Gary flashed his lightened smile. "I want you happy and comfortable. I don't push my clients. You got the doc off the hook. But Homestead is a different matter. Homestead stays on the hook. My legal advice? Sue the bastards."

"Tell me why," Christine said, taking a page from his book.

"I want to give you some background first." Gary held up an

index finger, with a manicured nail. "You need to know where I'm coming from. I'm Italian-American. My family came over in the 1930s, settled in Mystic, my grandfather was a plumber, my father was a plumber, my brother is a plumber. I didn't want to be a plumber. You know why?"

"No, why?"

"No stakes." Gary shrugged again. "Nobody cares. Nobody cries. Nobody does something wrong. Nobody does something right. You follow, ladies?"

"I'm following," Christine answered. It wasn't difficult.

"Me, too," Lauren chimed in.

Gary continued, "Also, plumbers, they're little guys. I come from a long line of little guys. In case you haven't noticed, I'm a little guy." He gestured down at himself. "So I feel for the little guy. I get the little guy. I'm feisty, and I'm loyal, and so I fight for the little guy." Gary gestured to the photographs of the lions on his wall. "I took those pictures. I go on safari every year. To Botswana, the Serengeti, I been all over Africa. I drag my wife Denise. I drag her best friend, since she's divorced. It's a whole thing. I don't shoot anything. I would never kill a lion. I'm a vegetarian. I take pictures. I have memories." Gary pointed to his head. "I remember the lions I take pictures of. The lion, he takes care of every member of his pride. You're my cub, now." Gary frowned. "You think you're in Connecticut, but you're in the jungle."

Christine waited, sensed he was coming to some relevant point. Or she hoped he was.

"Let me tell you the facts about the sperm banking industry, and believe me, it *is* an industry. It is a big, big, business. And in my opinion, it is lawless. As lawless as the jungle." Gary puckered his lips. "There are no laws governing the screening and testing performed by sperm banks in this country. The United States Food and Drug Administration has some requirements with respect to screening sperm donors, but they apply *only* to contagious or infectious diseases, like venereal diseases or HIV, which 3319 was screened for."

Christine perked up at the mention of her donor, and she began to realize that Gary had read their file, probably given him by Marcus.

"There are only two professional associations, the American Society for Reproductive Medicine and the American Association of Tissue Banks, that have anything to do with the screening and testing provided by sperm banks. They make guidelines for additional screening, like genetic screening, but they are only recommendations. Guidelines, not laws. They're not enforceable, they have no teeth." Gary glowered. "As a practical matter, sperm banking is a multibillion-dollar business, and they make their own laws. They're the boss. They're the king of their jungle."

Christine was starting to wonder if she had misjudged Gary. He might have been bombastic, but he was shrewd.

"To come specifically to the point"—Gary pointed directly at Christine—"there are absolutely *no* laws that require Homestead or any other bank to conduct psychological screening for sperm donors. And because it would cost them money to conduct such screening, they don't do it. Nobody tells them they have to spend money, so they don't. They're a business. They want to maximize their profit margins. They don't want to spend any money that they don't have to."

Christine swallowed hard.

"So they hire nice women to sit down and interview the donors. The interviewer is a college graduate. Is that enough? *No.* The interviewers don't have degrees in psychology. They don't even have a master's in social work. They're not a mental health professional, an MHP." Gary scowled. "Is an interview enough? No. That is *not* a psychological screening. That is *not* psychological testing. That's not the Personality Assessment Inventory Test, administered by a psychologist or other MHP, after an hour and a half of a clinical interview by a psychologist or other MHP."

Christine understood what he was saying and couldn't disagree.

"Some banks, like Homestead, administer a Myers-Briggs test. That's not the equivalent of a psychological evaluation. That's a test that reveals temperament or style, but it doesn't tell you any of the psychopathology of the putative donor."

"What does that mean?"

"It means a true psychological evaluation of the donor, exploring for disorders like depression or anxiety, to find out if the donor is hearing voices or the like, or manifests any issues regarding addictions or disorders like OCD and the rest. Some banks administer a phony-baloney test that somebody made up, which characterizes personality traits. You probably saw that online, with other banks. Did you?"

"Yes." Christine remembered.

"*None* of these interviews or tests constitute psychological screening to any reasonable standard of care in psychology or psychiatry. No nice lady with a liberal arts degree will be able to identify, much less stop, a sociopath."

Christine felt a chill run down her spine. Lauren looked over, but neither woman said anything.

"The other characteristic of a psychological test is that it has reliability and reproducibility. It's called 'test-retest reliability.' In other words, the test will reveal whether the donor has anxiety issues and the same result will occur if he is retested. Egg donors are routinely given those tests, but sperm donors are not."

"Why is that?"

"It began because egg donation is a more extensive, physically invasive process. Egg donors have to go through cycles of IVF, and they undergo the procedure by which the eggs are retrieved."

Christine understood. "Egg donation seems like a bigger deal."

"Yes, and, in the old days, you could donate sperm anonymously, or before the banking industry mushroomed, you could order the donations yourself. You could use a turkey baster, for real."

Christine had heard that from the techs at Families First.

"They didn't think about it downstream, in other words, no matter how differently the gamete—that is, the sperm or egg—is obtained, it's the same as far as the donor recipient is concerned. There is simply no reason that sperm donors should not undergo the same psychological testing that has become the ordinary standard of care for egg donation." Gary's eyes burned with a new intensity. "Moreover, the industry's record-keeping is also unregulated. Patients, or customers, like you are not required to report births or defects to the banks. The banks are not required to report births or defects to anyone above them, like the FDA. So if there's a flaw with the sample, they may not know, and they keep selling it." Gary shook his head. "To make matters worse, there's no regulation on how many times they can sell the same sample. There's no limit on the number of offspring produced by any single donor. That's left up to the banks. Some banks limit the number of offspring to 60. I've heard numbers as high as 170."

Christine shuddered.

"There's no financial incentive to make banks limit the number of times they sell that sample. The incentive is to use it more, you see? The banks pay a fixed cost for the minimal testing they perform on the donor. Most banks try to recoup that cost by requiring the donor to donate for a year."

Christine hadn't known that. She'd thought the donors could just donate once. Her head was spinning, and she knew Lauren's had to be, too.

"Because the banks rule their jungle, bad things happen to people like you, who just wanna be moms. You're vulnerable, you're weak. Some of you fight back. You sue. I can tell you about the case of the bank in Wyoming, who sold twenty-year-old sperm. The offspring was born with cystic fibrosis. Nobody tested for CF when the sperm was donated."

Christine recoiled.

"Let me tell you a recent case that's something like yours, involving Xytex. They've been in the business for forty years, a major bank. Do you know the name?"

"Yes, Families First uses it."

"Do you know that they were sued last year by a same-sex couple, two women, because their sperm donor became schizophrenic, dropped out of college, and was arrested for burglary?"

"Yikes." Christine thought it sounded a little like their case. "How did the women know it was their donor?"

"The bank told them their donor's identity by mistake, in an email. The women started playing detective. They had the name, they looked him up, they found out."

"My God."

"By the way, did you know that anonymous sperm or egg donation is illegal in the U.K.? They don't allow it. Interesting, no?" Gary nodded. "Anyway, to stay on point, Xytex followed the current standard of care, which is asking donors for three generations of family medical history, doing physicals, blood tests, and a minimal amount of genetic testing. And no psychological testing."

"Did the couple win?"

"Yes." Gary paused. "It illustrates another problem in their jungle. Even the best banks, like Homestead, don't follow up on the information to verify that it *remains* accurate. They don't follow up to see if any of the donors develop an illness or emotional disorder. They don't even try. The profile for 3319 that your husband showed me, that's just a snapshot. You follow?"

"Yes," Christine answered miserably. That was why they weren't sure their donor had gone to med school or not.

"There's no blood test or genetic marker for mental illnesses. So it's not easy, quick, and most important of all, *cheap* to screen for. Let me read you something." Gary pivoted to his laptop and hit a few keys, then read from his monitor, "The Director of Public Affairs for the American Society for Reproductive Medicine was asked about this, and he said, 'As technical capabilities to do genetic testing and screenings improve, the banks will do that. But it would be incredibly expensive to test for everything.'"

Christine inhaled, despairing. She understood why Marcus had wanted her to come.

"So you see, it's about money. It's business. They could be selling sneakers. It's all the same to them." Gary frowned. "They *could* hire a qualified psychologist to evaluate the donor, but they don't do that. Families First does, for egg donors. Correct. Props to them. But they don't do it for sperm donors because they're not in the sperm banking business. You might want to ask yourself why."

Christine blinked. "Why?"

"Davidow is doing only what he can do competently. Also, he wants to avoid the exposure. This is the next wave in med mal litigation. Infertility practice is the cutting edge, and there's going to be more of it, now that same-sex couples can get married."

Christine saw where he was going.

"So you see why I would advise that you and Marcus sue Homestead. They're doing wrong. Their wrong hurt you. They rule their jungle. They're not going to get away with it anymore, not under my watch." Gary paused. "It's your decision, but it's my advice that we file suit for negligence with respect to their psychological screening practices. Also for breach of contract, because you signed a contract with them, and implicit in that is a duty of reasonable care, and I don't think they exercised that."

"But how do we get the name of our donor? How do we find out if it's Zachary Jeffcoat?"

"We find out as part of a settlement. They disclose to us the identity of 3319, and they pay us money damages. If enough people sue them, in time, they'll change their ways. But I'm not fighting for the world. I'm fighting for you. I'm protecting you."

"I understand."

"Now, there's one thing we have to discuss, it's personal."

Christine couldn't imagine what was more personal than the conversation already.

"Your husband told me you would not consider terminating the pregnancy." Gary put up his hand again, before Christine could say anything. "Please, I'm only bringing it up to talk to you about timing."

"What about timing?" Christine asked, but she felt wary.

"This lawsuit is not going to happen overnight. I can file it next week. They have thirty days to answer. They'll ask for an extension. I won't give it to them. I'm going to pressure them from the get-go. I'm going to hold their feet to the fire."

"So then why do you bring up time?"

"Because you're not going to have your answer about your donor's identity right away. Best-case scenario, it's going to take a month or two, especially if we don't sue Davidow. If we had Davidow as leverage, it could get done faster. I don't care what he told you, he would put his thumb on the scale, believe me. But if you're not terminating the pregnancy, you're not in a rush."

"That's true," Christine said, still taken aback.

"The question I have for you is, why do you want to know if Jeffcoat is your donor when you're not gonna do anything about it, that is, terminate?"

"Why does that matter?" Christine asked, confused.

"Suing somebody takes effort. It takes persistence. I need my clients to stay strong." Gary eyed her, newly critical. "When you appear in a deposition, you need to mean what you're saying. I don't want you to go south on me, whether I'm defending you in a video deposition or if I put you on the stand. So. Answer my question, please."

"I want to know because I have an outside hope that our donor isn't Jeffcoat."

"Okay, I get that. Then everybody's happy." Gary shook his head. "Let's say you got the wrong answer. How are you gonna react? Give up the lawsuit?"

"Oh." Christine's heart sank. She didn't know what to do if she got the wrong answer, and Gary must've read her hesitation because he started talking again.

"Here's why you want to know, even if it's the wrong answer. You want to know because if Jeffcoat is the biological dad, then your child's going to need to be psychologically evaluated and tested every year, to make sure he's mentally on track and not showing signs of mental illness. If he begins to show signs, then you'll need to get him treatment. That's going to cost money." Gary tented his fingers. "You shouldn't have to pay that. Homestead should, because their lack of psychological screening is what caused you to have a child with a mental illness. So, Christine, you need to know if Jeffcoat is 3319, whether he is or not, do you understand?"

"Yes." Christine hadn't thought about evaluating or treating the baby, going forward. "But what's involved in a lawsuit?"

"Discovery, then trial, if we have to go the distance, which we won't."

"Will they take my deposition?"

"Yes, first thing. I welcome it. I can't wait. You'll be a great witness." Gary beamed, but Christine grimaced.

"How do you know that? I've never had my deposition taken."

"I'm looking at you. You're adorable. You're pregnant. You're an elementary-school teacher. That's a home run."

Christine couldn't manage a smile. "But it makes me nervous."

"I'll prepare you. I'll be with you. So what, you'll be a little nervous." Gary shrugged, again. "That's fine. It's true. It's authentic. And it's vulnerable. I want it on video, so Homestead knows that if this case goes to trial, the jury will see the big bad corporate lawyers upsetting the nice pregnant schoolteacher."

"What about Marcus? Do they take his deposition, too?"

"Yes, of course. I'll prepare him, too. He won't be nervous. He's as cool as a cucumber, your husband. *You're* the case. *You're* the sympathy. *You're* the reason they're going to settle and tell us."

"You really think so?" Christine felt her hopes lift, torn. It was good news and bad news, both.

"Yes, but one last thing. You will have to agree that the settlement is confidential. All of it must be confidential. The fact of it, that they told us the donor's identity, and the amount of the money. No Facebook, no nothing." Gary turned to Lauren with a sharp eye. "Even you, best friend. The best friend can't know about it. If the best friend is told about it, I don't want to know that. You follow, ladies?"

"Yes," Christine and Lauren answered, in unfortunate unison.

Gary returned his attention to Christine. "So, fish or cut bait. Can I count you in as a plaintiff with Marcus?"

Christine looked over at Lauren, who shot her a grim thumbs-up.

"That's a yes from the best friend." Gary turned to Christine. "Well?"

"Yes," Christine answered, praying she was doing the right thing.

Chapter Fourteen

After the meeting with Gary, Christine had mixed emotions, but kept them at bay. She lay on the examining table with a paper sheet covering her from the waist down, waiting for her OB-GYN to come in and start the ultrasound. Her obstetrician was Dr. Terry Frazier, who practiced with a women's health group unrelated to Dr. Davidow and Families First. Lauren stood beside her, and they had already done the initial workup with the nurse.

"You must be hungry," Lauren said, smiling down at her. "After this, I'm treating you to Clam Cottage. Fried things make the best celebration."

"What are we celebrating?"

"This, the ultrasound." Lauren smiled, looking down at her. "This is a big deal!"

"Right." Christine tried to relax. This was supposed to be a happy occasion. She was having a baby, something she'd wanted her whole life long. She tried to put the donor lawsuit out of her mind.

"I'm sorry Marcus couldn't be here." Lauren puckered her lip, sympathetically.

"I know." Christine had thought about texting him but hadn't.

He hadn't texted or called her this morning, and she wondered how he was doing. She prayed they weren't having a major rift. They'd been through so much, but this was a crisis. They had to get past this, somehow. She looked up at Lauren. "I'm glad you came, though."

"Me, too. Honey, I know you're worried, but you're doing the right thing suing Homestead. You need to know who your donor is, whether it's good news or bad."

"I know. I'm better off prepared."

They both looked up at the sound of a soft knock at the door, and Dr. Frazier entered. An African-American woman in her late fifties, she had a steely halo of gray hair that made a neat frame to her round face. Her dark eyes were soft behind rimless glasses, and she smiled sweetly.

"Sorry to keep you waiting, ladies. It's all about emergencies today. I have somebody in labor at the hospital, so you're my last appointment of the day." Dr. Frazier squirted some sanitizer on her hands, then slid on purple latex gloves. "We don't have to guess about your conception date. I checked your file, and your procedure was April 16, correct?"

"Yes." Christine knew Dr. Frazier meant the IUI procedure, by which she was inseminated with Donor 3319's sperm. Dr. Frazier knew that Christine had conceived using a donor, but nothing about the latest developments and the lawsuit. Christine briefly considered telling her, but decided against it. She wanted to keep this experience pure and untainted.

"So this is your first ultrasound, correct?"

"Yes." Christine nodded. "Do I hear the heartbeat today?"

"That's the plan," Dr. Frazier answered, and Christine heard the caveat in her voice, in that not every ultrasound would confirm a heartbeat. She'd learned to prepare for the worst and hope for the best.

"Good."

"Okay, let's get started." Dr. Frazier sat on a rolling stool and rolled into position. "You'll feel some pressure, but that's it. Keep your eyes on the monitor. That's the show."

"Okay." Christine turned to the boxy monitor on top of the ultrasound machine. Though the screen was black, she felt her heartbeat quicken. She'd seen this scene in movies and read about it in her books. She'd always wondered if she would ever be the pregnant lady on the examining table and now finally, she was. She hated that Marcus wasn't here, but Lauren was, and girlfriends were forever.

"Ultrasound, as you may know, uses sound waves to show us an image of the baby." Dr. Frazier spoke as the monitor screen blossomed into a grayish mess of static, and Christine felt some discomfort but was distracted by the image. She couldn't tell what she was seeing though she felt vaguely nervous and thrilled, both at once.

"Is that the baby?"

"Not yet, stay tuned," Dr. Frazier answered, then the image changed and shifted, gray and black, but still all static.

"It doesn't hurt the baby to do this, does it?" Christine couldn't tear her eyes from the monitor, watching the dark and light patches come in and out of view.

"No, this is perfectly safe." Dr. Frazier started pressing buttons on the keyboard of the machine. The image enlarged once, then twice, and Christine felt tears come to her eyes, her heart recognizing the image before her brain did.

"That's a heartbeat!" Christine cried out, joyful. "Isn't that the heartbeat? That thing, like, fluttering?"

"Yes." Dr. Frazier pressed more buttons. "So we can confirm this pregnancy, for sure."

"Oh my God!" Christine yelped. "Look at that! That's amazing! Lauren, look!"

"I know!" Lauren squeezed her hand. "Honey, you got yourself a baby."

"I do!" Christine's eyes brimmed. "I really do!"

"Let me explain what you're seeing." Dr. Frazier nodded toward the monitor. "See the circle, and the outer edges of the circle are grainy and gray? That's the lining of your uterus."

"Okay." Christine wiped her eyes, trying to focus through her emotions.

"Inside of the grainy edges, it's black, which is fluid, and in the middle of the fluid is the white spot, which is the baby. See how it looks like a figure eight? Or one circle attached to the other?"

Christine nodded, too overcome to speak.

"That's because, at this point, the head and body are about the same size. Sometimes you can see arm stems, but that's hard to see right now. And, as you said, the fluttering is the heart."

"Wow." Christine wiped her eyes again.

"Everything looks copacetic. You're nine weeks along." Dr. Frazier returned to the ultrasound machine and pressed more buttons. "I'm going to take some measurements, and we will be done in a few minutes."

"Thanks." Christine sniffled at the screen, riveted by the delicate white fluttering, like the most gorgeous of butterflies beating its wings, delicate but terribly fragile. She felt overwhelmed with a fierce protectiveness, as well as the greatest happiness she had ever known, suffusing her with the warmth, strength, and power of life itself.

"Hold on, for the finale." Dr. Frazier hit a button on the machine, which made a few ticks and in the next moment, printed a photo, which she handed over. "Baby's first picture."

"This is amazing!" Christine brimmed with new tears as she accepted the photo, her fingers shaking. Holding the photo was almost like holding the baby in her hands, proof of a dream realized, before her eyes. She made a silent vow to love the baby, to take care of it, and to shield it from any and all harm. Because it wasn't Rosemary's Baby, it was *her* baby, and she was its mother.

In time, the ultrasound ended, and Christine dried her eyes, came out of her reverie, and got dressed. She and Lauren waited together at the billing desk while she paid her co-pay, then they walked to the car. They were talking the way they always did, bantering back and forth, exchanging views about the ultrasound, but Christine felt as if she were also in a world of her own, a world that now included only her and her child, inside her. She had never felt that way in her life, and it struck her, as she piled into Lauren's Jetta and they drove off, past the pretty houses and tall trees toward the Clam Cottage, that she had never realized how incredible it was to be pregnant, that it truly was a miracle, and that this miracle had happened to her.

The sensation stayed with her like a state of grace, even as she climbed out of the car, went inside the restaurant, sat down, and ordered. All of the emotion she was experiencing resonated deep within her, as if being her baby's mother was the best thing she could be doing in the world, as if her heart had gotten what it had always wanted, even before she had even been born and filled out her body, to give her soul a home.

"Christine? Pass the ketchup, please." Lauren frowned from across the narrow Formica table, tilting her head. "Earth to Christine. I've asked you for the ketchup, like, three times."

"Sorry." Christine smiled, shaking it off.

"What's up with you?"

"I don't know." Christine shrugged, nonplussed but happy. "I didn't realize my ultrasound would be a spiritual experience."

Lauren burst into laughter. "OMG, you are so freaking hormonal."

"Thank you for coming with me." Christine almost choked up again but blinked her tears away.

"I'm happy I was there." Lauren took a big bite of her lobster roll, which was hot and dripping with butter, making her hands greasy.

"Are you so happy you got your lobster roll?"

"I'm unbelievably happy I got my lobster roll."

"I'm unbelievably happy I got my onion rings," Christine said, taking a bite. The batter was light, and the onions had been sliced thin, so it was like heaven on earth. "These are so good it's not even funny."

"We're eating for two."

"And nobody can stop us."

The Clam Cottage was a more humble establishment than its name would suggest, one large room with ten Formica tables around the windows on the perimeter. The cashier, take-out counter, and kitchen were situated on the right side of the room, where the menu was posted on a fading chalkboard that nobody needed because only locals ate here. A flat-screen TV played a soap opera on mute, and retirees watched, though it didn't have any closed captioning. Christine was relieved that it wasn't on a news station though Jeffcoat lurked behind her thoughts, darkening her happiness like a shadow.

"I feel so free." Lauren munched away on her lobster roll. "My mother-in-law picked up the kids at the bus. Let's go buy things for the baby."

"Good idea." Christine got distracted by the soap opera, where a gorgeous young couple were in bed. "Where do they get those people? They look unreal."

"They're all models." Lauren turned to the TV, and the scene changed to a lawyer in his office, lined with fake books. "That's Dan, the assistant D.A."

"How do you know?" Christine asked, surpised. "Do you watch this?"

"Of course. Not." Lauren laughed.

"When do you get time to watch soap operas?"

"I DVR them and watch when the kids do their homework." Lauren pointed at the screen. "See Dan? He lost his big case, so the killer's going free."

"Oh," Christine said, but her thoughts turned to Jeffcoat.

"Dan is also sleeping with the killer's twin sister, which he can't figure out even though they look alike."

Christine kept her eyes on the screen, thinking about Zachary Jeffcoat, in prison outside Philadelphia.

"They're even played by actors who are fraternal twins. You know how fraternal twins can sometimes look alike, even though they're not identical?"

"Yes, sure." Christine couldn't focus on the show. The idea that had been forming in the back of her mind was finally coming together, especially after what Gary had told her. "It's going to be really hard to wait two months to find out if Jeffcoat's our donor."

"The wheels of justice turn slowly."

"And in the meantime, we don't have an answer to a simple question."

"I know, it totally sucks."

"Maybe there's another way."

"What?"

Christine took a flyer. "We're trying to find out if Jeffcoat is Donor 3319, so what's the easiest way? What do we tell our students, every day?"

"Stop picking your nose?"

"No. We tell them, 'If you don't know something, ask.' "

"Ask who?" Lauren frowned. "Davidow doesn't know, and Homestead won't tell you."

"There's one person who knows. Zachary Jeffcoat."

"What are you saying?" Lauren's eyes flared in surprise.

"I'm saying that Jeffcoat knows whether he donated or not. He'll even know what his donor number is. If I want to know if Jeffcoat is Donor 3319, I should ask him."

"How?"

"Just, go. Drive down. He's in Philadelphia, not on Mars."

"Are you *insane*?" Lauren's eyes widened, horrified. "He's in prison."

"So? People in prison have visitors. I wouldn't have to wait two months. I wouldn't have to sue Homestead. I can just ask Jeff-coat."

"Are you seriously considering this?"

"Yes, why not?" Christine felt her heart lift.

"He's a *serial killer*. He's a *dangerous man*."

"They have him behind bars. The safest place you can meet a serial killer is in prison. The more I think about it, the more sense it makes. I can just go ask him."

"Would you tell him who you are?"

"I don't know, I'll figure it out." Christine thought a moment, remembering her conversation with William Magni, from the newspaper. "Who do prisoners talk to, besides their family and friends? Reporters. I could say I was a reporter."

"No, no, no. It's really crazy. What if you ask him and he doesn't tell you?"

"Then I go." Christine shrugged. "I haven't lost anything. Philadelphia's not that long a drive. I could leave in the morning and be there by the afternoon. Tomorrow."

"No!" Lauren said, hushed. "You can't, you shouldn't. It's scary."

"I don't see the harm. I can drive away. He can't get out. He doesn't know where I live."

"Marcus will *never* let you do that."

"Marcus doesn't have to know. He's away this weekend."

"You would go to a prison without telling him?"

"He went to a lawyer without telling me." Christine shrugged. The more she thought about the idea, the less crazy it seemed.

"But you're *pregnant*."

"By *whom*?" Christine leaned over the table, newly urgent. "I just saw my baby's heartbeat and I want to know who his father is. I want to know if it's Zachary Jeffcoat and I want to know if I can save my marriage. Why can't I investigate like that other couple did, the one Gary told us about?"

"But going to a *prison*? You're a *teacher*."

"Then think of it as a field trip. With really bad clothes."

Lauren didn't laugh. Her mouth made a tight little line, turning down so comically she looked like a sad-face emoticon. "You can't go alone."

"Yes I can."

"No you can't."

"Then don't make me," Christine said, with a wink.

Chapter Fifteen

M om, I'm home," Christine sang out, as soon as she entered the living room, because her parents would be in the kitchen and wouldn't hear her come in. They still left their front door unlocked, which drove her crazy. They still lived in Middletown where she grew up, and though it was safe, she felt lately that they were so vulnerable, protected only by an aging Chihuahua, Ralph Mouth. Christine found herself worrying about them, though her anxiety probably had something to do with her father's Alzheimer's. Everything seemed so precarious lately, so fragile. She closed the door and twisted the deadbolt, locking out all harm.

"In the kitchen!" her mother called out, unnecessarily since it was the only room in the house they ever used, from as far back as Christine could remember, just the three of them huddled around a Formica table in the sunny kitchen she always thought was cozy. She didn't realize that it was cramped, or indeed how *small* the house was—a white clapboard with two bedrooms, a "sewing" room, and one bath on the second floor—until middle school, when she visited her friends' houses. They had living rooms *and* family rooms, as well as a kitchen, but Christine didn't see the point because in the Murray house, the kitchen *was* the family room and the living room.

"Hey, guys!" Christine entered the kitchen, dumped her purse, tote bag, keys, and phone next to the toaster oven, then went to her mother, who rose from her seat next to Christine's father, lifting her arms for a hug.

"Here's my girl, how are you feeling, honey?" Her mother gave her a big hug, then let her go, smiling at her. The former Georgina Maldonado, she was cute enough to be Homecoming Queen at Windsor High in her native Providence, R.I. They'd called her Gidget because she could have passed for the actress Sally Field, with her big, friendly smile, wide-set, warm brown eyes, and bouncy, dark brown hair, typically gathered into a girlish ponytail, even now.

"I feel good, okay, Mom. How are you?"

"We're good, good." Her mother had turned sixty-five last week but had the energy of a much younger woman, and her smile was dazzling. She stayed trim by walking on her treadmill in the basement, but silvery-gray strands sprouted at her forehead, a sign of recent stress. It broke Christine's heart that just when her parents retired, her father had fallen ill and her mother had become his caregiver.

"Will you please lock the front door, from now on?"

"Nah, pssh." Her mother waved her into the chair. "Sit down, get off your feet. You're always running around."

"Mom, guess what, I'm finished with school."

"Oh my, already?" Her mother pushed bangs from her eyes, surprised. "You okay to be leaving teaching? Or are you sad?"

"I'm okay."

"I bet, I can't wait for the baby."

"Me, neither." Christine went around the side of the table to greet her father, though she wasn't sure he knew her. Sometimes he remembered her name, but she wasn't sure he knew she was his only child. He sat in his place next to her mother, behind a folded newspaper that he didn't read and a flowery paper plate that held a grilled cheese sandwich, cut into small squares. There was a plastic fork in his hand, though her mother had started feeding him to save time. She still had him hold the fork, giving him the dignity that his awful disease was determined to strip him of.

"Paul, Christine is here." Her mother leaned over, smiling in his face to get his attention. "Christine's here to say hi to you. Look, it's Christine."

"Hi, Dad, it's Christine." Christine leaned close to her father, so close she could smell his breath. She used to think it was infantilizing to get right in his face, but they had learned it was finally necessary. She and her mother had attended a seminar at the hospital, as part of her support group for caregivers, where they had been taught the basics by an instructor who had not only a degree in social work but was taking care of her husband at home.

Now, don't ask factual questions like, "Did you eat yet?" Or, "Did you go to the doctor?" They don't remember the answer, and it could agitate them. Go with questions there's no right or wrong answer to. Something that doesn't elicit a fact. Try, "How are you feeling?" "Are you having a fun day?" "Would you like a glass of water?"

"Hi, Dad," Christine said, smiling. "It's Christine, your daughter. How are you feeling? Are you having a fun day?"

"What?" her father said, his hooded brown eyes shifting upward, to her. His gaze was unfocused, and Christine wasn't sure he recognized her. He was only sixty-five, but the illness had aged him mercilessly, so that his forehead was more deeply lined and the folds from his aquiline nose to his fine lips more pronounced. The shape of his face was long, but his cheeks looked hollow. His bristled hair was cut close in a salt-and-pepper buzz cut, which her mother said would keep him cooler in summer but was really easier to help her shampoo him, in the shower.

"Dad, it's Christine, your daughter. Great to see you, Dad. I love you."

"Christine?" His lips curved into a smile. His lips were dry. "Christine."

"Right, Dad!" Christine leaned over, heartened, and kissed him on the cheek, which was slightly grizzly. He'd had a five o'clock shadow in his younger days and still did, though his beard came in gray, and her mother didn't bother shaving him again until the next morning.

"Honey," her mother said, touching her arm. "Talk to him about the baby."

"The baby is doing good, Dad," Christine said, following her mother's cues.

"Honey, let him feel your belly again. He liked that the other day, he told me. He talked about it."

"Really?" Christine felt her hope lift, another of the illness's cruel tricks. It was impossible to predict what would get through to her father and what wouldn't, and so she would try anything, only to reach him on Monday and have it fail on Wednesday. It was the connection to him that she missed to the depths of her soul, because she had been a Daddy's Girl from day one.

"Dad?" Christine picked up her father's free hand and placed it on her belly. "Dad, can you feel the baby? Do you want to feel the baby? There's a baby in there. Your grandbaby's on the way."

"Christine, Christine," her father repeated, leaving his hand against her belly and looking up at her with his warm smile. He'd taught Language Arts in the local high school, and she'd gotten her love of reading from him; and he used to take her to the library and got her hooked on the old English mysteries that were his favorite. His students called him Sherlock Holmes, and it killed Christine to think that his brilliant mind, as well as his gentle heart, were being eroded day by day. She felt as if she mourned him even while he was alive, hating that he didn't have their shared memories anymore, of trips to Lyman Orchards for the apple pie they both loved, or their annual pilgrimage to Gillette Castle, the East Haddam estate of William Gillette, the actor who had played

Holmes on the stage. Christine tried to enjoy every day she had left with him, which was why she had come over tonight to visit them though she was exhausted. Because she didn't know how many days they had with him.

"Dad, hold on, I brought you something." Christine went around the side of the table and got her purse. "Mom, wait'll you see this. Look."

"What?" Her mother reached for her bright red reading glasses, which she called her Sally Jessy Raphael glasses though nobody knew who that was anymore. She even had her Hartford Whalers T-shirt on, though the Whalers had left in the nineties, which didn't matter to true fans like her parents.

"It's the baby's ultrasound, they gave me a picture." Christine slid the photo from her purse, and her mother took it, her dark eyes lighting up.

"You had your ultrasound today? Great!"

"I saw the heart. It was great." Christine pointed to the whitish figure eight in the photo, which was reasonably visible. "See, this is the baby, the head and body are about the same size."

"Honey, I'm so happy for you!" Her mother beamed. "It's official now!"

"I know, I cried."

"Of course you did!" Her mother laughed, her eyes shining, and handed her back the picture. "Show it to your dad."

"Dad, this is the ultrasound, I had an ultrasound." Christine brought it over to her father, holding it in front of his face. "The white parts are the baby. You can see—" She stopped short when she saw her father looking away. He'd turned his head, staring at the counter, which was cluttered with crossword puzzle books, newspapers, mail, bills, and brown plastic bottles that were his medications, neatly categorized in separate Ziploc bags by her mother.

"Dad?" Christine said, but she straightened up, letting it go and setting the photo aside. Another thing they had learned from the seminar was to take cues from the patient, and she had learned it the hard way.

Agitation, hostility, and even physically striking out are not unusual in the memory-impaired. Don't take it personally or let it hurt your feelings. Remind yourself that it's the illness talking, as if the person were inebriated, and you would say "it's the whiskey talking." Learn to see the signs before hostility breaks out. Then, stop.

"Honey, you want a grilled cheese?" Her mother was already bustling to the stove, where the fry pan still sat on the grate.

"Okay, sure, thanks."

"What did Marcus say when he saw the baby?"

"He couldn't go, he's out of town. Lauren went with me."

"Oh, he'll be so sorry he missed that." Her mother's voice still bore the distinctive Rhody accent, in the flattish O of "sorry."

"Hold on, I brought another present, one for you." Christine dug inside her tote bag and pulled out a new book, Dr. Seuss's *Which Pet Should I Get?* "Did you see this? There's a new Dr. Seuss book."

"Oh my goodness! I didn't know that!" Her mother turned from the refrigerator and accepted the book, running her finger-pads over the smooth blue cover. "How did they do this? I mean, he's been dead for how long?"

"His wife found it and they published it. Isn't it great?"

"This is wonderful, honey." Her mother opened the front cover, marveling. "What a treat! Dr. Seuss, it isn't just for kids."

Christine smiled, remembering that was her father's mantra when she was growing up, that children's books weren't just for kids. Nutmeg Hill Elementary had plenty of Dr. Seuss in its library because Christine had bought the copies herself.

"Dad will *love* this."

"I figured." Christine nodded. These days, her mother read to her father at night, but mysteries had become too complex for him to follow. He'd grow agitated, unhappy, or simply fall asleep, so her mother had moved on to children's books, which he seemed to enjoy, perking up at the rhymes and pictures.

"Here, sit, let me make your sandwich," her mother said, pressing her into a chair, and Christine sat down because it made her mother happy. While her mother cooked, they both talked about the last day of school, trading stories and comparing notes, occasionally trying to include her father, who nodded and smiled but eventually returned to staring at the medications on the counter. The kitchen had a southern exposure, so it was bright during the day, but it began to darken as the day wore on.

"Here, honey," her mother said, putting the grilled cheese in front of her on a paper plate, with potato chips on the side, like she used to for playdates.

"Wow, yum, thanks."

"You okay? You seem kinda sad." Her mother sat down to her right, leaning on her forearm and looking at Christine dubiously. "Is it because you're leaving teaching? It has to be bothering you, just a little, I know."

"A little, yes." Christine felt grateful for the cover story. She picked up the half sandwich, cut in a neat triangle with the mustard on the top.

"God closes a door, and he opens a window."

"Right." Christine took a bite of her sandwich, which tasted delicious.

"And when the baby comes, there'll be so much to do." Her mother's face lit up again. "That's really something to look forward to, isn't it?"

"Yes, it really is."

Her mother leaned forward on her elbows. "Did the doctor say if it was going to be a boy or a girl? You can't tell yet, can you?"

"No, she didn't say." Christine chewed her sandwich, eyeing her mother. "Mom, you really don't care if it's a boy or girl, do you?"

"No, I don't. Do you?"

"No, not really. I'm just excited about having a baby."

"Me, too!" Her mother clasped her hands together, giving her little body a wiggle. "Can you imagine how much fun that will be? A little baby running around here? I think it will help your Dad, too, I really do."

"It just might," Christine said, noncommittal. She didn't want her mother to get her hopes up, and at some level, they both knew that Dad was never going to come back, even for a new baby. Neither of them needed a seminar to tell them that.

"Does Marcus still want a boy?"

Christine felt a twinge. Marcus still hadn't called or texted, and she hadn't either. She hated feeling so disconnected from him. Still, she couldn't tell him she was thinking about driving to Philadelphia to see Zachary Jeffcoat. "He never said he wanted a boy. He just says he wants a golf partner."

"That means a boy." Her mother rolled her eyes. "I wasn't born yesterday."

"Girls play golf, Mom."

"I can't imagine your husband playing golf with a woman. Does he play with any women now? No!" Her mother chuckled, and Christine joined her, because it was true.

"Mom, let me ask you a harder question. Does it really not matter to you that we used a donor?"

"It really doesn't matter to me at all," her mother answered, easily.

"Is that because you know that the child is genetically mine? Or half-mine? Is that why?"

"No." Her mother shrugged. "I didn't care if you adopted, I didn't care if you got a baby from China. I don't care if it's yours and not his, or his and not yours. You know why, honey?" Her mother paused, musing. "Because as I've gotten older, I've come to understand that there are very few things that are as big a deal as we think. *This* is what matters." Her mother gestured to her father, then to her. "All I care about is around my kitchen table, and that's all I ever cared about. As long as we have each other, nothing else matters. And your baby, whether it's a boy or girl, or whatever it is, it's going to sit right here and we're gonna love it to *pieces*!"

Christine felt relief flooding back to her at her mother's words, and they talked some more, sitting at the kitchen table where they always had. It struck her that she couldn't have foreseen what would happen to her parents, or to her and Marcus, her father getting Alzheimer's and Marcus infertile, both men betrayed by their bodies. She never would have realized, until she'd lived it, how the ripple effects of those illnesses would change her and her family, for all time.

And later, when coffee was ready, and Christine watched as her mother carefully cooled each teaspoonful before she placed it in her father's mouth, she realized that love could endure almost any obstacle. Real, abiding love. It was right before her eyes, lifelong, in them.

And she knew she had to go to Pennsylvania, if only to save her marriage.

Chapter Sixteen

Christine was loading the dishwasher when her phone on the counter rang. It was Marcus calling, and on the screen was an old photo she had taken of him, from their first trip to Presque Isle, where his family used to have a vacation house. The Nilssons sailed, and Marcus loved to work on the boat; in the photo, he was hand-sanding its wooden hull with the boombox blasting. What Christine loved about the photo was how carefree he looked, his grin loose and relaxed, his shirt off, his back tanned, his muscles defined, his body effortlessly sexy in the way of twenty-one-year-olds. They had been crazy in love then, with their future ahead of them, their successes merely assumed, their struggles unforeseen. She ignored the lump in her throat to answer the phone.

"Christine? Hey, how are you?"

"Okay." Christine could read his voice instantly, like any wife. He was still remote but too tired to be angry. "How about you?"

"It was a bitch of a day."

"I bet." Christine knew it was code for he was sorry he hadn't called earlier.

"So did you go to Gary?"

"Yes, Lauren came with." Christine would've bet that he had

already talked with Gary, but she was tired, too, and in no mood to play games. "Gary said that we don't need to sue Davidow but we should sue Homestead, and I'm going along with it."

"Good, great, well, thanks. I know that was a concession and I appreciate it."

"You're welcome." Christine could tell that he was trying to be nice. It made her want to tell him about the ultrasound, but she didn't want to risk a fight, and she had a lie to tell. "You know, since you're not coming home, Lauren and I were thinking about making a girl trip to New Jersey this weekend."

"Really, what's going on?"

"Well, you know her parents have a house there, on Long Beach Island?"

"Right, yes." Marcus sounded vague, and Christine knew he didn't remember. She barely remembered it herself. It was the only story that she and Lauren could come up with that was virtually uncheckable.

"Yes, her parents have a house there and all the kids use it. You know, one of those deals where they divide the summer into weeks and they rotate?"

"Okay."

"Anyway, she always gets stuck closing it, but this year she gets to open it, which is a helluva lot easier. She asked if I wanted to go with her. Take a weekend. Just take a break, you know, with all that's been going on."

"Of course, right." Marcus's voice softened.

"Right." Christine felt a wave of guilt. "Jessica down the street can take care of the animals, so I think I'm going to go."

"Sounds like a good idea."

"We'll leave tomorrow morning and come back Sunday."

"Fine. I won't be home until Sunday night myself. Remember, it's my dad's birthday Monday night?"

"Oh, right." Christine rolled her eyes because she could get away with rolling her eyes on the phone. She disliked her father-in-law, the insufferable Frederik Nilsson.

"We'll go out to dinner. I made reservations at that Thai place he likes, so you don't need to cook. Sound good?"

"Yes, that's great."

"Okay, I'm beat, so I'm going to turn in."

"Me, too."

"Love you," Marcus said, and for a brief second, he sounded almost like himself.

"I love you, too," Christine said, touched, but she could hear the defensiveness in her own tone.

"Hey, good night then. Give Murf the Surf a kiss for me."

"How about Lady?" Christine said automatically, their call-and-response, because he preferred the dog to the cat.

"Her, no. Drive safe tomorrow. The Jersey Shore is a long haul. Good night."

"Good night." Christine hung up, then stood still at the counter, the dishwasher door hanging open. She realized she had just lied to Marcus twice, once by omission and once by commission, her old Catholic catechism rising to her consciousness; she had lied about where she was going and she hadn't told him about the ultrasound. She couldn't remember the last time she had lied to him, if ever.

Christine looked out the kitchen window, into the darkness of the backyard, and suddenly the motion-detector light went on, which meant that Murphy was at the door, ready to come in. She shook some Cascade powder into the little boxes in the dishwasher door, closed it, and pressed ON, then went to retrieve the dog, so they could both go upstairs and end this hellish day.

Chapter Seventeen

It took Christine and Lauren until three o'clock to reach Pennsylvania, because the driver was pregnant and had to stop every hour to go to the bathroom or eat McDonald's French fries, salads from Sbarro, and an iced lemon cake from Starbucks, plus assorted drinks. The sky was sunny and cloudless, and it would've been a pleasant drive if they hadn't been so tense about where they were going or why they were going there.

They drove through the town of Collegeville on Route 29, a winding two-lane road, and continued past colonial vintage houses, then rolling hills and pastured horses. The farmland turned into a vast open space, and Christine sensed they were approaching the prison. "I think we're almost there," she said, glancing over.

Lauren straightened up in the passenger seat. "How do you know? It looks like more farms."

"I read on the website. The prison is set on seventeen hundred acres."

"So it's in the middle of nowhere. What else did you read?"

"Well, it's Pennsylvania's largest maximum-security prison."

"Oh, great. Go big or go home."

"It has about thirty-seven hundred adult men who have committed felonies, because that's who gets sent to maximum-security. It also has one of the two Death Rows in the state."

"Now there's an idea for summer vacation."

"It has a Facebook page."

"Whoa." Lauren chuckled. "Facebook for felons."

"Its profile picture is a koala." Christine gave the car gas, spotting the massive concrete complex that had to be the prison in the distance, to her right.

"Why a koala?"

"I've no idea."

"And you're sure Jeffcoat will see us?"

"I called ahead and asked to be put on his visitors' list, which he has to approve, so, yes."

"He must want the company."

"Or the press. Remember, I told them we're freelance journalists."

"Okay. No comment."

Both women fell uncharacteristically silent as the prison complex loomed larger, and Christine took a right turn when the GPS told her to, even though there was no sign. She steered onto a long, asphalt road that divided an open field, and they came to a fork in the road; to the right was a visitors' parking lot, which was signed, but to their left, the road led to a massive concrete prison rising behind a fifty-foot-high wall of concrete, topped with coiled barbed wire. At the corners of the building, guard turrets pierced the blue sky.

"Oh boy." Lauren grimaced. "Can we go home now?"

"Not yet." Christine steered into the parking lot, which was about half-full, parked, and shut off the engine. "Here are the rules. We're not allowed to bring phones or handbags, but we need to show IDs. Apparently they have lockers for the car keys, and we're allowed to bring in our pads but not pens."

"Can I bring my gun?"

"Do you even own a gun? It might be the one thing I don't

know about you." Christine looked over, sliding her laminated driver's license from her wallet.

"Of course not. I'm Jewish. Words are our weapons."

"Good thing you're a reporter then." Christine handed her a fresh legal pad. "Here."

"Oh right, I forgot." Lauren took the pad, then got her ID from her wallet.

"Remember, I'll ask the questions. All you have to do is take notes. They give us the pencils inside." Christine slid the keys from the ignition, and they got out of the car.

"Here goes nothing." Lauren squared her shoulders, walking around the front bumper.

"Thanks for doing this." Christine met her, trying to ignore her case of nerves.

"It's okay. It'll be interesting." Lauren patted her on the back.

"To say the least." Christine shot her a shaky smile, and they fell into step, heading up the road toward the prison. It loomed even larger as they got closer, its high wall even more forbidding; up close the concrete looked stained and aging, and its barbed wire glinted sharply in the sunlight. The turrets at the corners of the building were of smoked glass, so she couldn't see the guards inside. The air felt so humid it was almost claustrophobic, but that could have been her imagination.

They reached the parking lot in front of the prison, passing a black van with white lettering that read, CORONER'S OFFICE, MONT-GOMERY COUNTY, then a row of idling Department of Corrections buses, with wire grates over their windows. The women climbed the steps to the entrance, which had a grimy concrete overhang, and walked to the smudged glass doors of the entrance.

Christine opened one door, which was old, its wood frame weathered, and let Lauren go first, then followed her into a dingy reception room that was a very long rectangle, dimly lit by flickering fluorescent lighting and small windows at the far end. The air smelled warm and dirty; if it was air-conditioned, it was too weak to do any good. A smattering of visitors talked quietly as they waited on old-fashioned wooden benches, under a sign that read NO SPANDEX, NO HOODIES. Tan linoleum covered the floor, and old beige lockers ringed the far side of the room. The place gave off the overall impression of being stop-time, circa 1960s, and oddly small-town for a maximum-security prison.

Christine spotted a large wooden reception desk across the room, staffed by a female officer wearing a black uniform with the yellow patch of the Department of Corrections, which looked incongruous with the pink scrunchy around her light brown ponytail. Christine took the lead to the reception desk, placed her driver's license on the counter, and introduced them both, then said, "We're here to see Zachary Jeffcoat. We called ahead to be put on his visitors' list."

"Sure. Sign in, please." The corrections officer smiled as she slid a clipboard with an old-school sign-in log across the counter, and Christine signed in while Lauren handed over her driver's license. The corrections officer examined the licenses. "You ladies come all the way from Connecticut?"

"Yes."

"What newspaper you with?"

Christine told herself to remain calm. "I'm freelance, I'm a stringer."

"Oh. You're the third reporter today."

"Really?" Christine asked, surprised. She realized it helped her credibility as a cover story, too.

"Mr. Jeffcoat is our celebrity inmate. He made the Most Wanted List. We don't get many of those. He's here in our holding area, on account of his dangerousness. He should be at Chester County Prison but they're minimum security." The corrections officer slid their driver's licenses back across the counter. "His mail already started, too. He had some waiting before he got here. Wait 'til you see him, you'll know why." The corrections officer lifted a plucked eyebrow, then gestured at the lockers. "Car keys go in there, then take a seat. He'll be brought up in a minute. He just was sent back down after his girlfriend visited."

"His girlfriend was here?"

"Yes, you just missed her. A pretty redhead." The corrections officer winked. "He's a busy boy."

Christine and Lauren exchanged glances, then went to the lockers, stowed the car keys, and sat down on the bench. There were ten benches half full of people, of all races and sizes. Christine caught snippets of a variety of languages, English, Spanish, and others she couldn't identify. Children fidgeted on the benches, swinging their legs or playing with toys, which made her despair. She tried not to think about what the life of her child would be like if Jeffcoat was her donor. Her hand went reflexively to her belly, and she prayed her baby didn't end up here, in a maximum-security prison.

"Zachary Jeffcoat!" a male corrections officer called out, as he stuck his head out a doorway on the left.

Christine and Lauren rose together, and the male corrections officer motioned them forward toward a grimy metal door, which he opened with a loud *ca-chunk*. They passed through the doorway together and entered a narrow room that held an old wooden table with wooden bins, in front of a metal detector.

"Ladies, take off any belts, shoes, and jewelry, and put them in the bins. Put your notepads in, too."

"Thank you." Christine and Lauren complied, the both of them in their agreed-upon outfit of jeans, white shirts, and dark blazers, which they had on with flats. They passed through the metal detector, grabbed their legal pads, were handed two yellow golf pencils, and had their right hands stamped and read by an ultraviolet light, then they were led through one locked door, then the next, under the gaze of prison guards silhouetted behind a smoked glass panel. The two women were escorted to a narrow staircase with painted cinder-block walls and descended concrete steps. The air grew hotter the lower they went, as if it were hell itself, and a standing fan with grimy white plastic blades provided no relief, merely circulating hot air.

They walked down a short hallway that led to a large, harshly lighted visiting room the shape of an L, filled with old, mismatched chairs. A smattering of young women, kids, and older women sat talking with inmates in brown jumpsuits who wore no handcuffs. A sign read, **Inmates and Visitors May Embrace When Meeting and Departing Only.** A brawny young corrections officer stood guard, sitting on an elevated wooden chair against the wall, wearing a white short-sleeved shirt and black pants with a gray line down the side. His eyes scanned the room under the black bill of his black cap, a walkie-talkie crackling in its belt holster.

"Ladies, this way. This is general visiting. You're in the back." The male corrections officer ushered Christine and Lauren past the chairs, and Christine spotted an incongruous mural on the wall, depicting an idyllic stone archway with a cobalt-blue river winding into the distance.

"That's unusual," she said, pointing to the mural.

"It's a fake backdrop. Inmates can use it when they take pictures with their families."

"Oh." Christine took in the amateur art hanging on the cinderblock wall beside the mural, presumably by the inmates; a moonlit ocean, a pastoral landscape, Elvis, an Eagles logo, and a still life of red wine with cheese.

The corrections officer pointed to the left. "If you like murals, outside is one the Mural Arts Program did for us."

Christine looked to her left, where tall windows overlooked an outdoor area with old picnic tables and ratty blue-and-white umbrellas. On one side was a children's playground with a bright yellow slide and blue monkey bars, which would have been cheery but for the gray concrete wall topped with spiky concertina wire. On the wall was a colorful mural depicting children at play, which read CHERISH THIS CHILD.

Christine thought again of her baby, then the ultrasound image of its fluttery heartbeat, delicate as gossamer. Her heart beat faster with each step closer to where she would meet Jeffcoat, who could be the baby's father. She never would have believed she would get to meet their donor, much less in a prison, and the conflicting emotions wrenched at her gut; on the one hand, she was excited to meet the donor, but on the other, horrified that it was in here.

"Ladies, you'll be in the back booths, for no-contact visits. Jeffcoat is here on a special hold."

"Oh, I see." Christine tried to suppress her emotions and get her bearings.

"Here." The corrections officer stopped outside two white metal booths built into the wall and opened the metal door of the first one. "Wait inside and he'll be brought down."

"Thanks." Christine and Lauren squeezed inside the cramped white booth, where the air was so warm it was hard to breathe. They sat down on the two gray metal chairs, in front of a scratchy Plexiglas divider with a scored hole in the center and a white metal counter underneath. On the other side, barely three feet away, sat a single empty chair, where Jeffcoat would sit.

"Wait here," the corrections officer said, shutting the door.

Christine set down her pad and braced herself to get the worst news, or the best news, of her life.

Chapter Eighteen

Christine composed herself as the door opened on the other side of the booth, and Zachary Jeffcoat was admitted to the secured side, his arms handcuffed behind his back. He was tall, blond, and so handsome that he looked as out of place in the orange jumpsuit as an actor in a soap opera, a blond romantic lead miscast in the role of a felon.

Jeffcoat was tall and well-built, with broad shoulders and muscular biceps, shown by the short sleeves of his jumpsuit, but Christine zeroed in immediately on his face, visualizing the donor's adult photo. His eyes were wide-set, round, and blue, he had a straight nose, vaguely upturned, and a smallish mouth with thin lips, and his hair was a fine, ashy blond.

She had the instantly horrifying impression that Jeffcoat looked like Donor 3319, or at least his adult photo, but she resisted the conclusion with every fiber of her being. It bewildered her to see him in person, especially because her emotions roiled within her. She felt fear and confusion, at the same time as an intense, undeniable curiosity to know the truth. The very notion that she could be in the same room with the father of the baby she was carrying sent her into a tailspin.

Christine broke into a sweat, made worse in the hot room, and she felt her heartbeat accelerate. Her face burned, her thoughts raced. She wondered if her baby would look like Jeffcoat, if he was her donor, or if their baby would look like her, or what the combination would be, the amalgam of features and traits that made up a human being.

Jeffcoat looked up, meeting her eye for a split second before the corrections officer turned him around to uncuff him, and Christine recognized the look as the one from the CNN video, just before Jeffcoat had been put into the cruiser. A jolt electrified her system as she realized that Jeffcoat was a serial killer. It appalled her to think that he could be the father of her baby, and she felt like crying, screaming, raging, and suing everybody she could. But she told herself she had to get a grip on her emotions. She would only have twenty-five minutes with him, under prison rules, since she wasn't his attorney. She had to find out the truth, one way or the other, today.

"Hi, I'm Zachary Jeffcoat." He rubbed his wrists and met her eye, nodding almost shyly, as he sat down. "And you're a reporter? Christine Nilsson?"

Christine shuddered to hear her name coming from his lips. She made herself calm down. "Yes, a stringer, a freelancer."

"Which newspaper do you freelance for?"

"None, really." Christine reminded herself of her cover story, which she'd kept as close as possible to the truth in case he looked her up online. "I find stories that interest me, write them up, and try to sell them. This time I'm thinking of a book. My day job is a teacher, a reading teacher, and I always loved books, and I think this would be a great one."

"I understand, okay." Zachary nodded, inhaling. He pursed his lips, his strain evident. "So you're trying to make something happen."

"Yes." Christine put her legal pad on the counter, then gestured to Lauren. "This is Lauren Weingarten, a friend of mine. She's a teacher, too, but she comes along on my research trips."

Lauren said, stiffly, "Hi Zachary, if I can call you Zachary."

"Of course." Jeffcoat turned to Christine with a deep frown, a premature furrowing of his brow under feathery blond bangs. "Listen, I swear to you I'm not a serial killer. I'm not the Nurse Murderer, or whoever they want to call him. I didn't kill Gail Robinbrecht. I didn't murder anyone, I never would. I'm innocent, and I need to get out of here."

"So you're innocent?" Christine repeated, fumbling for her footing. She hadn't expected to talk about the murder right off.

"Absolutely, totally innocent, I swear it." Zachary held up a palm.

"First, before we begin, do you have a lawyer?"

"Yes, a public defender, but I haven't heard much from her. Her name is Mira Farooz. That's pretty typical of defenders, from what I hear. They handle, like, fifty cases at once, and I need a good lawyer, a private lawyer. Can you help me get one? I have to get out of here."

"Sorry, no, I can't." Christine wrote down *Mira Farooz*, to gather her thoughts. She hadn't anticipated him asking for her help.

"I'll tell you what I told the other reporters. I'm innocent and you have to help me. Please." Zachary leaned over, urgently, on his side of the divider. "The cops think I did it because they found me there in Gail's apartment, but she was already dead. I was the one who called 911. I didn't do it. Why would I call 911 if I did it?"

Christine wrote down, *he called 911*. She didn't know if it was prudent of him to be telling her so much about his case, but she didn't have time to ponder. She tried to ask a question that a reporter would. "How did you know her? Gail Robinbrecht."

"I didn't. We hooked up the night before she was killed, that's it." Zachary pursed his lips, shaking his head. "I have, or had, a girlfriend, I know. I feel terrible about that, I know it was wrong. But I would never kill anyone."

"What's your girlfriend's name?" Christine's ears pricked up. Donor 3319 had a girlfriend, but she didn't know if it was the same one.

"I don't know if I should tell you that. I don't want you to print that." Zachary's skin flushed a rosy pink, but Christine couldn't say for sure that it was *creamy*, like on the online profile.

"I won't use her name if you don't want me to, but why not?"

"I think it would make her look bad, right now. She's in medical school."

Christine swallowed hard. So Zachary's girlfriend was in med school. It was uncomfortably close to Donor 3319, who should have been in med school. She hoped it was a coincidence. "Why don't you tell me her name, but I promise not to print it?"

"Still, no. She'd hate that. She was just here, she broke up with me." Zachary flushed again, frowning. "I don't blame her, she has to distance herself, with all this. Her family, her career, anyway, we were in trouble for a long time."

"Oh, my. Sorry." Christine remembered the corrections officer upstairs, telling her that the girlfriend had been here today. She tried to think of more questions, so she could see if his background matched Donor 3319. "Can I ask, does she go to med school in Pennsylvania?"

"Yes, Temple."

Christine made a note, *Temple Med*. "Do you live together?"

"No. She lives in town, in Philly, and I live in Phoenixville. I travel for days at a time, to my accounts." Zachary paused, hesitating. "Do we have to talk about her? If this is about me, we should talk about me."

Christine nodded, trying to get on track. She was running out of time. "Okay, first, how old are you?"

"Twenty-four, and I didn't even know Gail Robinbrecht, not

really. I met her randomly and asked her out. I'd been with her the night before she was killed, and I was going to meet her again, but when I went to her house, like I say, she was dead. The police came and saw me there, and they thought I had done it."

"Do you have any idea who would kill her?"

"No, I don't even know her, it was a hookup. That's it. I *didn't* do it."

Christine tried to get to the point. "Why don't you tell me a little about yourself? Not about the murder, about you."

"Okay, if you want." Zachary frowned. "I'm an only child, and my parents have passed. My father was a pastor, and my mother worked however she could. Pastors, obviously, make no money. Her last job was in a high-school cafeteria."

Christine knew it matched the profile, in that Donor 3319's parents were religious. She remembered him writing that they would not approve of his donation, which was why he was requesting anonymity. "And where did you grow up, if I may ask?"

"We moved around because my father changed churches. We were Baptist and we went where the powers-that-be sent us. By the time I was fifteen, I had lived in twelve different states."

"Oh my. Could you name a few of them?" Christine was wondering if one was Nevada. Donor 3319 had said that he was from Nevada, but he hadn't mentioned anything about moving around.

"Let me see. New Mexico, Arizona, California for a lot of the time, then Colorado."

"That's a lot of moving around for a young child," Christine said, relieved not to hear Nevada, but the list was incomplete. "Did you have a happy childhood?"

"No," Zachary answered, without self-pity. "It wasn't horrible, but it wasn't great. My parents were very strict. It wasn't a happy household. It was disciplined. They had high goals for me. High expectations."

"That must've been difficult," Christine heard herself say, the words coming oddly naturally. Years of teaching had trained her to be empathetic, and she couldn't untrain herself in a day.

"In a way it was, but I understand the way my parents were. They weren't always that way."

"You mean they changed?"

"Um, yes." Zachary hesitated again. "Do you need to put this in the story? Like, is this for your story?"

Christine smiled at him, trying to put him at ease. "No, I won't print it if you don't want to. It's off the record. I'm just trying to understand your background."

"Well, okay, my parents changed after my baby sister died."

Christine blinked. None of this had been on the online profile of Donor 3319. "I thought you said you were an only child."

"I wasn't always, I had a little sister. Her name was Bella. She passed away when she was four, in an accident. It was awful." Zachary sighed, pursing his lips. "There was a development we lived in, like a townhouse development in Denver, that had a retaining wall at the back. After a really bad rain, water would fill up there."

Christine tensed, guessing where the story was going. Still, it wasn't on the online profile, so she was hoping that it proved Jeffcoat wasn't Donor 3319.

"Anyway, my mother was working two jobs then. She had the day job at the cafeteria, and at night she worked in a hospital, working for a janitorial company."

Christine made a note to stay on track. *Mother worked in hospital.*

"My mom had worked the night before and she was really tired, and she was playing with Bella and reading to her out back on the blanket, like they always used to do. I remember, I used to go with them." Zachary swallowed hard, his Adam's apple traveling visibly up and down. "Anyway, my mother fell asleep, she dozed off on the blanket. She had worked so late, she had only gotten two hours' sleep. Bella must have walked to the water and fallen off the retaining wall, and she drowned."

"I'm so sorry," Christine said, surprised to find herself meaning it. The story had an emotional power she couldn't deny, and it threw her off from making her mental note of comparisons with Donor 3319.

Lauren shook her head. "That must've been awful, I'm so sorry."

"Thanks. I came home with my dad, and I found them. My mom was asleep, and I'm the one who found Bella. I jumped in but I couldn't save her. It was horrible. For Bella, for my mother." Zachary shook his head, stricken, and Christine could see grief etching lines into his handsome face, which made it hard to believe he was a sociopathic serial killer.

Zachary continued, his tone quieter, "We were never the same after that, as a family. We fell apart. My dad tried to understand it, make sense of it in God's plan, all that. My mother was a woman of faith, too, and she prayed and prayed for forgiveness." Zachary's blue eyes glistened, but he blinked them clear. "She blamed herself for falling asleep, for letting it happen, for being careless. But she wasn't careless, it could have happened to anyone. It was a mistake. She was only human, overworked, underpaid, doing it all. She became very depressed. They died two years ago, they were hit by a drunk driver."

"I'm so sorry," Christine said, again. She hadn't expected to hear such a moving story.

Zachary shook his head, his lips puckering. "That was when I lost my religion, that day. I was ten but I was old enough to doubt. I don't believe in God anymore. I don't believe in a God who would let my little sister drown."

Christine reeled, trying to make the comparisons on the fly, so moved by his story of his sister's death. She remembered that Donor 3319 had said he was an agnostic or atheist. Maybe this was why. Maybe Zachary really was Donor 3319.

"Anyway, that's why I don't blame them. It was a hard thing to go through, as a family, and I was happy when we moved away. That's when we went to Nevada, and I graduated from high school in Reno."

Nevada. "Where did you go after that, did you go to college?"

"Yes, I was a good student. Math comes really easily to me, all sciences do. I'm a logical thinker."

Christine masked her dismay. Donor 3319 was good in math and logic. She didn't seem to have to ask anything for Zachary to keep talking.

"I graduated from the University of Arizona *magna cum laude*, which is pretty good." Zachary allowed himself a brief smile, and Christine smiled back, eager to latch on to a piece of good news.

"Well done, that couldn't have been easy. What was your major?"

"Chem."

Christine told herself to remain calm. Donor 3319 had been a chemistry major. "What did you do after graduation?"

"I worked, trying to save up the money to go to med school, but that was a dumb way. You can't do it without loans."

Christine held her breath at the mention of medical school, but she didn't interrupt him. She knew Lauren would be thinking the same thing.

"I got into medical school at the University of Nebraska, Creighton. I was so excited about being a doctor. I really wanted to work in a research capacity, like try and cure something."

"Like what?" Christine forced a smile, but her head was exploding. It was all adding up, just like Donor 3319, but she couldn't bring herself to reach that conclusion. She just couldn't.

"Something, anything to help society. Advance society. But the money was an issue for med school. The tuition was $65,000 a year, and I couldn't get enough loans. The textbooks cost way too much, like $300 a pop, even if you buy used or e-books." Zachary leaned forward, the conversation flowing more easily now that the harder subject had passed. "I worked every job I could get. Grocery bagger, math SAT tutor, research assistant. But I couldn't come up with tuition. I got accepted, but I never went."

"That's a shame." Christine realized it explained why the news reports hadn't said he was in medical school. He had never gone. Had Donor 3319 or was he Donor 3319?

"I hope I get back someday, but I have to get out of here." Zachary's forehead buckled, his desperation plain, all over again. "I'm innocent, they have the wrong guy, I swear to you. I had a life, I had a future. I don't belong in jail. You have no idea what it's like in here. It's scary as hell." Zachary's gorgeous eyes flared. "Please, I'll tell you anything you need to know. Do you think you could help me get a private lawyer?"

"I don't know," Christine answered, unprepared for the question. "I'm here to write about you—"

"But you're not, like, a real journalist with a real newspaper." Zachary hesitated, frowning in an apologetic way. "I didn't mean that the way it sounded. I meant, the other reporters told me that they have ethical guidelines. They can't help me get a lawyer. But you can, you're on your own."

"But I don't know any lawyers here. I'm not from here. Don't you know somebody, or maybe you could just investigate a private lawyer?"

"Not from inside, all they have are defenders, and they're not good enough." Zachary looked from Christine to Lauren with a new urgency. "Please can't you guys help me? I can pay, I had a job selling medical instruments. I was making $65,000 a year."

"Medical instruments?" Christine was thinking of the medical saw in the kill bag, which she'd read about in the news reports.

"Yes, I work for Brigham Instruments in West Chester, they make medical and surgical equipment. I've been working for them for two years, I have money in savings." Zachary placed his hands on the counter, leaning closer to the Plexiglas, desperate again. "Please, can't you find me a private lawyer? I need somebody good. You're on the outside. Go into West Chester or go online.

Find me a lawyer in Chester County." Zachary met her eye, his blue eyes plaintive. "You're the only reporter who asked me about myself, who asked about *me*. You're obviously a caring person."

"Thank you." Christine felt touched, oddly.

"If you find me a lawyer, I'll give you the exclusive. I'll cooperate with your book, and only yours. I'll tell you anything you want to know."

Christine's ears pricked up. *I'll tell you anything you want to know.*

Lauren interjected, "Zachary, I have to ask, in the newspaper accounts, it said that they found things in your trunk that incriminated you, like the bone-cutting saw."

"It's my *job* to have saws in my trunk." Zachary's blue eyes flew open, pleading. "My trunk looks like the inside of an operating room. I drive around with samples. I demonstrate bone saws to doctors and surgeons. I don't use my samples to *kill* anybody."

Lauren paused. "Did you tell the police that?"

"My lawyer told me not to. She told me not to say a word to the cops. She told me not to answer any questions. I told you more than I told them."

Christine found herself almost believing him. She could see the sincerity in his eyes and hear it in his voice. His whole manner seemed genuinely upset. The notion confounded her, but she didn't know whether to trust her judgment, and she still wanted to know for sure if he was Donor 3319.

Lauren interjected, "Zachary, what about the other things they found in the trunk? The shovel, the garbage bag, they said it's called a 'kill bag'—"

"That's no *kill bag*," Zachary shot back, urgent. "My territory includes central Pennsylvania. You ever go out there in winter? You need a shovel to get out of that snow. I keep the garbage bags because I put them under the tires when I get stuck. I practically *live* in that car, I carry everything I need." Zachary's head swiveled from Lauren to Christine. "Listen, I swear to you, on the soul of my sister, I didn't kill Gail Robinbrecht or anybody else, no matter what they say. It's a rush to judgment, just because I was there. I never killed anybody. I'm no serial killer!" Zachary shook his head, anguished. "That's just a story to sell more newspapers. I haven't been linked to any of those murders by any authority. None of the police from any of those states or the FBI has gotten in touch with me or my lawyer. None of it's true. None of it!"

Suddenly there was a loud rap at the metal door on the other side of the Plexiglas, and the corrections officer reappeared, taking stainless-steel handcuffs from his thick utility belt. "Jeffcoat, your time's up."

"Coming." Zachary rose reluctantly, anguished. "Please, Christine, get me out of here. I'll give you the exclusive. Find me a lawyer, please."

"I understand," Christine said, off-balance. She had run out of time to ask him, and she couldn't go home without finding out. "Maybe we could talk again tomorrow? Would that be possible?"

Lauren looked over but said nothing.

"Yes, yes, anytime." Zachary offered his wrists to the corrections officer behind his back. "We can talk every day if you want. Just help me, please. I'm begging you."

Chapter Nineteen

Christine headed to the exit doors of the prison with Lauren, shaken to her very foundation as they followed the others out. She wiped sweat from her brow, and her mouth had gone dry. Her mind reeled, her emotions churned. They went through the doors, and Christine felt hit by a wall of humidity, with the sun high in the sky and no trees to shade the prison entrance. They went down the steps and passed the Department of Corrections buses, which were still idling, their engines throwing off heat, making wiggly waves in the sweltering air.

Christine tried to recover as they walked through the official parking lot, neither woman speaking because they weren't alone. A man and a woman whom she had seen in the visiting room walked in front of them, tugging a toddler along, who had her little arm curved over a plush pink rabbit like a piece of macaroni. Christine noticed the woman walking too fast for the child, who had to scurry on the tiptoes of her sandals to keep up, and she would never understand the casual cruelty of some mothers, who had no idea how precious a gift they'd been given, in a child.

"Are you okay?" Lauren fell into step beside her after the women and the child went to the left toward a battered minivan.

They headed out of the official lot, walking downhill along the road.

"I don't know, I think so. It was so strange."

"Why didn't you ask him? Did you chicken out?" Lauren looked over at her, her brown eyes bewildered. Her long, dark hair stuck to the nape of her neck, curling in damp tendrils.

"No, I'm sorry, I didn't chicken out, I even had a plan of how to bring it up." Christine wiped her forehead with her hand, trying to process what had just happened. "I was warming up, finding out the background information, trying to see if it matched the online profile, but then, when he told that story about his sister dying, it threw me off track."

"I knew it. I could see, I knew something was happening. All of a sudden you went quiet."

"I felt *terrible* for him. For his sister, for his mom. Poor child, poor woman."

"Well? Do you think it's him?"

Christine couldn't answer, her emotions catching up with her all at once. Tears sprang to her eyes. She stopped in her tracks, stricken. She wanted to scream. It was too much. It couldn't be. She covered her face with her hands, even holding the car keys.

"Oh honey." Lauren hugged her gently.

"I think it's him," Christine heard herself saying, her heart speaking even as it was breaking. "I think he's our donor. I think he's my baby's father."

"You don't know that for sure." Lauren soothed her, then let her go. "You don't."

"Oh my God." Christine was trying not to cry. She had to keep it together. She lowered her hand with the car keys. "How did this happen? This can't be happening."

"It might not be. We don't know for sure until you ask him." Lauren held Christine by the shoulders, bracing her and looking directly into her eyes. "Remember that. We don't know for sure."

"Right. We don't know for sure." Christine repeated the words, almost involuntarily, trying to convince herself. Maybe if they could say it enough, over and over, they could make it true.

"Lots of people look like other people. Just last week, I got an email from Britney Keen, you know her, and she thought she saw me in the movies, and I wasn't at the movies."

"Right, people look alike sometimes." Christine sighed heavily, and Lauren let her shoulders go.

"Let's get out of here."

"Okay, yes, right." Christine wiped her face and started walking, with Lauren falling into step beside her.

"Why do you think he's your donor? Because he was accepted into med school?"

"Yes, and that he's a chem major, he's logical, he looks like him, he has religious parents . . ." Christine let her list trail off, trying to collect her thoughts.

"Don't get carried away, though. None of that is definitive."

"I know, but there's more. He said that he did a lot of things to earn money during med school, and in the profile it said he donated it for the money, so he could pay for med school."

"Most students need money during school."

"I know, but it's the sense I had, being in the same room with him—"

"You weren't in the same room with him." Lauren's eyes looked worried, as they walked along.

"I kind of was, I mean, we were. Anyway he *felt* like the father."

"Oh boy. Now you're talking crazy." Lauren snorted, walking beside her, as they traveled downhill.

"I know. It's just a sense. I can't deny it. It's a hunch. A sensation, intuition." Christine knew it was crazy, but she felt it inside. She hadn't realized it until this very moment, but she had to admit it to herself. They were almost at the visitors' lot, and she spotted her car, baking in the sun.

"It was voodoo? Pregnancy voodoo?"

"Whatever, I felt *connected* to him. I felt like he was the father." Christine aimed the key fob at her car, miserably.

"*Biological* father."

"Right." Christine meant biological, it was a shorthand. "What do you think? Do you think he's Donor 3319?"

"Honestly?" Lauren sighed, her heavy chest rising and falling slowly. "I hate to add fuel to the fire, but I thought he might be. The facts fit the online profile."

"Oh no." Christine breathed in deeply, suppressing her tears. She went to the driver's side of the car, opened the door and climbed inside, starting the ignition to turn on the air-conditioning to MAX. The temperature on the dashboard read ninety-six degrees.

Lauren got in the car. "It's going to be okay. We'll figure this out."

"Right." Christine grabbed a half bottle of water from the console and took a sip, but it was hot. "I'm sorry I said we'd go see him tomorrow. We didn't plan on that. I figured if we go in the morning, we'll be fine. Is that okay?"

"Sure." Lauren paused. "You know what's bugging me? I didn't understand why he told us about his sister."

"Because I asked him, I asked about his childhood."

"No you didn't, not really. You asked him about himself, and he told you a sad story from his childhood. He just offered it."

"I guess he felt comfortable with us." Christine finally began to cool down, feeling like herself again. "To leave it out would be an omission, wouldn't it?"

"Not necessarily. I just want you to be objective about him." Lauren met her eye, her lips in a grave line. "Do you believe him, that he's innocent?"

Christine sighed, ragged. "I don't trust anything I'm feeling right now. I'm not objective."

"I get that."

"But you know what, I think he might be innocent. I recognize that he could be guilty, but I just didn't feel like I was in the presence of someone who could kill someone, much less be a serial killer." Christine searched her best friend's troubled expression. "Did *you* think he's innocent?"

"He could be, yes. But what do we know about serial killers?" Lauren exhaled, deflating.

"Yeah." Christine's heart was still racing. "I'm a mess."

"Let's get out of here." Lauren patted her arm again. "Are you okay to drive?"

"Yes, I got it." Christine pulled out of the space and steered toward the exit road.

"You want to go to the hotel, check in? Grab some dinner?"

"Not just yet," Christine answered, getting her bearings as she turned left onto Route 29.

Chapter Twenty

Christine sipped water and pressed END to hang up the call. She felt somewhat better after a salad and French fries at a drive-thru MacDonald's, and they were making phone calls from the idling car, parked on the street near the courthouse in West Chester, which was a quaintly charming town with funky boutiques, restaurants with sidewalk seating, and a tiny business district that had a confusing number of one-way streets. It had the feel of a college town since it contained West Chester University, reminding her of where she had grown up, since Middletown had Wesleyan. It had taken them an hour to drive here, and on the way, they'd called local criminal lawyers that Lauren had found online. Unfortunately, it was five thirty on a Saturday night, and none of the lawyers was in.

Christine sighed, worried. She'd just called the sixth lawyer and got another no answer, leaving messages on voicemail. "I'm striking out here. Do we have more names?"

"Just a few. Look." Lauren clicked to get another website, then showed her the phone screen, munching away. Napkins, used ketchup packets, and a crumpled white bag joined the other food debris on the floor of the backseat.

"On it." Christine pressed in the number of Melinda Norate, Esq., who according to her website, had been practicing for twenty-two years, representing felons in distinctly rural Chester County, which as far as Christine could see, could include horse thieves. A bronze historical plaque on a pole by the car read, **Chester County— One of Pennsylvania's three original counties, formed in 1682 by William Penn**.

"I can't believe we're doing this."

"Getting him a lawyer? You heard him. He said he'd tell us anything if we helped him. Tomorrow, I will find a way to ask him if he's Donor 3319." Christine straightened up, and the phone stopped ringing, but it didn't go to voicemail.

"This is Melina Norate," a woman answered, sounding harried.

"Yes, hello!" Christine said, hopeful. She put the call on speaker so Lauren could hear. "I'm calling for Zachary Jeffcoat, who needs a criminal lawyer. He's—"

"The serial killer who killed Gail Robinbrecht."

"Allegedly," Christine answered, surprised. "Would you represent him?"

"No."

"But you practice criminal law, don't you?"

"Yes, but I'm too busy. That's why I'm here on a Saturday night." Norate paused. "You're never going to be able to get Jeffcoat local representation."

"Why?"

"Are you from here?"

"No."

"Okay, West Chester is the proverbial small town. Everybody here knows everybody else. Gail Robinbrecht had a lot of friends, she worked at the local hospital. Haven't you seen the white ribbons people are wearing?"

"No. I just got into town."

"Any lawyer who defends her murderer will never get new business, ever. He'll be a pariah."

Christine hesitated. "But what if Zachary Jeffcoat isn't guilty? Doesn't he deserve a defense?"

"In theory, but law is a business . . ." Norate didn't finish her sentence.

"Can you recommend anybody who would take him?"

"You know who I would try? Francis Xavier Griffith. He goes by Griff. He's semi-retired, but he's the best."

Christine took heart. "Is he local?"

"Yes."

"So why would he do it, when others wouldn't?"

Norate chuckled. "Give him a call. You'll see. Don't be put off by his demeanor."

"Okay." Christine started scrolling through her phone for Griff's website. "Thanks."

"Bye."

Christine hung up, found the website, which was barebones and had no photo, but she pressed CALL, and the phone rang a few times.

"Griff," a man answered in a grumpy voice.

"Yes, hello." Christine introduced herself, then said, "I'm calling on behalf of Zachary Jeffcoat, who needs a lawyer. He's charged with the murder of Gail—"

"I know who he is. I'm old, not stupid. Who are you? Are you family?"

Christine cringed. She was family, in a way. "I'm a freelance journalist and—"

"Lord, deliver me. Journalists are bad enough. Freelance means you couldn't get hired by anybody."

Christine and Lauren exchanged looks.

Griff said, "I heard Jeffcoat had a PD."

"PD?" Christine didn't know what that meant. To her, PD meant Professional Development, or homework for teachers.

"Public Defender."

"Yes, but he wants a private lawyer. Would you represent him?"

"I don't know. I'm trying to retire. My daughter says if I do, I'd make everybody miserable. But I already make everybody miserable. So."

Christine wasn't sure how to respond. "Well, please don't retire, because we need a lawyer."

Griff sighed heavily. "I don't do this over the phone. Come in Monday morning."

"Can I come in now? I'm only available for the weekend. I see that your office is on Market Street. We're in town, near the courthouse."

"Then get here before I change my mind."

"See you in five—" Christine said, but he had already hung up.

Five minutes later, Christine and Lauren were sitting in an office that was as different from Gary Leonardo's as a mousehole from a lion's den. The law firm of F.X. Griffith, Esquire, was a single room in the back of the first floor of a converted row house, which Griff evidently rented from a large estates practice; the office was a medium-sized rectangle with a single window in the back wall, containing brown bookshelves, a gray file cabinet, a plain wooden desk with an old desktop computer, and two maroon leather chairs opposite the desk, in which Christine and Lauren sat. The bookshelves held faded photographs of grinning family members, and the lawbooks were leather-bound, their spines broken and their tops feathered. The framed diplomas and court admission certificates on the wall dated from the 1970s.

"So, fill me in." Griff narrowed his eyes, which were gray-blue and cloudy at the edges behind old-fashioned tortoiseshell glasses. His thick, chalk-white hair shot straight up from both sides of his part, and he had unruly eyebrows to match. He had to be seventy-five years old, given the number of age spots on his temples, the depth of his crow's-feet, and the fissures etched into his face, bracketing his flattish lips. Still, he had sunburned cheeks and a small red nose, which made him look like an outdoorsy Methuselah.

Christine answered, "We just met with Zachary, and he asked us to find him a private lawyer."

"He too good for a public defender?" Griff wore a dingy white polo shirt with baggy khaki pants, and when he leaned forward on his desk, his arms were covered with spidery white hair.

"I guess he wants somebody better."

Griff frowned. "Public defenders are good. I started my career there."

Christine wondered when but didn't ask. "Well, he wants a private lawyer."

"What he should want is a local lawyer." Griff leaned over the desk, picking up a dirty rubber band. "Somebody who lives in Chester County. Knows the judges and the bar. Knows how to pick a jury, what appeals to them and what doesn't. Knows how to reach them, speaks their language. Has the same accent."

Christine noted that Griff had a farm-y accent. "So you'll do it?"

"I didn't say that."

Christine felt nonplussed. "Okay, can you tell me about yourself? How many murder cases have you handled?"

Griff frowned in thought. "Can't tell you. Lost count."

"Can you ballpark it?" Christine was trying to evaluate him as a lawyer.

"Handled up to thirty felonies a year in my salad days. Practiced criminal law for fifty years. You do the math."

Christine got the gist. "How many cases did you win?"

"Nobody keeps count, nobody worth knowing." Griff held up a thick finger. "Wait. Four."

"You won only *four* cases?" Christine glanced at Lauren, worriedly.

Griff shook his head. "No. Four death-penalty cases. That's all anybody keeps track of. Got life without parole for all four. That's four victories." Griff nodded, satisfied with himself. "Two of my guys are at Graterford. I wouldn't recommend you say hello."

Christine shuddered. "Do you have staff to help you on this case?"

"Used to. These days I'm a one-man band."

"Can you handle this case on your own?"

"Jeffcoat's got no money for staff, does he? He's not a rich kid, is he?"

"No. But do you have a paralegal or a secretary?" Christine hadn't even seen a receptionist's desk

"I know how to answer a phone. See?" Griff reached for his beige telephone and held up the clunky receiver, then hung it up again.

"You have a cell phone, don't you?"

"No. No email, either. The government taps our phones and email. NSA admits as much. You know what NSA stands for? No Such Agency." Griff permitted himself a crooked smile, showing yellowing teeth. "You ask me, politicians are the real criminals. Wholesale violations of the Fourth Amendment, every day. Unreasonable searches and seizures. Dragnetting of information, which is *exactly* what our forefathers warned against. Why the citizenry consents to it, I don't know. Not me. I *don't* consent."

"So how do you work?" Christine asked.

"I use the computer for word processing. I type my own briefs and motions. I don't *e-file*. I wouldn't have the website, but my grandson made it for me."

"Do you have Internet?" Christine had to draw the line. She would accept a Luddite, not a crackpot.

"No. Too easy to hack into. I've been saying it for years, but you see it on TV now. Everybody getting hacked into." Griff pointed to the door. "If you don't like it, do me a favor. Go. Let me retire. I was about to. Also my bunions hurt. I have two now. My feet are tripods."

Christine didn't think he was kidding.

"Now, to business. Can Jeffcoat pay? Freedom isn't free. My retainer is low because I have no overhead. $5,000. He'll pay fifteen grand with someone else. Twenty-five in Philly."

"He says he'll pay. So what happens, next, for him?"

Griff linked his fingers. "In ten days, if we don't ask for an extension, the Commonwealth will have to appear at a preliminary hearing and show its *prima facie* case."

"What does that mean?"

"You don't know Latin?"

"No."

"Too bad." Griff sniffed, his disapproval plain. "*Prima facie* means first face or first impression. The Commonwealth has to show its first impression of the evidence against Jeffcoat, sufficient to make out the crime of capital murder. Then there's a formal arraignment date, where he'd enter a plea, and we'd ask the Chester County D.A., for mandatory disclosures."

"Which is?" Christine felt like she was pulling teeth.

"The photos they took, autopsy reports, blood and DNA tests, review of physical evidence, reports of forensic evidence, and the like. They have to turn it over, but not until later. Jeffcoat will have to enter a plea, yay or nay. Pretty soon, the FBI and the other state jurisdictions, Maryland and Virginia, will want to interview him about the other murders. It's fun messing with the government." Griff smiled sideways again. "Messing with the press, even better. They're calling him a serial killer. It prevents him from getting a fair trial."

Lauren interjected, "What does the FBI have to do with this?"

"The FBI sticks its nose where it doesn't belong. In a situation with multiple killings over multiple states, every state has jurisdiction over the murder that took place within its borders. The FBI shouldn't investigate a murder unless it happened on a government property, an Indian Reservation, a federal building, national park, military base, or involves a U.S. citizen abroad. They're supposed to have a nexus, a jurisdictional hook, but they try to find one. Remember that spree killer, Cunanan? Shot that famous Italian designer, back in '97?"

Christine tried to remember. "You mean Gianni Versace?"

"Right. The FBI got involved because he also killed a caretaker of a park in New Jersey. It turns out that in the middle of the park, there was a one-acre cemetery deeded to the federal government. That gave the Feds their nexus. Cunanan eventually killed himself, so he wasn't prosecuted."

Christine listened, interested. When Griff talked law, his words took on an authoritative ring.

"Whether or not the Feds find a nexus in Jeffcoat's case, their behavioral science people or a profiler will work with all three jurisdictions. The profiler would be assigned to the Philly FBI Office but he could travel anywhere covered by the Philadelphia Division. He'll meet with both state police departments and the prosecutors from the Chester County D.A.'s office. He might also get input from a unit at Quantico." Griff rolled his hooded eyes behind his glasses. "Big deal. Jeffcoat's *advocate* would have to shield him from the FBI and other jurisdictions. I would sideline the Maryland and Virginia cases. Focus on the Robinbrecht case. Investigate it. Decide whether he pleads out or goes to trial."

Christine sensed Griff would take the case, though he hadn't said as much yet.

"This case alone will be difficult enough. They've already leaked incriminating information, like the kill bag."

"He has an answer for that. He's a medical equipment salesperson at Brigham Instruments."

"In town? He told you that?" Griff lifted his furry eyebrows.

"Yes."

Griff didn't say anything for a moment.

Christine filled the silence. "I heard that not many lawyers in town would take his case. Why would you take it if they won't?"

"I don't care what anybody thinks. I only care about the law. I only care about the Constitution. I care about the rights of the individual against an oppressive and corrupt government. No lawyer worth his salt gives a *damn* what anybody thinks." Griff stopped playing with the rubber band, eyeing her and Lauren. "Why are you doing this?"

"I got interested in this case for a freelance article or a book, and I wanted to meet Jeffcoat." Christine stopped herself from calling him Zachary, then wondered when she had started thinking of him as Zachary, not Jeffcoat. "He said he'd give me the exclusive for my book if I found him a private lawyer."

"So you've spoken to him about the facts of his case?"

"Yes."

"What did he tell you?"

Christine answered truthfully, telling him about Zachary's date with Gail Robinbrecht and finding her dead in her home, which was when Griff's mood soured.

"He shouldn't have said anything about his case. If he hires me, I'm going to advise him not to talk to you. Ever again."

"You're putting me in a difficult position," Christine said without elaborating.

"So?" Griff snorted. "If I take Jeffcoat on, my interest is what's good for him. Not you."

"Why shouldn't he talk to me?"

"Anything he says to you is discoverable. If you're taking notes, your notes are discoverable. You can be called as a witness at trial by the Commonwealth. You have no privilege to protect that conversation." Griff pointed to Lauren. "Did she go with you to see him?"

"Yes."

"Then she can be called, too. That's true whether I put Jeffcoat on the stand or not. He has nothing to gain by talking to anybody but me, and only my conversations with him are privileged. Or somebody who works for me. By the way, where did you say you were from?"

"Connecticut."

"How did you hear about the case? You saw it on TV or something?"

"Yes," Christine answered, because she was tired of lying.

"Don't be surprised if the FBI comes knocking on your door. Or hers."

"Why?" Christine couldn't imagine what Marcus would do if the FBI showed up at home.

"They may want to talk to you as part of their investigation. It's within their purview."

"How would they know where I live?" Christine realized the answer as soon as she'd asked the question.

"You signed the visitors' log at Graterford. You showed your driver's license. They're the FBI. Even they can find you if they have the address." Griff chuckled at his own joke. "So, if you want to write a book after the trial, that's up to you and Jeffcoat. But for right now, it's no-go." Griff hunched over his desk. "So now, decide. I'll take the case, but if you hire me, you got no book. Do you care about Jeffcoat or do you care about your book? Who are you *advocating* for?"

Christine thought fast. "I have to see him one more time, tomorrow morning. To tell him about you."

"One and done?"

"Yes."

"Okay." Griff eyed her behind his bifocals. "You're putting his interest above your own?"

"I guess so." Christine could feel Lauren's eyes on her but didn't look over.

"Hmph! Can I trust you not to talk to him about the case?" Griff wagged an index finger at her, his knuckle as gnarled as the knot of a tree.

"Yes."

"You give me your word?"

"Absolutely."

"That was easy," Griff said, with a derisive snort. "You sure you're a real reporter?"

Chapter Twenty-one

The two women walked down the street from Griff's office, with Christine mulling over the meeting, preoccupied. The sun still burned in the sky, and the air still felt humid. The only shade came from tall trees that lined the sidewalks, which were of red brick. They passed an antique store with a window display of painted cast-iron doorstops and a barber shop with an old-school barber pole mounted on its brick façade. The town seemed busier, with more traffic clogging the narrow streets, couples strolling hand-in-hand to restaurants, and young people bopping around, toting backpacks, icy Dunkin' Donuts drinks, and smart-phones. Christine spotted people wearing white ribbons pinned to their clothes, and more than one shop window had a sign that read GAIL, YOU WILL BE MISSED!

"Mission accomplished," Christine said, after a moment. "We got Zachary a lawyer."

"Yes, and I like Griff."

"You mean Gruff?"

Lauren laughed. They passed a hair salon with a sign that read STUDENT CUTS ONLY TWELVE DOLLARS, since West Chester was home to West Chester University. "He knows what he's talking about, even if he reminds me of those Muppets in the balcony."

"Staler and Waldorf?" Lauren laughed. "Exactly. He's Waldorf."

"Right." Christine smiled, but it faded. "So we only have one meeting left with Zachary. I have to ask him tomorrow morning."

"You can do it. And you need to since you're too nice to convince anybody you're a reporter. I bet Waldorf is Googling you right now."

"He doesn't have the Internet, remember." They turned the corner, passing a local bank, and spotted her car down the street.

"You must want to get off your feet. Let's go to the hotel and check in."

"Right." Christine got her car keys from her purse and chirped her car unlocked as they approached since it was on their side of the street. "Did you hear what Griff said, that Zachary hasn't been linked to the other murders? It was the same thing Zachary said."

"What's your point? That he's not a serial killer?"

"I guess," Christine answered, but she didn't know what her point was, truly. Her emotions were bound into a knot that she was too tired to unravel.

"If you kill even one person, that's too many."

"I agree." Christine went around the back fender of her car and waited for traffic to pass until she went to her door. "But what if he's innocent? What if it's not him? He seems too emotional to be a sociopath, doesn't he?"

"Then we just got him a good lawyer," Lauren answered before she got inside the car.

"I'm worried." Christine turned on the ignition and went through her air-conditioning routine.

"You'll feel better after you shower and rest, we both will." Lauren buckled on her seat belt. "Oooh, I want to use towels I don't have to wash, then put on a bathrobe that's nicer than mine."

Christine only half-listened, pulling into traffic and stopping at the red light, on the road that led to the highway back to Collegeville.

"I wonder if our hotel has room service. I want to lie in bed and have people bring me food. It's like a hospital for moms."

Christine's thoughts churned, and she felt like she needed a sounding board. "The problem is that there are so many possibilities, and I can't figure out which ones are true."

"Like what?" Lauren looked over.

"Let's start with whether Zachary is Donor 3319. We both think he might be, but that's based on our intuition and some facts."

"Not a lot of facts."

"Right." Christine watched the traffic light burn red. "Tomorrow we find out the answer, but there's a part of me that doesn't want to know."

"Because you're afraid it's him?"

"Yes." Christine had a second thought. "But the only reason I'm afraid it's him is because he's in jail, charged with murder, a serial killer. If he's innocent, I'd *like* it if he was our donor. He's a nice guy. He's smart, personable, and he's so good-looking."

"I get that. I understand."

"So I'm not crazy?" Christine hit the gas when the traffic light changed, going forward.

"Not at all. This is a hard situation, and I'm proud of you. You're doing a great job, considering all you've had for sustenance is saturated fats."

"Ha." Christine glanced over at a street sign, which read WARWICK STREET. "Warwick Street? How do I know that name?"

"I don't know."

"I read it somewhere." Christine braked slowly, causing the car behind her to start honking. "I remember, in the newspaper article online. Warwick is the street that Gail Robinbrecht lived on. Where she was murdered."

"That's weird." Lauren grimaced.

"Not really. It's a small town. We've seen it ourselves, you can *walk* places here." Christine stopped the car, her eyes on the WAR-WICK STREET sign, letting traffic flow around her. "Can you get her address for me, on the phone?"

"Does this mean we're not going to the hotel?"

"Not yet." Christine got a second wind as she turned onto Warwick. "Aren't you curious?"

"As between a murder scene or room service? No." Lauren chuckled, but she was already scrolling though her smartphone. "Here we go. Robinbrecht's house number is 305."

"Thanks." Christine drove down Warwick Street, slightly downhill, and they entered a residential section of West Chester. Well-maintained colonial-vintage row houses with Victorian porches lined block after block, each home with brick façades and paneled shutters painted in tasteful Williamsburg hues of light blue, grayish browns, or daffodil yellow. Most of the front doors sported decorative wreaths, and colorful glazed pots of impatiens and petunias sat atop the front steps. The houses had no front yards because they were built directly on the sidewalk, as they would have been in the 1700s and 1800s, reminding Christine of the older sections of Mystic and Marblehead.

"This is pretty."

Christine looked ahead to the next block, where there seemed an unusual amount of traffic slowing in front of one of the houses. "I think that's 305, her house."

"Oh man. People are stopping by to pay their respects."

"Right." Christine was getting the idea that the murder of Gail Robinbrecht might have disappeared from national headlines, but the story was heartbreakingly alive in West Chester.

"Look, a memorial." Lauren pointed to the right, and as Christine drove closer, she spotted in the middle of the block a lovely three-story house with moss-green shutters. People stood in front, gathering around a sad grouping of flowers, candles, stuffed animals, and homemade signs. Cars lined the block, and some double-parked in front of number 305, with their blinkers on.

"That's sad." Lauren shook her head. "I hate to think that people can be that evil."

"I know." Christine was wondering if Zachary could be that evil and if evil was inherited. She drove slowly as she approached the house, then navigated around the double-parked cars, glancing over at the signs. WE WILL MISS YOU, GAIL, read one handwritten placard with a bunch of signatures, and another sign had a picture of a lovely young woman, presumably Gail, but Christine couldn't see much detail from her side of the car.

"You sure you want to do this?" Lauren asked, looking over. "This reminds me of Sabrina, remember?"

"Yes," Christine said, her throat tight. Sabrina Bryfogle had been one of the most beloved teachers in the fourth grade, passing last year from breast cancer. The faculty had been stricken to lose her, and they'd called in grief counselors for the students. Sabrina's memorial tree grew by the soccer field, and Christine would never forget the outpouring of emotion at the memorial service.

"I hate cancer."

"I hate cancer, too."

"But I hate murder more."

"I do, too. I hate that anybody has to die, ever." Christine was thinking of her father. She turned the corner, looking for a parking space that she wasn't sure she wanted to find. "Maybe we should leave. I don't want to bum you out."

"No, that's okay," Lauren said, rallying. "We're here, and I see a space at the end of the block. Go park, it's okay."

"Okay, thanks. I don't know what I'm expecting to find, I'm just curious." Christine drove forward to the space, which was at the corner, where she parked and cut the ignition. They got out of the car, and Christine crossed behind it to the sidewalk, where she fell into step with Lauren. They passed a woman with over-processed bright red hair sweeping the sidewalk, a cigarette clamped between her teeth.

"Hello," Christine said politely.

The woman straightened up with a deep frown. Her eyes were a bloodshot blue, and her nose was vaguely reddish, like a drinker. She was dressed in a vintage Ramones T-shirt, cutoff shorts, and pink flip-flops, and blurry tattoos blanketed her arms. "Going to see Gail's?"

"Yes."

"You from Connecticut?"

"Yes," Christine answered, surprised. "How do you know?"

"The license plate." The woman motioned toward the car with her broom. "I've been seeing all kind of plates, you're not even the farthest. People came down from Québec yesterday. They don't even know her. People, they're ghoulish. It's sick."

"Not really," Christine said, defensive. "They're just trying to be nice, I think. Don't you?"

"Hmph." The woman turned her back, returning to sweeping, while she talked to herself. "What's nice about it? Come see where the lady was killed by the Nurse Murderer? Everybody in town's talking about it. Everybody's saying the same thing, 'I just saw her, she was just here.' Everybody locking their doors now. We never used to have to lock our doors around here. *Never!*"

Christine and Lauren exchanged glances, but neither of them said anything, and they resumed walking again. They came to a break in the row houses, and a skinny asphalt street that ran behind the row houses, each of which seemed to have a backyard. Blue recycling bins and numbered trash cans lined the spiky privacy fences along the back wall of the yards. Most were also fenced on the sides by more tall wood, white picket, or old-school iron, separating one neighbor from the next, and some yards contained pretty gardens around bistro tables, but others were paved over, converted to a driveway.

The women kept walking, and Christine felt an increasing sadness the closer they got to the house, and by the time they turned the corner and walked partway up the block, she regretted having come. A small group of forlorn people clustered around the memorial, their heads bent over a pastel pile of sympathy cards, scented and votive candles, and more than one SpongeBob Square-Pants; Gail Robinbrecht must have been a fan, which touched Christine, showing that the nurse had had a sense of fun. Photographs of Gail covered the signs; candids showing her in navy scrubs at the hospital, hiking with three other women on a hillside covered with wildflowers, or cuddling a chubby calico near a bookshelf full of books.

Christine felt an ache in her heart. She prayed to God that Zachary hadn't been responsible for the brutal death of this lovely woman, then caught herself, realizing that Zachary might not have been her donor at all. Either way, she felt terrible if Zachary had killed Gail, or that anybody had killed her. She heard snatches of the sorrowful talk around them: ". . . how could this happen . . ." ". . . she was so dedicated . . ." ". . . I'll never forget how she helped my son when he had his tonsils out . . ." ". . . she was the best, just the best . . ."

Suddenly a woman started to cry, holding a Kleenex to her blotchy face as she was comforted by another woman. They must have been coworkers of Gail Robinbrecht's because they both had on blue scrubs and each wore a laminated employee ID from Chesterbrook Hospital on a green lanyard.

Christine wasn't surprised to see Lauren's eyes glistening, and she touched her best friend's arm. "Let's go," she said softly.

"Right." Lauren fell into step with Christine, and they walked stiffly away.

"Sorry I dragged you here."

"It's okay. It puts things into perspective, doesn't it?"

"How so?" Christine asked quietly as they turned the corner and headed toward the car.

"That life is short, and sweet. You have to live it in a way that makes you proud." Lauren wiped her eye, blinking back her tears. "That's it, that's all I got."

"That's pretty good," Christine said, patting her on the back, but ahead they both spotted the tattooed woman, still muttering to herself as she swept. She was either drunk or crazy, so they gave her a wide berth, but just as they were passing, the woman stopped sweeping, turned, and straightened up, glaring at them.

"Well, girls? Did you see what you wanted to see? Did you get your jollies?"

"No, really, please," Christine started to say, raising her hand, but the woman's eyes flared with anger.

"Did you shed a few tears, did you have a good cry? Boo-hoo! Boo-hoo!"

Lauren fended her off with a hand. "Look, that's uncalled for—"

"Is it?" the woman demanded, stabbing her broom into the sidewalk. "How the *hell* would you know? You don't know her! You hear she was a nurse, you think she was a saint! But I'm telling you, that woman was *no saint*! She was a *slut*!"

"Please, we have to go," Christine said, shaken. She didn't want to hear the woman speak ill, much less slut-shame, and Lauren hustled away to the car.

"She lived back there!" The woman shook the broomstick toward the backyards. "You see that second floor, the duplex with the yellow door, where the stairs go? That's where she lived!"

Christine looked back toward the yellow door, only because she hadn't realized that Gail Robinbrecht had lived in a duplex. None of the newspaper articles had said that, and Christine spotted the bright yellow door, which had a stairwell that zigzagged down the back of the row house, standing out against the brick because it was of unpainted lumber.

"That's right! Take a good look!" the woman shouted at her. "I live *right* across from her door. My kitchen's across from hers. You know how many different *men* I saw come up and down the stairs late at night? *Plenty!*"

Christine's eyes flared, but she couldn't stop listening. She scanned the back walls of the other houses, and she could see that wooden stairwells had been added to many of them, so they all must have been duplexes with the entrances around the back.

"One man after the other, all different, they were *booty calls*! That's what they're called! *Booty calls!*" The woman shook her head, her lips making a bitter line. "What did she expect was gonna happen? You gonna bring home strange men? You're gonna let them in? That's Gail the *saint*!"

Christine listened, appalled, but she started to think about the implications for Zachary. He could've been one of several men that Gail hooked up with, maybe even one of many. Maybe he had been telling the truth, that he'd found her dead already.

"The neighbors on the front of the street, they don't see what I see! You know what I think? She was a slut and a hypocrite! You play with fire? Sooner or later you're gonna get burned! That's what I—"

"Miss," Christine interrupted, "what's your name?"

"Linda Kent. Mrs. Kent! I'm a widow!"

"My name is Christine Nilsson, and I'm wondering if you saw anything suspicious or unusual on the night she was murdered. Did you see any man, or men, on her back steps?"

"See something, say something! See something, say something! I already called the police! They said they'd call me back and get my statement." The woman brandished the broom, her eyes wild. "Now get lost! Get back to Connecticut!!"

Christine turned away, then hustled for the car.

The woman could have been drunk, or crazy.

Or she could've been correct.

Chapter Twenty-two

Christine called Griff as soon as she got in the car, driving away from Warwick Street. She hit the SPEAKER button so Lauren could hear, then stuck her smartphone on the Drop-Stop sticker she kept on her dashboard, so she could talk hands-free.

Griff picked up after two rings. "What?"

"I was just at 305 Warwick Street, Gail Robinbrecht's house. I found out that she lived in a duplex, and a neighbor around the back said that she used to have a lot of men going up the stairs at night."

"You went to the crime scene?" Griff asked, surprised.

"Well, I went to her house. I couldn't get inside, it was taped." Christine cruised through the leafy residential area of West Chester. "But I thought you could follow up on that for the defense. It suggests that there may have been other suspects, other than Zachary. I mean Jeffcoat. He could have been telling the truth."

Lauren looked over, rolling her eyes, since she hadn't been inclined to credit Kent's ravings.

"His defense is my job, not yours. Assuming he retains me."

"I know, but I thought I could help, and I'm sure he's going to retain you." Christine caught sight of the business district up ahead and hit the gas. "The woman's name is Linda Kent and she lives on Daley Street. She tried to tell the police what she saw, if anything, but they didn't get back—"

"I have to go. Call me after you meet with Jeffcoat. Tell me if he wants to retain me." Griff paused. "Remember, no talking to him about the case. Don't tell him what you just told me."

"Why not?" Christine turned right, onto the main road, and traffic was moving along steadily out-of-town. People strolled on the sidewalks, window-shopping or waiting in line for restaurants, and folk music wafted from the open door of a bar, under a banner that read, HAVE A GR8T SUMMER, WCU STUDENTS!

"I told you already. What are you, stupid? Conversations between you and Jeffcoat are not privileged. They're discoverable and admissible."

"Okay, okay, I got it." Christine glanced at Lauren, who was trying not to laugh.

"God in heaven! You're stubborn!"

"No, I'm not, I'm just curious."

"Curiosity killed the cat." Griff hung up, and so did Christine, pressing END on the mounted phone.

Lauren looked over, chuckling. "You're driving him crazy."

"Because I'm curious? Curiosity is a good thing."

"Not for cats. You heard him."

"Right." Christine fed the car some gas as traffic broke up, steering out of the town for open road.

An hour later, Christine and Lauren arrived at the hotel, checked in, took turns showering, and flopped in matching bathrobes on the bed, then ordered Greek salads with no onions from room service and a first-run Melissa McCarthy comedy from the Spectravision. The two women enjoyed the movie, tacitly agreeing not to talk about the day, but Christine felt anxiety gnawing at the edges of her consciousness. She tried not to think about Zachary, Gail Robinbrecht, or the other murdered nurses, but they were in the back of her mind. She also knew that she'd have to talk to Marcus to say good night and she dreaded lying to him.

Night fell outside the large smoked-glass windows, and, by the time the movie ended, Christine knew she couldn't put off the phone call any longer. She found the remote, aimed it at the TV, and muted the credits as Lauren looked over, her dark eyes tired and her curly topknot slipping to the side. She had spent most of the movie answering texts from her mother, husband, and sons, who were getting ready for a travel baseball game and couldn't find clean socks, the new cleats, or the dog's Prozac.

"You going to call Marcus?" Lauren asked with a sigh.

"It can't be avoided, can it?"

"My advice, keep it short. You're a bad liar."

"Good advice." Christine picked up her phone, and Lauren rose slowly, with a soft grunt.

"I'll leave you alone. I'm going to the bathroom."

"You don't have to, you can stay."

"Are you kidding?" Lauren looked back with a smile. "I get to sit on the bowl in peace? I've been looking forward to this all day."

"Have fun," Christine called after Lauren, who trundled off to the bathroom, then she speed-dialed Marcus's number, and he picked up after the second ring.

"Hey, babe, how you doing?" Marcus asked, still in cool mode.

"Okay, but tired," Christine answered, which wasn't a lie. "I just wanted to call you quick before I went to bed. I can barely stay awake."

"I won't keep you," Marcus said quickly, and Christine felt a twinge, getting the impression that he didn't want to talk to her.

"How's it going on the site?"

"The usual crap. We'll be able to straighten it out, but it puts us behind schedule, and you know how that goes. It's expensive. How's the weather? You getting any beach time?"

"Not really, I'm helping out in the house. We have to get all the sheets out and the towels, and sweep up." Christine scrolled quickly to her Weather Channel app, plugged in Long Beach Island, New Jersey, and saw that it was partly cloudy there. "It's not that nice a beach day anyway."

"Too bad. It's been raining all day, down here. I think I actually ruined my suitpants."

"That sucks," Christine said, her mood spiraling downward. She couldn't believe they were reduced to talking about the weather in their respective locations, one of which was fraudulent.

"You feeling any better about the Homestead lawsuit?" Marcus's tone softened, which only made Christine feel guilty, so she faked a yawn to bail on the conversation.

"Yes, I am, but let's not get into it tonight, okay? I'm so tired, and I'm tired of thinking about it. I just want to get to bed."

"Okay, I get it." Marcus's tone stiffened again, now that he had been rebuffed. "Sleep tight, and take care of yourself."

"Love you," Christine said, then she realized that he hadn't said it first.

"Love you, too."

Christine hung up first, then tossed the phone aside. A wave of sadness overwhelmed her, so she closed her eyes. She didn't want to think about Marcus, Zachary, or anything bad, any longer. She placed the palm of her right hand over her belly and focused on her baby. Because that was everything good, growing every day, bigger and stronger, right inside her very body.

Her breathing grew soft and even, and every muscle in her surrendered, and she drifted into an exhausted slumber before she could even begin to worry.

About what tomorrow morning would bring.

Chapter Twenty-three

Christine sat with Lauren in the cramped white booth, waiting for Zachary. The room was stifling, but she had already thrown up, as well as having showered and changed into the pink shirtdress that she had worn to her first appointment with Dr. Davidow. She'd packed it because it was one of her nicer casual dresses, which meant it didn't have any pen marks or stiff patches of glue from school. Somehow, it seemed fitting for today, when she would learn if Zachary Jeffcoat was Donor 3319.

"Do you know how you're going to ask him? How you are going to bring it up?" Lauren asked, her brow knit. She was already sweating from the heat inside the booth, which made her worry lines glisten. She'd showered, but had to put on the same clothes as yesterday, because she hadn't had time to pack herself, having packed three boys, their sports gear, two dogs, and the dog's Prozac, for their weekend of travel baseball.

"I think I'm going to try to engage him, like I would any one of my students."

"Really? How so?"

"You know my theory, I let them read anything they want to, just so they read. I try not to judge. I build up their self-esteem and create a safe and nurturing environment, so we can build a rapport and they can learn." Christine had been thinking about that last night. "So I'm going to do the same thing with him. Get him talking about something he really loves, and he'll feel good about himself. Then I'm going to look for a way to bring up the subject."

"Sounds good." Lauren smiled, in an encouraging way. "Do you want to rehearse it?"

"No, thanks." Christine knew that rehearsing would bring her jitters to the fore, not only the nervousness she had about asking him but from the fact that this was the last time she would see him. It wasn't that she wanted to see him again, but she didn't like the idea that she would never see him again, and her emotions hung somewhere in the middle, in a netherworld between attraction and repulsion. She'd tossed and turned last night, trying to visualize how this final meeting would go. And she couldn't help but think that he could be innocent, especially after she'd learned from Linda Kent that he wasn't Gail Robinbrecht's only hookup.

"You're stressing, I can tell." Lauren's lower lip puckered. "Why don't you just come clean? Tell him the truth. Tell him that the reporter thing was a lie to meet him and find out if he was your donor."

"No, I don't feel comfortable with that."

"Why? It will be easier than trying to get him to say it. So what if he knows you lied? You're never going to see him again."

Christine didn't like the sound, *never going to see him again*. "But the fact that we used a donor is still a secret. You and my parents are the only ones who know. My *in-laws* don't even know. I hate the idea of the exposure."

"Oh, right."

"Marcus doesn't even know that I told my parents. He wanted to wait to tell the rest of the family, maybe until after the baby's born. You're the only one who's allowed to know."

"I'm so special." Lauren smiled.

"Exactly." Christine knew Lauren was trying to lighten the mood. "It feels weird to me that he should know before my in-laws do. I want as few people to know as possible."

"I get it," Lauren said, nodding. "Strictly need-to-know, like the CIA. But don't you get tired of the family secrets? We have them, too. My aunt knows things my mother doesn't know, my mother knows things that my sister doesn't know. It's hard to keep it all straight."

"Sometimes it's necessary." Christine spotted Zachary's blond head bobbing behind the guard in the secured part of the hallway and she straightened up in the hard chair. "He's here."

"Remain calm. You can do it."

"Fingers crossed." Christine caught Zachary's eye, and he smiled. He looked genuinely happy to see her, and she didn't think it was her imagination.

"I see him," Lauren said, and they both watched as the guard unlocked Zachary's handcuffs and showed him into the secured side of the booth, where he sat down, with a new smile.

"Good morning, Christine. Hi, Lauren. You two look nice."

"Thank you." Christine placed her legal pad and golf pencil on the counter, as if reestablishing her journalistic bona fides. "I have great news for you. We found you a really good lawyer."

"That's great!" Zachary's eyes widened, his relief plain, and he beamed. "How did you do that so fast?"

"We got busy. He's from West Chester, and he's a very experienced criminal lawyer. His name is Francis Griffith but he goes by Griff. He knows about your case and he really wants to take you on. He gave me a business card, but they wouldn't let me bring it in. So I'm going to have to tell him to contact you, is that okay?"

"Sure, that's great. You sound like you know him."

"No, but we met with him and really liked him. We talked about your case—"

"You told him I was innocent, right?" Zachary interrupted,

newly urgent. "I don't want one of those lawyers who thinks it's fine to represent somebody guilty. I'm *not* guilty."

Christine thought again of what Linda Kent had said and took a quick detour. "Zachary, can I just ask you, how well did you really know Gail Robinbrecht?"

"Honestly, I told you, I didn't know her at all."

"The first day you met her was the night before she was murdered?" Christine knew she was treading into forbidden territory, after the warning by Griff, but she couldn't help herself.

"Yes."

"Did you exchange emails with her or texts before you met her?"

"No, I met her in the cafeteria, chatted her up, and she said she was free that night, so we made a date. I didn't even have her phone number."

"How did you know where she lived?" Christine could feel Lauren trying to catch her eye, warning her off the questions.

"She told me the address."

"You don't know if she had a boyfriend or was seeing anybody else?"

"I have no idea. I know she wasn't married, that's all. Why?"

"Just curious," Christine answered, avoiding Lauren's disapproving eye. "Now, anyway, to get back to the lawyer, I told him what you told us and he completely understood. I'll have him visit, or contact you; he probably knows how to do that."

"He probably does. I don't. I know I can get email, but they didn't give me my email address yet. They're saving all the email. They screen it before it goes to me."

"Oh, even the lawyer's? He said that would be privileged."

"I don't know. They told me most of the email is from media people and women who write the Death Row inmates here, whatever." Zachary rolled his eyes, like a goofy teenager.

"The other thing Griff said is that he needs a retainer of $5,000."

"Oh no." Zachary grimaced.

"I hope that's not a problem. I told him that you would pay him."

"But five grand? I didn't think it would be that much. I don't know how I'm going to get the money. I have, like, $2,300 saved. I'd have more than that, but I'm paying off my student loan debt. Could you find someone cheaper?"

"Not that I know of, it's the weekend. He said it's low and I believe him."

"Will he take less?" Zachary's eyebrows lifted, with hope. "He should be able to get money later, like those lawyers on TV. They say they only get paid if you get paid."

"That's not the same kind of case, that's a civil case," Christine answered, touched by his naïveté.

"Can you lend me the money? I would put in my $2,300, and maybe you could put in the rest?"

"I don't know." Christine fumbled, off-balance.

"I would pay you back. When you finish the book and sell it, then you could just take it out of whatever you're going to give me. You were going to give something, weren't you, like a consultant?"

"I have to think about it."

Zachary turned to Lauren. "Could you put in some? I'll pay you back out of the book sales, I swear to you. Right now, there's nothing I can do, there's no way I can make money to pay for my defense."

"I don't think so, Zachary." Lauren shifted in the chair, and Christine felt guilty for having gotten her into this spot.

"Zachary, Lauren is only helping me as an assistant, she's not even getting paid. If it's going to come from anybody, it should come from me."

"So can you?"

"As I said, I have to think about it. I'll go home and think about it."

"Then you'll let me know?"

"Yes, I'll let you know." Christine had to move on. "Let's table the money discussion for now because there's one more important thing I have to tell you, and it came directly from Griff. He said that this should be our last meeting. He doesn't want you to be discussing your case with anybody except him."

"Why?" Zachary asked, his eyebrows sloping down unhappily.

"He said that all these conversations are admissible and so are my notes." Christine gestured at her pad, for effect. She'd practiced this part of the conversation in her mind.

"We're not supposed to meet anymore?" Zachary's lips parted in disappointment.

"No, this is it." Christine knew he was disappointed but couldn't let it show.

"What about your book?"

"He said it will have to wait, and I understand that, I really want what's best for you." Christine wasn't lying about that part.

"But I *like* talking to you. I like you." Zachary turned to Lauren and back to Christine. "I like you, too. It's nice to have somebody to talk to, somebody normal."

"I like talking to you, too." Christine kept her emotions in check. She had a purpose for being here, she was on a mission. "It was so interesting yesterday, to get to know you better, to hear your life story. But I couldn't live with myself if your defense was compromised because I want to write about you. That wouldn't be right. I couldn't sleep at night."

"I appreciate that," Zachary said, blinking. "That's unselfish of you."

"Thanks." Christine kept her expression impassive, though she felt a twinge of guilt. "He also said you shouldn't meet with anybody else, no one from the press, none of the other reporters or book people."

"Even the movie people?" Zachary frowned. "They were from Los Angeles. They said they're coming back."

"Not even them."

"But one of them knows somebody who knows J. J. Abrams. They know really famous people."

"I understand, but Griff would say no."

"They would *totally* have the money for a lawyer. They wanted to option my story for a movie. They said they would get me an agent and everything."

"Ask Griff when you see him." Christine hesitated. "Anyway, Griff said I could meet with you this one last time, and I was allowed to talk to you only about your background, but not about the case. That's all I was really interested in anyway, I really wanted this to be more about you."

"That's cool." Zachary brightened.

"We better get started." Christine picked up her golf pencil. "First, let me say that we were both very moved by your story about your sister. We don't have to go over that again, because I don't want you to have to relive that."

"Okay. I appreciate that."

"We were both amazed that, given the circumstances, you managed to get yourself to college, graduating with honors."

"Don't forget it was *magna cum laude*."

Lauren interjected, "I graduated *magna cum laude*, but my father always said it was *magna cum* loudly."

They all laughed, and Christine could see that Zachary eased back in his chair on the other side of the Plexiglas.

"Now, Zachary, you said you always wanted to go to medical school. Why?" Christine held her golf pencil poised over her pad, ready to take fake-notes.

"I want to help people, to help society. I thought it would be rewarding, to cure something."

"So I guess we could say that you're unselfish, too."

"Right." Zachary's bright blue eyes met Christine's with warmth, and again, she couldn't deny the connection she felt with him, wanted or no.

"What was your favorite subject in school?"

"Hmm," Zachary smiled, tilting his head in thought. "You know, I would have loved gross anatomy. My girlfriend took it first year, and I used to help her study. There's a lot of memorization, and I used to quiz her. She even took me to lab with her once though she wasn't supposed to."

"Lab?" Christine didn't understand the turn that the conversation was taking.

"Anatomy lab. I loved it, even though it's the hardest because you spend so much time in lab, dissecting and learning the structures you dissect. My girlfriend showed me how they started on the cadaver's back, then flipped the body over, then you can see the face. That makes the experience seem even more real." Zachary paused, but his expression didn't change, almost pleasant. "She told me they dissected the thorax, upper extremities, lower extremities, then the abdomen, then sawed off the leg—"

Lauren blurted out, "She *sawed off* a leg?"

Christine felt troubled by his lack of emotionality but didn't let her judgment show since Zachary was lowering his guard.

"You have to, to dissect the pelvis, then the face, which had a bunch of tiny sets of dissections. Eyes, nasal cavity, ear canal, and a bunch of nerve structures run through the face, especially the facial nerve and all its branches." Zachary paused, reflecting. "She told me it took forever. Then she sawed off the skull with a bone saw and removed the brain. She used the brains and brainstems in neuroanatomy in the spring semester."

Christine felt her stomach turn over, and it wasn't only the graphic nature of what he was saying. Zachary seemed to go into loving detail about the human anatomy. "I would think that would be difficult to hear about at dinner, much less see."

"No, I could compartmentalize it. When she showed me the cadavers, they were all lined up in steel boxes and each had an index card with their occupation, cause of death, and age taped to their case. She didn't even know how to put the scalpel blade on the shaft, I had to show her."

"How did you know?"

"From work. I know all about scalpels. Brigham makes thirty-seven different types, at three different product lines and price points." Zachary nodded. "For the first slice into the flesh, and depending on where the flesh is or how thick, you use a different scalpel. I won't bore you with details, it's shop talk. But once you pierce the skin, the scalpel should glide with ease until you hit a bony structure or muscle, with the exception of the face. You really have to peel that, and fat is yellow and greasy, almost like a really ripe mango."

"Yuck," Christine heard herself say before she could stop herself. She understood that a prospective medical student would revel in the details of human anatomy, but Zachary was sending shivers up her spine. Lauren must have felt the same way because she leaned away from him.

"Sorry you asked?" Zachary smiled, warming to his topic. "My girlfriend showed me her notes, and the professor said that the trick to anatomy is finding the right fascial plane, the layer of fascia where you could freely separate the muscles from one another or from a structure. My girlfriend said, finding a good plane could be the difference between a two-hour dissection and a four-hour dissection that she had to superglue together."

"Superglue?" Christine asked, thinking she had misheard him.

"Yes, everyone in med school stashes superglue in their table." Zachary chuckled in a knowing way. "It's inevitable you'll rip a nerve when you're moving a muscle out of the way, or working too fast with your scalpel down a fascial plane. A little bit of superglue, and the nerve will innervate the muscle again." Zachary leaned back, relaxing. "You know what I'd love most of all? Heart dissection. It's probably the coolest of all. I'd have loved to be in cardiology research."

"Why?" Christine asked, shocked. She was remembering the detail about Gail Robinbrecht's murder and the other nurses, killed with a single stab wound to the left ventricle. She didn't understand why Zachary would even go there, given that he must have read the same accounts, but she didn't stop him. She wrote a note, *cardiology*, so he couldn't see her expression.

"You cut the rib cage open to get into the thorax, then go through the pericardial sac, which the heart sits inside of." Zachary made a cutting motion with his hand, demonstrating by holding an imaginary scalpel. "You cut one major vessel at a time—coronaries, aorta, pulmonary vein—and once you've cut all of the connecting structures, you deliver the heart from the pericardial sac." Zachary paused, his smile spreading. "And then you're holding a human heart in your hands."

"How do you know this?" Christine asked, horrified. "Did your girlfriend tell you?"

"Yes, and then I got to observe heart surgery in the hospital. The surgeons let me, and my boss came, too. We had to see how the instruments performed in the OR. The most surprising thing? The heart is small. It seems so small to have such a huge role in your life, it's smaller than your liver and your lungs by a lot." Zachary's blue eyes lit up. "You examine the outside and the four chambers, and how they circulate from the body to right atrium, then to the right ventricle, via the tricuspid valve." Zachary made a loop de loop with his hands, in the air. "Then to the pulmonary artery and lungs, then back via the pulmonary vein to the left atrium and to the left ventricle, via the mitral or bicuspid valve. The left ventricle is the powerhouse. It pumps to the entire body's systemic circuit, via the aorta."

Christine couldn't take it any longer. "You know, that's the way Gail Robinbrecht was murdered, the way they all were murdered, stabbed in the left ventricle."

"I'm aware, and the newspapers say the killer must have been a doctor or a med student, but if he was, he wasn't a very good one." Zachary's tone turned superior. "It's true that you can kill somebody by stabbing the left ventricle, but that takes a lot of force. The heart is tucked in under the lungs, and the left ventricle is the bottom right, here, called the 'apex of the heart.'" Zachary pointed at his chest. "The killer would have to aim between the second and fifth intercostal space, between the ribs on the left side, then angle it up and in to reach the apex of the heart."

Christine kept her expression impassive, but Zachary continued, oblivious.

"The intercostal spaces are only an inch or two between each rib, that's why it would be hard to have perfect aim with the first stab, without getting stopped by a rib. That's why your ribs are there, after all, to protect your thorax and mediastinum." Zachary's eyes lit up. "The human body is a beautiful thing, the way it's designed, all of it intended to protect the heart, to keep the person alive. So obviously, you *could* kill somebody that way, but it doesn't make sense." Zachary shrugged. "That's how you know I'm innocent. I know better than this serial killer. If I wanted to kill somebody with a stab wound, I would stab the carotid, or the second-best, the right kidney. It's above the right hip, lower than the left kidney. If you stab somebody there, that would send them into shock, and they'd bleed out and die."

Christine flip-flopped, changing her mind. Zachary might have known about anatomy, but maybe he truly was innocent. He seemed to be saying that someone who knew about anatomy wouldn't have killed the nurses the way they'd been killed, meaning he was innocent.

"The other problem with stabbing someone in the left ventricle, or anywhere in the heart, is that the heart is so strong it will initially try to contract to hold the gap closed, but the more wide and gaping the stab wound to the heart wall, the more blood will leak out. It would pump out of the chest with each heart beat after the stabbing."

Christine recoiled.

"Then the heart will start beating harder and faster to try to get blood to the aorta and to the body. Most of it would be leaking out of the wound, of course, but it's a beautiful thing, the way the entire body is structured to protect the heart and the way the heart would try to save itself, save its body. Once you know the anatomy, you appreciate it even more, don't you?" Zachary seemed to come out of his reverie. "I would have loved med school. I would've done anything, worked any job, to get the money for tuition."

Christine hoped she could get him back to her point. "What did you do, to get the money?"

"Everything, anything. I had three jobs. I was a movie usher, I was a math tutor, and I waited tables. I sold a futon on eBay. I sold my car, too. I even sold my plasma."

"You can sell plasma?" Christine sensed they were getting closer.

"Sure, I sold blood, too. I even sold—" Zachary stopped himself, and Christine held her breath.

"You sold what?" she asked lightly, though her heart was thundering.

"I'd tell you, but you can't put this in the book. This is off the record." Zachary glanced over his shoulder, then leaned closer to the hole in the Plexiglas. "I sold sperm, too. They call it donating, but I don't know why. They pay you."

Christine felt her heart stop. She had rehearsed this moment last night, how she would react if he told her, yes or no. She was *this* close to finding out the answer, she could feel it within her grasp. She was dying to know, and she was terrified to know. She told herself to get her act together. She made herself continue. "You were a sperm donor? I always wondered how that worked."

"I assume you know how it *works*." Zachary chuckled. "Hey, it's random, but I did it. It paid really well. They put you in a program, you do it for a year. I didn't tell anybody. I thought it would help people, but I really needed the money. I knew my parents would kill me if they found out. My parents thought if people aren't meant to get pregnant, they don't get pregnant. They would think that was playing God."

Christine felt herself reeling, as he spoke. Everything he was saying corroborated his online profile. She had to keep him going. "Zachary, how much did they pay you?"

"I made a thousand dollars that year, and I liked the people at the bank."

"Bank?" Christine said, as if she were unfamiliar with the term.

"Sperm bank. It was called Homestead."

"Oh?" Christine squeezed her golf pencil, masking her reaction, which was almost violent, her emotions in tumult.

"It had an office near campus. I donated anonymously. That's the only way I'd make the deal. I gave them two pictures of me, because they kind of pressure you to do that. But they don't release your name when they put it online. They give you a number."

"A number?"

"Yes, a donor number."

"What was your number?"

"Why?" Zachary frowned, surprised.

"I'm just curious."

"My number was 3319."

Chapter Twenty-four

Christine heard Zachary answer, confirming that he was Donor 3319, and she understood that he was her donor, *their* donor, the father of their baby, the *biological* father of their baby, yet she had a million thoughts flying through her head, setting her brain on fire, electrifying her senses, overloading her circuits.

She didn't know what to say or do. She felt herself falling away from the world, the way she had the other day, having an out-of-body experience, observing herself hearing the news at the same time that she experienced hearing the news, and it was all she could do not to throw up, faint, start crying, or otherwise show her hand.

Her reaction felt like it lasted ten minutes, but it must've only been a moment or two because she noticed that Lauren was taking over the situation, leaning close to the Plexiglas, smiling at Zachary, and asking him a question, and then Zachary was smiling back and saying words that Christine was too freaked out to hear. Her heart hammered, she broke a new sweat in the sweltering booth, and her mouth went completely dry.

She had been right, all of her research and even her hunches had been right, and Zachary was Donor 3319, and now she didn't know what to do. Because the father of her child was wanted for murder, even a string of serial killings, and she thought he might be innocent, but she also thought he might be guilty as sin.

The corrections officer walked over on the other side of the Plexiglas, and she realized that it was time to go, time to leave Zachary, even to say good-bye. She wanted to get her act together, to be wholly present, but she felt such a powerful conflict of emotions, like two gargantuan waves crashing into each other, because she had just found out that he was her donor at the same time that she would have to let him go, forever.

She could see Zachary turn to the guard behind him, and the guard bringing the handcuffs forward, and Lauren continuing the conversation, and Zachary talking back to her, the two of them smiling, and Christine struggled to come around, tuning in the sound of their talking, but she couldn't fake joining them, stricken. The handcuffs made a jangling sound as the corrections officer carried them over, and Christine watched as Zachary offered his wrists, and the handcuffs snapped mechanically into place, *ca-chink*, and somehow that sound brought her to her senses and she realized that if she didn't get it together, she wouldn't get to say good-bye.

"Zachary?" Christine rose.

"Bye, Christine." Zachary smiled. "Please, can you please lend me that money for the lawyer? When my trial's over, we can get the book done, and I'll pay you back out of the royalties, I swear. Please?"

Lauren interjected, "She'll look into that, and we'll get back to Griff. Hang in there. Best of luck. Bye!" Lauren stood beside Christine, turning to her and flaring her eyes meaningfully. "Say good-bye, Christine."

"Good-bye, Zachary," Christine said, on cue, her heart in her throat.

"Please!" Zachary called back, as the corrections officer took him by the elbow and escorted him out of the booth, locking the door behind them.

Lauren grabbed her arm and escorted her from the booth, almost the same way that the guard had escorted Zachary on the other side, and neither woman said a word because the other corrections officer was sitting on his chair and the visiting room was already beginning to fill up, with families seeing inmates.

Christine felt herself in a sort of shock, stunned enough to let Lauren steer her down the aisle through the mismatched chairs, past the oil paintings on the left, and the windows overlooking the courtyard on the right, with the mural CHERISH THE CHILD.

My number was 3319.

A corrections officer at the door of the visiting room led them in silence up the stairwell and through the metal detector to make sure they weren't smuggling out contraband, and Lauren guided Christine out of the security room through the locked door and into the waiting room full of men, women, and children, talking among themselves in a variety of languages.

Christine tried to get a grip on her emotions as Lauren took her to the lockers, wordlessly sliding the key from her pocket, opening the locker to retrieve the car keys, then replacing the locker key, only to retake Christine's arm and guide her out through the dim reception area toward the glass double doors, blinding with sunlight.

"This way, honey," Lauren said under her breath, just as two uniformed corrections officers walked past them.

Christine raised a hand against the sunlight, taking a deep breath as they walked through the official parking lot, though the humidity made it impossible to breathe.

"You're okay, Christine." Lauren squeezed her arm, keeping her in motion, saying nothing more because families were all around them, walking past them to the prison.

Christine nodded, trying to recover as they walked along, trying not to think about what she had just learned, or what she would do about it, or whatever was going to happen next. She took each step as if it were a deliberate action, knowing that each footfall carried her farther away from Zachary, and at the same time knowing that while she wanted to leave Zachary, she also wanted to stay, because she was undeniably connected to him, now. She was carrying his baby.

She spotted her car, the first in the lot because they had gotten here so early, and the sight of it anchored her in reality, taking her outside of her thoughts. It was her car. She paid the car loan every month. She had a life. She had a husband, a mortgage, a dog, and a cat in Connecticut. She had to go back home. She wanted to go back home.

My number was 3319.

But she understood, at the same time, that no external change could alter the inner reality. Zachary was a part of her, fully half of the child she carried inside her very body, and it was that inside-out feeling, that disconnect that was nevertheless connected, which confounded her, bollixed her up, rendered her incapable of parsing any of the feelings she was having, but still she kept moving toward her car.

Christine realized as Lauren aimed the key fob, chirped the car unlocked, and led her to the passenger side, that she was in no shape to drive, and it was then that the tears started to come. Lauren's timing was perfect and she opened the passenger door, stowed a weeping Christine inside, and even buckled her into the seat, so that by the time they had turned onto Route 29 heading home, the shoulder harness was the only thing holding Christine up.

Chapter Twenty-five

Christine waited for Marcus to come home, finding reasons to stay downstairs, puttering around the kitchen. She hadn't bothered changing when she got home, and she wasn't crying anymore because she cried out all her tears, and then some. She could never thank Lauren enough for what a great friend she'd been the whole weekend and told her so when she dropped Lauren off at her house, where they gave each other a final hug. They'd both agreed that it was time to tell Marcus, but only one of them would have to do the telling.

She'd gone through bills, then wiped out the plastic container they kept under the counter for trash, her least favorite task. She'd always try to ignore the stinky smells when she put in a new fresh white plastic liner, and she always bought the scented to try to combat the stink, but she could never bring herself to wash out the actual plastic container the way she did now, awkwardly scrubbing the tall plastic bin in the kitchen sink, then turning it over with difficulty, trying to rinse it out using the spray hose beside the faucet.

The garbage smells made her nauseous, mixing with her hormones, or the dread of what was to come when Marcus got home.

It was past nine thirty, which was her pregnancy bedtime, but something told her to stay downstairs. Keep on her feet. Talk to him eye-to-eye, not flat on her back, lying in bed. She felt as if she were in a sort of suspended animation until he came home, felt in the very air as if the entire home held its breath, but that could have been her imagination. Murphy was typically oblivious, curled up at the end of his dog bed, with his butt spilling onto the floor because Lady was hogging the middle in a way that only cats can and only dogs permit.

Christine tilted the trash bin on its side upside down, letting the water run out into the sink, but it went too slowly. It wasn't worth wasting paper towels for, so she grabbed a sackcloth and wiped down the inside, shoving her arm so far inside to reach the bottom of the bin that she got water on the shoulder of her shirtdress.

Suddenly she heard the front door being unlocked, then opened, in the entrance hall. Murphy raised his head from his paws and swung his nose toward the entrance hall, evidently not sleeping as soundly as Christine had thought, but Lady didn't stir, only resettled after the interruption.

"Honey?" Marcus called out, then there was the jingling of his car keys tossed onto the console table and the rumble of his roller bag, which he would roll to the bottom of the stairs to be brought upstairs, later. By habit, he did things the same way every time, so that he rarely lost his keys, his wallet, or his phone. Christine didn't have to wonder how such an orderly man would take such disorderly news, which is what worried her.

"In the kitchen!" Christine spread out a dishcloth flat on the granite counter, so that she could turn the trash can upside down to drain overnight.

"Mmph," Marcus said under his breath, a soft noise that Christine knew reflected mild surprise that she was still downstairs. She heard the sound of his footsteps coming her way, a tapping that told her he had his loafers on, and the rhythm of his footsteps was steady and slow as usual because he had long legs and a strong stride, so he got wherever he wanted to quickly and never had to hurry.

"Hi," Christine said, and she was about to turn to face him, but the trash can wobbled on the dishcloth and she jumped to prevent it from falling.

"I can help you with that." Marcus came over, standing behind her as she hastily righted the trash can. She wasn't ready to be physically close to him yet, or maybe she knew he wouldn't want to be close to her after this conversation, and she backed away, turning to him.

"How was your trip?" Christine asked, backing toward the counter, and as soon as she said it, she knew everything was wrong.

"Honey?" Marcus looked at her funny, first with some surprise, then with concern, his handsome features softening. "Are you okay? Have you been crying?"

"Yes." Christine swallowed hard. She didn't know where to begin. She had rehearsed it but she wasn't sure where to start.

"Babe, listen. We don't need to fight about this anymore." Marcus took a step toward her, with a conciliatory sigh. "I've been thinking, the whole way home on the plane. I think best on planes. I get some of my best ideas on planes, you know that."

Christine nodded. "I know but—"

"No buts. I really think this is going to work out. I spoke with Gary today, and he has our lawsuit all ready to go. He put it to the top of the pile, he said. We have an appointment to go in tomorrow morning to sign it, and he'll file it. It's not against Davidow, only Homestead, and—"

"Marcus?"

"I know what you're going to say, but here's what I decided. This lawsuit is going to help us both. We're going to delegate this, the stress of it, the worrying about it. We don't need this, we don't need to fight about this."

Christine wanted to break in, but Marcus was trying to finish his point.

"We can let Gary handle it, that's what lawyers are for. We have the money, will pay him what it takes. Let's turn him loose and let him find out about our donor. It's his job, not ours."

"Marcus," Christine said more firmly, unable to take the irony, but Marcus barely seemed to hear her.

"What I also realized on the plane is that we're dealing with too many hypotheticals. We're getting worked up over a hypothetical. Jeffcoat could turn out not to be our donor, but we're acting like he is. There's no reason to worry until we have to—"

"There's something I need to tell you." Christine braced herself, pulling out the tall cherrywood stool at the kitchen island, feeling that she had to sit down. She flashed on those scenes in the movies, when the person with the bad news says to the person who doesn't know, "you need to sit down," but the truth was, she was the one who needed to sit down. Because in that moment she realized that the only thing worse than hearing the worst news of your life is being the person who has to deliver the worst news of your life.

"What? Is something the matter?"

"Yes."

"Okay, what?" Marcus stood tall, facing her, looking every inch the Suburban Dad he so wanted to be in his blue oxford shirt and khakis, but something about the way he was standing, his long arms hanging loose at his sides, his chest open and exposed, made him so vulnerable. She almost couldn't tell him, and she flashed on Zachary telling her that the human body was a thing of beauty because so many structures protected the heart, but she realized that the human heart simply couldn't be protected, not by muscle, not by bone, not by anything.

Christine took a deep breath. "I went to Graterford this week-end and met with Zachary Jeffcoat and he told me that he's Donor

3319. We don't need a lawsuit to figure that out. We already have the answer."

Marcus blinked, once, then again, though he remained standing, absolutely motionless, and for a moment, Christine was afraid that he would fall backwards like a cardboard cutout, like the Flat Stanley that the kids in school took everywhere, taking pictures with something that looked like a man but was only a drawing of a man.

"Marcus, I know this is a shock, and I know it's awful news, but there it is. I wanted to know and I found out."

"Are you *serious*?" Marcus asked, his tone hushed. His shock was so complete that it becalmed him, and Murphy, who had been waiting for Marcus to come over and pet him, lowered his head to his paws, knowing that something was wrong.

"Yes, I'm serious," Christine answered simply. "I can tell you the whole story—"

"Hold on." Marcus held up a large hand, showing her his palm. "Are you telling me you weren't in Jersey this weekend?"

"I wasn't in Jersey."

Marcus winced slightly, and for some reason, Christine knew she had wounded him, as surely as if she'd stabbed him in the heart, in fact. She could see the impact of the revelation that she had lied to him land even more vividly than she could see the impact of the first revelation, that Zachary was their donor.

"Was Lauren with you?"

"Yes, we went together."

"How did you get there? Where did you stay?"

"I drove and we stayed at a hotel near the prison." Christine understood that Marcus had to come up to speed, asking her questions about the details before he began to deal with the headline.

"This was where? Somewhere outside of Philadelphia?"

"Collegeville. It's in the country."

"So when we spoke on the phone, you were really in a hotel near the prison?"

"Yes."

Marcus winced again, wounded a second time, but she had to get him past the preliminaries. "Did Lauren tell Josh where she was?"

"Yes," Christine had to admit. "Marcus, I'm sorry that I lied to you, I know that was wrong, and I'm sorry about that. But let's talk about what we learned, which is that he's our donor. He really is our donor. He told me, completely unprompted. He didn't know who I was—"

"What did you tell him? Who did you say you were?" Marcus frowned, pained, though his voice remained even and his questions made sense. Christine realized that was probably why he was so good at his job. He could fly down to a job site, elicit the problem by asking questions, then figure out a solution. The only problem was, this time, there was no solution.

"I told him my real name, but I didn't tell him why I was there. He doesn't know that he was our donor."

"You actually *met* him?" Marcus's eyes rounded like blue marbles. "You went inside a prison and you met a *serial killer*?"

"He's not a serial killer, he hasn't been linked to the other—"

"Are you kidding me? Am I really hearing this?" Marcus stepped back, flabbergasted. "Did you meet with this serial killer alone?"

"Lauren was there—"

"*Lauren* was there, and you and Lauren met with a *serial killer* and you determined that he's our donor. You found this out just by asking?"

"Yes, and—"

"You tricked him? You didn't tell him who you really were, or why you wanted to know? You assumed a *false identity*?" Marcus's mouth dropped open. He looked at her with utter disbelief.

"Now we have the answer to the question, the truth—"

"How do you know he told you the truth? He could be lying. The man's a criminal, a serial killer." Marcus started shaking his head, in a state of shock.

"He wasn't lying. He would have no reason to lie. He didn't even want to tell me about it. I had to get it out of him."

"I can't believe I'm hearing this. This isn't like you at all! You've never done anything like this."

"I've never been in this situation before, and maybe we don't need a big lawsuit now to figure out that he's the donor, because he is. Maybe Gary can just call them and tell them that we already know it, and they'll make a settlement with us, just in case the baby needs evaluation and help, like he said."

"Are you trying to tell me *that's* why you did it? *That's* why you went down there? So we don't have to file a *lawsuit*?"

"No, I went down there because I had to know, I couldn't not know any longer, and I knew a way to find out. That's why I did it." Christine fumbled for words, trying to organize her thoughts. "I expected you to be upset, and I know this seems really strange, and I'm sorry I lied to you, but I met with him, twice—"

"*Twice?*" Marcus kept shaking his head.

"He's nice, he's smart. He's easy to talk to, he's charming—"

"*Charming?*" Marcus's face reddened. "Honey, Ted Bundy was charming. I can't believe this. I can't believe I'm hearing this."

"He's not like Ted Bundy, Zachary's—"

"*Zachary*, now? You call him *Zachary*? Are you on a first-name basis? Does he call you *Christine*? Does he call you by your first name? *Zachary and Christine*?"

"Marcus. We talked, we had a conversation—"

"I don't understand what you're thinking. I don't know how you expect me to hear this." Marcus started edging away. He wasn't angry; he was anguished.

"I know it's a lot to process, but now we know who our donor is. Now we can put a face and a name to him, and I'm not even sure he's guilty of murder, I think he might even be innocent and—"

"I don't want to *know* who our donor is!" Marcus kept backing away, stricken.

"What do you mean? Of course you do." Christine got off the chair, in confusion.

"No I don't. I *liked* it anonymous. Don't you get it?"

"No, I don't. You wanted us to *sue* to find out his identity. It wasn't going to be anonymous any longer—"

"That's different, that's *Gary* finding out, that's lawyers finding out, that's corporations battling in court, and on phones, that's insurance companies." Marcus shook his head, nonplussed. "That's not *you* finding out, my *wife*, meeting him."

"What's the difference who finds out or how? Now, we know and we—"

"I don't want you to meet him. I don't want you to lie to me about it. I don't want you to be the one who finds out the real father of the baby you're carrying."

Christine's mouth went dry, hearing the jealousy in his voice. She had expected that he would be angry, even furious, but she hadn't expected that he would be hurt and jealous. "Marcus, it's not like that—"

"You're carrying his child, Christine. You went to see the man whose child you're carrying."

Christine felt his words hit home, and she felt terrible. "Marcus, I'm sorry—"

"We spent so much time in therapy saying he's just a biological donor, and that's all I wanted him to be. That was the deal." Marcus shook his head, edging out of the kitchen, his forehead knotted with pain. "Maybe *Zachary* wanted anonymity, but you know what? So did I. It worked for me, too."

Christine kept going toward him, not wanting him to be so hurt, seeing how much pain he was in. "Marcus, you're getting the wrong idea."

"No, I'm not. It was never the deal that you would go running off to meet him, that you would lie to me about that." Marcus's eyes glistened suddenly, an agonized blue. "Whose wife *are* you? Whose *woman*? His or mine?"

"Marcus, of course, I'm your wife—"

"But you're having his baby. Zachary. You don't even care that he's in jail for carving up nurses. You're already on his side."

"There's no sides—"

"Yes there are sides! You're on one, and I'm on the other. Correction, you and Zachary and the baby are on one, and I'm on the other."

"No, that's not true!" Christine cried out, but Marcus turned away, left the kitchen, and walked into the entrance hall.

"Leave me alone. Just leave me alone."

Christine went after him. "Marcus, I'm sorry, I didn't think of it that way, that's not the way I meant it."

"That's the way it is." Marcus kept walking away from her, into the living room, flicking on the light. "I'm tired, I've been traveling all day. I had a shitstorm to deal with this weekend. I want to sleep downstairs, I need time to think alone."

"Marcus, we can still talk about it—"

"I don't want to talk about it. I want to think about it, by myself." Marcus held her off with a straight arm, so Christine stopped, motionless until Murphy came wandering in, his toenails tapping and his tail wagging slowly, confused because nobody ever went into the living room.

"Are you sure?"

"Yes, absolutely." Marcus motioned to the stairwell. "Please go upstairs. I'm sleeping downstairs. We'll see Gary in the morning."

"Okay," Christine said, heartbroken.

"Murph, come." Marcus whistled to the dog, who trundled in after him.

Chapter Twenty-six

Christine and Marcus waited for Gary in his office, sitting in the chairs across from the lawyer's ornate desk, having been served coffee in real china cups and saucers by his niece Theresa. Christine and Marcus had barely exchanged a word this morning, avoiding each other while they'd showered and dressed for the meeting, Christine into a blue oxford shirtdress and Marcus in a tan suit with a silk tie because he was going to work later. She was going home afterwards, so they had driven here separately, which was merciful. Christine imagined that a car ride together would have been miserable.

"Hello, Nilssons!" Gary boomed, clapping his hands together as he entered his office, scampered around his desk, and plopped into his ergonomic throne. "Sorry about that! Nature called! Ring, ring!"

"Good to see you, Gary," Marcus said stiffly.

"Yes, hi, Gary," Christine added.

"Glad you could come in. I love that we're jumping right on this, no waiting." Gary opened a manila folder on his desk, extracted two slim packets of papers from inside, and slid them across his glistening desk, one to Marcus and another to Christine. "I'll take you through our suit papers, so you understand them completely."

"Gary," Marcus said, calmly, "before we do that, there's something you should know. I could explain, but I'll let Christine."

Gary turned to Christine, his good cheer clouding over. "Don't tell me you got cold feet. Did you get cold feet, Christine?"

"No, it's not that." Christine braced herself. "This weekend, I went to Graterford Prison with Lauren, and we interviewed Zachary Jeffcoat. I pretended I was a reporter and I didn't tell him who I really was. He told me that he's Donor 3319."

"Are you for real?" Gary blinked in astonishment, then broke into a grin.

"Yes, it's true," Christine answered, confused. She hadn't anticipated a favorable reaction. She was expecting that Gary would be as angry as Marcus, except for the jealousy part.

"That's amazing! You went right to the source, eh? You used self-help, I love it. I didn't know you had it in you, teach."

"Neither did I," Christine blurted out, with an abrupt laugh, like a release of pressure.

Gary laughed. "With clients like you, I'd be out of business."

Marcus looked from Christine to Gary, incredulous. "What the hell? Are you two insane?"

"Hold on." Gary held up a hand. "Let me get the facts—"

"Gary, what facts? What other facts do you need?" Marcus shook his head in disbelief, which seemed as fresh as last night. "Don't you realize how dangerous that was, what she did? Going into prison? I looked it up online last night, it's maximum-security. You know the animals that are in there?"

"Whoa, whoa, whoa. Slow your roll." Gary leaned over the desk, his smile fading. "I told you before about the plumbers in my family. That's my father's side. My *mother's* side, they're crooks. Petty crooks, not mobsters. Not mob. Not Mafia. Not every Italian-American is connected, is what I'm saying."

"What's your point?"

"That people in prison are still people. I spent my childhood visiting my uncle and my nephew in prison. They were nice guys. They made mistakes. One was an embezzler, the other got into a fight in a bar."

Marcus bristled. "I'm entitled to be concerned about my wife and her safety."

"Your wife was safe. She visited an inmate. People do it every day. She didn't walk around naked in the exercise yard."

"Gary, the man is a *serial killer.*"

"In a cage. The man is a serial killer in a *cage.*" Gary gestured at his pictures from the Serengeti. "You put a *lion* in a cage and he can't hurt you—"

"Enough with the lions. We're talking about my wife. She didn't even tell me she did it."

Gary didn't bat an eye. "Marcus, I understand you don't want your wife to do stuff like that without your knowledge. That's a different issue. Don't get your issues confused."

"But it ruins the lawsuit now, doesn't it?" Marcus motioned at the white papers on the desk.

"No, if anything, it helps the lawsuit." Gary slid the papers back toward him. "If Jeffcoat told Christine that he's 3319, then I would argue to Homestead that he's waived his right to confidentiality. In other words, I would argue that they don't have to keep his identity confidential because he's already disclosed it. If he didn't follow the agreement, then they don't have to follow the agreement."

Christine brightened, surprised. She hadn't thought she'd hurt the lawsuit, but she hadn't thought she'd helped it, either.

Marcus stiffened. "But what about the fact that she tricked him, that she got that information by false pretenses?"

"That's irrelevant, legally." Gary frowned, seeing that Marcus remained not only unconvinced, but unhappy. "Marcus, it's all about what a court would do. It's contract law. The reason Homestead wouldn't disclose the identity before was because they signed a contract with Jeffcoat to keep it confidential. Once the other contracting party, namely Jeffcoat, discloses, then the only other person who would sue them for breach drops out. Jeffcoat could never sue in court for breach of confidentiality to an agreement that he'd already breached. The court would say he has 'unclean hands' and throw the case out."

Marcus shook his head again, nonplussed. "Then what effect does it have? What do we do now? I don't want to drop the lawsuit. I want to hold Homestead responsible for their negligence. It's ruining our lives, our marriage."

Christine swallowed hard, realizing that Marcus was right. It was ruining their marriage. She could feel it, too. She had to admit it to herself. They were in crisis. This was all happening, to them. To her. To their new family.

But Gary only shrugged in response. "Marcus, who said we're dropping the lawsuit? We're not. Now, what I would do is pick up the phone and see if we can do this quickly and more efficiently. I'm going to tell Homestead we have bad news for them— their donor waived, and they need to settle with us. Confidentially. Quietly. Just like before, nobody will be the wiser, they pay us to go away."

Marcus fell silent.

Christine's thoughts raced. "Do you think they'll settle?"

"I would, if I were them." Gary paused. "But, but, but. Here's the caveat. There's a possibility that they won't, depending on what their insurance company tells them or their parent company. If they don't agree, then we file our papers, just like before. We haven't lost anything." Gary slid his computer keyboard in front of him and hit a few keys. "But let me back up a minute. Christine, I need to get the facts about what you learned from Jeffcoat. Tell me what he told you."

Christine filled Gary in, telling him that Jeffcoat had applied but hadn't gone to medical school, about the religious parents, even the death of his baby sister. Gary typed as she spoke, and Christine could feel Marcus listening hard, realizing that he hadn't gotten any of the details last night. She had a vain hope that hearing the full story might soften him up, which might have been a pipe dream. She also told them how Zachary told her his exact donor number. She didn't say anything about going to Gail Robinbrecht's house because it didn't seem relevant to the fact that Zachary was their donor—and she didn't want Marcus to hit the ceiling. Also she remembered not to call Zachary by his first name.

"So, that's it?" Gary looked up expectantly, his small, slim fingers poised over his keyboard.

"Basically, yes."

Marcus sipped the last of his coffee but didn't say anything, replacing his cup in the saucer with a loud *clink*.

Gary started typing again. "Christine, do you know if Jeffcoat is represented? I like to know who my opposition is."

"Yes, he had a public defender but I think he might be getting a private lawyer." Christine realized that Zachary would be meeting with Griff right now, at the exact same time that she and Marcus were meeting with Gary.

Gary kept typing. "How do you know that, did he tell you?"

"I think he's going to hire a local lawyer named Francis Griffith, from West Chester."

"Good to know." Gary typed away. "Griffith's a criminal lawyer, right?"

"Yes," Christine answered, aware that Marcus was weighing her every word. Suddenly her phone rang in her purse. "Sorry, I should have turned it off."

"No worries, I'm no phone Nazi." Gary typed away.

Christine reached down and slid her phone from the outside pocket, seeing that the screen read GRIFF. She pressed the red button to decline the call, but Marcus saw the screen, too.

"Wait," he snapped. "Isn't that the name you just said? Griff? Is that a nickname for Griffith? Jeffcoat's lawyer?"

"Yes." Christine slipped the phone back in her purse, kicking herself for putting Griff in her contacts list.

"Why is he calling you? How does he have your number?"

"I helped Jeffcoat get him," Christine answered because there was no reason to lie.

"What do you mean? How did you help?"

"He had a public defender and he wanted somebody local, so I helped."

Gary stopped typing, listening to them both, his head of glossy black hair swiveling back and forth, shiny under the lights.

Marcus frowned, confused. "You didn't know any local lawyers, did you?"

"I made a few phone calls, it wasn't that difficult," Christine answered, without elaborating.

Marcus's lips parted. "*Why* would you help him?"

"Because he said he'd tell me anything I wanted to know if I helped him, and I wanted to know if he was our donor, so I helped him." Christine glanced at Gary, who sat listening, his hands still.

Marcus's eyes flared. "He's a serial killer, he manipulated you, don't you see that?"

"No, he didn't," Christine answered, trying to reason with him.

Gary put up a hand. "Marcus, let me handle this. We need to keep it on a legal track."

"Why? I can talk to my own wife."

Gary turned to her. "Christine, did Jeffcoat ask you to help him get a lawyer?"

"Yes."

"Did he ask you anything else?"

"Yes." Christine hesitated, but whatever, it was too late now. "He asked me to pay half the retainer, which is $5,000."

"What?" Marcus shifted toward Christine in his chair. "How could you even think of helping him?"

"I didn't."

"But did you consider it? How could you?"

"How could you not?" Christine thought it was time to stand up for herself. "Let's assume that he's innocent and behind bars for a crime he didn't commit. That means our donor could spend the rest of his life in prison, wrongly accused. Am I just supposed to turn my back on him?"

"Yes," Marcus answered instantly.

"Yes," Gary added, a second later. Both men exchanged glances, then Gary turned to her. "Christine, let me explain the legal reason you can't help him. You're about to sue Homestead because of their negligence in using Jeffcoat as a donor. Even if Jeffcoat isn't technically a party to this litigation, his interest is adverse to yours. He's on their side."

Marcus interjected, "That's what I tried to tell her."

Gary kept speaking to Christine. "I understand why you went to see him, and you got good information. But my legal advice to you is, this far, and no further. *Capisce?* Understand me?"

"I understand you."

"Good." Gary leaned over the keyboard, newly urgent. "Now for my non-legal advice, Christine. I've been in more prisons than you. I've known more inmates than you. I've known more con artists, bullshit artists, and every other artist there is. Everybody in prison says they're innocent."

Marcus interjected again, "Exactly."

Gary ignored him, his dark eyes trained on Christine. "Even my uncle and my nephew, when they went before the parole board, they said they were innocent. Take it from me, they weren't. Now, a guy like Jeffcoat, he's in a heap of trouble. He will grasp at any straw and he can manipulate, deceive, and use you to get what he wants."

"He asked for $2,500 for a lawyer. It's not like he asked for the moon."

"So far. That could just be the beginning. Besides, it might not be money that he wants from you. He can want a willing ear, a sympathetic shoulder. A friend. You're a nice lady, and he's got nothing but time."

Marcus interrupted, speaking to Gary, "She doesn't even consider that he could be lying about being our donor. Why should we even take his word for it?"

"We're not going to, Marcus," Gary answered calmly. "When I call Homestead, I'm going to tell them what we know and how we know it, and I'm going to ask them to confirm or deny."

"Good." Marcus nodded, sitting back in his chair. "He's taking advantage of her, and she's falling for it."

Christine looked over. "No, I'm not, Marcus."

"*Silenzio*." Gary waved them both into silence. "You two have to get on the same page. You're in this together. Go out to coffee, talk this over. You're going to get through this together, you'll see. Now, meeting's over."

"Thank you," Marcus said, rising, but Christine knew it was only because he finally felt validated.

Her cell phone rang again, so she pulled it out, and when the name GRIFF reappeared, she hit the red button.

Marcus frowned. "I don't want you to return his call, obviously."

"Why not?" Christine stood up, getting her purse.

"We're going to leave Jeffcoat to his own devices. You got him a lawyer, and now you have to wash your hands of him."

Christine didn't like being told what she could and couldn't do. "Griff is not going to represent him if he can't pay the retainer."

"It can't be our problem."

Gary rose, flashing a forced smile. "Okay, *basta*! Get out of my office, you crazy kids. Go out, have a cuppa coffee together. You can figure this out. I have faith in you."

But Christine didn't.

Chapter Twenty-seven

That was enlightening," Marcus said, exhaling, when they were outside the tony brick building that housed Gary's offices. It was located on the business end of Main Street, which morphed into one of the most expensive shopping blocks in town, containing ritzy boutiques, interior designers, a custom wedding-cake baker, and imported English antiques so exclusive that a sign in the window read BY APPOINTMENT ONLY.

"Marcus, maybe he's right, we should just go sit down and talk a minute."

"I can't, I have to go, my car's over there." Marcus gestured to the right, where there was a small parking lot between restaurants that opened only for lunch. Dappled sun shone on the sidewalks, which were neatly swept or hosed down for the day, and the stores were just beginning to open. A pretty young salesgirl unfurled a navy-and-white striped awning over the gourmet chocolate shop, her long hair swinging each time she turned the old-school brass crank.

Christine said, "Let me walk you to your car. We can talk on the way."

"No, where's your car? You shouldn't walk that much, and we don't need to talk any more."

"Marcus, please. Don't you think—"

"I can't talk right now. I have to get to work."

"Marcus, you own the firm, you can be late. You're clearly pissed."

"Yes, I am. What are you going to do about it?" Marcus eyed her, his lips pursed.

"I can't do anything about it except help you understand it."

"I don't need your help, and I do understand it. I disagree with you."

"What do you disagree with?" Christine asked, pained.

"Everything you did. That you went there. That you're fine with that. Even that *he's* fine with that." Marcus nodded in the direction of Gary's office. "He thinks he understands, but he doesn't. You think you understand, but you don't."

"Then make me. Explain it."

"How do you think that makes me feel, finding out that you helped Jeffcoat get a lawyer? That the lawyer is calling you? That you call him by his *nickname*? That you would even consider giving him *our* money?"

"I wasn't going to use our money, I was going to use my own, and I didn't."

"Still," Marcus shot back, and the young girl looked over, having unfurled the awning.

"Marcus, I'm sorry if it makes you feel bad."

"Try humiliated."

"It shouldn't be humiliating."

"Well it is." Marcus's blue eyes looked wounded and tired. "Didn't we learn in therapy that you're not supposed to tell me how I should feel? Isn't that what I learned from you and Michelle? What do you want from me?"

"Okay, well, I'm sorry you feel humiliated." Christine felt for him, because she could see he was hurt, not angry. "I didn't mean to humiliate you."

"Fine, but that's not the point either."

Just then, Christine's phone began ringing in her purse. "Sorry, I'll send it to voicemail."

Marcus stepped closer. "Check your phone. I want to see if it's that lawyer."

"Fine." Christine bristled, but she slid her phone from her purse. They looked down at her phone screen, which read: GRIFF.

Marcus pursed his lips. "Man, he wants his money. Are you going to help pay for his defense?"

"I don't know." Christine's hands fumbled as she hit the button to decline the call.

"You better not give him a cent, Christine. Not one cent." Marcus's tone turned bossy, and Christine looked up sharply.

"Don't speak to me that way."

"What way, like a good husband? I'm trying to protect you."

"I'll spend my money the way I see fit, and I'll take the calls I want to. I'll decide about the retainer, but it's a bigger issue than that." Christine tried to think of a way to reach him. "We can't ignore reality. We used a donor, we agreed to. We know his name now. He exists, and we can't pretend he doesn't."

Marcus stepped away, waving her off. "I have to go to work. Everything blew up this weekend and I have to deal with it."

"Then we can talk about it tonight?"

"No, we're going out to dinner with Dad and Stephanie, remember? It's his birthday."

"Oh, right." Christine had forgotten or maybe blocked it. An evening with her in-laws would be the perfect end to a perfect day.

"I got him that putter, but if you could pick up a card, that would be great. You have the time, right? I have to go, bye." Marcus walked away without another word.

"Good-bye," Christine called after him. She watched him go, then realized her car was in the opposite direction. She turned around and walked the other way, trying not to see it as symbolic.

Chapter Twenty-eight

Christine sat in her car in the parking lot, letting the air-conditioning blow on her face. She took a sip of an overpriced iced tea she'd bought on the way. She still had another half-hour on the meter and she was eyeing the phone in her hand. Griff had called the first time at nine forty-five, so she assumed that it was right after he'd met with Zachary. She would have to make a decision about the retainer, now.

Christine mulled it over. After what Gary had said, she wasn't sure she should contribute, but she did want to call Griff back, even though Marcus didn't want her to. Griff was only following up on something she'd asked him to do, and she hated to drop out of the picture without any explanation, even a fake one. She took another sip of tea, wondering if she should call Lauren to see what she thought. They hadn't talked much on the way home since Christine had fallen asleep after her crying jag. She scrolled to FAVORITES and pressed Lauren's cute profile picture. Any reason was a good reason to call your best friend in the world.

"Hey, honey!" Lauren said, picking up after the first ring. "I was just about to call you. How are you?"

"I've been better. Just got out of Gary's."

"Ruh roh. Did you get yelled at? And what happened last night? Tell me fast, I'm picking up Seth at the orthodontist."

"The headline is I didn't get yelled at, but they don't want me to call Griff and pay any retainer. Griff called."

"What did he say?"

"I couldn't get it. Marcus was right there, and we had a fight."

"Oh no." Lauren groaned.

"Oh yes." Christine sighed.

"Christine, I don't think you should help with the retainer. Paying, even lending him money, is crossing some line I don't want you to cross."

"I get that, but what about calling Griff back? Can't I call and tell him that? The lawyer said not to and so did Marcus, but they just don't want me to get involved. I felt majorly bossed around."

"Aw." Lauren clucked. "They're not the boss of you. So what, you want to call Griff?"

"Yes."

"Then call him, but make sure it's the last time." Lauren paused. "I have to tell you, Zachary scared me yesterday with all that talk about how you cut into a heart. That was creepy, you have to admit. I started to wonder if he was guilty."

"I know, but then again, it shows he's not the killer, or he wouldn't even go there."

"So are you completely sold?"

"No, but I'm inclined to think he's innocent, that's why I feel so crappy about washing my hands of him. Gary gets it, but Marcus doesn't. Last night is a story you don't have time for."

"Okay. Call me later, I want to hear."

"After dinner with my in-laws."

"Big Frederik and his trophy wife? Lucky you."

"You got that right. Bye, love you."

"Love you, too." Lauren hung up, and Christine pressed END. She took another sip of tea, scrolled to recent calls, and pressed Griff's number. It rang twice, then he picked up.

"Griff."

"Yes, hi. It's Christine. Did you get to see Zachary this morning?"

"Yes. I'm going to represent him, if he can get the retainer."

"Griff, about that." Christine hesitated. "I don't know if I can give him half of it."

"His girlfriend's lending him the other half."

"Really?" Christine felt confused. "I thought they broke up and—"

"Gah," Griff growled, impatient. "I don't care. I didn't call you to talk about romance. I called about that woman you told me about. The neighbor who told you Robinbrecht used to have men up all the time. Did she see anything that night?"

"I got the idea that she did, but she wouldn't say."

"What was her name again?"

"Linda Kent. She lives around the block from Warwick Street, but I don't know her house number."

"Then it is the same one. The house number is 505. I went over there. She's dead."

"*What?*" Christine asked, shocked.

"It was an accident."

"How? What kind of accident?"

"She fell down her staircase. Her neck was broken."

"How horrible!" Christine tried to visualize it, from what she remembered of the backstreet. "Do they know how she fell, or what happened?"

"At midnight or so. She probably slipped on the stairs. Neighbors say she drank like a fish."

"But why would she be out on her stairwell at night?"

"How the hell do I know?" Griff grunted. "I don't have time to shoot the breeze."

"She said she had a clear view of Gail Robinbrecht's steps, in the back. That's the only entrance to a duplex, isn't it?"

"Yes. Typical West Chester. The realty companies came in,

chopped the houses into duplexes. Kent lived in one. So did Robinbrecht."

"Doesn't that seem strange to you, that Mrs. Kent dies in an accident, just a few days after the woman who lives directly across from her is murdered?" Christine was thinking out loud. "I mean, we know that Kent could have seen something that night, or maybe the killer simply thought she did. Kent looked at Robinbrecht's apartment all the time, and the back stairs. If she told that to me, a complete stranger, how many other people do you think she told it to? Anybody who went to Robinbrecht's, like Lauren and I did that night?"

"Oh boy. Speculating. I gotta go."

"But wait, please. Think about this. A person who thought he was seen by Linda Kent going up Gail Robinbrecht's stairs, or who might have believed he was seen, would have a motive to murder Linda Kent. Maybe he's the real killer, not Zachary. The killer would be somebody who knew, or suspected, he was seen and didn't want to take any chances." Christine's thoughts raced. "Zachary's in prison, so it couldn't have been him. Don't you think that's worth following up on? I think that's the kind of thing that can really help the defense, don't you?"

"Leave Jeffcoat's defense to me—"

"I am, I'm just saying that this seems like an unusual turn of events. Don't you agree?"

"I don't want to discuss it with you. Now will you please let me hang up? I'm trying to remain a gentleman—"

Christine couldn't let him go just yet. "One last question. Now that you met with him, do you think he's innocent? He told me that he wanted a lawyer who believed in his innocence."

"Well, all he's got is me," Griff answered, then hung up.

Chapter Twenty-nine

Christine tugged a weed from between two purple coneflow-ers, trying to clear her head. She hadn't known what to do with herself after the phone call with Griff, and she couldn't seem to shake the notion that Linda Kent's death might not have been an accident. She needed not to think about it anymore, and the same went for Zachary. She took out another weed and tossed it in the red plastic bucket she used for plant refuse.

She had started the garden three years ago, back when they couldn't figure out why she wasn't getting pregnant, and even then she was self-aware enough to know that she wanted to grow something, even if it wasn't a baby. They had a small yard in the front and back of the house, but she had located the garden in front by the driveway, so she could see it every time she came home.

Their house, the New Construction, was actually set perpen-dicular to the road, not facing it, and a tall hedge bordering their street gave her privacy while she gardened, so she could wear whatever she wanted, like the tank top and gym shorts she had on now, even braless. She'd never felt so constrained by a bra before she had gotten pregnant, and last week, before all hell had broken loose, she had happily begun to notice her breasts swelling, newly sexy on her tomboyish figure. Ordinarily, she would've spent the afternoon shopping online for the least-ugly nursing bra, but shopping for the baby had been tainted by the events of the morning.

Christine pulled another weed, but it came with too much dirt and she shook it out before she tossed it into the bucket. The garden was just beginning to bloom, and she could see that it was going to be a good summer. She'd planted only perennials because they'd come back every year, saving her a lot of work since she'd hoped she'd be busy when their baby finally arrived. When that looked like it was going to take longer than anticipated, she made peace with the perennial decision, if only because she loved the unruly wildness to coneflower, some with delicate purple petals and others with a dusky pink, and rudbeckia, or black-eyed Susans, whose bright golden petals stood out like yellow caution lights in the mass plantings she favored.

She pulled another weed. Elsewhere in the garden she had planted groupings of purplish Japanese anemone, tall white phlox, and some pale blue delphinium, which she couldn't wait to see bloom. Along the border, catmint was already beginning to spread, and she felt happy that she had at least one plant that deer and rabbits wouldn't eat. She hadn't begun to spray yet, pumping the rotten egg and pepper repellent that obliterated the sweet perfume of the yellow roses and the fresh earthen smells of the dirt, but it was a price every gardener had to pay.

She plucked another weed from the coneflowers and tossed it into the bucket. She was one of those strange birds who loved weeding, seeing it as a way to nurture the garden entire, and usually it transported her and she would lose her worries in the performance of a simple task, but she couldn't find her weed groove today. She was too preoccupied by everything. She couldn't help but wonder about Linda Kent and shuddered to think of the woman's being pushed down the stairwell to her death.

Christine tried to puzzle out why Kent would be outside on the stairwell at night, anyway. Having a smoke? Looking at the stars? She tried to remember if she had seen any plants or flowers on Kent's stairwell, maybe something that needed watering, but she couldn't remember anything like that. Kent could have gone out to answer the door. But for whom?

Christine kept weeding, imagining the awful scene. There would be a knock at Linda Kent's door, and she would go to answer it, maybe after a few drinks. She would open the door, either recognizing the man or not, even assuming it was a man, but what if it wasn't a friendly visitor? What if the man had thrown her down the stairs? Would neighbors have heard it? Would anybody have seen it?

Christine keep weeding and thinking. She didn't have any answers. She didn't remember any streetlights in the street behind the houses. Maybe there was security lighting or motion detectors. Maybe somebody saw something but hadn't reported it to the police. Or maybe the police had made a mistake and not asked enough questions, so they'd ruled the death an accident. Kent might not have had the chance to tell them about the men going up Gail Robinbrecht's stairwell, so they would have no reason to consider anything suspicious about her death.

Christine pulled another weed, shook off the extra dirt, and tossed it into the bucket. Wondering why she was wasting her time, at home.

But she still had dinner with her in-laws to get through.

Chapter Thirty

Christine sat alone at the table, nursing her ice water while she waited for the others to arrive. The restaurant was called Bangkok Dream, a pricey favorite of Marcus's father's, with floor-to-ceiling draperies of tangerine silk and scrolls of antique Japanese art bordered by red calligraphy. Pendant halogen lights glistened off the polished teak tables, each set with exotic chopstick holders, and the food was Thai, Japanese sushi, and other Asian fusion, even the smells of which did not appeal to Christine in her current state. She wished for a strong margarita, but of course she hadn't ordered one. She was already worried that her baby was going to have enough strikes against him. Or her.

Sitar music played in the background, which was Thai enough for the suburbs, and the coveted tables were filled. The other diners were well-dressed middle-aged couples, and Christine was glad she'd dressed up. She'd showered after gardening because she was ridiculously sweaty and she'd even blown her hair out completely, applying Moroccan oil to give it some shine. She had on her nicest summer dress, of lime-green silk, and for once she was glad she wasn't into maternity clothes. She hadn't dressed to impress Marcus or his father, though Frederik Nilsson was the type of man that women tended to dress up for. She was dressing for herself, to improve her mood and put the day behind her.

She looked up when the restaurant doors opened, her attention drawn by a flash of bright sunlight. In the doorway she spotted Marcus's silhouette, followed by an almost-identical silhouette of her father-in-law Frederik, with his wife Stephanie. Christine smiled and gave a pleasant wave, and Marcus waved back. He walked toward the table, though his father and Stephanie lagged behind, greeting the restaurant owner, who came out to shake Frederik's hand.

Frederik Nilsson was a star architect, or "starchitect," who lived in Avon and owned his own architecture firm in Hartford, Nilsson International, which he had started by designing modern glass homes for the wealthy residents of Greenwich and Darien. After one of his houses appeared in *Architectural Digest*, his client base expanded to national proportions, though Christine thought his glass shoeboxes reminded her of a fourth-grader's diorama. Frederik touted his "design aesthetic" as his "Scandinavian architectural voice," but to her, it was cookie-cutter for a five-million-dollar cookie.

Christine truly didn't begrudge her father-in-law his success, though she wished he wore it with more grace, for Marcus's sake. Frederik always acted as if architects were true artists, while architectural engineers were boring number-crunchers. Frederik gave lip service that engineering was equal to architecture, but Marcus knew his father was disappointed in him for choosing engineering over architecture. It came to a head five years ago, when Frederik had asked Marcus to join his architectural firm, to provide it with an adjunct engineering arm. Marcus had declined to move under his father's thumb, which Frederik took personally, and the competition between father and son formed a constant undercurrent of tension.

"Hey, honey," Marcus said, leaning over and giving her a quick peck on the cheek, and she realized that he hadn't touched her in days.

"Hi, good to see you."

"God, what a day." Marcus sat down next to her but avoided eye contact, and Christine could feel him being gingerly around her, his feelings still hurt. They hadn't spoken since Leonardo's office, not even a text.

"Busy?"

"Totally, but it looks like North Carolina settled down." Marcus loosened his tie. "Dad's in a great mood."

"Good," Christine said in a way that she hoped sounded pleasant and not relieved. Frederik could be temperamental, and his moods tended to dictate the mood of the evening, if not because he enforced it but because everyone around him became accustomed to acquiescing.

Christine and Marcus looked up as Frederik and Stephanie had finished with the owner and were coming over, with Frederik making a great show of walking between the tables, smiling at the diners as if he knew them, wheeling his head of cool, longish ash-blond hair this way and that. The man had presence, projecting that he was the kind of man you should know, expensively dressed in a dark gray Italian suit tailored closely around his lean torso and waist, which he'd paired with a black silk shirt worn open at the collar, with no tie. His eyes were a fiercely intelligent light blue, sharp against his light tan, and he kept flashing a smile with aggressively large top teeth that Christine always thought of as Kennedyesque, but in a bad way.

"Christine, how's our girl?" Frederik boomed, finally reaching the table, leaning over, and giving her a quick kiss on the cheek.

"Great, thanks. Happy Birthday!"

"Don't remind me! Sixty-five is for speed limits, not men!"

Christine chuckled, then leaned over to smile at Stephanie, who, at about five-ten, was nevertheless hidden behind her husband. "Hi, Stephanie, great to see you!"

"You, too!" Stephanie said with a warm smile, sitting down at the table. Christine liked Stephanie, having gotten over the fact that she was the proverbial trophy wife, some twenty-five years younger than Frederik. The former Stephanie Wooten had caught Frederik's eye when he started taking a Pilates class she taught, after he had injured his back. Stephanie was kind, thoughtful, and artsy but happy to let others take the spotlight, namely her husband.

"You look amazing!" Christine said, meaning it. Stephanie had worked as a catalog model in Europe and was beautiful in an exotic way, with almond-shaped brown eyes, and tonight, her long brown hair slicked back into a chic high ponytail. She wore almost no makeup except for lip-gloss, letting her ethereal beauty just be, like a Zen goddess. Delicate gold hoops hung from her ears, and she looked effortlessly elegant in a sheath of taupe jersey with a dramatic halter neckline, which hugged every inch of her ballet-lean body, all the way down to her flat, Roman sandals.

"How are you feeling?" Stephanie asked, smiling at her sweetly.

"Thanks, I'm fine except for the morning sickness," Christine answered, compromising somewhere between the truth and completely fake small talk.

Frederik grinned his toothy grin. "What a great way to celebrate this birthday, with two beautiful women! Marcus tells me school's over for you, Christine. What are you going to do with yourself until the baby comes?"

"Read without guilt?"

"Great idea, rest up for the baby!" Frederik grinned, then glanced over his shoulder. "Where's that damn waiter? We need to get this celebration started! I ordered champagne!"

"He'll be here soon, Dad," Marcus said, looking for the waiter.

Frederik leaned on the table hard enough that the glasses tinkled. "I had a life-changing event this week. I was in a G V."

"Wow!" Marcus said. "Cool. A G V?"

"What's a G V?" Christine joked. "Is that like a Gee Whiz?"

Frederik chuckled. "It's a jet. The G stands for Gulfstream, and the V is for the Roman numeral five. Thus, G V. It's the new one, after the G IV. I've never seen anything quite like it."

Stephanie rolled her lovely eyes. "Here we go. Boys and their toys."

"Dad, what was the ride like?" Marcus asked, his tone encouraging, and Christine sensed he was trying to be nice because it was his father's birthday.

"It was *unreal*. So smooth. Have you never flown in one, Marcus?"

"No, never."

Christine bit her tongue. Frederik knew that Marcus's clients weren't sending private jets to pick him up.

"The design of the cabin? Art. The finishes, top-of-the-line."

Stephanie was smiling slyly. "Christine, you're supposed to ask him whose jet it was. He wants you to ask and he's not gonna be happy unless you do."

Christine smiled. "Frederik, whose jet was it?"

"Before I answer, it's incumbent upon me to make clear that she's not my client yet. Mine is only one of the firms she's considering. But if she picks those hacks at Scheller Whiting, I'll shoot myself." Frederik glanced over his shoulder again, and the waiter was hustling over with a bottle of champagne in one hand and a white napkin over his arm. "Finally!"

"Okay, so whose jet was it?" Christine repeated.

"Also, to be completely accurate, I'm not sure if she owns the G V. She might have rented it. A lot of these Hollywood people buy contracts in networks to share jets. Very few actually own their own jet."

Christine caught Stephanie's eye, and Stephanie smiled.

Frederik continued, oblivious. "A G V costs God-knows-how-much new, and it's not all of the expense of the purchase, but running it that's the expense. They may not fly enough to justify it."

"Mr. Nilsson, sorry about the delay," said the waiter, arriving at their table. He showed Frederik the bottle in a formal way, resting it against the napkin on his forearm. "Mr. Nilsson, is it to your liking?"

"No," Frederik answered flatly, his disapproval plain. "I asked for the '96 Salon. This is a special occasion."

"Apologies, Mr. Nilsson." The waiter pivoted on his heels and hustled away.

Frederick shook his head. "The '96 Salon. What else? A sommelier wouldn't have made that mistake. Salon has its own plot of land in the Champagne province. They're their own grape producer, so they have better control. They release the vintages very late—"

"Dad, you were saying—" Marcus interrupted, and Christine knew that it was a diversionary tactic, designed to avert his father's making a mountain out of a molehill over the waiter's bringing the wrong champagne.

"Yes, right." Frederik smoothed back his bangs, which were feathery and thick for a man his age. The gray at his temples blended with his ash-blond hair in a way that only made him a more striking figure. "What was I saying?"

Marcus answered, "You were telling us about the client you took the jet for, the G V."

"Yes, of course, it's a teardown in the Hollywood Hills, with a view of Los Angeles on the better side. It's on eight acres, all wooded. Phenomenal. And at night, with the lights, it's indescribable."

"Whose jet was it already?" Christine asked again. She got along best with Frederik by acting like a clueless audience, so he could explain things to her that she didn't care about or already knew.

"In a minute." Frederik held up a long, slim finger, keeping them in suspense, making them hang on his every word. "I can't tell you more about the job because I signed a confidentiality agreement, and you know that I take such things seriously, even among family."

"Of course," Marcus said quickly, but Christine flashed on

the other confidentiality agreement, the one that had kept Zachary's name confidential. She wondered what he was doing now and imagined him in prison. She didn't know if Griff had what it took to get Zachary acquitted. She hadn't liked how Griff had answered her, when she'd asked him about whether he believed Zachary was innocent.

Frederik was saying, "I must tell you, in the past six or seven years, I've signed more confidentiality agreements than I can count. Used to be that you signed them only when you got the job, or at the earliest, visited the site. Nowadays, you have to sign them as soon as you get the phone call, and the phone calls are placed by some fifth assistant."

"Really," Marcus said, undoubtedly noticing Frederik shifting in his chair, preoccupied by his waiter search.

"I'm sure he'll be here soon," Christine chimed in, in a soothing tone. "I still want to hear who the G V belonged to."

Frederik frowned. "Where is our champagne? This is a very special night! I want to celebrate!"

"We will," Christine said.

Marcus nodded. "We will, Dad. We just got here."

Frederik scowled, unplacated. "But I have big news, and I don't want to wait another minute!"

"What, Dad?"

"My beloved bride has just given me the best birthday present ever." Frederik broke into his toothy smile. "Guess what it is?"

Marcus answered, "Please, not a new putter."

Christine chimed in, "A G V?"

Frederik guffawed. "We're pregnant! Stephanie's going to have a baby!"

"What, really?" Christine exclaimed, shocked. It was such a weird situation, and Stephanie and Frederik had always said they didn't want children. Christine couldn't organize her emotions. She and Marcus had gone through such a struggle to conceive that she couldn't feel immediately happy, and she knew Marcus would feel much worse. It was just another way that his father proved superiority over him, although that was something only Christine and Marcus knew. Marcus hadn't told his father or Stephanie about their infertility problems. Frederik and Stephanie knew only that it took Christine and Marcus a while to conceive, but then they got pregnant, end of story.

"Congratulations!" Marcus said, after a moment. He was smiling, but his forehead creased into a frown, as if the top half of his face and bottom half couldn't agree on an emotion. "So this means I'm going to have a . . . brother or sister? At thirty-five years old?"

Frederik burst into hearty laughter again. "Better late than never, don't you think?"

"Ha!" Stephanie flashed a grin. "Your father thinks this is so funny, but the joke's on me. I already have morning sickness, I'm the most exhausted I've ever been in my life, and when I don't eat, I feel like crying."

"I know, right?" Christine said, trying to come around. "We're the ones"—she almost said *left holding the bag*—"who have to do all the work. How far along are you?"

"I'm only a week behind you!" Stephanie's dark eyes lit up with uncharacteristic excitement. "We're going to be pregnant together!"

"Oh my God!" Christine laughed, getting used to the idea, as strange and awkward as it was.

"We'll have such a great time!" Stephanie squealed in a way that Christine had never heard from her before. "You have to tell me everything, Christine. You're the pro. I know you have all those books. You know everything!"

"Girl, I will hook you up. I memorized those books, and I can barf on cue."

Stephanie laughed. "I didn't think I would be this excited, but I am!"

"Wait until you get your ultrasound, that's amazing. You can hear the heartbeat and see the heart." Christine realized as soon as she'd said the words that she hadn't told Marcus about the ultrasound. He glanced over at her, blinking, but didn't say anything. His smile looked frozen in place, but his frown was deep.

Marcus turned to his father. "Dad, I have to admit, I'm surprised. I didn't know you guys were even thinking about having kids."

"Tell me about it!" Frederik flared his eyes, comically. "We *weren't*. I was sure my days of that foolishness were over. But the one time we slipped up, *bam*!"

"Just like that?" Marcus kept smiling, but Christine knew this had to be killing him, not only because he had mixed feelings about having a new sibling, at his age.

"Just like that! At my age, can you imagine!" Frederik puffed up his chest in an exaggerated way, then bent his arms and flapped them like a rooster. "Cock-a-doodle-doo!"

Stephanie recoiled, laughing, and gave him a playful shove. "Frederik, really? Could you keep it classy? You're embarrassing yourself."

"Congratulations, Dad," Marcus said again. "I have to say, this is a hell of a way to celebrate your birthday. I'll hand it to you, I didn't see this coming."

"Never a dull moment, right?" Frederik laughed heartily, throwing his head back and displaying his carnivorous teeth. "I'll be in a walker by the time the kid's out of high school, if I'm lucky!"

Stephanie nodded in happy agreement. "You know the expression, 'Man plans, and God laughs.'"

Frederik looped an arm around Stephanie's slim shoulders and kissed the top of her head. "I'm happy. I admit it's a surprise, but I'm so happy. We're happy. Right, honey?"

"Right." Stephanie looked up at him with a beautiful smile.

"Awww." Christine nodded but felt a tinge of envy. Both Stephanie and Frederik looked over-the-moon, and Christine couldn't help but feel that they were having the happiness about the pregnancy that she would've wanted for her and Marcus.

"Damn, where's that waiter now?" Frederik said, looking over his shoulder, but Stephanie's lovely gaze settled on Christine, and her grin faded.

"I'm . . . sorry, Christine," Stephanie said, nervously. "I didn't mean to be so insensitive."

"How were you insensitive?" Christine asked, confused.

"Well"—Stephanie glanced at Marcus and then back again at Christine—"Marcus shared with us why you had problems conceiving, that you didn't produce enough eggs, and that's why it took you so long to get pregnant."

Christine said nothing, shocked that Marcus had told them such a lie.

Stephanie's glossy lips puckered with regret. "I didn't mean to brag about getting pregnant so fast. I'm sorry, it wasn't nice. You know we love you."

Frederik's smile faded, too, and his gray-blond eyebrows sloped down with unusual empathy. "Yes, we love you guys. We didn't mean to show off. I know I tend to, but Stephanie's making me mend my ways."

"That's okay." Christine plastered on a smile.

"All's well that ends well, right, Christine? We're reproducing like rabbits now! Nilsson babies are taking over the world!" Frederik cranked his neck to look over his shoulder. "Now where the *hell* is that waiter?"

Chapter Thirty-one

M arcus?" Christine called out, as soon as she hit the house, closing the door behind her. She'd stewed the entire car ride home since they had driven separately to the restaurant. She tossed her purse, keys, and phone on the console table, glancing around the entrance hall, but the house was quiet and felt still. She hustled into the kitchen, but Marcus wasn't there and Lady jumped up on the kitchen island, her tail curling into a question mark.

"Marcus?" Christine headed for the sliders to the backyard. One of the doors was open, and the outside light was on over the back patio, recessed into the bottom of a pent roof. She stepped outside, and the motion-detector light went on instantly, casting a cone of bright white in the middle of the yard, where Marcus stood looking down at his phone, his features lit from below. Murphy trotted around at the back of the yard, visible only because of the glowing red disc that dangled from his collar. The night air felt cool and calm, but Christine was anything but.

"Marcus, why did you lie to your father and Stephanie?" Christine walked toward him, not bothering to check her frustration.

"Lie to them about what?" Marcus turned, lowering the phone.

"You know exactly what I'm talking about, so please don't lie to me, too."

"You mean about why we can't get pregnant?"

"Yes, that's exactly what I mean. You told him it was because of my eggs."

"What's the difference?" Marcus shot back, and just then the motion-detector light went off, so Christine could barely see his face in the ambient light from the neighbors' houses. There was no moon out, and the sky was black, opaque, and starless.

"The difference is that you lied."

"So, why does it matter?" Marcus's tone was sharp. "That's what you told me, wasn't it? It doesn't matter whose fault it is. So why should it matter if they think it's your fault and not mine?"

"Marcus, I agreed when you didn't want to tell them anything, only because it's your family, but lying to them is something else. You told them an outright lie, and that's just wrong."

"This, from the woman who lied to me about where she was the entire weekend?" Marcus slid his phone in his pocket, where it glowed. "That's not the reason you're mad. The real reason is that you blame me because we couldn't have our own child. No matter what you say, you blame me because we couldn't get pregnant."

"I *don't* blame you for that."

"Yes you do. You know it, and I know it. And so do I. I blame myself, too." Marcus raised his voice. "Do you have any idea what that's like for me to sit there and listen to my father, who got his *second* wife pregnant by *accident*, when I couldn't even get you pregnant once? Do you know what that feels like, as a man? As a husband?"

"I know, but this isn't about you."

"Of course it is. We wouldn't be in this mess with Jeffcoat if I had been able to get you pregnant. You wouldn't have a baby in you *right now* that has half the DNA of a *serial killer*. We're not having a *Nilsson baby*, that's the reason you're pissed."

"No, that's the reason *you're* pissed. You're the one who has a problem with that, not me."

"Oh, right. You're fine with it because it's *Zachary's* baby. Your new boyfriend."

"How dare you!" Christine's blood boiled, and she felt suddenly exasperated with Marcus, with his jealousy, with his insecurities, and with him. "Do you know what bothers me? What bothers me is that tonight at dinner, I was sitting across from your father and Stephanie, and he's completely supportive of her. He's as excited about their pregnancy as she is, and they didn't even plan it. She's having the pregnancy that I wanted."

"That's exactly what I just said! You wanted a nice, normal pregnancy. You're angry because you didn't get one. You feel cheated because we had to use a donor."

"No, that's not true." Christine finally understood her own feelings, and they were coming to a head. "I'm angry because you're not supportive of this pregnancy."

"I've been supportive. I drive you to your car. I get whatever food you want. I bring you water. I hold your hair when you throw up—"

"I'm talking about *emotionally* supportive. You didn't buy in from the start, and now that you found out about Zachary—yes, I call him by his first name—now, you can't get past it. You wanted me to have an abortion." Christine couldn't stop now that she'd said it aloud. "How is that supportive?"

"I don't want that anymore—"

"Still, that's the barest minimum. I'm talking about your being *in* it with me and sharing the joy with me, but also the hard parts. So we're having a hard part. We got dealt a bad hand, but I'm the only one trying to solve it—"

"How, by running off to see Zachary? By lending him money? By making sure he has a lawyer?"

"Yes. That's all part of it. I was just going to the source, like Gary said, and I feel connected to him. I want to help him."

Christine heard herself admit it aloud and understood something more, almost like an epiphany. "But the answer isn't for me to ditch Zachary. The answer is for you to be part of this *with* me. He's our donor, and we have to figure out what we're going to do about that—"

"We're going to sue the bastards!"

"That's not all, not nearly. It's all about taking care of this baby, because it's on its way." Christine understood everything with a new clarity. "Marcus, if we found out this child had cystic fibrosis, we'd be in it together. We'd be buying equipment. Medication, nebulizers. We'd be seeing the best doctors we could afford. We'd figure that out before the baby came. Why treat a physical illness but not a mental illness? This is no different."

"Of course it is!"

"No it isn't; and anyway, it doesn't matter. The baby's coming, and I'm going to be its mother. You've evidently decided you're not going to be its father."

"You think Zachary is the father. You went to see him, why?"

"To find out if he was the biological father, our donor." Christine knew that Marcus was half-right, but she wasn't about to admit it because she was right about the whole thing. "I wish you'd gone with me. I wish you were handling this whole thing differently. I wanted to get to know him, to learn things about him, about his family medical history, who had mental illness, who didn't—"

"We already have more information about him than most people have before they get married. We have three generations of medical history on him."

"That's not the point, it's not the same thing." Christine thought fast. "You can have a résumé, but it's not the same thing as meeting them. You could meet somebody online, but that's not the same as a real date."

"Excuse me if I don't want to *date* Zachary. Excuse me if this whole thing is completely galling and mortifying and humiliating, and all you do is think about yourself!"

"No, you're exactly wrong." Christine felt resentment and bitterness welling up from deep within. "All I do is think about you. Since the day of your diagnosis, all I have done is worry about your feelings, your emotions, how embarrassed you were, that you felt ashamed and humiliated. I lied to my friends at school, and I didn't even tell Lauren until I couldn't keep a secret anymore. Everyone around you is protecting your feelings and your ego just because you have a medical condition you can't own up to. Because you never accepted that it's biology, not manhood. I'm *sick* of worrying about you. I'm officially done worrying about you. I'm tired of saving your face for you. Grow the hell up!" Christine stood her ground. "And you know what else I realized? That being a father is a *decision*. It doesn't have to do with DNA or anything else. Zachary is the biological father of this child, and right now, what I'm saying is that this child doesn't have a father—"

"I'm the father!"

"Then *act* like it. You have to care about this baby, and you have to take care of this baby—"

"I do care about the baby. That's why I want to sue Homestead."

"That's not why you want to sue Homestead. You want to sue Homestead because you're angry. You're angry at them for picking Jeffcoat. You're angry at yourself because you're infertile. You're angry at the *world* and you're taking it out on Homestead! You don't really care about the baby."

"And you say you care about the baby but you really care about Zachary. You admit you have a connection with him. How am I supposed to deal with that?"

"Admit that *you* have a connection to him, too." Christine was freewheeling, but it was her heart talking. "Because if this is going to be our child, and you're going to be the father, then you *do* have a connection to Jeffcoat. Share it with me."

"What are you talking about? What are you asking from me?"

"Zachary is down there, he's in prison. He's our donor and he could be in jail for a crime he didn't commit. I'm not going to turn my back on him."

"You didn't, you got him a lawyer!"

"And I'm not going to wash my hands of him just because I did that." Christine felt like it was finally time for her to face her feelings. "I'm worried about him. I feel bad for him. I think he's innocent. I don't think he committed that murder—"

"Christine, you're being naïve. You heard what Gary said."

"Either way, I have to find out for myself." Christine knew what she wanted to do, and it wasn't stay home, obsess about Zachary, and weed her garden. "I want to go back down there and see how I can help him. I want to make sure he has what he needs—"

"*What? Are you serious?*"

"I am asking you if you would come with me."

"No!" Marcus snapped. "Absolutely not. I'm not going down there."

"Marcus, please. Come with me." Christine tried to think of an argument to persuade him. She felt a glimmer of hope that if they could go together, they could get their marriage back on track. "When this baby grows up, do you want to tell him that his biological father is behind bars, a murderer? Would our baby feel good when he finds out that his biological father was in jail for a crime he didn't commit? And that we didn't help him when we could? Do you know what that can do to a child? Can't you think ahead? Can't you get past the fact that we needed a donor?"

"Christine, enough. You're asking too much. You're just asking too much of me."

"I can deal with it, why can't you, Marcus? I can't deny that he exists and that he's in trouble. Come with me or not."

"You can't go!"

"You're my husband, not my principal." Christine folded her arms. "Are you coming with me or not? It's your choice."

Chapter Thirty-two

The next morning, Christine crossed into New Jersey, glancing at the dashboard clock, which read 9:15. She'd gone to bed last night without another word to Marcus, who'd slept downstairs with Murphy and Lady. She'd packed some clothes and sneaked out at five thirty, with nobody even stirring, which didn't surprise her. Marcus was the heaviest sleeper in history, with the dog a close second. She suspected the cat saw her go but didn't care.

Rain pounded on the windshield, and the wipers flapped to keep it clear. Her stomach had finally stabilized after a bout of morning sickness, and she was making excellent time driving south on I-95 in remarkably light traffic. Marcus hadn't texted or called, and she wasn't about to contact him. But she had some bases she had to cover.

Her phone was on its holder on the dashboard, and she waited until it was safe to dial, then pressed the phone screen for her mother's number. The phone rang only once, and her mother picked up. "Hey, Christine, how are you this morning?"

"Great, I just wanted to see how you guys were."

"Your dad's having some breakfast. We're out of ketchup, so he's not a happy camper."

"But how are you?" Christine asked, making it a point. Her mother had become such an excellent caregiver that she routinely placed her needs second.

"I'm fine."

"Did you sleep okay?" Christine knew her mother had been having trouble sleeping.

"Great. We had the air conditioner on. So what are you doing? You sound like you're in the car already."

"I'm having fun." Christine felt a twinge of guilt but let it go. She had to keep lying or her mother would worry. "I'm going back down to Lauren's family's house for a few more days. She had to go back, but I'm staying to decompress after school."

"That's a wonderful idea! Good for you! You do so much, you need the break. Is Marcus going to join you?"

"No, he has to work, and Lauren can't leave the kids."

"So you're all by yourself?"

"Yes, but I'm looking forward to it. I bought a bunch of books and I'm going to read myself into a coma on the beach."

"Oh that does sound wonderful," her mother said, and Christine could hear the wistfulness in her tone.

"I wish I could've brought you, Mom." Christine realized her parents hadn't taken a vacation since her father had been diagnosed, five years ago. Changes of scenery and routine disturbed her father, so they stayed home.

"Another time."

"Yes, another time," Christine said, knowing that there would be no other time. Her mother knew the same thing, but they said the words anyway, a comforting call-and-response between a loving mother and daughter.

"I better go, I need to help your dad with breakfast."

"Can I say hi to him?"

"Not just now, okay, sweetie? I want him to finish his meal."

"Of course. Tell him I said hi and I love him."

"I will. Love you. Drive safe. Stop if you get tired. Don't go in the water after you eat."

Christine smiled. "Yes, Mommy."

"What a comedian." Her mother chuckled, then hung up, and Christine pressed the button to end the call, then called Lauren, who picked up after three rings.

"Christine! Sorry it took me so long. I'm trying to pack two bicycles in the back of the car and they got tangled up, the pedal of one got stuck in the spokes of the other." Lauren sounded exasperated. "I told Josh we need a bike rack, but does anybody listen to me? No."

"So it's that kind of morning."

"Yes, in other words, typical. What are you up to?"

"I'll tell you if you won't worry, because I'm on my way."

"Where?"

"Do you want to hear about the fact that my father-in-law is becoming a father again, the tattooed alcoholic we met in West Chester is dead, or that I'm on my way back to Pennsylvania?"

"*What?*" Lauren said, astonished, and for the next thirty miles, Christine filled her in on what had happened. Lauren had the reaction Christine had expected, which was generally "are you really sure," "you need to be careful," "I'm not sure if you should be doing this," and stopping just short of, "wait an hour before you go in the water." But after Christine told Lauren what her plan was and convinced her that it was safe, or at most a waste of time, her best friend came around, reluctantly. Which was why the two women were best friends forever, because each one always believed in the other.

Lauren said, "You have to promise me you'll be careful."

"I'll be careful, I'm careful. But don't you think it's suspicious that Kent turned up dead?"

"I don't know why you think it's suspicious if the police don't."

"Because they have no reason to believe her death is suspicious. They don't know what she saw, they never called her back."

"True."

"Let's assume Kent was murdered because she saw the killer on the stairs the night Gail Robinbrecht was killed, or because the killer *thinks* that she saw him. That means that Zachary isn't the serial killer."

"You're creeping me out with all this talk of Kent getting murdered and serial killers."

"It happens."

"Not in our world. Our world is kids and bicycles and Crayola and standardized testing."

Christine smiled. That used to be her world, but she didn't know where her world was any longer. She wasn't a teacher anymore, and her previously happy marriage was in trouble. She knew she wanted to be a mother, and she knew she wanted to be the mother of the child she was carrying. But that loop kept leading her back to Zachary Jeffcoat.

"I'm worried about you and Marcus."

"Me, too." Christine drove on, rain pounding against the windshield. "I know this is going to sound strange, but that's part of the reason I'm going. I wish I could pretend Zachary doesn't exist, but he does, and I'm not going to be happy unless I try to help him, one way or the other."

"What if you can't help him?"

"Then at least I tried. Unless I try, it's going to bug me. You know how I am."

"Curious."

Christine smiled.

"But what about Gary? Does this mess up your lawsuit?"

"No, I don't think so. I'm doing what you call self-help."

Lauren sighed. "How long do you think you'll be down there?"

"I don't know, a couple of days? I'm going to play it by ear. If my mother calls you, back up my story. I'm at your house at the Jersey Shore."

"The house is getting a lot of use for a house that never gets any use." Lauren chuckled. "What does Marcus know?"

"I didn't lie. I told him where I was going."

"What'd he say?"

"He's angry. So be it." Christine knew she sounded tougher than she felt.

"So what do I tell him if he calls here?"

"He's not going to, but if he does, tell him to call my cell. I made a reservation at the Warner Hotel in West Chester."

"That town has a hotel?"

"Just the one, it's a converted movie theater."

"So no Jacuzzi."

"Not likely. It looks nice online." Christine braked when the downpour intensified, and a passing truck sprayed her with grit and water. "Okay, I should go. The rain is bad."

"Stay in touch. I'll give you a call to check on you."

"Take care, talk soon. Love you."

"Love you, too." Christine hung up, with only one more phone call to make. She pressed Griff's number, and the lawyer answered on the first ring.

"Christine. I'm busy."

"Can I meet with you this afternoon?" she asked, with hope.

Chapter Thirty-three

Christine walked down the hall toward Griff's office, gearing herself up. It was one thing to have a plan and another to put it into action, especially when it required convincing Griff the Gruff. She reached the end of the hall and opened the door just as he hung up his landline.

"Why are you here?" Griff frowned, and Christine was pleased to see he was better groomed than the other day. His hair was almost tamed with something pomade-y, and he had on a white oxford shirt, a red-and-blue bow tie, and a boxy blue-and-white seersucker suit, like a demented Atticus Finch.

"Thanks for seeing me, Griff. You look very spruced up."

"Did I ask you?"

"No, that's called being polite." Christine sat down. "You should try it sometime."

"I'm too busy."

"On Zachary's case?" Christine scanned the desk, which was newly cluttered, strewn with pencils, pens, and yellow legal pads covered with scribbled notes. To the right of the computer keyboard was a stack of expandable accordion files stuffed with papers and Xeroxed cases.

"None of your business. Why are you here? I'm busy."

"Good." Christine reached into her purse, pulled out a manila envelope, and slid both across the desk. "My résumé is inside. I'm married, thirty-two years old, and I've been a reading teacher at an elementary school for the past eight years."

"Why do I care?" Griff didn't even glance at the envelope.

"I want to be your paralegal. At no cost to you."

"No." Griff pushed the envelope back. "Good-bye."

"Why?" Christine had prepared for the reaction. "You're busy, you need help. You said you're a one-man band. You don't have to be."

"This is about your book. Admit it."

"No, it's not." Christine cringed inwardly. "I put Zachary's interest ahead of my book, didn't I? That's already been established. I just want to help Zachary and I'm interested in the case."

"Why?" Griff's eyes narrowed behind his glasses, which were remarkably unsmudged.

"I think he's innocent."

Griff harrumphed. "That's proves you're not qualified to work in criminal law."

"You don't think he is?"

"I'm not discussing the case with you."

"Okay, but I'm qualified. You don't need a degree to be a paralegal. I have a degree in education. I'm a college graduate, University of Connecticut. I can be taught to do legal research, and factual research is common sense."

"Voltaire said common sense isn't common."

"Luckily, Voltaire's not here. After what happened with Linda Kent, I think something suspicious is going on and I want to get to the bottom of it."

"No. Good-bye." Griff's phone started ringing, but he ignored it.

"Be practical. You can't do it all, and there's no money to hire staff. Somebody needs to follow up about Linda Kent." Christine gestured at the ringing phone. "I'm sure the FBI's calling you, and the other state jurisdictions will want to talk with you, just like you said. You can't do it all yourself, can you?"

Griff pursed his dry lips but didn't reply. The phone stopped ringing.

"I promise I'll be completely loyal and I'll keep everything we learned confidential. I'm much more responsible than anybody you'd get off the street, and I already have a rapport with Zachary."

Griff didn't say anything, so Christine kept talking.

"I'm good with computers, unlike somebody we know. The FBI and other authorities will need to email you. They're not all going to be able to call you on the phone, especially if you don't answer. You have to be realistic, if not for your sake, then for Zachary's. If you stay in the Dark Ages, that's not going to serve your client. Let me help."

"I don't think so." Griff shook his head, and the phone started ringing again.

"Aren't you going to answer that?"

"No."

Christine half-rose, reaching for the phone. "Let me, I can take a message."

"No. Sit back down. I know who it is."

"Who?"

"None of your business."

"Why aren't you getting it?"

"Phone calls are always somebody else's agenda. Remember that." Griff held up a knotted index finger. "People would get more done if they would ignore the phone calls of others. Work their own agenda. Like me. I have my own agenda. Do you know where the word agenda comes from?"

"I'm guessing Latin?"

"Of course. Actually it is a Latin word, the neuter plural of *agendum*. It means 'things that need to be done.' As in, answering the phone is not my *agendum*, my thing that needs to be done. My *agendum* is my client."

Christine resorted to Plan B. "I'm going to do factual investigation on this case, whether you like it or not. You can't stop me."

"So do it. Why bother me?" Griff shifted his knobby shoulders inside his jacket, which was too big, undoubtedly from his younger days.

"Because if I do it as your employee, then it's privileged, isn't it? I wouldn't have to reveal it to the FBI or in court. That's what you taught me, am I right?"

Griff didn't reply except to frown, a fissure between his unruly eyebrows.

"But if I do it on my own, it's not privileged and it's not confidential. I have to answer questions about it, and I can also tell anybody I want to. I could print anything I wanted to. I could go to the newspapers myself. I could put it on that crazy new thing called the *Internet*." Christine paused to let it sink in. "The only way you can control me is if you hire me. Either way, I'm going forward. It benefits Zachary if we work together, not against each other."

Griff kept frowning. "That's blackmail."

"No, it's cooperation." Christine couldn't give up on teaching, even at his age. "Our cooperating is in Zachary's best interests. We both want the same thing, which is to see him acquitted. What do you say?"

Griff sighed, unhappily. The phone stopped ringing.

"Griff, you have no money. You have no staff. You can't do it by yourself. Please, be practical. Use me."

Griff paused, pursing his lips.

Christine waited. "Please?"

"You have to do what I say," Griff answered, after a moment.

"I will." Christine felt her heart lift.

258 | LISA SCOTTOLINE

"Don't write or talk about the case, except to me. No books, no Facebooks, no leaks. Do I have your word?"

"Yes."

"You're covered by Rule 1.6, which means that anything you discover while you're working for me is work product, protected by attorney-client privilege. Keep it that way."

"I will." Christine shifted forward in her seat. "Okay, so tell me, you meet Zachary?"

"You're asking questions already?" Griff's hooded eyes widened.

"If we're going to work together, we have to share information. Sharing and cooperation, Griff." Christine felt like she was talking to a fourth-grader, only hairier.

"What's to share? I went over on Sunday and met Zachary."

"And what do you think of him?"

"It doesn't matter."

"It doesn't matter what you think of him?"

"No." Griff met her eye behind his glasses and sealed his lips into a flat, if wrinkled, line.

Christine let it go. "Do you think he's innocent?"

"That doesn't matter either. I'm his lawyer, not his Creator."

Christine had no idea what that meant. "Did you ask?"

"Of course not."

Christine didn't understand. "So what happened in the meeting? How do you have a meeting where that doesn't even come up? Isn't that the elephant in the room?"

Griff sighed theatrically. "I asked him what happened the night of the murder. He told me the same story he told you. I took notes." He gestured at his legal pads. "Somewhere in here."

"You didn't ask if he did it?"

"Do I have to repeat myself?" Griff frowned, recoiling. "Is this what it's going to be like? You bothering me with stupid questions, *ad nauseam*?"

"Zachary called 911 that night, you know. He was the one who reported the Robinbrecht murder."

"So?" Griff shrugged. "Serial killers have been known to do that. Robert Durst called 911. So did the BTK killer. They like the game. They toy with the cops. They like to tease. Show their superiority."

Christine held up a hand. "Okay, I'll move on. What else have you done so far on the case? Catch me up."

"I filed an Entry of Appearance, which puts everyone on notice I represent him. I cleared his visitors' list at the prison of everyone but me. I'll have to put you back on. I went to the scene."

Christine gasped. "You went to Robinbrecht's apartment?"

"Robinbrecht's apartment is the scene, so, yes." Griff flared his cloudy gray eyes. "How is it I don't need a hearing aid but you do?"

"How did you get in?"

"How do you think? I called the D.A. Detectives take you. They stand watch. You look around."

"Did you see anything helpful?"

"No."

"I wish I had gone." Christine couldn't imagine what it had looked like, but she wanted to know.

"Then go. I'll set it up for tomorrow morning."

"Really?" Christine felt her pulse quicken. It would be grim, but maybe she would see something that Griff had missed.

"Hold on." Griff dug under his accordion files and produced a single-lens reflex camera, which he passed her over the desk, dragging the black strap across his papers. "I took pictures."

"Thanks." Christine rose, took the camera from him, and turned it over to look through the pictures, but the back was sealed. "It's not digital?"

"No, it's not. Human beings are digital, not cameras. See these?" Griff wiggled his arthritic fingers. "They're called digits. Know why? From the Latin, *digitus*, meaning fingers or toes."

"Really?" Christine sat down with the camera. "You learn something new every day."

"I don't, but you do." Griff waved at the camera. "Get that film developed. That will be your first assignment as my paralegal."

"Okay, but I do have something I want to do first. In fact, right now."

"Already, you're not listening." Griff frowned.

"I'm listening, I'm just not obeying."

"You said you'd obey."

"No I didn't." Christine hadn't even said that in her wedding vows, which was turning out to be a good thing. "Let me tell you what I want to do, and if you give me the go-ahead, I'll go. How about that?"

"No."

But Christine didn't obey, and told him anyway.

Chapter Thirty-four

Christine dropped off the film at a drugstore, which unfortunately didn't have one-hour developing, then went on to Warwick Street, arriving at six o'clock, which was perfect timing. It was still light out, so she could see the lay of the land, and residents were returning home from work. She circled the block, noting that some were finding parking spaces in front of their houses but others were driving down the block, taking a right turn on Warwick, and turning into the skinny driveway behind the houses on Warwick.

She pulled into a space a few doors up from Gail Robinbrecht's house and parked the car. She cut the ignition, grabbed her purse, and got out of the car, chirping it locked behind her. She walked to 301, two houses up from Gail's, and scanned Warwick Street on the fly. All of the houses, from 301 to 307, which was at the corner, were redbrick row houses, the same except for the paint color of their shutters, window treatments, and plantings.

Number 301 had petunias and pretty black window boxes, with a black door to match, and Christine could see from the two front windows on the first floor that lights were on inside the house. She walked up the two front steps, knocked on the door, and reminded herself to act like a paralegal, which was basically a teacher with a better pay scale.

The door was opened in a few moments by a good-looking, if scruffy, young man in a purple WCU T-shirt and gym shorts, with red Dr. Dre earphones on. "Hi," he said, lifting one from his ear.

"Hi, I'm Christine Nilsson, and I'm a paralegal working for an attorney in town." Christine slid one of Griff's business cards from her pocket and gave it to him.

"Okay, I'm Phil Dresher." Phil tugged the earphones off and let them rest around his neck, but his rap music was loud enough that Christine could still hear the shouting.

"Phil, I just have a few questions about Linda Kent, who lived around the block at 505 Daley. Did you happen to know Ms. Kent?"

"No, not really. I know the neighbors on this street. We have block parties and stuff, it's cool. But I don't know around the block, on Daley Street."

"You may have heard that Ms. Kent was killed in an accident on Sunday night. She fell down the back steps."

"Oh that sucks. I didn't know." Phil frowned.

"Yes, we're investigating the matter, and I was wondering if you saw or heard anything that night, perhaps saw her fall or heard her shout?" Christine wasn't exactly lying, and neither she nor Griff wanted to do that. But if she led with what happened to Linda Kent, rather than what happened to Gail Robinbrecht, residents would assume it was about a negligence lawsuit and be more likely to talk.

"No, I don't think so. What time did it happen?"

"We think midnight."

"No, heard nothing."

"Do you generally hear noises out back? Does your house go all the way through?"

"Yeah, we rent the whole house. All the houses go all the way back, I think."

"Do you have a backyard?"

"Yeah."

"So if there'd been some noise, do you think you would've heard it?"

"Not really." Phil gestured to his earphones. "I study with these on or listen to music. My other three roommates play video games. We keep the AC on and the windows shut, so the neighbors don't bitch about any noise we make. They're always looking for an excuse to get students out of this end of town." The young man turned toward the back of the house. "I can show you, we do have a backyard, and we sit out there sometimes, have some wine, you know. That's what we did Saturday night with some friends. But we were out Sunday night since one of my roommates is graduating."

"Congratulations." Christine smiled. "By the way, I'm sorry about what happened to your neighbor Gail Robinbrecht."

"Wow, I know, it's horrible, really horrible." Phil frowned in a way that made him look older than a college student.

"Did you know Gail?"

"Sure, me and my roommates, we liked her. Gail was the organizer of the block parties, she knew how to make it fun. My girlfriend liked her, too, and she's really freaked. She wants us to start a neighborhood watch."

"That's a good idea." Christine saw her opening. "Did you see anything suspicious that night around her house? It was last Monday night."

"No, not at all."

"Were you home?"

"Yeah, I was, but I didn't see anything. I had the game on. We already told the police."

"Great, good. Thank you very much."

"You're welcome." Phil closed the door, and Christine walked to 303, Gail Robinbrecht's next-door neighbor. They had a Norway spruce in a blue glazed pot, and the front door was of natural wood with a brass knocker. Louvered shutters covered the windows, but classical music played inside, so someone was home.

Christine knocked, and the door was opened by an older African-American woman with wire-rimmed glasses and a graying topknot, in a white silk blouse with a navy skirt, evidently part of a suit. She was barefoot, as if she'd just kicked off her pumps.

Christine smiled, gesturing at her feet. "I do the same thing, the first thing when I come in the door."

"Ha!" The woman smiled, warmly. "Heels aren't shoes, they're torture devices."

"I agree." Christine introduced herself, handing her Griff's business card. "I'm a paralegal for an attorney in town, and we're looking into the accidental death of Mrs. Kent, who lived around the block on Daley."

"Nice to meet you. Anita Noxubee."

"Anita, did you know Linda Kent, by any chance?"

"I knew her, but not well. Most of us at this end of the block run into her, from time to time." Anita pursed her lips. "I had heard that she passed. I'm sorry about that."

"Yes, it took place on Sunday night around midnight. Did you hear anything that night, maybe a shout or someone cry for help?"

"No, I didn't. We were asleep by that time. My husband and I go to bed early because he teaches an early class at Widener."

"By the way, did you know Gail Robinbrecht?"

"Yes, we both did. She was such a lovely woman, so full of life. She arranged block parties every summer, and everybody went. We were going to have one in July." Anita's expression changed, folding into lines of fresh grief. "It's awful to think about how she died. We all know how dedicated she was."

"You didn't see or hear anything unusual or suspicious at her house that night, did you?"

"No, not a thing. We told the police."

"I see." Christine peeked past her, where delicious smells of curried something wafted from the kitchen. "Does your house go all the way through, with a backyard out back?"

"Yes, but it was paved over when we bought the house. We use it to park."

"Well, thank you. Again, my condolences." Christine stepped away from the house, heading past Gail's, where the front door to the house, the alley beside it, and the sidewalk were cordoned off with yellow crime-scene tape.

The memorial was larger, with more candles, bouquets of flowers, homemade signs, and a bunch of heart-shaped Mylar balloons floating in the breeze. Christine recognized the same two nurses from Saturday in front of the memorial, both in scrubs, with their laminated employee IDs around their necks on green lanyards; the one was young, perhaps in her twenties, with her silky black hair in a braid down her back, and the other looked older and was heavyset, with auburn hair chopped into neat layers and pearl earrings that dressed up her scrubs. They glanced up as Christine approached, their pained eyes meeting hers, their expressions changing as they seemed to recognize her.

"Hello," Christine said uncertainly. "I'm sorry for your loss."

"Thank you," the older one said.

The younger one nodded, wiping her eyes. "Yes, thanks."

Christine asked, "Did you work with Gail at the hospital?"

"Yes. We were on the same unit, orthopedic surgery. We saw you here Saturday, didn't we?"

"Yes."

"You didn't know Gail, did you?"

"No, I didn't." Christine thought fast, gesturing behind her. "I'm a paralegal for a lawyer in town. We're looking into the fatal accident that occurred Sunday night, in which one of the other neighbors, on Daley Street, Linda Kent, died. I don't know if you heard."

"No, what happened?" the older nurse asked, concerned.

"She fell down her back steps and was killed."

"Oh, that's terrible. How old was she?"

"In her forties," Christine answered, guessing. She switched tack. "Gail seemed like a really great person. When I was here the other day with my friend, I heard you saying how dedicated she was."

"Yes, she loved nursing, and everybody at the hospital loved her."

"Her family must be really upset," Christine said, fishing. "Are they local?"

"No, they live in Minnesota. They'll be coming in for the vigil."

"Vigil?"

"Yes, the hospital is holding a special service, tomorrow afternoon at three. Everyone's been grieving, and our administrator thought it would be a tribute to her and help us heal. It's open to the public, too. She had so many friends, and the neighbors want to come."

The younger nurse wiped her nose. "I don't know how I'll get through it."

The older nurse put an arm around her. "You can do it, honey. You'll do it for Gail."

Christine's chest tightened, seeing their pain, but she couldn't forget her mission. "I know she lived on the second floor. Do you know who lived on the first?"

"Yes, an older woman. June Jacoby, she's a sweetheart, just turned eighty. Gail always checked in on her. She had diabetes."

"Do you know where she is?" Christine wondered if she would have seen or heard anything.

"She went to her sister's in Atlanta. She was so sad about Gail, but she had to leave her apartment since the police taped it up as a crime scene."

"I see. Do you know when she'll come back?"

"No." The older nurse shook her head, sadly. "Dink will have to get Gail's things out of the apartment. She was her best friend."

"Dink . . . ?" Christine was fishing for the last name.

"It's a nickname. We all work together in orthopedic surgery. Dink's a wreck. A wreck."

"I'm sure." Christine made a mental note of the nickname. "I read that Gail wasn't married. Did she have a boyfriend?"

"No, she didn't," the older nurse answered.

"She didn't?" Christine allowed her voice to reflect her surprise. "She was such a beautiful woman. I'm surprised she wasn't seeing anyone."

"She did about three years ago, but he was killed in Iraq and she never got over it."

"Oh no," Christine said, caught short. She was getting a fuller picture of Gail Robinbrecht, who must have been trying to regain her emotional footing after a terrible loss. It made the nurse's murder all the more poignant because, by all accounts, she seemed like the type of woman who would have gotten back on track, in time.

"She was so dedicated and she spent a lot of time with us and with her other friends. She was a really great girlfriend. Anything you needed, she would be there."

"It's nice to have a girlfriend like that." Christine was thinking of Lauren. "I was here with my best friend on Saturday. I couldn't get through life without her."

"That's what I always say." The older nurse nodded with a game smile. "I tell my husband, 'marriage may not be forever, but girlfriends are' an—" She caught herself mid-sentiment, realizing the irony only belatedly.

"Still," Christine said quickly, "girlfriends *are* forever. People are forever. We never lose the people we love."

"That's true." The older nurse looked over at the younger one, who began to tear up again.

"I'll leave you alone, I have to keep going anyway. Good-bye." Christine walked away stiffly, burdened with a guilt that she couldn't identify. She walked to 307, the last house on Warwick, which had a red-lacquered front door, black shutters, and a wreath of dried flowers on the front door. She knew someone was home because she could hear children giggling on the other side of the door. She knocked, and the door was opened by an adorable Indian-American girl, with dark eyes and eyelashes for miles.

"Hi!" she said with a big smile, and Christine smiled back.

"Hi, is your mommy or daddy home?"

"Emma, don't answer the door!" someone called out in mild alarm, and the next moment, a woman rushed to the door, presumably Emma's mother, taking the little girl gently by the shoulder and placing her protectively behind her. The mother was a short, slender Indian-American woman in a gray Penn T-shirt with cutoff shorts, who blew a dark tendril of curly hair from her eyes. "Hello. How can I help you?"

"Sorry to disturb you." Christine introduced herself, handed over the business card, and told the same cover story.

"Hello, my name is Jerri Choudhoury."

"I'm wondering if you heard or saw anything unusual the night Linda Kent was killed?"

"No, I didn't."

"Did you hear her scream or even fall? This would be Sunday, around midnight."

"No. I must say, I'm sure there's no basis for a negligence lawsuit." Jerri shook her head. "You can ask any of the neighbors, Linda had a drinking problem and I'm sure that's why she fell. I didn't allow the children around her for that reason. Her language was often inappropriate. She used to scare my little boy. You probably know, she didn't work. She was on disability, for her back, or so she said."

Christine made a mental note. "Were you home the night she had her accident?"

"With two young children?" Jerri chuckled ruefully. "Of course. My husband and I never go anywhere. If we didn't have On Demand, we would never see a movie, and we never get to watch the entire show."

Christine smiled, not bothering to explain that she prayed for that very life. "But you didn't hear anything?"

"No, we were asleep. My husband uses a sound machine."

"By the way, my condolences on the loss of your neighbor, Gail Robinbrecht. That must be so upsetting."

"Horrifying!" Jerri's dark eyes flew open, and she leaned closer to Christine, lowering her voice. "It's *horrifying* to think that a serial killer struck so near. If they hadn't caught him, I'd never have slept again."

"I'm sure." Christine had her standard last question. "By the way, did you notice anything unusual that night, out back of Gail Robinbrecht's house?"

"Not that night, but I told the police what I saw."

"What did you see?" Christine asked, keeping her tone light.

"I saw the *serial killer*," Jerri answered, eager to share. "The one they arrested!"

"You did? What was he doing?" Christine let her face show the surprise she felt.

"I saw him going up the back stairs to Gail's apartment on the Thursday before she was murdered."

"Really?" Christine hid her confusion. Zachary had told her that he had met Robinbrecht for the first time on Sunday, the night before she was murdered. "When did you see him, what time?"

"At about eleven thirty at night. After the news."

"My God, how did you know it was him?"

"I saw him, clearly." Jerri glanced behind her, checking on the giggling children, then turned back, warming to her story. "Our backyard is in the back, and I was putting out the recycling. I happened to look up, and I saw Gail opening her door and a very handsome blond man coming into her apartment. I saw her give him a hug, then they went inside."

"Wow. How did you know it was him? It would have been dark, right?"

"I could see, easily. When he came inside the kitchen, it was light and I could see." Jerri's eyes lit up. "He's a *ve*ry good-looking man. I thought 'oh, good for Gail, she's seeing such a hottie!' I was happy for her. We always go to the block parties, and we liked her so much. Emma adored her, she was wonderful with children."

"And you told the police this, about seeing the man?"

"Certainly. When they arrested the man, Jeffcoat, I saw his photo on the TV, and when they came around asking, I told them, I saw him before. I went to the police station and gave a statement."

Christine made a mental note. "Did you know if Gail was seeing anybody else?"

"No, I don't. My hands are full." Jerri looked back over her shoulder as the children started to fuss. "I should go, I'm sorry."

"Please, just one last question. Did you generally notice visitors going up and down the stairs to her apartment?"

"Gail's? No, but I'm never in the backyard. Richard takes out the recycling and the trash. The night I saw the killer, Richard had fallen asleep on the couch, and I didn't have the heart to wake him up. I'm never out back otherwise."

"I see. Well, thank you very much, I appreciate it."

Christine left the house and walked down the street, troubled that Zachary had lied to her about meeting Gail Robinbrecht before. She wondered if Thursday was the first time he had been there, or if he had been seeing her earlier. And if it was the first time he had lied, as well. This wasn't the time to figure it out, because she had her work cut out for her, hoping to find more answers around the corner on Daley Street, where Linda Kent had lived.

And died.

Chapter Thirty-five

Christine kept walking to the end of Warwick Street, turned the corner onto the cross street, Latham, and walked along Latham until she reached the skinny backstreet that ran between the houses on Warwick and Daley Streets. She walked partway up the backstreet, taking pictures of the back of Linda Kent's house. She confirmed that it was directly across from Gail Robinbrecht's apartment, so that Kent would have a perfect view of men going in and out of Robinbrecht's.

Christine slid her phone back in her purse, left the backstreet, and turned right on Latham toward Daley. She passed the very spot where she had met Linda Kent sweeping up, and it struck her for the first time that she didn't understand why Kent was sweeping so far from her own house, essentially around the corner. She made a mental note though she wasn't sure it mattered, and turned onto Daley, scanning the street.

Daley was almost identical to Warwick, lined with cars parked in front of well-maintained brick row houses, each with different shutter and door colors, outdoor decoration, or foliage. She started with the house on the corner, number 507, feeling hopeful.

The house was the best kept so far, with a buttercup-yellow door and matching window boxes, bursting with English ivy.

Christine knocked and waited, and the door was answered fairly quickly by an attractive brunette in her fifties, who had on a white polo shirt, tan riding britches, and black boots. Christine introduced herself, gave out the business card, then said, "I'm working for a lawyer in town, and we're looking into the fatal accident involving Linda Kent."

"Oh yes." The woman's face fell, her brow knitting. "That was really unfortunate. How awful. I'm Rachel Cannonette, by the way."

"Hi, Rachel. We're looking into if there was some problem with the steps, perhaps some negligence in construction or repair that could've caused her fall."

"I see. She did rent, the duplexes are rentals. It would be their responsibility to repair the steps, but the Realtor is Cobblestone, and they do a really good job. The man who owns the company lives in town, it's not as if he's an absentee landlord. So, in terms of fault, it's not on Cobblestone." Rachel arched an eyebrow. "I don't like to speak ill, but Linda Kent was an alcoholic."

"I have heard that." Christine thought of something. "I know that she used to sweep close to your house. Did you ever see her do that?"

"All the time." Rachel half-smiled. "That's why my boyfriend calls her the 'wicked witch.' She was always with her broom."

"Why did she sweep here, if her house was at 505?"

"I'm not quite sure." Rachel shook her head. "She used to sweep all the time, almost compulsively. I know she didn't work, she had nothing else to do. My boyfriend thought she used the sweeping to spy on all of us."

Christine thought it answered her question. "Did you know her?"

"No. Truth to tell, I avoided her. She tended to filibuster. Otherwise, I had no problem with her because she policed these houses like nobody's business."

"What do you mean?"

"Cobblestone has a lot of rules for renters in the duplexes. No pets, no partying, no smoking. The rules work fine for me because I like it quiet. I'm a public-interest lawyer, I work long hours and so does my boyfriend. In summertime, I ride at night, so I get home late and I don't want partying. We don't want this part of town to turn into the other part of town, where the WCU campus is."

"I understand completely. By the way, did you hear any noise, like a shout or a scream the night that she was killed? After all, she fell down the stairs."

"No, I didn't hear anything." Rachel averted her eyes in thought. "My boyfriend wasn't home, just me. He was out of town."

"How did you find out what happened?"

"When I left the next morning, one of the neighbors told me."

"Who?"

"The girls who live on the first floor of her house, Kimberly and Lainey Merzinka. They're sisters, waitresses. By the time I got out, the ambulance was gone."

"What time was that?"

"I was out by eight. I think Linda was found closer to dawn."

"Do you know who found her?"

"No." Rachel checked her watch. "I hope that helps. I've got to get to the barn before it gets too dark."

"By the way, I'm sorry about Gail Robinbrecht."

"I know, isn't that so awful? I thought she was so nice. She always made a point to include our street in her block parties, and it's shocking to think that a serial killer struck so close to home. I lock my door and my car, now. I never did before."

"I'm sure."

"I'm so glad they caught him. I'm not a fan of the death penalty, but I hope he rots in prison."

Christine shuddered but kept it to herself. "Did you see or hear anything unusual that night Gail was killed? I noticed that you have a view of her back staircase."

"No, the police asked me that, too, but I was at the barn that night. I stayed late because my horse was colicky."

Christine hadn't known that horses could get colic, only babies. "Did you ever see the man they locked up, Zachary Jeffcoat, at Gail's before?"

"No. Okay, well, I have to leave. Thank you."

"Thanks." Christine stepped away, feeling a tingle of anticipation as she approached the next house, 505. That was Linda Kent's house, and if anybody had heard or seen anything on the night Linda was killed, it would be her downstairs neighbors, Kimberly and Lainey, the sisters.

Christine went to the door, which was black and matched the shutters, and she was about to knock when suddenly the door was flung open, and a blonde and a brunette in their early twenties came out, tottering on wobbly black platform shoes, enveloped in a cloud of powdery perfume.

"How funny!" the blonde squealed. "I didn't know you were there, did you knock?"

"No, I'm sorry, I was about to." Christine introduced herself and gave her a business card and quick cover story.

"Okay, hi, I'm Kimberly, and that's Lainey." The sisters had on matching uniforms, a black-and-white checked vest with no shirt underneath and black satin shorts. Lainey closed and locked the door behind them.

Christine said, "I was wondering if you could help, I just have a question or two about Linda Kent."

"Sorry, we can't talk, we're late for work." Lainey aimed the fob at an old red Jetta parked on the street. An oversized white purse dangled from the crook of her arm, and her skin glistened with glittery moisturizer.

"I'll walk you for a minute." Christine fell into step with them. "I'm sorry about your loss. It must be sad to have a neighbor die, so suddenly."

"Oh, yeah, that's sad," Kimberly said, with a glossy pout.

"Really sad," Lainey added. "She wasn't even that old."

Christine asked, "How well did you know Linda?"

"Not very well, because of our hours," Kimberly answered, while Lainey went to the driver's side of the Jetta. "We work at night, at Burnsie's on 202? When you work at night, you sleep during the day. We don't know many of the neighbors."

"Were you home the night she fell?" Christine walked Kimberly to the Jetta, where she stopped at the back fender.

"No, our only night off is Wednesday."

Christine made a mental note. "What time did you get home Sunday night?"

"Not 'til four. We went over a friend's house after work and got in really late. We didn't even hear the ambulance come the next morning, on Monday. It didn't run the sirens, that's why."

"Who found Linda then, do you know?"

"Our next-door neighbor, Dom. They live right there, at 503." Kimberly pointed with a manicured acrylic nail. "Yo, I appreciate you work for a lawyer and all, but you know Linda fell because she's a total drunk. You knew that, right?"

"I had heard she had a drinking problem." Christine switched gears. "By the way, the night that Gail Robinbrecht was murdered, did you see anything unusual on her staircase?"

"Gail was so the coolest! We loved her parties, and it's horrible that she's dead. We can't even deal." Kimberly grimaced. "Our mom freaked the hell out, too. She wants us to move home now."

"Did you see anything unusual at Gail's the night she was murdered?"

"No, we were working that night, too. We weren't home, and I'm so glad they caught that guy. So horrible!"

Christine couldn't let it go. "I'm asking because the back of your apartment is directly across from Gail Robinbrecht's."

"I know, but we never go in the backyard. We just use it for trash, and that's where Linda used to hang, on her stairs. She smoked there."

"Really?" Christine sensed something wasn't adding up, but she couldn't put her finger on it.

"Yes, the landlord's big on the rules. No smoking in the apartments. Linda smoked outside, a lot."

"I wonder if that's why she was out on her steps that late? Because she was smoking?"

"Prolly."

"When did she usually go to bed, do you know?"

"I only know from my night off. She smoked her last cigarette at midnight, usually. I know because I could smell it. I used to smoke so I didn't mind." Kimberly dug in her oversized black purse. "You said you work for her lawyer, right?"

"Well, uh—" Christine started to say, but before she could answer, Kimberly had rummaged around in her purse, wedged a key from her key ring, and handed it over.

"Here, take it. She gave us her key in case she got locked out, but would you give it to her lawyer?"

"Yes, thanks." Christine hid her excitement as she pocketed the key.

"We gotta go, nice talking to you." Kimberly turned to the passenger door, then stopped. "Oh wait, here's Dom now. Dom, come here a second!"

"Great," Christine said, as Kimberly flagged down a trim, compact man in aviator sunglasses and a khaki suit, who was getting out of a parked blue BMW. Dom waved back, then walked over, hoisting a leather messenger bag to his shoulder. He slid off his sunglasses with a hooked index finger, revealing bright blue eyes and a lean, tanned face, with short gray hair.

"Hey, Kimberly, how are you doing?"

"Good." Kimberly hurried to the Jetta, talking to him on the fly. "Dom, I have to go to work, but you should talk to this lady. Her name's Christine and she's a paralegal and she's asking about Linda. Do you mind? We're super late for work."

"Not at all, take care." Dom turned to Christine with a polite smile. "Dom Gagliardi. Nice to meet you. Which law firm did you say you were with?"

"I'm Christine Nilsson, a paralegal with Francis Griffith." Christine handed him the business card.

"Griffith?" Dom eyed the card with a frown. "I don't know his firm. I work in corporate insurance, in Philly. We use a lot of civil firms in West Chester, but I don't recognize this one."

Christine wanted to change subjects. "We're looking into the circumstances of Linda Kent's death, whether there was any negligence involved in her fall. Kimberly said that you found Linda. Do you think you could show me where?"

"Sure, follow me." Dom turned toward the house. "You get to the second-floor apartment through this alley, here. Obviously, the front door's only for the first floor."

"Right." Christine fell in behind him, and they walked through the long alley between the two row houses, which was only wide enough to hold a single person. "Do you know if there are any security cameras around here?"

"No, I doubt it. There's not even security lights. It's safe, or it used to be. People don't even lock their doors. I do, but I grew up in Queens."

"What about surveillance cameras, nothing like that?"

"No, it's residential. Downtown or the campus may have, but not here." Dom chuckled. "West Chester is a stop-time. My wife calls it Mayberry. She's from the area."

"Any traffic cameras that you know of?" Christine realized the answer as soon as she asked. "Oh, whoops. There's no traffic lights."

"Right, it's great for runners. I never worry about getting hit, like I used to in Manhattan." Dom stopped as the alley ended in a wooden stairwell and pointed down to the concrete at the bottom of the stairs. "Here. This is where I found her, at the bottom of the stairs."

"I see." Christine didn't see blood or other marks on the concrete, and she scanned the small, narrow backyard, which was completely paved. Trash cans and recycling bins sat on the right, against an old privacy fence. There was a back privacy gate with a barrel lock, and a sign read PROPERTY OF COBBLESTONE REALTY MANAGEMENT.

"It was really pretty horrible."

"I'm sorry," Christine said, sympathetic. "I hate to ask you, but what did Linda look like? I mean, could you tell how she had fallen?"

"No, I couldn't." Dom grimaced. "I knew right away she was dead, because her neck was bent and her eyes were open, staring upward."

"Was there blood or anything?"

"No blood." Dom shook his neat head. "Her legs didn't look broken, but they were bent underneath her, like she had fallen down the steps."

"Was she lying faceup?"

"Yes, she was, and her head was right here." Dom stepped over to the base of the steps. "Her head was facing near the steps, and her legs were toward our house."

"What was she wearing?"

"Shorts and a T-shirt. She was barefoot, I did notice that."

Christine made a note. "How did you happen to find her?"

"I run every morning before work. It's a long commute with the traffic on 202, so I leave early. I get up and run at five thirty."

"What were you doing out back?"

"I stretch in the backyard, then I leave by our back gate." Dom gestured over the privacy fence to his grassy backyard with a bistro table, which ended in an iron gate. "I was stretching and I happened to look over the fence. You can see it's not that high, and there she was. I went over to do CPR but she didn't have a pulse. Her skin was cool." Dominic wrinkled his nose in distaste. "I called 911, and they got here with an ambulance."

"So do you know when it happened, did the police give you any indication of that?"

"You could probably get that information from the coroner, but I think I heard them say that they think it was around midnight."

Christine noted that it dovetailed with what she already knew. "Did you hear any sound around midnight, that night? Any cry for help or even her bumping down the stairs, as grisly as that sounds?"

"No, but I go to bed early and I take Ambien. So does my wife. There's a lot of stress on my job."

Christine made a mental note, using the pause to switch tack. "By the way, my condolences on the loss of your neighbor, Gail Robinbrecht."

"I know, Gail was a nice person, and we both liked her. We went to her parties, she included everyone, and she was so good to my neighbors on the other side, the Davidsons."

Christine's ears pricked up. It was the next house she was going to.

"They're a retired couple, but they're never home these days. They have a new grandbaby in Toledo and they've been there for three months."

Christine crossed that one off her mental list of houses to visit. "How did she know them?"

"Bill Davidson had a procedure at Chesterbrook, and Gail went out of her way to make sure he was okay. It was just thoughtful, and Bill really appreciated it." Dom frowned. "We're so glad they got the guy who did it. It blows my mind to think that he was right here. Lately there's been too much bad news."

"Did you hear anything or see anything suspicious the night Gail was killed?"

"The police asked us, too, but we didn't. Like I say, Ambien works."

"By the way, did you ever notice people going to visit Gail Robinbrecht's house, coming up the back steps?"

"No, but about Linda Kent, if your boss is looking for somebody to sue, he's barking up the wrong tree. Insurance is my business, and people don't realize that when you sue an insurance company, you're still suing somebody." Dom gestured at the staircase. "Take a look at those steps, they're in fine condition. It didn't rain that night, and there was no reason for them to be slippery. Linda had an alcohol problem, everybody knows that. That's why she fell. It wasn't negligence."

"I did hear that." Christine's heart sank at the consensus, and the alcohol issue made her doubt Linda Kent's reliability as a witness to anything on Robinbrecht's back stairs. "Did Linda use the back steps to smoke?"

"Yes. She sat up in her chair up there, with the crossword puzzle, chain-smoking. It drove us nuts." Dom pursed his lips. "We kept our back windows closed, and when my wife mentioned it to her, she called us 'health nuts' and blew the smoke in our direction. Now, if you don't mind, I have to go get dinner before I start answering phone calls from our West Coast office."

"No, I understand completely. Thanks, I appreciate your time."

"Bye." Dom left by the alley.

"Bye, thanks." Christine turned toward the steps.

Linda Kent's apartment key was burning a hole in her pocket.

Chapter Thirty-six

Christine took pictures as she ascended Linda Kent's staircase and stopped at the landing outside the apartment door, where Kent had set up a smoking area. There was a gray folding chair with worn cushions set against the wooden railing on the right, and to the left, nearer the door, was a metal tray table with newspapers folded to the crossword puzzle, a few red Pilot pens, and an overflowing beanbag ashtray.

The date of the newspaper on top was Sunday, and the crossword puzzle was half-completed, sadly. She took photos of the sitting area, then turned to her left, taking more photos and confirming that Kent had not only a perfect view of Robinbrecht's staircase and back door, but even into her kitchen, which had a window across the way, though it was darkened now.

Christine put her phone back into her purse, took out the apartment key, opened the screen door, and unlocked the front door, though she hesitated at the threshold, at the violation of Kent's privacy. Christine didn't know what she expected to find, but she wanted to learn as much as she could while she had the chance. She resolved to do a quick walk-through and she closed the door behind her.

The front door opened into a small, square kitchen, which was surprisingly neat. White wood cabinets ringed the room, but looked as if they had been wiped down regularly, because they and the buttercup-yellow countertop, of Formica, showed absolutely no dirt, crumbs, or even pen marks. If there was liquor around, it was hidden. On the counter next to the door was a pack of Virginia Slims, with a transparent blue lighter on top. A toaster oven, a cof-feemaker, and a small television sat next to the refrigerator, and the dish rack was empty. A round wood table in the center of the room was equally clean, holding only a stack of napkins, and a salt-shaker.

Christine swallowed hard, chastising herself for barging in, but made herself stay on task. She took her phone from her purse and snapped a few pictures, then walked through the kitchen, getting the layout of the apartment. To the left was a bedroom, to the right the bathroom, and beyond that was another bedroom that Mrs. Kent had converted to a living room.

Christine walked through, taking pictures, but nothing she saw seemed helpful. The furniture in the living room was in-expensive and generic, and there were no magazines or books around, except for stacks of crossword puzzle and Sudoku books on the coffee table. Christine realized she was looking at the evidence of a life that was lonely, and she wasn't seeing anything that Kent did to nurture herself or feed her interests.

Christine left the living room and walked into the bedroom, but she stopped at the doorway, not wanting to invade Kent's pri-vacy more than necessary. She took a picture of a bedroom that was as neat as the rest of the house, with a carefully made bed and a bare wooden chair that contained a stack of freshly folded and laundered clothes. A pair of pink flip-flops sat side by side in front of the bed, where they had been taken off, presumably.

Christine left the bedroom, heading back toward the kitchen, mulling it over. If Kent usually had her last cigarette around midnight, and the police had estimated that the time of death was about that time, it made sense to think that Mrs. Kent fell after she smoked her last cigarette or while she was smoking. Then Christine realized something didn't jibe.

Kent's flip-flops were beside her bed, as if she had just taken them off. So why did she take them off before she went outside for her cigarette? The landing of the stairwell was wood, and most people would have been wary of splinters, which meant that Kent would've kept her flip-flops on. But Dominic had said that she was barefoot when he found her at the foot of the stairs.

Christine tested her theory by viewing it the opposite way. Kent could've gone outside barefoot, and it fit with her profile, too. It's not as if Kent were so conventional; her arms were covered with tattoos. She liked the Ramones. So the fact that she was outside barefoot probably didn't mean anything.

Christine walked to the kitchen, opened the door, and was just about to leave when her gaze fell on the pack of cigarettes with the lighter, sitting on the counter by the door. Christine thought about it a moment, trying to reconstruct what happened that night. Kent presumably fell during or after her last cigarette of the night. So why would her lighter still be inside, on top of her pack of cigarettes?

Christine considered it, wondering. The landlord's rule was, no smoking in the apartments. So Kent had gone outside to smoke. But people who smoked outside didn't light up inside, did they? Christine wasn't a smoker, but her late mother-in-law had been and her mother-in-law hadn't smoked in her house. Her mother-in-law kept her cigarettes and lighter by the door, and her smoking ritual was the same every time; her mother-in-law pulled a cigarette from the pack, then stepped outside with her lighter. Her mother-in-law lit up the cigarette outside, smoked it, came back inside, and put the lighter back on top of the cigarette pack.

Christine blinked, eyeing the cigarette pack and the lighter.

She considered the darker possibilities, the one she had come here to explore, that Kent's death hadn't been an accident, then tried to reconstruct an alternate scenario. If Kent wasn't killed while she was outside smoking, then there had to be some reason for her to be outside.

Christine thought about it. Perhaps Kent had already gone to bed, or was just about to, and had taken off her flip-flops but not her clothes. What if there was a knock at the door and she was going to answer it, but it had been the serial killer, coming to silence her because she had seen him go up Robinbrecht's staircase? What if the serial killer had entered as soon as she opened the door, pushed her inside, and silently broken her neck?

Christine realized that that scenario made perfect sense, and it also answered the question that had been bothering her, why hadn't the neighbors heard anything? Some of the neighbors had been asleep or on Ambien, but not all of them. Somebody should've heard *something* when Kent slipped and fell down the stairs; a cry for help, an exclamation, profanity, or the horrible sound of someone falling down a wooden stairwell, a bumping as she rolled down the stairs.

Christine felt the realization dawn on her. No one heard that because none of that happened. The killer could have killed Kent in her kitchen, then carried her quickly down the stairs, placed her at the bottom, and left by the alley, with nobody seeing him. Christine felt the hair stand up on the back of her neck. She realized that the alternative scenario was completely possible, and it reconciled with what she had learned tonight from the neighbors.

She took one last look around the kitchen, then headed for the door.

Chapter Thirty-seven

Christine called Griff as she walked back to her car, her head swimming with what she had learned at Kent's apartment. She was feeling more right about her suspicions than ever and couldn't wait to talk it over with him. She listened to the phone ring again and again, then the ringing stopped. No voicemail or message machine kicked in. She'd have to go back to the office to talk to him.

She reached her car, chirped it unlocked, climbed inside, and started the engine and the AC. She felt a wave of fatigue and hunger but ignored them, steering out of the space. She had to go to the bathroom, but it wouldn't take long to get to Griff's. She plugged the address into GPS because West Chester had so many one-way streets, then she pulled out of the space, went straight, then turned right, following the directions.

Her phone started ringing on the dashboard, presumably Griff calling back, and she answered right away. "Griff, you're not going to believe this!" she said, but when she glanced at the screen, it wasn't Griff but Marcus.

"It's your husband, remember me?" he asked, bristling.

"Sorry." Christine kept calm.

"What is it that Griff isn't going to believe?" Marcus asked, his sarcasm undisguised.

"If you really want to know, I think I figured out that there was someone other than Zachary who was seen at the apartment and that a witness—"

"Spare me, Nancy Drew. Tell it to *Zachary*."

"Fine." Christine didn't want to fight with him. She headed uphill, past the pretty row houses. Runners ran by, now that the humidity had dissipated, and residents were out watering their plantings. Lights glowed from within the mullioned windows, and the sky darkened to a soft shade of periwinkle.

"Have you seen *Zachary*?"

"No." Christine ignored his tone. "How are you?"

"I'm fine. When are you coming home?"

"I'm not sure yet. I'll keep you posted. I'm fine, you don't have anything to worry about, and I'm doing something that matters to me."

"What *are* you doing?"

"Come down and find out."

Marcus scoffed. "So you won't tell me what you're doing and you won't tell me when you're coming home?"

"Marcus, if you really want to know what I'm doing, please, get in the car and come down. I'm staying at the Warner Hotel in town."

"No, I have work."

"You can take a few days off, and you know it."

"What you're doing is wrong. I'm not buying in."

"Then we agree to disagree." Christine swallowed hard. Part of her wondered if this counted as separation. It felt like one. They'd never been at such odds. She thought of what Marcus had said in Gary's office. *This is ruining our marriage.*

"I'm calling because Gary spoke with Homestead, and they won't confirm or deny that Jeffcoat is our donor without our filing suit. They aren't buying our waiver argument, at least not yet."

"So now what happens?" Christine took a left turn and braked behind a line of other cars, a long line of red stoplights.

"Gary's going to file the papers and show Homestead we mean business. He's hoping that will make them more inclined to settle."

"Good." Christine glanced around, stalled in traffic. She had left the residential neighborhood, and busy restaurants lined the street.

"I didn't tell Gary where you were. I covered for you."

"You can tell him where I am. I'm not ashamed of what I'm doing, and he's the one who said it was self-help, which it is." Christine fed the car gas when the traffic started to move, inching uphill.

"Christine, I really hope you're not damaging our lawsuit."

"Nothing I'm doing is going to hurt the lawsuit. Nobody here knows Zachary is our donor. Griff doesn't even know I'm pregnant."

"They will when we file suit."

"How? Zachary's in prison, Marcus. It's not like he has a phone, and I don't know if his email has been set up. They might not even try to contact him."

"He'll have Internet. It's public record. He can find out. Your buddy Griff can find out, too."

Christine couldn't help but smile, at the irony. Thank God Griff didn't have Internet. "I'll ask Gary how that works."

"No, don't. I don't want you to do anything that interferes with this lawsuit."

"It wouldn't interfere with the lawsuit. It would just be asking a question about what could happen. You heard what Gary said, it's a parallel track. What I already found out about Zachary improved our position. So the waiver argument didn't pan out, so what? Like Gary said, we haven't lost anything."

Marcus groaned. "It's embarrassing. This whole thing is embarrassing."

"Why? Because you couldn't control your wife? Like I'm not a person with a will of my own? Since when did you become so sexist?"

"I'm not embarrassed for my sake, I am embarrassed for your sake. You're embarrassing yourself."

"Thank you for that vote of confidence," Christine snapped, and on impulse, she pressed END to hang up, her throat tight.

The stalled traffic became a blur of red lights, and she tried to remember the last time she'd hung up on her husband. She'd never felt so separate from him, ever before. She wished she could have shared with him what she'd figured out about Linda Kent, so she could make him see that what she was doing was for a good reason. But she'd have to stop trying. Marcus had said it was too much to ask him to join her. With or without him, this was her mission, and she had to see it through, for her sake and for the baby's. It still didn't stop the tears from welling up in her eyes, but she blinked them away.

She had another call to make.

Chapter Thirty-eight

Traffic slowed, and Christine waited until it was safe to make the call. "Gary, do you have a minute?" she asked as soon as he picked up.

"I assume you talked to Marcus. Don't worry. Just because Homestead didn't cave on the phone doesn't mean—"

"That's not what I'm calling about." Christine took a deep breath, giving the car gas. "I need to clarify something. We're still going to file suit against Homestead, is that right?"

"Yes, that's correct."

"When are you going to do that?"

"Tomorrow."

"And my name is on the case, right?"

"The caption? Yes. The caption reads Marcus Nilsson and Christine Nilsson versus Homestead and its parent company, Homestead International. Is that what you're asking?"

"Yes." Christine could imagine it, having seen the papers. "Now here's my question. When you file that in court, is it public record?"

"Yes."

"So people can see it?"

"In theory, yes, but only in theory. Marcus asked me the same question since the fact that you used a donor isn't public knowledge."

Christine felt surprised since Marcus hadn't mentioned that detail to her.

"It's public but it's not easy for the public to know. It's not like the court sends out a bulletin to anybody. You have to know a lawsuit was filed before you even search for it, then you have to search for it on the district court's website, which is impossible to use if you're a layperson. Hell, it's not easy to use if you're a lawyer."

Christine breathed easier. "Right, okay, so how does Homestead get a copy?"

"I serve it on them."

"Does that mean you mail it?"

"Yes. I mail it to their lawyer. He's agreed to accept service."

"Do you send a copy to Zachary Jeffcoat?"

"No. He's not a party."

"Does Homestead send a copy to Zachary Jeffcoat?"

"No, I doubt it. As I say, he's not a party."

Christine breathed a relieved sigh. "So Zachary won't necessarily know that a lawsuit is being filed that involves him?"

"Correct, but let's be precise. As a legal matter, our lawsuit doesn't involve Zachary Jeffcoat. It involves only his donation. I doubt Homestead will notify him about the lawsuit."

"Why? They know, because of us, that Zachary is Donor 3319, and therefore they know he's in Graterford. Why don't they mail him papers?"

"They have no reason to. If this were a case in which Jeffcoat's donation was tainted or carried a disease, for example, if he carried Tay-Sachs or some other illness, then I could see them notifying him. But there's no regs or laws that require that. That's part of the problem we're dealing with in our lawsuit, the absence of laws in this area." Gary snorted. "They're hoisted on their own petards."

"So they wouldn't have any reason to notify him?"

"No. Besides, the only other reason parties to litigation reach out is to join others as codefendants or to seek indemnification against them for damages. In other words, to get money out of them. Homestead doesn't need to do that with Jeffcoat. It and its parent company have a deep pocket, and I'm sure Jeffcoat is judgment-proof."

"What does judgment-proof mean?"

"Broke. So I doubt they'll let him know. Why are you asking?"

Christine decided to come clean. "I'm back in Pennsylvania, working as a paralegal on Zachary's defense."

"For real?" Gary asked, surprised. "But you're a teacher."

"Never underestimate the power of a teacher."

"I'm not, but you're not trained in legal research."

"I'm not doing legal research, I'm doing factual research. It's common sense. Your wife is a paralegal, isn't she? Did she go to paralegal school?"

"No, she didn't. I trained her."

"Same here. The lawyer is training me."

"This Griff guy?" Gary chuckled softly. "Oh, man. But Griff doesn't know why you're really there. I get it, now."

"Yes, and I was wondering how much time I had before my cover was blown."

"You have time." Gary chuckled softly again. "I'm going to be in trouble with your husband, aren't I?"

"I'm your client, too," Christine shot back, firm. "Last question. This doesn't hurt our lawsuit in any way, does it?"

"No, it doesn't."

"I'm just engaging in self-help, like you said."

"I created a monster."

"No, it's not on you, it's on me." Christine felt the conviction in her words as she drove into town. "The more I learn about this case, the more I doubt that Zachary's really a serial killer."

"What does Marcus say?"

"He's not happy."

"But he knows where you are, you told him?"

"Yes, I asked him to come, and he said no. I know what I'm doing and I know why I'm doing it. I don't have to justify it to anybody."

"Okay, relax, I understand." Gary's voice softened. "You and Marcus are in a tough position. I don't want to get in the middle. My only word of caution is that Jeffcoat could be manipulating you. He's desperate right now, desperate to get anybody to help him, listen to him, or champion his defense. Don't be his sucker."

"I won't," Christine said, more confidently than she felt.

Chapter Thirty-nine

I brought you some carbohydrates," Christine said, leading with her pizza box as she entered the lawyer's office, which was dark. Night had fallen outside the window, and his desk lamp had an old-fashioned green glass shade, which glowed in a homey, throwback way.

"Trying to get on my good side?" Griff looked up from his cluttered desk, his eyes pinkish with strain and his eyelids heavy behind his tortoiseshell glasses, which needed cleaning again. The sleeves of his oxford shirt were ringed with wrinkles, and his bow tie angled on a slant, like a stopped airplane propeller.

"Hoping for a raise."

"Good luck. Though we did get paid."

"Really, how?" Christine cleared a space on the desk for the brown bag containing sodas, napkins, and plates, and the pizza, which wreathed the air with delicious tomato-and-mozzarella smells.

"The girlfriend dropped it off."

"Did you meet her?" Christine asked, intrigued.

"No. It came in while I was out. She left it at the front desk. They take hand-deliveries for me." Griff dug through the papers on his desk, which was messier than before, and produced a white envelope.

"Can I see?"

"Here." Griff handed her the envelope, which read F.X. Griffith, Esq., on the front, in handwriting. She opened it up and looked inside to see a cashier's check made out to F.X. Griffith, Esq., for $2,500.

"A cashier's check?" Christine said, surprised. "Did you ask her for this, as opposed to a personal check?"

"No." Griff slid off his glasses, set them aside, and rubbed his eyes, then tugged the pizza box toward him. He opened the box, raising an unruly white eyebrow. "You ate three pieces? Sheesh. You can really pack it in."

"Thanks." Christine didn't explain that she was eating for two, or that it was an excellent excuse. She set the check on the desk and sat down in one of the chairs.

"My wife ate like a pig, too."

Christine ignored the "pig" part since he said it with affection. Kind of. "You didn't mention a wife."

"She's dead," Griff said matter-of-factly. "Five years ago. Pancreatic cancer."

"Oh, I'm sorry."

"Don't be. She's in a better place, if you can imagine a better place than living with me." Griff took out a gooey slice of pizza, and before she could stop him, he turned over one of the legal pads and plopped the slice on its cardboard back, using the pad for a plate.

"Griff, there's a paper plate in the bag."

"This is fine."

"Napkins are in the bag, too, and a can of Coke."

"You got kids?" Griff took a bite, chewing noisily.

"None, yet." Christine felt her face flush, but Griff seemed not to notice, tearing into his pizza. Grease covered his lips almost immediately, but she didn't remind him about the napkins. "You?"

"Six. Three girls, three boys, twenty-one grandkids. You're married, aren't you?"

"Yes." Christine shifted forward in the seat, wanting to change the subject. "So I learned a lot tonight, and I want to fill you in. You can let me know if it helps the case."

"Good." Griff finally wiped his mouth. "You talk, so I can eat."

Christine complied, telling him about the flip-flops and cigarette lighter, then that Linda Kent's neighbor had seen Zachary at Robinbrecht's on the Thursday before the murder. By the time she was finished, Griff was sipping his Coke, having gone through three slices of plain pizza and nine napkins, crumpled on top of his desk like greasy origami.

Christine asked, "So what do you think?"

"I think the pizza didn't have enough cheese." Griff sniffed. "Next time get double cheese."

"I mean about what I found out. On balance, I think it helps us because it suggests that there was another person who might have done it." Christine's thoughts were racing. "And the cigarette lighter and the flip-flops show that Mrs. Kent could have let somebody into her apartment, somebody who killed her then carried her downstairs. What if that person was Gail's killer? That's very possible."

"True." Griff set down his Coke can.

"Is this where you say, 'Good work'?"

"No, I never say that," Griff answered, deadpan.

Christine chuckled. "You would be a bad teacher."

"Luckily, I'm an excellent lawyer." Griff blinked, eyeing Christine. "And you're ignoring the fact that Jeffcoat lied to you about when he met Gail for the first time. The police now have a neighbor, an eyewitness, who placed him there earlier."

"Maybe the neighbor was mistaken. They say eyewitness identifications aren't as reliable as everybody used to think. I know I read that in an article, somewhere."

"True, those articles come from cases that hold eyewitness

identification as being unreliable in situations that are stressful, such as when somebody robs a bank and people at the bank were asked to describe the perpetrator. Those cases support the proposition that people do not make reliable eyewitness identifications when they are emotional or stressed." Griff wiped his mouth. "That's not the situation with the neighbor. You're describing to me a woman who goes to put out the trash in her backyard. She looks up because she sees a handsome man calling on her neighbor. In addition, it sounds like the lighting was good. Interior lighting is a factor, as opposed to exterior or outside lighting, like from a streetlamp or moonlight."

Christine swallowed hard. "Maybe Zachary didn't lie, maybe he just misunderstood me. Or maybe he lied because he didn't know me that well. I wasn't working for his defense then. He'd just met me that day. Plus—"

"You're making excuses for him." Griff's aged gaze bored into Christine.

"I'm keeping an open mind."

"No, you're disregarding facts that inculpate Jeffcoat, that is, bad facts that point the finger of blame at him, and you're emphasizing facts that exculpate him, in other words, good facts that get him off the hook."

"No I'm not," Christine said, though she wondered if he was right.

"You believe he's innocent."

"Yes, I do," Christine answered, meaning it. "I'm not absolutely sure, but I do think he's innocent."

Griff lifted a furry white eyebrow. "I would fire you if you weren't working for free."

"Why?" Christine asked, surprised. "We're his legal team, we're supposed to believe in his innocence."

"No, that's only in movies and TV. Unrealistic ones, at that." Griff leaned forward, placing his elbows on the desk. "Jeffcoat does not need our subjective belief, one way or the other, yea or nay. Our job is to get him acquitted. The only way to do that is to be completely objective about the facts as we learn them. That's how we put ourselves in the shoes of the jury, and before that, the district attorney, the FBI, and the prosecutors in Virginia and Maryland."

Christine didn't interrupt Griff because he was on a roll, his gray eyes flashing with a conviction that she sensed had been dormant for a long time.

"If you understand the persuasive weight of the facts against your client, then you can think of an effective argument to meet them. If you don't give the bad facts the weight they truly deserve, then you will never be able to convince the person who does."

"Okay." Christine felt as if she'd just heard why Griff could be good in front of a jury. She rose, coming around the desk to see his notes, which were a mess. "You know, it wouldn't take me very long to read these and organize them. Then we could share the information."

"My old paralegal used to say the same thing."

"Where is she now?" Christine started gathering up the pads.

"She died."

"Sorry." Christine let it go, pointing at the stack of accordions that weren't there earlier. "What are those?"

"Legal research. Relevant cases I pulled out from my files in the back."

"What back?"

"There." Griff gestured vaguely to a side door. "That's where I keep my case files. In the old days I had this whole floor, but since I scaled back, I don't need it."

"Let me see."

"Don't go snooping back there."

"It'll just take a minute." Christine went to the side door, opening it onto a dark corridor, which ended in a back door. She flipped on the light, illuminating a wall of boxes on the left-hand side of the hallway, and on the right, she spotted something that gladdened her heart. "Is that a bulletin board?"

"What did you say?" Griff called from his desk, but Christine was already tugging the bulletin board from behind some old foamcore trial exhibits. She dragged it out of the hallway and into the office. Nobody could set up a bulletin board like a teacher, and she was getting a second wind.

Griff groaned. "What are you doing?"

"Organizing us." Christine rested the bulletin board on the side wall, which was bare. "What did you use this for?"

"My secretary liked to keep track of me. My calendar was up there, and a calendar from my associate, back in the day."

"You had an associate?"

"Yes. His name was Tom, I forget his last name. He was short. I called him Tom Thumb."

Christine let it go. "Do you have any paper towels?"

"No, why?"

Christine blew dust off the top of the bulletin board. "That's why. Please hand me some napkins."

"Why are you doing this?" Griff handed over the napkins.

"We need a bulletin board for the case. One place where all the facts can be collected, maybe a map so we can plot where the three murders occurred, as well as the date and time." Christine wiped dust from the bulletin board. "We need a list of the facts, like you said, the good facts and the bad facts, so that we can analyze them objectively. We need a chronology of the case, so we can fill in the facts."

Griff rolled his eyes. "You want a war room. Maps with little flags, like on TV."

"Yes, but they exist in real life, don't they? Didn't you used to have a war room?"

"War rooms are for lawyers who have an army. I only had me."

"What about Tom Thumb?"

"He lasted six months."

"He quit?"

"He died."

Christine wondered if it was suicide. "You don't play well with others, Griff."

"Don't try and change me. Women always try to change men. It never works."

"I'm not trying to change you. I'm trying to work with you." Christine tossed the dirty napkins into the trash can. "I still don't have most of the important facts of the case."

"But *I* do."

"Where?"

"In my head." Griff pointed to his fluffy gray temple.

"But I need to know things, too. We need to communicate." Christine shot him a look. "Can you get me another napkin? We're a team."

"I'll know more after tomorrow." Griff leaned over the desk, got a napkin, and handed it over. "I'm meeting with the detectives from Maryland and Virginia."

"When did that happen?" Christine wiped down the sides of the bulletin board.

"I set it up on the phone, while you were out. Must I account to you?"

"You have to inform me, not account to me."

"A distinction without a difference." Griff sniffed. "They'll be here tomorrow. Maybe the FBI, too, but I'll know better tomorrow morning."

"Should I meet them with you? It sounds interesting, but I'm not sure it's the best use of my time."

"It isn't. No sense in our duplicating effort. You should continue factual investigation. I can't get around as easy as you, with my bunions."

"Okay." Christine felt pleased that he seemed to be thinking about their working together. "I was thinking I'd go back to Zachary and talk to him about when he first met Robinbrecht, see why he lied. What do you think about that?"

"Do it. See him after the crime scene. Ask him any questions you come up with. See if you can find out if he lied. But only tell me good things."

"What's that mean?"

"When were you born? Yesterday?" Griff sighed theatrically. "If I know he lied, I can't put him on the stand. Lawyers can't lie, officially. Only Congress."

"Okay." Christine understood what he was saying. He wanted deniability.

"After that, pop over to his apartment in Exton. The landlord was expecting me at noon, but you go instead. Snoop around."

"Wow, okay." Christine hadn't thought she'd get to see inside Zachary's apartment. She liked the idea, even if she didn't learn anything about the case. The more she knew about him, the better. "Where does he live?"

"I wrote down the address somewhere." Griff gestured at his messy desk.

"See? That's why we need the bulletin board." Christine bubbled over, only half-kidding. "Organization! Communication! Sharing! Cooperation!"

"Go, team, go." Griff scowled.

"Ha!" Christine set the bulletin board against the wall. She'd need to buy tools to hang it up, plus office supplies, paper towels, Fantastic, and Windex. "Is there a Staples around here?"

"God knows."

"Why don't you look on the Internet? Oh, wait. You don't believe in progress." Christine smiled to herself.

"You're making me tired." Griff rubbed his forehead, leaving pinkish marks.

"So go home, let me take over. Where do you live anyway?"

"None of your business. Go."

"But I'm not tired." Christine would have been exhausted at

home, but fatigue hadn't hit, maybe because so much was at stake. She was curious, and her curiosity led her where it always did, to books. She crossed to the bookshelves and scanned the bound law-books, blue volumes with gold numbers, which read ATLANTIC REPORTER, SECOND SERIES.

"What are you doing now?" Griff asked, wearily, leaning against the desk.

"I wish I knew more about criminal law."

"Leave the law to me."

"It would help if I knew the basics, too." Christine pulled a book off the shelf.

"Don't touch that."

"Would it help if I read a few of these?" Christine opened the book, which had yellowed pages. The print was old-timey and small, and the paper so thin that she could read through to the other side. She read the first line: *this dividing line is significant in a discussion of the extent of riparian rights . . .*

"No. That's a casebook. Reports of decided cases, from all areas of the law. Not just criminal."

"Do you have any books about the basics of criminal law?" Christine closed the casebook and put it back on the shelf.

"You're talking about a hornbook. I have a criminal hornbook from law school."

"Is it still good?"

"Of course. Am I still good?"

Christine let it go. "Where is your hornbook?"

"In one of those boxes." Griff motioned to the hallway, reluctantly.

"Great." Christine went back to the threshold and peered down the hall. Stacked boxes lined the walls on either side, making a narrow walkway between, and there was a wooden door on the left. The boxes bore the printed name CHESTER SPRINGS BUSINESS ARCHIVES, but they weren't labeled on the side. "Are these labeled on top, so you know what's inside?"

"I know what's inside."

Christine didn't believe him. "Do you remember where the hornbooks are?"

"Far right. Second row. Third one from the bottom. But don't go in there."

"Just a minute." Christine walked down the hall, scanning the boxes. She went to the door on the left, opened it, and flicked on the light. It took her a moment to understand what she was seeing, as she took in the windowless white room about the size of a large storage room, with a neatly made single bed on one side next to a night table that held a small, open carton of milk and an unwrapped packet of half-eaten chocolate cupcakes. Next to the table was a dorm-sized refrigerator, a white IKEA cabinet, and a stainless-steel rack of suits—seersucker, light gray wool, heavyweight tweed three-piece—then a rack of striped bow ties and a row of wingtips on a wire shelf at the bottom, each shoe filled with a cedar shoe holder. Attached to the room on the left was a tiny bathroom with a shower. It was obvious that Griff was living here and didn't want her to know that. She felt a stab of sympathy for the old lawyer, and sadness that he had come to such dire straits.

"What are you doing?" Griff called from the office.

"I think I found the box!" Christine called back, closing the door quickly so he wouldn't suspect she had seen anything.

"Don't touch my boxes!" Griff called out from his office.

"I won't, I'm coming back!" Christine swallowed hard as she walked back down the hall and entered the office. "I think I found the right box, but I can't get it out. Do you have a hand cart?"

"Why would I have a hand cart?" Griff sighed, but he looked tired, his lids lower, and Christine knew it was time to go.

"It can wait. Tomorrow, can we borrow a hand cart from the other law firm?"

"Yes, good." Griff went back to his desk and eased into his desk chair slowly, with a squeak from its dry springs. "I'll finish up here. You go."

"You're the boss," Christine said, her throat tight. She went to the door. "See you after my morning stops. I'll keep you posted on what I find."

"Hold on, I almost forgot." Griff dug through the piles on his desk, found a manila envelope, and handed it over. "This is from the police. They didn't have to turn 'em over yet. They threw me a bone."

"What is it?" Christine took the envelope, intrigued.

"Look 'em over. But not before bedtime."

Chapter Forty

The Warner Hotel turned out to be as charming as the rest of West Chester, and Christine's room reminded her of a Victorian dollhouse; it was a cozy size, with a panel of mullioned windows that overlooked a horse pasture, so she didn't have to bother closing the curtains. She left the windows open since the night air was surprisingly cool and smelled fresh, if vaguely earthy. A bed with a chintz canopy and matching bedspread sat on top of a pink-and-green hooked rug, and the dresser and armoire were both carved antiques. Soft crystal lamps gave off a gentle light, lending the room a serene country feel, but even the lovely setting couldn't put Christine's mind at ease.

She couldn't shake the sadness that seemed to sink into her bones as she showered, wrapped her wet hair in a fresh towel, and cocooned herself in a soft terry bathrobe. She kept thinking about Griff's tiny quarters, stuck into what must have been a re-purposed storage room, and she found herself liking him, even though he was a complicated man. There was so much she didn't know about him, like how a man with so much family could be so completely alone, if not lonely. She respected him as a lawyer and admired the energy he was putting into Zachary's case, and she could forgive him his occasional crankiness, especially after what she had seen.

Marcus was always in the back of her mind, too, and Christine kept checking her phone to see if he had called or texted, but he hadn't. She'd held out hope that he would appear at the hotel, having reconsidered his position, but she knew that she was in denial. Marcus wasn't that kind of man, and this rift went too deep to be repaired quickly. She guessed that if he hadn't called yet, he probably wasn't going to; she glanced at the digital clock on the night table, which read 9:45.

Christine's gaze traveled from the clock to the ultrasound photo of the baby, which she'd left on the night table, and she picked it up and eased into a sitting position on the bed, eyeing the image. She felt a surge of the overwhelming protectiveness and love that she'd felt the first time she'd seen the image and every time she'd looked at it thereafter. She remembered the fragile heart she'd seen beating on the monitor, and her loving eyes took in the grayish figure eight of the baby's body, growing inside her. The sight of the baby renewed her strength and resolve. She had to stay strong and accomplish what she came for. She had come this far and she hadn't been wrong yet. If she could keep going, she had a chance of exonerating Zachary and putting her marriage back together.

Christine set the ultrasound photo aside, fetched the envelope Griff had given her, and climbed into bed with it. She sat cross-legged in the middle of the bedspread, opened the old-fashioned brass brad, and peeked inside to see a bunch of photos, which she shook out onto the bed. The top one landed faceup, and just one glance made Christine's gut wrench. She swallowed hard and picked it up, to see it more closely in the low light.

It was a photo of Zachary that the police must have taken after his arrest, the night of Gail Robinbrecht's murder. It appeared to be taken in a home setting, evidently at the crime scene, though an unusually bright light shone on Zachary and illuminated him in a clinical way, probably for evidentiary purposes. It showed clearly the blood that was spattered on his face, dotting his cheeks and forehead, obliterating his handsome features. There was even blood in the front of his hair, darkening and stiffening his tawny bangs. His round blue eyes looked directly at the camera, in mute shock. His lips were parted, and there was blood on his upper lip.

Christine sighed, and it only got worse as her gaze traveled downward in the photo. Blood covered Zachary's upper chest in his Ralph Lauren polo shirt, which must have been white before it was covered with gruesome crimson blotches, radiating from the center as if he had been shot in the chest. His hands hung at his sides but they were covered with blood, and there was blood on his forearms, too; some in droplets and others in smears, as if it had been rubbed or wiped. He was wearing khaki pants, and blood dripped down them in teardrop shapes. His shoes were brown loafers, but she didn't see any blood on them. She looked more closely, but still didn't see any blood on the upper of his shoes.

She set the photo down and picked up the others, counting them quickly. There were eight photos, and out of habit, she set them out on the bed, four in the top row and four in the bottom, the way she did at school, when she used flashcards for sight vocabulary with her younger students. Then she sorted the photos according to setting; there were four photos taken in the home setting, so she put them on the top row, and there were four photos taken in an institutional setting, probably the police station, with a bright white background, fluorescent lighting, and a gray-white counter and cubicles in the background.

Christine started with the top photos, which were front, back, and views of Zachary from both sides, showing the blood spatter that was all over his face, body, clothes, and skin. But not on the uppers of his shoes, and she didn't know if it was meaningful or chance. She examined each photo carefully, trying to look at it in an objective way but failing. Maybe it was her current mood or maybe it was the fact that she was just a teacher from suburban Connecticut, but she couldn't get over the horror of what she was seeing. She wanted to believe that Zachary wasn't guilty, but it was hard to do with so much blood on him, and she couldn't find a way to justify it to herself. His expression in each of the top four photos was basically the same; his eyes unfocused and oddly opaque, without any of the warmth she had seen at the prison or any of the connection she had felt there.

She picked up the second set of four photos, which were also front, back, right, and left views, and she experienced the same sensation of horror, mixed with despair. The bright institutional lighting made the blood shine cruelly and brought up its rich vermilion color, even though it had started to dry at the edges of most of the bloodstains, where it must have been thinner. Christine could see how it made stiff splotches on Zachary's polo shirt and pants, and it had even begun to clump his bangs together.

She scrutinized each photo, then set them down, so that all eight were looking back at her, and eight sets of blue eyes seemed to see through her, to her very heart. She thought of her baby's beating heart, so fragile and delicate in its gossamer ultrasound, and it sickened her to think that this was her baby's father. She looked at Zachary's eyes and she wondered if she would see them someday, looking back at her in the flesh, the eyes of her own little boy or girl. And even as she hoped that the genetics counselor was right, Christine couldn't help but wonder if Marcus was right, too, and a propensity toward violence of this deranged degree was somehow carried in the very DNA of her child, who would turn out to be a murderer, the same way that athletic skill, ability with numbers, and even a knack for languages were inherited.

Christine prayed that Zachary wasn't guilty, but even so, it was a nightmare to imagine that he was in this very situation, covered with the blood of an innocent young nurse who didn't deserve to die. Gail Robinbrecht had dedicated her life to the care of others, to saving lives, only to meet a horrific end in a random hookup with a deviant, even as she was trying to come to terms with the loss of another man she had loved and lost to the war.

Christine felt tears come to her eyes and didn't know who they were for, whether they were for Gail, Zachary, Griff, her baby, or Marcus. She couldn't help but feel that all of them were bound together somehow, tangled up in some flesh-and-blood ball, as if their veins, arteries, nerves, and DNA were wound around each other like so many rubber bands, forming a hard core that could never be torn apart, much less untangled.

Christine wiped her eyes, put the photos away, and sealed them inside the envelope. A wave of exhaustion and despair swept over her, and she set the envelope on the night table, then lay back on the stacked pillows, still in the cottony cocoon of her bathrobe. She had to keep it together, and it was time to get some sleep. She closed her eyes, tried to clear her mind, and let herself drift into sleep.

Because she knew it was going to get worse, before it got better.

Chapter Forty-one

Christine followed Detective Wallace, ducking under the yellow caution tape and walking down the alley beside Gail Robinbrecht's house. On the way, she snapped photos with her phone, trying to ignore the tension in her stomach. She hadn't slept well and she'd already barfed up her breakfast, but she'd showered and changed into a fresh denim shirtdress. It had a skinny leather belt, and for the first time, she'd had to move to an extra hole, a fact she noted with mixed emotions. She'd been waiting for her baby bump, but she felt differently now. She was about to see the aftermath of a murder that her baby's father might have committed.

Detective Wallace stopped at the end of the alley, waiting for her. He was in his forties, with short dark hair and wire-rimmed glasses, and he made a tall, trim, and professional appearance in a black polo shirt with the sewn-in gold emblem of the Chester County Detectives, which he had on with Dockers and loafers. He gestured at Gail Robinbrecht's wooden stairs, which Christine had only seen from a distance. "Here we go. It's upstairs."

"Thanks."

"Follow me." Detective Wallace ascended the stairway, she

climbed behind him, snapping photos of the backyard, which was also paved with concrete, lined on one side with trash and recycling bins, and bordered by the same wooden privacy fence as Linda Kent's backyard. It even had the same sign on the back gate, COBBLESTONE PROPERTY MANAGEMENT, and Christine gathered that the duplexes managed by the company would be generally uniform.

Detective Wallace asked, when they reached the top landing, "Before we enter the scene, did Griff tell you the rules?"

"No. Do you know Griff?"

"Everybody knows Griff. He's an institution." Detective Wallace smiled as he bent over and unlocked a square metal container with the county seal. "Can't say I care for his clients, but he does a lot of good for the department. He's the single biggest donor to the Widow & Orphans Fund. He gives to PAL, too. We'd do anything for him. How do you think you got in here so fast?"

"He has money?" Christine asked, surprised to think of Griff's sad little bedroom behind his office.

"He must be worth a fortune, but he gives it all away." Detective Wallace reached inside the metal container. "My wife's a librarian, and he gives them money, too. He just paid to renovate the reading room for the kids. He doesn't make a big deal about it. He didn't want his name on the reading room. They offered, too."

"Where does his money come from? Not from his family, I didn't get that impression."

"No, he's self-made, in commercial real estate. He owns the building his office is in."

"You mean he rents it to that other law firm?" Christine had thought it was the other way around.

"Yes. He owns a lot of office buildings in West Chester." Detective Wallace held a cardboard box of blue booties, tugged two from the box, and offered them to Christine. "Please put these on your shoes."

"Okay, thanks." Christine took the booties and slipped them over her espadrilles, thinking about Griff. The man was a paradox, that much was sure. Suddenly her cell phone began ringing in her hand, and she checked the screen. It was Marcus, so she didn't get it. "Sorry."

"You need to wear gloves, too." Detective Wallace returned to the box. "Are you allergic to latex?"

"No."

"Here." Detective Wallace handed her two purple gloves, and Christine put her phone in her purse and tugged them on.

"Thanks."

"Here are the rules. Please don't touch anything inside." Detective Wallace spoke as he gloved his hands. "No smoking or gum chewing. You may take as many pictures as you want. You may not make or receive cell-phone calls or texts." Detective Wallace went back into the metal box and pulled out a clipboard with a pen attached. "Please walk only in the areas I designate. You're entitled to see any rooms you wish, but you may not contaminate or disrupt anything. The scene hasn't been released yet, so it's still an active crime scene."

"When will it be released?"

"That, I don't know. It's not up to me." Detective Wallace made a note on the clipboard, which appeared to be a log of visitors to the scene.

"Who's been here already?" Christine peeked at the log, trying to read it. "Did the FBI come, or detectives from Maryland and Virginia?"

"That's police information." Detective Wallace put the clipboard back in the metal box, then pulled a key from his pocket, opened the screen door, and unlocked the wooden door. "If you have any questions, either you or Griff can call the district attorney. We're not meant to answer questions on these walk-throughs."

"Okay." Christine took the opportunity to look across the way at Linda Kent's apartment, directly opposite, and she snapped a few pictures.

"Follow me," Detective Wallace said, holding the door open, and Christine went inside, struck instantly by an intensely horrible odor. It was unmistakably blood, organic and decomposing, and it turned her stomach. She didn't know if the smell was more powerful because the apartment had been closed up or if it was because of her pregnancy, but she had trouble keeping her gorge down.

"Watch your step." Detective Wallace turned on the light, then pointed to the floor, and Christine looked down, appalled to see bloody footprints that led from the door, around the kitchen table, and out of the room.

"Ugh," she heard herself say, snapping pictures almost immediately because she didn't want to waste time. Some of the footprints were clearer than others, but she didn't have the heart or the stomach to parse it now.

Christine took a slew of pictures, looking around the small, pretty kitchen, its walls a sunny shade of buttercup yellow, with white cabinets and heartbreakingly charming details; above the sink was a narrow shelf with an array of photographs of Gail with her family and friends, everybody smiling and with their heads together, taken at a Great Adventure park, in bathing suits at the beach, and around a table in a restaurant.

Magnets blanketed the refrigerator, plenty of SpongeBob SquarePants, but more about nursing; one was shaped like a Band-Aid and read, NURSES MAKE IT BETTER, another showed a picture of a nurse in a cape and read, I'M A NURSE, WHAT'S YOUR SUPERPOWER? and a third one said, RN: CUTE ENOUGH TO STOP YOUR HEART, SKILLED ENOUGH TO RESTART IT. Christine felt her eyes tear up as she took pictures, but she suppressed them.

"Watch your step." Detective Wallace led her out of the kitchen, and she followed him, though the stench grew stronger and more nauseating.

"Look down. Don't step on that." Detective Wallace stopped, pointing down with an index finger, and Christine looked down, taking more pictures of the footprints tracking blood from the kitchen to the bedroom.

Detective Wallace turned on lights, and she noticed that the apartment was laid out the same way as Linda Kent's was, with the bedroom to the left and the living room to the right. Detective Wallace strode ahead to the bedroom and turned on the light, and Christine gasped.

Blood stained the flowery sheets of a queen-size bed, obliterating the pattern as it spread all over the surface. No longer red, it had dried a dark brown and even black in spots, spattered everywhere: on the brass headboard, on the white wall behind the bed, on the framed reproduction of van Gogh's sunflowers at the head, even on the floor beside the bed, where there was a pair of clog sandals, left where Gail must have taken them off. They were splattered with blood, too, and the pool of blood around them was disturbed by more footprints, in different directions.

Christine tried not to tear up again or even breathe as she took pictures of the horrifying sight. A human being had been slaughtered here, and the sights and smells revolted her to the depths of her very being. She realized that the bed was the first thing she had seen because the headboard was against the right wall, and the midsection of the bed was in direct view of the doorway, but then she noticed that there was a dark pool of blood at the foot of the bed, a dark red-black that had soaked into a blue twill rug, almost the color that Christine had in her bedroom at home.

She ignored the thought, taking pictures of the spot because even as a nonexpert, she could tell that that must've been where Gail had been stabbed. The blood was concentrated on that spot, and it had even spurted on the opposite wall, obscenely marking the mirror and pine dresser with teardrops of blood. Christine remembered that Zachary had told her how the blood would spurt out of a stab wound to the left ventricle, pulsing with each heartbeat, but she never would have believed it if she hadn't seen it with her own eyes.

She tried to stay in control of her emotions, trying to reconstruct the murder, whoever had committed it: from what she was seeing, it looked as if the killer must have confronted Gail at the foot of the bed, maybe surprised her by stabbing her with the medical saw. Perhaps he had it hidden in his back pocket or elsewhere. Her blood would have gushed all over him, as well as the mirror and the dresser, then he would have carried her to the bed, where he bound her at the wrists and ankles, either as she lay dying or even after she was dead.

Christine kept taking pictures, her brain filled with gruesome scenarios. She knew she would learn more after the autopsy reports were turned over, but she didn't need to be a coroner to know that the way she imagined the crime matched the blood that she had seen on the photographs of Zachary last night. Except for one detail: the fact that there was no blood on the uppers of his loafers. He should have had blood on his shoes if he had killed Gail in the way Christine had imagined. Unless it was just random that no blood had spattered there.

Detective Wallace kept an eye on her as she took more pictures, walking gingerly around the bedroom, taking in the girly perfume bottles, ponytail holders, pink-striped makeup case, and other bits and pieces of Gail Robinbrecht's tragically short life. Detective Wallace escorted her to Gail's bathroom, and Christine followed him, taking pictures of the bathroom, then the living room, and she knew that there was no substitute for seeing this scene with her very own eyes, even if her photos were like Griff's pictures, which wouldn't be ready until later today.

All of the darkest emotions from last night came rushing back at her, and she felt the deepest despair she had ever known at the notion that one human being could do this to another, much less that it was Zachary Jeffcoat who had done it to Gail Robinbrecht.

She wanted to punish whoever had committed this murder, even if it was Zachary, a feeling she had never had before this moment.

Christine finished going through the apartment, taking pictures as she breathed in the awful odor, her head filled with gruesome images and her heart full of anger, and by the time Detective Wallace led her finally outside, she stood on the landing of the wooden stairs, breathing in deep lungfuls of fresh air before she began to take off her gloves and booties.

Her head was swimming with questions, all of them for Zachary, and she couldn't wait to get to the prison.

Chapter Forty-two

Christine's mouth dropped open when she caught sight of Zachary, being escorted to the booth. He had been badly beaten; his forehead was puffy and pinkish, his right eye was swollen half-closed, and fresh scabs covered his right cheek. Dried blood clotted in his hairline at a cut that had been closed with butterfly bandages. The corrections officer uncuffed him, and Christine could see that red scrapes cross-hatched his arms and fresh bruises discolored his elbows. A gauze pad was adhesive-taped to his left forearm.

Christine couldn't imagine what had happened. Her chest tightened, and she remembered their blood connection. The father of her child had been assaulted, and she couldn't deny that she cared about him for that reason alone. It disarmed her on the spot; she had been upset and angry at him, having come from Gail Robinbrecht's, the stench of the murder still in her nostrils. Fresh in her mind were the bloody photos of him, and she had been geared up to confront him for lying. But her anger dissipated when he entered the booth and she saw his wounds close-up.

"Zachary, what happened?" Christine asked, stricken.

"Oh man, it was unreal." Zachary sat down stiffly, wincing.

"We were in lockdown yesterday because of it. They said they were going to call Griff. Did they?"

"I don't know. What was it? Were you attacked?"

"Kind of, we were out in the yard when it happened." Zachary shook his head, running a tongue over dry lips. "You don't know what it's like, I stand with my back against the wall. I try to stay out of everybody's way. The white guys hang with the white guys, the black guys hang together, the Muslims and the Mexicans, same thing. I avoid everybody. So I was standing there, and the CO—that's what they call the guard, for corrections officer—the CO was walking in front of me, keeping an eye on things. It was hot as hell out, and all of a sudden the CO grabs his chest right in front of me and falls to his knees. I knew exactly what was happening."

"What?" Christine asked in confusion.

"He had too much upper body weight, a big beer gut. He was sweating, and I knew he was having a heart attack."

"Right in front of you?" Christine grimaced.

"Yes, so I went to him right away and I started compressions on his chest. I knew I could save his life. I yelled out, 'call 911, it's a cardiac,' but the COs thought I jumped him, so they came running, pulled me off him, and put me on the ground. They slammed my head into asphalt and beat the crap out of me."

"Oh no!"

"I kept yelling 'he's having a heart attack, he's having a heart attack, call an ambulance, call an ambulance,' and the next thing I know, all hell broke loose. Gangbangers started throwing punches and, like, a SWAT team of COs dragged me away and threw me in ad seg."

"What's that?"

"Administrative segregation. Isolation. Solitary. They were even going to write me up until they got the CO to the hospital and they got it straightened out."

"What's 'write you up' mean?"

"Discipline me!" Zachary's eyes flared, though the right one stayed half-closed. "The only reason they didn't is because the EKG and heart enzymes showed he had a heart attack. It took them all day to realize I didn't jump him, and they backed off on the discipline, but I'm still in ad seg."

"Did he live?" Christine asked, astonished.

"Yes." Zachary smiled, exhaling.

"So you saved the man's life?"

"I guess." Zachary's bruised forehead eased momentarily.

"Wow." Christine felt a warm rush of validation. She'd seen compassion in him, and she'd been right. But at the same time, she'd also seen the bloody scene at Gail's. She wanted to know why he had lied to her.

"Right?" Zachary snorted. "Unreal. The COs are probably trained in CPR but none of them was as close as I was."

"So was there a riot, in the yard?"

"No, it didn't get that far, but they locked us down."

"Did they take you to the hospital?"

"No, they treated me here. It's only superficial."

"This wasn't in the newspaper or anything, was it?"

"I don't know. I didn't see any reporters. I hear the prison brass can keep things out of the papers."

"Still, you did the right thing. You saved a man's life."

"Are you kidding?" Zachary leaned close to the Plexiglas, looking at her like she was crazy. "It's *not* the right thing to save a CO, not in here. Gangs run this place, stone cold gangbangers. They would've let the CO die. They're keeping me in ad seg for my own protection. I'm the pretty boy who saves COs. I have a target on my back." Zachary raked his fingers through his hair, his knuckles red. "I hope they never move me back to gen pop, but ad seg is the *worst*. The guy in the cell next to me, he screams, rants, and raves all night. The guy on the other side hits his head against the wall. It's *cinder-block*." Zachary's good eye rounded, a bloodshot blue. "They had to put him in a restraint chair, with shackles and a spit mask, and they moved him to a psychiatric observation cell. He should be in a mental hospital, they all should. They're psychotic. *Insane*."

"My God." Christine grimaced.

"I sit in the cell twenty-three hours a day. I eat in the cell, all three meals. I talk to nobody, I see nobody. They only let me out for an hour, in a cage by myself. You *have* to get me out of here." Zachary shifted forward on his elbows. "Tell Griff about this, what happened in the yard. You're working with him now? They put you on my visitor's list."

"Yes, and I will talk to him about it, for sure." Christine resolved to buy Griff a cell phone, too.

"Please, do, maybe he can use it to get me out of here or sent down to Chester County Prison. It's minimum-security, a camp compared to here."

"Of course." Christine had to get back on track. She had so many questions, including the one about the lie. "Zachary, I just came from Gail's apartment, and there's a few things I need to understand about the murder. Can you tell me exactly what happened that night, in detail?"

"I told you, I came in and found her." Zachary blinked.

"I need to know in greater detail. What did you do exactly?" Christine wanted to hear his story and see if it explained the blood she'd seen on him in the photos.

"I went in—"

"How did you get in?"

"The door was open. Only the screen was closed. I went in. We had a date, so I figured that was okay, but I didn't see her in the kitchen. So I went to the bedroom."

"Were there bloody footprints from the kitchen to the bedroom?"

"Not that I saw at first. I wasn't looking down. I saw them later, after the cops came, and I'm sure a lot of the footprints are mine, pacing, walking around, going back and forth to let the cops in."

"So what did you do when you first got there?"

"I saw that there was something wrong in the bedroom, that she was lying there, so I went in, like, I went in to her."

"Was a light on in the bedroom?"

Zachary frowned in thought, shifting his butterfly bandages. "No, I think I turned it on."

"So how did you see in the dark?"

"There's a window on the other side of the bed and some light was coming in from it, moonlight or light from the houses, just enough to see something was wrong. And there was a funny smell. I knew it right away, from the OR. It was blood."

Christine knew it, too. It rang true. "What time was this?"

"Around ten o'clock."

"Why so late?"

"That's when she said she was free." Zachary shrugged.

"Then what did you do?"

"I went right to her, I grabbed her, I mean, I don't remember exactly. Blood was everywhere, all over her, the bed, everywhere." Zachary's brow furrowed, even with the red scrapes. "I leaned over her, I lifted her up, I called her name, I felt her pulse, her carotid. There was nothing. She was dead."

"Was she bleeding? Was blood spurting out?"

"No, not in the beginning. Her heart had stopped, so it wasn't spurting out, and I don't know why, I pulled out the saw. I just couldn't believe what I was seeing, it was like I wanted it not to be. I wanted it not to be in her." Zachary's lips curled in revulsion. "But when I pulled the saw out, blood came out, gushed out, more of it. I even held her up, like, hugged her, God knows why, I was so shocked." Zachary grimaced, recoiling. "Blood squirted all over me. It was horrible."

Christine thought it explained the blood that was on him, a credible alternative scenario to his being the killer. And she realized something else, it also explained why there had been no blood on the top of his loafers. His shoes would have been out of the way or under the bed, from the way he described what had happened. She kept going. "Before we move on, let me ask you, you called it a saw. Did you recognize it as one of the types that you sell?"

"No, not at first. It was too dark, and I was too, like, upset." Zachary shook his head. "I saw it had a stainless-steel handle. I thought it was a kitchen knife. When I pulled it out, the blood flew all over, I didn't notice what kind of knife it was. That was the last thing I was looking at. But then when the police came, and they took photos of me and the knife, I realized it was one of ours."

"Did you say that to the police?"

"No, I was, like, in shock, I was so freaked. I didn't realize they would arrest me. I mean, I didn't do it." Zachary leaned over, his battered face a mask of anxiety. "Please, I didn't. You have to know that."

"I believe you," Christine found herself saying. She thought that if Zachary was telling the truth, then he was terribly unlucky, being wrongly accused not only at the scene but in the prison yard. "Let's go back to the saw, as you call it. What type of instrument is it?"

"It's a metacarpal bone saw, for hand surgery or other small bones."

"So hand surgeons would have that?"

"Yes, all hospitals would in their ORs and ERs. It's for general surgery of the hand and other small bones."

"Are hand surgeons your customers?"

"My accounts? Yes, but I don't call on hand surgeons on their own. They're in hospitals or affiliated with hospitals. I sell to the purchasing people at hospitals, not the docs."

Christine had more questions about the saw and the customers he sold it to, but she wanted to get to why he'd lied to her about Gail. "Okay, sorry I interrupted. Then what happened, after you pulled the knife, or the saw, out?"

"I called 911, I told them what I saw, what I found." Zachary frowned, his scrapes buckling. "I don't know what I said, you can get the tape. Then the cops came."

Christine decided it was time to go for it, because she had to know. "Let me ask you, when was the first time you met Gail?"

"I told you. Sunday, in the hospital."

"Why were you there on a Sunday?" Christine tried to listen critically.

"It was the only time I could catch Dr. Malan-Kopelman. He's a top doc in thoracic surgery and he's wall-to-wall during the week. He's impossible to catch, so I went in. He does rounds starting at 6:00 A.M. that day."

Christine felt confused. "But when we were talking about hand surgeons, you just said you don't sell to docs."

Zachary blinked. "I do, when the docs have clout with purchasing. I don't know any hand surgeons who have that kind of clout. Malan-Kopelman is major."

Christine thought it made sense. "Okay, back to Gail. Do you know why she was there on a Sunday morning?"

"Nurses work every day. We were both in early. Her shift started at seven, and she was getting coffee. I was getting coffee because I was finished selling Malan-Kopelman. I got the order, by the way." Zachary half-smiled, but Gail couldn't be distracted.

"And your first date with Gail was that same night?"

"Yes, I told you."

"And you went to her apartment?"

"Yes?"

"And you slept together?"

"Yes." Zachary frowned, crumpling his bruises. "But why are you asking me all these questions? I told you all this."

Christine searched his face to see if his expression had changed, but it hadn't, and she couldn't tell if he was lying or not. "Zachary, what would you say if I told you that one of Gail's neighbors saw you at her apartment on Thursday night?"

"What? Who?" Zachary's lips parted in outrage, and his

blue eyes flashed like cold steel. "Are you trying to trap me? Whose side are you on? I thought you were working for me, not against me."

Christine recoiled, surprised. "I am on your side, I'm asking you—"

"You're not asking me anything!" Zachary raised his voice. "You're accusing me. You're calling me a liar!"

"No, I'm not. I'm asking you—"

"You're trying to trick me, catch me!"

"Zachary, calm down. I'm on your side—"

"The hell you are! You don't know what it's like in here! I could have been killed! I can't sleep, they scream all night! I feel like I'm going to explode! You have to get me out of here!"

The CO standing guard on the secured side swiveled his head to them. "Jeffcoat, no shouting!" he boomed through the window in the door.

Christine sat back in her chair, trying to regain her composure. His outburst rattled her because it was so sudden.

"I'm sorry," Zachary said, seeming to recover. He exhaled loudly, pushing his blond bangs from his cut. "I'm at the end of my rope. I'm losing it. I didn't mean to snap. I have to get out of here. I don't know what to do."

"It's okay," Christine said, though it was anything but.

"You don't believe me? Is that why you asked? Why don't you believe me?"

"I need you to tell me the truth," Christine said, because it was exactly how she felt.

"I told you the truth," Zachary shot back, but Christine could see him avert his eyes for a moment.

"If you're lying, come clean with me now. We can't help you if we don't know the facts. Is the neighbor right, that she saw you?" Christine kept her tone soft. If she had learned anything as a reading teacher, it was to create an atmosphere that was safe enough to make, or confess, any mistake. "Tell me the truth, Zachary."

"Okay." Zachary swallowed hard, pursing his lips. "I did see Gail Thursday night, but that was the first time, ever."

"How did that come about?"

"The exact same way I told you. I met Gail in the cafeteria on Thursday, that was the first day I met her. Same time, all else the same. I was trying to get Dr. Malan-Kopelman in the morning, but I missed him in surgery. I didn't get the order until Sunday, I kept at it." Zachary rubbed his face, wincing. "I saw Gail again on Sunday, but Sunday wasn't the first day we hooked up. Thursday night was."

"Why did you lie?" Christine kept the judgment from her tone.

"Because of Hannah, my girlfriend. I didn't want her to know that I cheated on her twice."

"What difference does that make? Cheating once is bad enough, isn't it?"

"Once could be, like, a slip-up, a mistake. But twice, I don't know, I knew she'd think it was worse. Not that it matters now." Zachary paused, his shoulders letting down. "I knew we were in trouble when she went to med school and I didn't. She got distant. At first I thought it was that our schedules were different, she was working all the time or in the lab, but it wasn't that."

"What was it?" Christine didn't know if he was deflecting or being honest.

"A medical sales rep isn't the same thing as a doctor, not to women. Especially not to women doctors, like Hannah. I felt like I got demoted in her eyes, and she looked for the upgrade." Zachary slumped. "Hannah's gone, so maybe I got what I deserved."

"I don't think that," Christine said, wanting to build on their rapport. "But I'm surprised that given the break-up, she would lend you the money for your retainer. She dropped it off last night, a cashier's check."

"I'm not surprised." Zachary managed a smile. "She really cares about me, or she feels guilty because she dumped me. I'll pay her back, and she knows that, if I get out of here. I loved Hannah, and if I could've had her back, the way she used to feel about me, I would've been totally happy."

"How can I reach her? I'd like to speak with her."

"Why?" Zachary frowned.

"She was your girlfriend. Who knows you better than your girlfriend?"

"I don't see the point." Zachary frowned again. "She's done enough for me, lending me the money."

"I'll know the point after I speak with her. I'm trying to turn over every stone for your case. She might have facts to help your defense."

"Christine, if you want to help my defense, talk to my boss. His name is Tim Foster and he's right in town. The Brigham offices are right outside of West Chester on Cardinal Street."

"Okay, I'll see him first then." Christine made a mental note to squeeze him in before she went to Zachary's apartment. "But how do I reach Hannah? I'd still like to speak with her."

"No, don't, please."

"I have to." Christine thought a moment. "You were dating her during the time of the other murders, weren't you?"

"You mean the other two nurses?"

"Yes." Christine felt bothered he didn't say their names, which she remembered. "Did you know them?"

"No, not at all. Bethesda General and Newport News are my accounts, but I didn't know those nurses. I never met them."

Christine couldn't tell if he was lying, but his plaintive expression looked so genuine, especially with the bruises. "Did you hook up with nurses at Bethesda General and Newport News Memorial?"

"I don't know, I'd have to think about it, but not those nurses." Zachary spread his hands, palms up. "Look, I'm not perfect. I'm a single guy, I hooked up on the road, when I was with Hannah. She was the one who turned away from me. I was just hanging on because I wanted to be with her. Sometimes you don't get what you need from someone you love. That's the truth."

Christine felt the words resonate but tried not to let it show. She knew exactly how Zachary felt, now that Marcus was turning away from her.

"I'm not proud of it, but I'm not going to apologize for it, either. But I didn't kill Gail or anybody else. I'm not a serial killer. I love nurses, I would never *kill* nurses."

"McLeane was killed in January and Allen-Bogen in April." Christine didn't have the exact dates since she didn't get to finish her bulletin board. "You were with Hannah during that time, and at some point, I'll have to talk with her about where you were those nights and establish an alibi."

"But she might not meet with you. Her parents want her to distance herself from me, and she'll be hard to get ahold of. Med school is super busy. You'll have to catch her between classes."

"Where does she go to school?"

"Temple. It's all the way in town. Philly."

"I'll drive in." Christine got her golf pencil and notepad from her pocket. "What's her number and email?"

"But please, don't push it if she doesn't want to meet you." Zachary rattled off a number and email address, then glanced behind him as the guard approached, signaling the end of their visit. "Christine, just know, I didn't kill anybody. I would never kill anybody. I'm completely innocent, and I need you to believe in me and get me out of here. It's worse than before, in ad seg."

"I understand," Christine said, believing him, in the end.

"Christine, please, help me. I'm counting on you."

Chapter Forty-three

Brigham Instruments was housed in a boxy new building of red brick, shaped like an L, and Christine stepped inside, glancing around the reception room. It was modern, with cheery blue wainscoting and an off-white wall covered with framed covers from the Brigham Hospital Catalog, General Surgery Edition, next to framed Better Business Bureau certificates and laminated newspaper articles. Two blue padded chairs flanked an end table that held an artificial plant, and to the right, Christine passed an open French door that read SALES/SERVICE over the top. She walked to the reception desk.

"May I help you?" an older receptionist asked, sitting at a panel counter about shoulder height. Her hooded eyes were gray-blue, almost the same shade as her straight gray hair, which she wore closely cropped with dangling silver earrings.

"I'm Christine Nilsson, the one who called about a meeting with Tim Foster."

"Of course, I was so happy when your call came in." The receptionist's expression changed, falling into concerned lines. "Please do everything you can to help Zachary. I *know* they have the wrong man."

"You do?" Christine's ears perked up.

"Absolutely, we all do, all the girls in billing and the ones in back, in the warehouse." The receptionist gestured behind her. "We think it's terrible that they arrested him. He didn't do it, we just know it."

"What makes you so sure?"

"I know that boy. I tell him, 'you're the grandson I never had.'"

Christine smiled, warmed. "How long have you known him?"

"Two years, since he started here. He's so handsome and so sweet, he does the nicest things for everybody here. We all love him. And he's so good-looking!" The receptionist's aged eyes flared. "My granddaughter calls him *dreamy*. The girls in back have a crush on him, and I don't blame them. It's not just that he's handsome. He's a good person, inside."

"What makes you say that?" Christine realized it was the first time she'd heard something nice about Zachary, and her heart lifted.

"He's so thoughtful. He remembers things about us. He knows I have a Chihuahua, Rico, and he always brings a box of dog treats for him, special for small dogs. And when he pays a call on his accounts in Delaware, he always brings Millie in the warehouse a box of salt water taffy. Oh, we all just *love* him." The receptionist's eyes narrowed. "He's not like some of the account managers, who are only nice to the bosses. He's nice to everybody, no matter whether they're a big shot or not. In fact, just last week, he visited one of the other girls in the hospital when she broke her arm. He knows she likes mysteries, so he brought them."

Christine made a mental note to talk to Griff about whether they could call these women as witnesses to Zachary's character at trial. "Does he have any friends here, like other account managers?"

"He was friendly with Tim, most of all, so he's probably the one you should talk to." The receptionist shifted her gaze to the open French door. "Oh, here he is. Tim?"

Christine looked up as a heavyset African-American man appeared in the sales/service door, motioning to her. He had a broad grin and large dark eyes set far apart behind gold-rimmed glasses. He crossed the room to shake her hand, dressed in a Brigham-blue polo shirt and neatly pressed khaki pants, with the perfect break over his shiny loafers.

"Christine, hello, I'm Tim Foster."

"Nice to meet you." Christine shook his hand. He had a strong grip, and such a convivial way about him that she liked him instantly. "Thanks for meeting with me."

"Happy to. Come this way, we can talk. I have a half an hour before I have to leave. Everyone's at lunch, and I wanted to fit you in."

"Thank you so much." Christine followed him through the open door and past a row of tall blue cubicles, which were empty except for family photos, Eagles and Phillies sports schedules, and miniature American flags.

"This is where our inside salespeople sit." Tim spoke freely as they walked down the hall. "They're the only ones who get cubicles. Brigham has fifty-five employees and fifteen account managers. We supply medical instruments nationwide and we're a medium-sized player. It's a family-owned business, started by the Brigham family about sixty years ago."

"Did Zachary have a cubicle?"

"No, he was an account manager. His office was in his house. We mail our account managers anything they need, so he only comes into the main office one to three times a month to pick up samples, supplies, or for a meeting. We do send the big paper catalog home, but we're encouraging more of our accounts to order online, as you can imagine."

"Yes," Christine said, as Tim let her into a small corner office with a dark wood desk and a narrow window that overlooked a loading dock, where a white container truck was reversing in. A stack of blue Brigham catalogs sat on the corner of his desk, next to a flat monitor, and Tim gestured at a wall chart that read BRIGHAM PREMIUM INSTRUMENTS, above PREMIUM GRADE, MIDGRADE, AND FLOOR GRADE, with an array of shiny, stainless-steel instruments.

"We make fifteen thousand medical instruments of all types. Three different product lines, each with its own scissors, hemostats, forceps, needle holders, retractors, and whatnot. We manufacture instruments for all surgical fields. Cardiac, gynecology, rectal, urology, ophthalmology, microsurgery, you name it. We even make instruments for plastic surgery, which change fairly often. Please, sit down."

"Thanks." Christine sat and slid her pad from her purse. "Do all the account managers sell all of the types?"

"Yes, they do." Tim eased into his desk chair. "That's what's difficult about the job. It's a challenge to keep abreast of the product lines. We make twenty-seven different types of scissors, alone."

"I was curious what kind of an employee Zachary was."

"He was the best." Tim nodded. "He really was. He was the golden boy. No pun. Yes, he's a good-looking kid, he's been employee of the month more than anybody else. Eight times in two years."

"Does he report directly to you?"

"Yes, and I report to the vice president of sales, who reports to the president of sales. They're not in today. I knew Zachary better than they do, so you're not missing anything."

"Did you review his performance?"

"Yes, he's gotten a bonus for going beyond his quotas, every quarter."

"Could I see his personnel file?"

"Unfortunately, not. I thought you might ask that, so I checked with Legal, and they said no. You need to have his lawyer write us a letter."

"I'll do that."

"Good. Legal said I could talk to you, and we'd like to help

Zachary if we can. No way in the world is he guilty." Tim puckered his lower lip, shaking his head. "No damn way."

"What makes you so sure?"

"He's a good guy, all around. He always worked without complaint, he filled in when guys got sick. Like when Stan, one of our other account managers, got prostate cancer, he filled in for him while he was in the hospital. Zachary's just that kind of a kid. He's the youngest account manager here, and he's interested in medicine. He got into med school but didn't have the money to go. It helps him with the doctors and the purchasing people. It's all good."

"Did you know that he was dating nurses who worked at these hospitals?"

"No, but that's his business, he's single. I don't blame him. I met my wife on this job. She's a bookkeeper at Riddle Memorial." Tim shrugged his heavy shoulders. "That's who we meet at our accounts. Doesn't mean he killed anybody. I can't picture him doing that."

Christine wanted to believe him, but she remembered that flash of anger she'd seen today. "Did he have a temper?"

"No, not that I saw."

"Did you trust him?"

"Absolutely. I like him and trust him."

"How about the accounts?"

"They all did. The docs, the purchasing people, everybody. I've been getting calls since he was arrested, and none of them believe that he did it." Tim spoke with conviction. "He's such a *good* guy. Did what I asked, even the things that I get pushback on from some of the others."

"Like what?"

"Perfect example, I ask my account mangers not to have a Facebook page. I don't want our accounts looking up my managers, finding out whether they're Republican, Democrat, or anything about them, personally. You never know who you turn off these days."

Christine thought it explained why Zachary didn't have a Facebook page, which Lauren had thought was strange. "What about the fact that the killer used your instruments?"

"So what?" Tim's dark eyes flared. "You know how many people come in contact with those instruments in the hospital or doc's office? Everybody from the docs, to the nurses, to the orderlies, to the techs, to the people who unpack the boxes. Anybody could use our instruments."

"What was his region?"

"Mid-Atlantic. Maryland, Virginia, Delaware, and Pennsylvania. It's a big region, but he handled it. I was grooming him to succeed me. He was a real go-getter. Look at this." Tim turned to a black bag on the floor, then lifted it onto the table and opened the top flap. "This is what they called his 'kill bag' or 'hit kit' in the papers. It's the sample bag we give to our account managers. They said in the paper that it was a plain black bag, that's intentional. It doesn't say Brigham because these instruments cost a couple hundred bucks a pop. We don't label the bag so they don't get stolen." Tim extracted a black nylon folder from inside the case and opened it to reveal an array of different tweezers on a field of blue velvet, held in place by black elastic bands. "This is what it looks like inside."

"And these are . . . tweezers?"

"No, forceps. Top line of forceps, tissue forceps, Adson forceps, Adson-Brown forceps. It's a typical sample bag for forceps."

"Was this what Zachary had in his car?"

"Not specifically. He had our surgical general kit for top-of-the-line operating rooms. It includes a Langenbeck metacarpal saw, named for a Bernhard von Langenbeck, a Prussian army surgeon. Unfortunately, many surgical advances and instruments come from wars."

Christine remembered what Zachary had said. "Was that the murder weapon? A saw used by hand surgeons?"

"Yes, I have one to show you." Tim stuck a hammy hand into

the bag and pulled out a long, shiny saw that had a serrated edge, then handed it over with care. "Watch out, it's sharp."

"Yikes, and it's heavy." Christine eyed the jagged edge, which gave her the creeps.

"It has to be. It's nine and a half inches long, including the blade, which is four and a half inches long. The tip is part of the blade, the saw has no curvature, it's straight. It's stainless-steel, reusable, rigid, and strong enough to saw through small bones. It can also punch through a chest, but anybody could've had this." Tim pointed to the saw. "This is a very common saw in an OR, and any trauma surgeon, hand surgeon, orthopedic surgeon, or podiatric surgeon could have these instruments. It costs about $160, so it's not even as expensive as many medical instruments. So you see, there is a perfectly reasonable explanation for Zachary's having it in his car. It doesn't mean he's a serial killer."

"How about the tourniquets?"

"Same, very common, everywhere. I pulled those for you, too." Tim dug in a pocket of the sample bag and extracted a roll of bright turquoise bands. "You can find these a zillion places. We sell them, and so do a lot of other people."

Christine knew as much. She got her yearly blood test, and her local Labcorp used the same tourniquet. "And the tourniquets are used by hand surgeons, but not only by hand surgeons?"

"Exactly."

"Can laypeople buy these things?"

"No. We sell only to hospitals, hospital supply companies, and medical professionals." Tim frowned. "I see our metacarpal saws on eBay sometimes, but that's resellers."

"May I take these things and some catalogs, to read through them later?"

"Sure." Tim packed the saw, tourniquets, and some catalogs in the black nylon bag and flopped over the top flap.

"Did the police talk to you about Zachary?"

"Yes, they talked to my boss, too. I told them what I told you. Zachary's not a serial killer."

"Did they ask for his personnel file?"

"Yes, and we gave them a copy. Legal said we had to." Tim frowned. "It won't hurt him any, and we complied. The fact that whoever killed those nurses used our instruments isn't helping, public relations–wise. We got tons of calls from the media the first week. We even hired a PR firm. The Brigham family isn't happy. The sooner this is over with, the better."

"Did Zachary have any enemies that you know of?"

"No, not at all." Tim cocked his head. "Uh, one of the other account managers wasn't a fan. But that's between us."

"I'll keep it confidential. What is his name?"

"Dan Pepitone."

"Is Dan here today?"

"No, he's calling on accounts. The managers are always on the road, remember? They never come in."

"Right." Christine made a mental note to follow up and meet Pepitone. "Why didn't Dan like Zachary?"

"Zachary came into Dan's region. I needed to bring somebody new. All of our regions are large, and there's hundreds of accounts, we're spread pretty thin. Dan's in his late fifties."

"Are you saying that Zachary was brought in as Dan's successor?"

"That's about the size of it." Tim buckled his lower lip. "Dan is slowing down, he's just burned-out. It's not easy being a road warrior. When Zachary came in, the numbers went way up. Zachary made Dan look bad. That's sales."

"What do you think makes the difference?"

"Zachary tries harder. He charms everybody. He's always closing, that boy." Tim frowned slightly. "But Dan thought Zachary was a BS artist, which I get."

"What do you mean?"

"I'm in sales. I manage salesman. It's a mentality. Some salesman, they're made. Others are born." Tim smiled. "Zachary was a born salesman. He could sell ice to the Eskimos. It's a cliché, but it's true about him."

Christine didn't know if she wanted her baby to be a born salesman, and if that was a good thing or not. "What makes a born salesman?"

"In my opinion, it's a knowledge of people. Zachary can clue in on what somebody wants and give it to them. He knows how to work people."

"That's manipulative." Christine couldn't help but wonder if Zachary was manipulating her, like Gary had warned.

"It is and it isn't." Tim shrugged again. "Sales requires you to understand people and to a certain extent, yes, manipulate them. To tell them what they want to hear, so you can close."

Christine thought it sounded worse and worse. "So is he a liar?"

"No more than I am." Tim chuckled. "We're just trying to sell you something. You need it, and we make it, so it works out. There's no harm, no foul. Zachary's very good at his job, the best young salesman I've seen in a long time. Zachary was a star. Not everybody likes that. Dan thought Zachary was arrogant, but I want my account managers to be arrogant. You know who are the most arrogant people on the face of the earth?"

"No, who?" Christine asked, because he seemed to wait for a reply.

"Surgeons. Surgeons think they're God. They will cut into the human body without hesitation. They will save a life. They're brilliant men and women, and they don't respect dumb. I want my account managers to be arrogant and confident enough to earn the respect of surgeons."

Christine understood. "Could Zachary?"

"Yes, totally. He could walk into a hospital, collar a surgeon when he's on his way to the OR, grab whatever three minutes he can, and convince him that we make a better instrument than the next guy. If my guys don't have that confidence, I'm not gonna be able to feed my family."

Christine tried to understand. "So Zachary's arrogant and manipulative, but you like him anyway?"

"No." Tim smiled. "Zachary's arrogant and manipulative, and I *love* him anyway."

Chapter Forty-four

Christine hurried down the busy sidewalk, crowded with students carrying backpacks, businesspeople scrolling through smartphones, and Temple University employees in red lanyards, hurrying back to their offices after lunch. It had taken her almost an hour to drive into the center of Philadelphia, then another half an hour to fight the traffic going up Broad Street, which was evidently the city's main artery. Hannah had said she only had twenty minutes between classes, so Christine had driven like a maniac, sensing that Hannah didn't want to meet with her at all.

The air was impossibly humid, and Christine wiped the sweat from her brow as she passed a bustling campus bookstore, then made a beeline for the cheesesteak place that Hannah had specified. She threaded her way to the restaurant, pushed open the door, and breathed in the delicious smells of sizzling steaks. Her eyes adjusted to the dim, cramped rectangle, mostly a take-out joint with an order counter, open griddles, and cooks on the left, and on the right, two rows of small brown tables.

A young girl sitting in the back waved to Christine, but it didn't make sense. The young girl was tall and thin, with long dark hair, which didn't fit the description of Zachary's girlfriend that

Christine had gotten from the CO at the prison, the first day. Christine remembered the CO describing Zachary's girlfriend as a "redhead" and "a pretty little thing," and the woman standing up was neither little nor a redhead, though she was adorably pretty. She had a soft, round face, with dimples and a turned-up nose, full lips, and a dazzling smile, with perfect teeth.

"Christine!" the young girl called, impatiently motioning her forward, and Christine walked past the noisy crowd lining up at the counter and headed for the back of the restaurant.

"Hannah? I thought you were a redhead."

"No, why would you think that?" Hannah sat down, brushing smooth the hem of a summery purple sundress with skinny straps. "Please sit, I don't have long."

"The guard at Graterford told me you had red hair."

"How would they know? I've never been to Graterford."

"But you visited Zachary, didn't you?" Christine sat down, bewildered.

"No, no way." Hannah shuddered. "A maximum-security prison? Uh, no thanks."

Christine didn't understand. "But the guard said his girlfriend was there."

"He has no problem getting women. Such a player. Whatever, dude." Hannah snorted. "Why would I visit him? We broke up. We're over."

"Well, I was under the impression that you cared about him as a friend."

"Where did you get *that* impression?" Hannah drew back.

"From him. He said so."

"Ha! He's *so* full of himself!" Hannah rolled her eyes, which were a lovely shade of hazel, with only light makeup.

"It's a reasonable conclusion, given the fact that you're lending him money for his retainer." Christine felt unaccountably defensive on Zachary's behalf.

"What?" Hannah looked at Christine like she was crazy. "I'm not doing that. I'm not lending him any money, ever again."

"Wait, hold on. Let me get this straight." Christine felt confounded, beginning to realize why Zachary hadn't wanted her to meet with Hannah. "You didn't lend him $2,500 toward his retainer, in a cashier's check? You dropped it off at his lawyer's office?"

Hannah scoffed. "Are you kidding? No, not at all. My days of paying his bills are so over."

Christine couldn't get her bearings. Zachary had lied to her, but she didn't know why. "I guess I was misinformed."

"Welcome to the world of Zachary Jeffcoat. I don't know what angle he's working with you, and I don't know what he told you. But if he's talking, he's lying." Hannah sipped soda from a tall, plastic tumbler. "Don't ask me why he'd lie about something that was so easy to catch him on. He's usually better than that."

"He didn't know I was going to meet you."

"Right, that's it, and he would know that I would avoid meeting with you, which I totally tried to do."

Christine had called Hannah five times, not about to give up. "I had that impression. Why, though?"

"My boyfriend getting arrested as a serial killer?" Hannah shook her head, newly somber. "I want nothing to do with that, believe me. I *have* nothing to do with that. It's horrible, it's embarrassing, it's scary. My parents went ballistic. They liked him. They're both doctors in town, in family practice. They're beside themselves."

"When did you break up with him?"

"The night they arrested him. He called me from the police station in West Chester. I went with my dad."

"And you broke up with Zachary right then?"

"Totally, it was a no-brainer." Hannah chuckled, without mirth. "He was sitting there in handcuffs and a white paper jumpsuit. He had washed up, but there was still *blood* under his fingernails and in his hair. I'm not one of those dumb women who stand by their man, no matter what. It was a long time coming, anyway. We hadn't been that happy for a while."

Christine wondered if she had become one of those dumb women. "Do you think he's guilty?"

"Possibly, okay?" Hannah shook her head, curling her nose in distaste. "I hate to think I was with somebody who was that sick and didn't know it. My dad is sending me links to articles about serial killers whose girlfriends and wives didn't know it. It's so freaky. I think they're right. It could've been me."

"Where was he the night of the murder? It was last Monday, June 15."

"I have no idea. I was in town, at my apartment. Zachary told me he was on the road in Maryland. Liar."

Christine felt dismay at yet another lie. "Did you speak with him that night?"

"No, he texted me, saying he was working soooo hard. Boo-hoo. What a joke."

"What time did he text you?"

"About eight o'clock. I was studying with my friends."

"Can you just tell me briefly about your relationship? You started dating Zachary when, when you entered med school?"

"Yes, the summer before first year. We met at an orientation mixer for accepted students, at a bar in Society Hill. I fell for him, like, *bam*. He is so hot." Hannah smiled slightly. "It was good that summer, I'll give him that. It was great when we thought we were both going to school."

"Then what happened?"

"To start with, it was a problem that he never had any money, he had no help with tuition, and it was a constant issue. He worried all summer about making enough for tuition. He had, like, five jobs."

"Do you know if he did anything else to make money?"

Christine was wondering if Hannah knew that Zachary had been a sperm donor.

"Like what?"

"I don't know, sell blood? Donate sperm, like some students do?"

"No, I have no idea if he did any of that." Hannah shrugged it off. "But he did need money. I paid for a lot of things, I didn't mind, my family has the money. But then Zachary couldn't come up with the tuition." Hannah shook her head. "He was mad when I wouldn't ask my father for a loan. We had a huge fight. He lost his temper, out of nowhere."

Christine flashed on Zachary's sudden temper, which she'd experienced.

"He called me names, too. Basically 'rich bitch.' It wasn't nice."

"Did that happen often?"

"No, but I didn't forget it. I wouldn't put up with that." Hannah frowned. "He started making noises like he couldn't register because you can't register until your tuition is paid. So he conceded the obvious and got a job at Brigham, but he was bummed. He loved medicine more than I do. I mean, it sucked, and I was feeling guilty."

"So then what happened?" Christine thought it was the flip side of what Zachary had said about their relationship, that he felt demoted when he didn't go to med school.

"He was jealous that I was in med school and he wasn't. He was on the road for three and four days a week for Brigham, and I was in lab, so we never saw each other. He resented me, and it started to come out in strange ways."

"What ways?"

"Like sex. It got weird. He started to want to do things that I didn't like."

"What things?" Christine kept her tone gentle, seeing that Hannah was reluctant to continue.

"Like he wanted to tie me up, to be submissive. I'm not an idiot, I could see why. He resented that I was doing better, so he had to assert his power. His dominance." Hannah pursed her lips. "He wasn't in control of his life, so he tried to control what he could. Me, in bed."

"Did he say how he wanted to tie you up?" Christine shuddered, knowing that it dovetailed with the serial killer's MO, tying up the nurses.

"Yes, at the wrists, in front." Hannah's expression darkened. "I know, when I read that's what the serial killer did, it freaked me the eff out. I mean, when I first knew him, I never would've thought he was capable of killing anybody, much less being a *serial killer*." Hannah flared her eyes in disbelief. "But then, when he got arrested, I thought about how he got so weird in bed, toward the end. I could've been his *next victim*."

Christine felt sickened, but she had to press on. "Did the police interview you?"

"They tried to, but my father called our lawyer and she said no way. I don't want to get involved. The cops might try again, but she'll handle it."

"So the police don't know any of this?"

"No. You won't tell them, will you?"

"No, of course not." Christine realized the information was what Griff had called bad facts.

"I don't know if he did it or didn't. I just don't want to be involved in this. Zachary's just a guy I dated, and it was good while it lasted, then it fizzled." Hannah met Christine's eye directly, straightening. "Don't involve me. Don't even think about calling me to testify for him. I wouldn't be a good witness for him, you can see that."

"Yes, I understand," Christine said, though she felt more confused than ever. She had gone from believing in his guilt, to believing in his innocence, then back again to guilt.

"Now that it's over, I'm starting to think that I didn't really know him. He liked to travel. He likes moving around. He never sits still. He doesn't let anybody get to know him. He deflects really hard questions. He won't answer stuff about his past. I think he used to tell me stories just to get my sympathy, like about his sister dying."

Christine remembered. "But that's a true story, isn't it?"

"Yes, I think it is." Hannah nodded, pained. "But even if it's a true story, what I figured out about Zachary is that he tells it for a reason. He tells it to make you feel sorry for him, and he's so good-looking, and nice, and smart, the combination is irresistible. I said to him once, 'you're the kind of guy who wins *The Bachelorette.*' With him, there's just no there, do you know what I mean?"

"Maybe," Christine answered, truthfully.

"I have to go." Hannah checked her phone, then stood up. "Take everything he says with a grain of salt. Even that he's innocent."

Chapter Forty-five

Christine phoned Griff as soon as she got in the car, driving out of the city on the highway. It took her three calls in quick succession to reach him, but he finally picked up. "Griff, we need to talk. First, you need a cell phone."

"I don't want a cell phone."

"Too bad. I'm buying you a cell phone." Christine thought of what Detective Wallace had told her about Griff's money. "Or you're buying one for yourself. Either way, you need a cell phone because Zachary was injured at the prison yesterday and they couldn't reach you."

"I heard, today. It's over."

"He saved the guard's life. Can you use that to get him moved to Chester County Prison?" Christine steered ahead in the fast lane, whizzing past a wide river that ran beside the highway. Brightly painted Victorian boathouses lined the far bank of the river. It was a lovely sight, but she was no tourist.

"No, they won't do it."

"But he's in isolation, in ad seg."

"It's hell, but it's safe. Pick your poison." Griff didn't sound happy. "Now what do you want?"

"I went to the crime scene, then I met with Zachary, his boss, and his girlfriend and—"

"You want applause?"

"No, but I was hoping I could fill you in and we could talk it over. I could use a sounding board, like last night."

"I want to die without being anybody's 'sounding board.' "

Christine let it go. "How about I just fill you in? I'll begin at the beginning, because it's complicated—"

"What's the headline?"

Christine collected her thoughts, driving into the sun as the highway curved to the left. She flipped her visor down. "Zachary lied about when he met Gail because he didn't want his girlfriend to know he cheated twice—"

"Good answer."

"—but the woman who used to be his girlfriend is no longer his girlfriend. His old girlfriend's name is Hannah Dolan, but she's not the woman paying half of his retainer."

"Don't care. Deposited the check. Can the old girlfriend give him an alibi for the night of the murder?"

"No."

"Can she give him an alibi for the other murders, Allen-Bogen and McLeane?"

"I didn't ask her, or him."

Griff snorted.

"I'll ask him next time."

"What about the new girlfriend? Can she give him an alibi for any of the murders?"

"I don't know. I didn't know about the new girlfriend until I met the old one—"

"Find out."

"But I don't know her. I'll have to ask Zachary, unless your receptionist got the name of the woman who dropped off the cashier's check."

"I have no receptionist."

"Whoever accepted the hand-delivery of the check, then."

"Phyllis? She'll do me no favors. That woman is a harpy."

Christine let it go. "I'll ask Zachary then."

"Don't tell me what you're going to do, do it. That's why you make the big bucks." Griff chuckled at his own joke.

"Oh, you're a laugh riot." Christine accelerated. Traffic was thick but moving fast. If it stayed that way, she would make the vigil on time.

"Did the old girlfriend talk to the police?"

"No." Christine considered telling Griff about the sex games that Zachary had tried, but she wasn't sure if that fell into the category of good news. Also she didn't want to give him a heart attack.

"How about the new girlfriend? Did she talk to the police?"

"I don't know."

"Where are you?"

"On the way back."

"Pick up a pizza, double cheese this time."

"I'm not going to the office. I'm on my way to the vigil for Gail Robinbrecht." Christine checked the dashboard clock, which read 1:32. "It starts at three o'clock."

Griff sighed. "Okay. Good-bye and good luck—"

"No, wait, don't hang up. What happened today? You were going to meet with the detectives from Virginia and Maryland."

"I did."

"So?" Christine joined the fast-moving traffic past the City Avenue exit, where the highway expanded, heading west.

"I also met with an A.D.A. from Chester County."

"So tell me what he said. This would be communicating. We're communicating."

Griff groaned. "I don't like to yap on the phone. I'll tell you later."

"I don't want to wait. Just give me the headline." Christine figured that turnabout was fair play.

"Bottom line, Chester County has significant trace evidence that ties Jeffcoat to Robinbrecht. They have his hair on her, fibers from his shirt on her, and they have his fingerprints on her skin and in her apartment."

"But that's explainable," Christine said, defensive. "He found her. He touched her. He's been with her. He's been in her apartment twice. He told me all about it, how her blood got on him. I saw those pictures, and there's no blood on his uppers, which corroborates his story—"

"No matter. Juries love hard evidence. He was found there and the knife and tourniquet are his merchandise. It's strong circumstantial evidence."

"But Zachary's boss told me that Brigham's bone saws are available in any hospital and you can get the tourniquets anywhere."

"It's not enough. Plus the Chester County coroner took a swab from Robinbrecht, and though the test results aren't back yet, we know it is going to be Jeffcoat's DNA. Again, it's strong circumstantial evidence."

"So they had sex, he admits that." Christine knew more about Zachary Jeffcoat's DNA than Griff could imagine.

"Still, DNA establishes the link, the connection."

Christine didn't need that explained. She understood the connection at soul-level.

"And now we know that it wasn't his first visit to Robinbrecht's apartment. They don't know that we know that."

"What about Maryland? What did those detectives say?"

"The murdered nurse was Susan Allen-Bogen at Bethesda General. Maryland can prove that Bethesda General is an account of Jeffcoat's and that he was there that day, April 13, calling on them. Jeffcoat's boss supplied copies of his hotel and gas reimbursement receipts. The police got him on EZ Pass cameras, and the hospital has him on its parking garage cameras."

Christine's heart sank. "But why would Zachary put in for reimbursement on a trip in which he killed somebody?"

"He has to. His boss knows he sent him there, and Jeffcoat regularly puts in for reimbursement. He wouldn't be fooling anybody if he didn't ask for reimbursement."

"Well, the important thing is that Zachary doesn't know Susan Allen-Bogen. He never met her. He never met either of the other nurses."

"They have him in an elevator talking to Allen-Bogen, three hours before she was murdered. The security camera in the elevator got the footage."

"Really?" Christine asked, aghast. "Did they show you this footage?"

"No, of course not. They told me they have it. I believe them even though they're prosecutors."

Christine tried to understand the legal procedure. "Why do they tell you what their proof is, in advance?"

"They do it to persuade me to let them talk to Jeffcoat. I got my free discovery, then I said no."

Christine wondered if Zachary had lied about knowing Susan Allen-Bogen or if there was another explanation. "Maybe Zachary didn't remember meeting Allen-Bogen. Maybe he didn't even get her name. It's circumstantial."

"Uh-huh." Griff was noncommittal. "Except that it's the same pattern as Robinbrecht. He met her in the cafeteria that day, no text or phone call, and he shows up at her house that night. And Allen-Bogen was killed the same way, with the same MO, using the Brigham knife and tourniquet."

Christine didn't bother to tell him that it was a metacarpal saw. "Do they have trace evidence in Maryland, like they have in Chester County?"

"Don't know yet. They're waiting on the results to see if it's a match."

"How about Virginia?"

"Virginia can prove that Jeffcoat was at Newport News Hospital the day Lynn McLeane was murdered, January 12. Found killed with the same MO in her apartment, in bed. They can prove that the hospital is one of Jeffcoat's accounts, and his boss has already turned over the hotel receipts Jeffcoat turned in. They have the camera in the parking lot that got his license plate. So did the EZ Pass."

"But can they link Zachary to McLeane? He doesn't know her."

"They have him on security footage talking to her in the cafeteria line, the morning of the day she was murdered. They said he was very chatty."

"Do they have audio?"

Griff sighed heavily. "Of course not. What do you expect? A body mike?"

Christine's heart sank. "But once again, we don't know if he actually knew McLeane. He'll admit that he talks to nurses in the cafeterias. He hits on nurses at his accounts. We don't know if he remembers McLeane's name or actually knew her, much less went back to her apartment and murdered her."

"Uh-huh," Griff said again.

"What about the hard evidence, or trace evidence, or whatever it's called?"

"The tests take longer, and they're waiting for the results."

Christine tried to put it all together. There were too many facts to analyze on the fly, and her gut was churning. She had believed Zachary when he said he didn't know Allen-Bogen or McLeane. So either he lied or made a simple mistake. "So what does this mean for Zachary?"

"Bottom line, Virginia, Maryland, and Pennsylvania feel very good about their cases against Jeffcoat. They 'like him,' which is police-talk for they believe he's the Nurse Murderer. The fact that he was in all three hospitals on the day the three nurses were murdered, and were seen with him, is strong circumstantial evidence.

It won't get to our jury, but it's enough to get the FBI and the other two jurisdictions champing at the bit."

Christine's mind reeled. Even if Zachary hadn't lied, he was in worse trouble than ever. "What did the FBI have to say? Did they meet with you?"

"No. The FBI doesn't meet with defense counsel."

"Then how do you know what they said?"

"The detectives from Maryland and Virginia told me, trying to make me shake in my boots." Griff chuckled. "The Feds are on board, lending them a profiler out of the Philly office."

"What did the profiler say, did they tell you?"

"The profile they developed is that the killer likes and respects women. He gets along great with them. The praying hands is a reference to nurses as angels on earth. They think he's a ladies' man."

Christine listened, disturbed. The description fit Zachary to a T. "But if he likes nurses so much, why does he kill them?"

"Because they're not appreciated on earth. They're too good for this mundane world. That's why he does no sexual violence, unusual for a serial murderer. He delivers them to heaven. That's what the profiler thinks."

Christine couldn't begin to wrap her mind around the twisted logic. She didn't know if it sounded like Zachary. "What do you think?"

"I think I missed lunch. I'm hungry. I'm hanging up."

"Okay, good-bye," Christine said, but Griff had already hung up.

Christine hung up, her thoughts racing. Could it be a coincidence that Zachary was in the same three places at the wrong time? How unlucky was he? Was he being framed? It horrified her to think that he really was a serial killer, but she knew she had to allow it as a possibility.

She tried to focus on the road. Traffic was speeding. She still couldn't bring herself to believe that Zachary was guilty. She didn't want to believe that the father of her baby could be so evil, so depraved. She squeezed the steering wheel to hold fast to something palpable, to tether herself to reality.

She headed west, driving into the hot white sun.

Chapter Forty-six

Chesterbrook Hospital was a massive modern complex of boxy tan buildings with orange tile rooftops, sprawling with associated medical offices, blood-testing labs, a physical rehab center, and parking lots and garages. Christine got out of the car and joined the stragglers heading to the vigil. She was running late because traffic had turned heavy, so she'd parked in the ER lot, which was the closest to the vigil, which was being held outdoors, behind the hospital, on the South Lawn.

The sky had clouded over, which seemed appropriate for such a solemn occasion, and Christine walked along the walkway, following people to the South Lawn. A hospital employee stationed at the lawn entrance handed her a bottle of water, a white program, and a white ribbon, which she didn't have time to pin to her dress. Even if she had, it would have felt wrong. She thought about using a blue Porta John on the route, but it reeked, and she was late.

She entered the South Lawn, a lush green carpet where a few hundred people stood facing a temporary wooden stage with forest-green skirting and a matching backdrop covered with CBH logos. At its center was a podium with a microphone, several folding chairs with seated men and women in suits, and uniformed West Chester police officers, in front of an American flag and a forest-green flag bearing the hospital logo.

Christine joined the back of the crowd, looking around. She'd come hoping to learn more about Gail Robinbrecht, and hospital employees were out in such force that they looked like an army of lab coats, blue, green, and maroon scrubs, green lanyards, and clogs. Everyone wore a white ribbon, and each face bore the traces of sadness. There were fresh tears from nurses who must've known Gail personally, and still others who carried green balloons and homemade posters with Gail's picture: GAIL, WE MISS YOU! FOREVER IN OUR HEARTS! CBH FOREVER RIP GAIL.

Christine caught snippets of conversation around her, either from employees talking about Gail—"dedicated nurse," "so sweet," "still can't believe it," "seems unreal"—or talking about Zachary, who had become the focus of their collective anger—"heartless bastard," "sick pervert," "they should fry him," "he'll never hurt anyone else." She felt like an interloper among them, her white ribbon tucked into her purse and the child of the man they all hated growing inside her very body.

The program got underway, and two massive screens flanking the stage came to life, broadcasting a magnified close-up of the speaker, a middle-aged man in a gray suit, at the podium. Some of the crowd ahead of Christine surged forward for a center view of the stage, but others flowed around the right side of the stage, settling for a parallax view, if closer to the front. She joined the latter group and noticed a group of downcast nurses in patterned scrubs in the front row of the crowd, their arms linked together as they stood. Among them she recognized the older nurse and the younger Asian nurse from the memorial, and Christine realized that they were the orthopedic surgery unit, where Gail had worked. Next to them was a reserved section, cordoned off by a green sash, which held a grief-stricken older couple who had to be Gail's parents, sitting with their other family and friends. They

raised their glistening eyes to the stage when the man at the podium tapped the microphone.

"Good afternoon, ladies and gentlemen," he began to say, his
voice solemn. He had on rimless glasses and a shaven head, a masculine look he managed to pull off. "My name is Dr. Adam Verbena, CEO of Chesterbrook Hospital, and I welcome you to this
program, at which we will remember one of our dearest colleagues,
nurse Gail Robinbrecht. Gail worked for the past nine years in our
orthopedic surgery unit and was beloved by all of us and by her
patients. Today will be a celebration of her life and of all she
gave to those around her, because that's what nurses do, and that's
the way she would've wanted it, as those of you who knew her
the best will agree."

Christine glanced at the orthopedic surgery nurses, who nodded
in approval, and there were sniffles throughout the crowd. Everyone faced front, except for a handful of children who fidgeted,
and Christine realized that the public must have been invited.
Older people sat on folding chairs that had been set up on the
other side of the crowd, and she spotted a hugely pregnant woman
sitting with them, wondering how she felt. Off to the side, she
recognized the group of Gail's neighbors, sitting together: Kimberly
and Lainey with their neighbor Dom, Rachel the brunette horse-
woman with her boyfriend, Jerri the Indian-American wife, who
had seen Zachary in Gail's kitchen, sitting with her husband, and
Phil the good-looking WCU student with the headphones, sitting
with his girlfriend and his roommates, who lived two doors down
from Gail.

On the stage, Dr. Verbena was saying, "Today, we will have
only three speakers, after Father Lipinski leads us in a moment of
silence. You will then hear from Dr. Milton Cohen, CEO of the
Suburban Health System, Dr. Grant Hallstead, Chief of Orthopedic Surgery, and Ms. Rita Kaplan, Chief of Nursing, who will recall
the day that she hired the young Gail Robinbrecht." Dr. Verbena

stepped aside. "Father Lipinski, would you lead us in a moment of silence before your speech?"

Christine took a sip of water, and when her stomach growled unhappily, she found herself wondering how long the program would be. She was regretting not having used the Porta John on the walk down. She looked around for another, but the only one was way in the far back of the crowd and the line was long.

A black-robed Father Lipinski came to the podium, then adjusted the microphone. "Ladies and gentlemen, friends of the hospital community and neighbors, please join me in a moment of silence for Gail Robinbrecht."

Everyone's head bowed, and Christine felt vaguely dizzy as she looked down, noticing that her feet were swelling, puffing out of her espadrilles. It must have been due to all the running around she was doing, though it hadn't happened before. She thought the books had said that her feet wouldn't swell until the eighth or ninth month.

The moment of silence ended, and Father Lipinski continued, "Thank you, ladies and gentlemen. At times like this, it is difficult to trust in God's wisdom, for one of our brightest lights has been taken from us. In addition, at times like this, we may find ourselves questioning His ways . . ."

Christine began to lose focus as the pastor spoke, and her thoughts strayed to the evidence against Zachary and how he'd been filmed talking to Allen-Bogen and McLeane, though he'd told her he didn't know them. There was too much evidence to dismiss, even though Christine didn't want him to be guilty, with every fiber of her being. She shifted on her feet, which were beginning to ache.

Father Lipinski ceded the podium to Dr. Milton Cohen, who was tall and good-looking in a corporate way, with dark hair going silvery gray at the temples. He began to speak, and Christine tried to pay attention, his speech sounding sadly like the others;

"wonderful nurse," "always a smile," "upbeat attitude," "made every patient feel special."

Christine started looking around for a bathroom, noticing that the physical rehab building was across the parking lot, not that far. Its entrance hall was a box of glass, and she could see hospital personnel and people in street clothes inside the lobby. The first floor had to have a bathroom, but she didn't know if she could sneak away from the vigil without being noticed or rude. She tried to hang in and pay attention.

The next speaker was Dr. Grant Hallstead, and he was younger than she would have expected for someone so responsible. His light reddish hair was cut in layers, and his eyes were brilliant blue, magnified on the screen. He spoke with a preppy accent, his vowels plummy as he added to the consensus; "an excellent nurse," "brought cheer to our unit," "always a kind word," "took extra shifts even when she wasn't asked," "had a brilliant future stolen from her."

Christine couldn't pay attention because her bladder was filling. She had to get to a bathroom, and the physical rehab building was the closest. She backed away from the crowd and hustled past the stage, noticing more men and women in suits conferring in low tones behind the green curtain.

She hurried off the grass, reached the concrete sidewalk, and scooted through the parking lot of the physical rehab building, ducking a passing Cadillac. She made a beeline for the entrance, threw open the glass door, and mouthed to the security guard, "Ladies' room?"

"To the right," he answered, pointing.

Christine hurried past him, made her way through the lobby, then followed the signs to the restrooms. The men's room was first, and the ladies' room predictably down a long hall. She scurried along, reached the ladies' room, and pushed open the door, startled to find three women in suits, looking over some notes for the vigil program.

"Oh, I'm sorry!" Christine said, almost banging into them.

"Excuse us," said one of the women, stepping back. "We shouldn't have been so close to the door."

"No, my fault." Christine headed to the last stall, to give herself some privacy if they were going to use the ladies' room for their meeting. She closed the stall door, practically threw her purse at the hook on the back, and slid off her underwear just in time to sit down.

Outside the stall, the women were saying, "Tell Rita that Gail's mom and dad are in the crowd. They're sitting in the first row on the right, the far right."

"Got it," the other woman said. "What are their names again?"

"John and Hilda Robinbrecht."

"Hilda, really?"

"Yes, okay, let's go," the other woman answered, then Christine heard the sound of the ladies'-room door opening and heels clattering out, leaving her finally in peace.

Christine let herself relax on the toilet seat, in no hurry to get up because it felt so good to finally sit down. She looked at her feet, which were still swelling. She straightened her legs to elevate them, and in the next moment, she heard the ladies'-room door bang open again, then came more clattering shoes and the sound of a woman bursting into tears.

"What a jerk!" the woman cried out, between hoarse sobs. ". . . he has some *nerve,* really that man has the gall of ten men . . ."

"It's okay, honey, it's okay," another woman said, her voice soothing.

"No it's not . . . I should go out there and bust him . . . standing up there in front of all those people . . . so proud of himself . . . I should tell everyone what a fake he is, he's friggin' *married*!"

Christine kept her feet up, so they wouldn't know the stall was occupied. It was hard to do, but it was too awkward to reveal that she was there. From the sound of the conversation, someone had been having an affair with a married man. She didn't want to embarrass them or herself.

"Honey, you have to get a grip. We have to go back out there. People are going to notice you're not there."

"They know I'm her best friend . . . they'll expect me to cry . . . he doesn't deserve to speak at her service . . . he didn't deserve *her* . . . I know she really loved him . . . but I told her, 'he's using you, he's never gonna leave his wife, ever' . . ."

Inside the stall, Christine couldn't believe what she was hearing. "*Her* service?" The two women must have been talking about Gail. Gail must have been the one having the affair, and the married man must be one of the speakers at her vigil. Christine flashed on the orthopedic surgery nurses at the memorial. They had told her the funny nickname of Gail's best friend. *Dink.*

Outside the stall, the sobbing resumed. "It's so unfair that she died right now . . . when she was going to end it for good . . . she was trying to date . . . she knew I was right . . ."

"Wash your face, come on. We have to go back out. Keep your cool. Do it for Gail. She would want you to, Dink."

Dink. Christine had been right. She couldn't wait to hear more. If Gail had been having an affair with a married man and had wanted to break up with him, then the married man could be a suspect in her murder. It was certainly possible. Christine made herself keep her feet high, so they wouldn't know she was there.

Dink's sobbing began to subside. "He would never let her go . . . but he wouldn't commit to her either . . . he wanted it both ways . . . the *ego* on that man . . . he's a total narcissist . . . I should tell everybody that he's a fraud . . ."

"No, don't do that. That won't help now, and it will just upset her parents. Here, blow your nose. Let's go."

Inside the stall, Christine's thoughts raced. So one of the speakers could be Gail's killer, but which one? They were all in hospital administration, all about the same age, and all of them were decent-looking. She couldn't remember any of their names. She wished she could get her vigil program from her purse but didn't dare. She strained to keep her feet up, then she heard the sound of water running and the mechanical whirring of the paper-towel dispenser.

"Honey, hurry, really, we should go. They're all out there."

"That bastard!" Dink heaved a final sob. "He wasn't worth her tears—or mine. You're right, Amy. Screw him!"

"That's the spirit! Ignore him! Take the high road. You won't be sorry."

Christine realized that the existence of a married boyfriend also explained why Gail wasn't seeing anybody. Maybe Gail had been getting over the loss of someone in Iraq, but she had fallen in love with a married man who was stringing her along. Christine heard some nose-blowing outside the stall, then the door opening and shoes clattering as the women left the restroom.

Christine jumped up, dug inside her purse, and pulled out the program for the vigil, which was folded in half. On the right was a list of speakers, and there were three male names: Dr. Adam Verbena, Dr. Grant Hallstead, and Dr. Milton Cohen. One of them could have been Gail's killer.

A serial killer.

Christine reached for her phone, hurried out of the stall, and flew out of the restroom.

Chapter Forty-seven

Christine called Griff, praying that he answered the phone, as she hurried down the hallway. She wanted to keep track of Dink and Amy, but the hallway was already empty. They couldn't be far ahead of her. She had to catch them.

"What now?" Griff asked, picking up the phone. "I saw it was you on caller ID. I answered anyway."

"Griff, this is important." Christine hustled down the hallway. "Gail had a married boyfriend, one of the higher-ups at the hospital. She was about to break up with him or she may have, because he kept saying he would leave his wife but he wouldn't—"

"What is it with the romance—"

"—Griff, it's relevant—"

"—this one's girlfriend, that one's boyfriend—"

"If she were going to break up with him, maybe he killed her to stop her, or out of anger. What can we do with that information? Can't we call the police and tell them that he could be a suspect?" Christine reached the end of the hallway and entered the lobby, which was bustling with more hospital employees and patients arriving for physical therapy. She assumed the vigil had ended.

"Who could be a suspect?"

"The married boyfriend." Christine lowered her voice, so she couldn't be overheard. She didn't see Dink and Amy, but she didn't know what they looked like. She hadn't even gotten a chance to see their shoes. She looked for a woman who looked as if she'd been crying, but didn't see one as she headed for the exit.

"What's the boyfriend's name?"

"I don't know. He's one of three speakers at the vigil. If we tell the police all three names, they can investigate, can't they?"

"Who told you about this boyfriend?"

"I heard it in the ladies' room."

"Gossip." Griff scoffed.

"Trust me, it's true." Christine figured that only a woman would know that a ladies' room could be a goldmine of information.

"What's the best friend's name?"

"Dink." Christine left the building and looked ahead for Dink and Amy as she hurried across the parking lot, careful of the cars pulling out of spaces, having used the lot to park during the vigil. Still no luck.

"Dink is a name?"

"It's a nickname."

Griff sighed heavily. "What's the real name?"

"I don't know, but I bet I can find her." Christine reached the grass and made her way toward the South Lawn, where the crowd was dispersing. People scattered toward the various parking garages, and others flowed into the hospital entrances, returning to work. Some remained behind, standing, talking, and wiping their eyes in somber groups, clinging to each other for comfort. She spotted the group of Gail's neighbors leaving together, and Kimberly was crying, being comforted by her sister Lainey and Dom, trailed by Jerri and Rachel. Phil, the handsome WCU student, spotted Christine and gave her a friendly wave, and she waved back, preoccupied. She scanned nurses who looked like they'd just come off a crying jag, but none of them seemed as upset as Dink had been.

"What's her last name?" Griff was asking.

"I don't know that either, but I can find out. She works at the hospital in the same unit as Gail."

"How do you know it's true?"

"Because I overheard it, and it makes sense. That's who Gail must've been seeing. She was trying to break up with him. She was trying to get her life back on track to meet somebody new. That's probably why she hooked up with Zachary." Christine passed the back of the dais behind the green curtain, where the hospital officials gathered, and she eyed the group hard. She didn't see Dink or Amy but she did spot the three male speakers: Dr. Verbena, with the shaved head and the glasses, who was talking to a township official; Dr. Hallstead, the tall ginger with the preppy accent, who was talking with the priest; and Dr. Cohen, the tall one with the graying temples, who was talking with a group of women in pastel suits.

"Is that all you got?" Griff was saying.

"That's a lot! Can't we call the police and tell them? He could be the person who killed Linda Kent, too. He would've worried that Linda Kent had seen him. If he was Gail's married boyfriend, he was probably at her house plenty of times." Christine hurried past the stage, where folding chairs were being put away by workmen. She scanned the crowd for the orthopedic surgery nurses because that was the likeliest place Dink and Amy would be.

"No. It's not enough to call the D.A. with."

"Why not? Why don't you try?" Christine remembered what Detective Wallace had told her earlier. "I heard you're a big contributor. They told me they'd do anything for you."

"Who told you that?"

"Does it matter? Call them." Christine threaded her way through the crowd, looking for the orthopedic surgery nurses.

"They don't investigate leads as a favor. But if you get the best friend's name and get her to come forward . . ." Griff's tone changed, taking on an earnestness it hadn't had before. "I could take that to the D.A. I would, too. Right away."

"On it." Christine kept moving toward the back of the crowd. Ahead she caught a glimpse of the older nurse and the young Asian nurse from the orthopedic surgery unit, standing in the middle of a group that clustered around a crying woman.

"Then call me when—"

"Bye." Christine hung up and beelined for the nurses, joined the back of the cluster, wedged her way next to the older nurse, and got her attention. "Hello," she said, with a smile. "Remember we met at Gail's, at the memorial in front of her house?"

"Oh, yes, I do." The older nurse smiled back at her, her hooded eyes glistening. "From the other day."

"I'm so sorry for your loss." Christine glanced over the older nurse's shoulder toward the center of the cluster, where a short nurse with a head of short blond curls stood out because of the brightness of her hair. She was comforting Gail's parents, their lined faces downcast and their narrow shoulders slumped together, a heartbreaking sight. Christine assumed the nurse was Dink and she had to get to her. It had started to drizzle, and Christine couldn't lose her chance.

The older nurse was saying, "Thank you, it was a wonderful service, wasn't it? I really felt as if Gail got her due."

"Yes, it was." Christine spotted the Asian nurse, looking over with teary eyes, and extended a hand. "Again, my condolences."

"Thanks," the young nurse nodded, then glanced up at the sky, which had clouded over, a dark pewter. "Looks like it's going to rain. The vigil ended just in time. It's so great to see such a large turnout, all for Gail."

"Yes." Christine pointed at the curly blond nurse. "That poor woman who's so upset, is that Dink, her best friend? Remember you told me about her?"

"Yes, that's her, with Gail's parents." The older nurse looked at Dink and Gail's parents, shaking her head sadly, and as they watched, it appeared that two township officials were trying to make their way toward Gail's parents, touching her father on the shoulder and waiting for him to turn around, which Christine saw as her opening.

"I feel so bad for Dink, and like I said, girlfriends are so important. I think I'll take a moment to pay my respects."

"Oh, okay," the older nurse said, blinking in puzzlement, but Christine wasn't waiting for permission. She waded into the cluster of orthopedic surgery nurses, and just when the township officials managed to get the attention of Gail's parents, she reached Dink and touched her forearm.

"Dink, hi, my name's Christine Nilsson, and I'm so sorry for the loss of your friend. Gail seemed like an amazing person."

"She was, thanks." Dink wiped her eyes with the soggy Kleenex, but her tears had been spent. She had hazel-brown eyes, but they were puffy and bloodshot, and freckles everywhere on a wholesome, pretty face. She was trim in a black linen dress instead of scrubs.

"You don't know me, but could I speak with you for just a minute, about Gail?" Christine gripped her forearm lightly. "Privately?"

"Sure, what is it? Why?" Dink frowned slightly, but was upset enough to let Christine lead her out of the cluster, though some of the other nurses looked over curiously.

"Dink, this is going to sound random, but I was in the ladies' room just now and I overheard you crying and saying that Gail had a married boyfriend—"

"Oh my God!" Dink's hand flew to her mouth. "I didn't check under the doors. I was just so upset."

"I know, and it's okay, but here's the thing." Christine didn't want to start with the fact that she was working for Zachary's defense. "Did it ever occur to you that Gail was killed by her boyfriend?"

Dink recoiled, shaking her head. "No, they caught the guy

who killed her. His name is Jeffcoat. He's a serial killer, the Nurse Murderer."

"But what if they got the wrong guy? What if the real killer is Gail's boyfriend? Gail wanted to break up with him, right? What if he wanted to stop her or was angry at her, for wanting to end it?" Christine talked fast. "I say this because I found out that Linda Kent, the woman who lived directly across from Gail on Daley Street, was killed in an accident Sunday night."

"Oh no, I know Linda. I met her. She was always out back. I didn't hear she was dead." Dink frowned, confused, but she was listening.

"Right, I met her, too. She was always out back, spying on the neighbors. She told me that she saw other men on Gail's back steps, and I think she saw one of them on the day of the murder."

"Not Jeffcoat?" Dink's lips parted in surprise.

"No." Christine's phone started ringing in her purse, and she checked it quickly. It was Marcus calling, so she didn't answer.

"Who then?"

"I don't know. She didn't tell me. She called the police to tell them, but they didn't call her back, and she was killed."

"Oh, man," Dink said, hushed, her bloodshot eyes widening.

"She fell down her stairs, supposedly by accident, but I looked into it and found some things that made me think she was murdered."

"What things?"

"It's a long story, but I think she was murdered because she knows who the real killer is. I don't think the real killer is Zachary Jeffcoat. The real killer could be Gail's boyfriend."

"But that would mean he's a serial killer." Dink shook her head, frowning. "He's a jerk, but I don't think he's a *serial killer.*"

"How do you know? You can't tell somebody's a serial killer just by looking. They can be very successful. They're selfish. Narcissists. Isn't that how you described him in the ladies' room? Doesn't that sound like her boyfriend?"

"Well, yes, it does." Dink nodded, newly tense.

"Or, think about this possibility." Christine was thinking aloud. "Maybe he's not the serial killer, but what if he killed Gail the same way the Nurse Murderer killed the other nurses, so the police would *think* the Nurse Murderer had killed Gail?"

"Like a copycat, like on *CSI* or something?"

"Yes, he knew about the Nurse Murderer, didn't he? It was on the national news."

"He knew, we all did." Dink's eyes flew open with a sudden realization. "Oh my God, he sent an email to us nurses three weeks ago, warning us about the Nurse Murderer and saying that we should be on the lookout."

"Three weeks ago?" Christine's thoughts raced. "What if he was setting himself up to kill her? What if he planned the whole thing? Did he know she wanted to break up with him?"

"Yes, totally." Dink met Christine's eye, a horrified expression coming over her face. "She told him she wanted to break up with him, over and over. He wouldn't take no for an answer. He's used to getting what he wants. He could have killed her, and nobody would believe it was him because of who he is."

"Who is he? Which of the speakers was he?"

"Grant Hallstead," Dink answered, glowering.

"The preppy one with the blue eyes?"

"Yes, that *bastard*." Dink's bloodshot eyes glittered. "The head of our unit, orthopedic surgery."

Christine thought fast. "As an orthopedic surgeon, would he have access to a Langenbeck bone saw? Do you know what that is?"

"Of course." Dink's mouth twisted with bitter anger. "He could have killed her. I wouldn't put it past him."

"So we have to go to the police. Let's go together. They'll investigate him and—"

"No." Dink shook her head, flatly. "That's so *not* what we're doing."

"Why not?" Christine asked, but in the next minute, she got her answer.

Dink had turned away and was stalking off in the direction of the stage.

"Dink?" Christine called out, hustling after her. "Dink!"

Chapter Forty-eight

Christine took off after Dink, realizing what was happening. The nurse was going to confront the man who she now believed had killed her best friend. Christine had to stop her. It wouldn't help Zachary unless Dink went to the police, and worse, it would alert Hallstead to the fact that he was suspected of Gail's murder. Christine shouted, "Dink, no!"

Dink ignored her, jogging through the crowd, her blond curls bouncing, her arms swinging, her stride strong and determined. She ran past the other orthopedic surgery nurses, who looked at her curiously, their heads turning in confusion.

One of the nurses, a tall African-American woman, grabbed Dink by the arm, trying to slow her step. "Honey, what's going on?"

"Amy, let me go. I know exactly what I'm doing."

"Dink, wait! Hold up!" Christine reached the nurse, touching her other arm, flanking her. "Don't do it this way. You're just going to tip him off. He'll get a lawyer, he could leave town. Let's get him the right way. Let's go to the cops."

"I don't care!" Dink didn't break stride or even look over. "I'm gonna call him out! I'm gonna bust him in front of everybody! He's going to pay for what he did to Gail!"

On the other side, Amy hustled to fall into step with Dink, her dark eyes flaring behind wire-rimmed glasses. "Dink, don't do this! You're going to get fired! He could even sue you!"

"He's a killer, Amy! He killed Gail! He killed her because he didn't want to let her go!"

"*What?*" Amy said, shocked, hustling to keep up with Dink. "What are you talking about?"

"Dink, no!" Christine grabbed the nurse's elbow, but she wrenched it away.

"Don't try and stop me! You didn't know Gail and you don't know me! Stay out of it!"

"Please, no!" Christine shouted, running beside Dink. People began to notice the commotion they were making, three women shouting and running through the astonished crowd. Nurses swiveled their heads to them in alarm, other hospital employees craned their necks to see what was going on, and people at the periphery looked askance, wondering who would disrupt such a solemn occasion.

Suddenly Dink broke into a run, her curls flying as she bolted forward, ignoring Christine's and Amy's shouts to stop. Amy outpaced Christine, who ran as hard as she could on her swollen feet.

"Dink, no!" Christine hollered futilely, as she watched Dink sprint around the right side of the stage and disappear behind the curtain, where the speakers had been. Christine picked up the pace, panicked as she ran through the crowd, which had parted to let them through. She veered around the side of the stage, where she saw that the speakers had dispersed, but Dink was running after them full-tilt as they walked toward the hospital entrance near the ER, Dr. Hallstead, Dr. Cohen, Dr. Verbena, with Rita Kaplan, some other men, and the women in pastel suits.

"Grant, Grant!" Dink shouted as she ran, but the group didn't hear her, crossing onto the sidewalk toward the entrance.

"Dink, stop!" Christine yelled, catching up with Amy, and the two of them ran side by side, shouting for Dink, who ignored them.

"Dr. Hallstead, Grant!" Dink hollered, and Grant Hallstead whirled around, his lips parting in shock. Dr. Cohen, Dr. Verbena, Ms. Kaplan, and the rest of the group turned around, too, confused and bewildered.

"You killed her!" Dink screamed. "You killed Gail because she wouldn't be with you! You're not going to get away with it! Not while I draw breath!"

"What are you talking about?" Hallstead asked, his eyes flaring.

"Don't you give me that crap! You were having an affair with her and you killed her because she wanted to break up with you!"

"No, no that's not true!" Hallstead's mouth dropped open, and the women gasped. Dr. Cohen looked over, frowning.

Dr. Verbena faced Hallstead in anger. "Grant?" he demanded, in an undeniably authoritative tone. "What is she talking about?"

"It's not true, it's not true!" Hallstead insisted, edging backwards.

Christine and Amy froze, watching the spectacle since there was no other choice.

Dr. Verbena gestured to Dink. "You may not know, Dink is my niece, Dolores Verbena. I've known her since birth. She doesn't lie, and she and Gail were the best of friends."

Christine bit her tongue, thrilled and dismayed. She wished she'd had this confrontation in the police station, but she never would've guessed that Dink was related to the CEO of the hospital. It gave her accusation instant credibility.

Hallstead was shaking his head. "I would never kill anybody, I would never kill Gail. I was with Milt the night she was murdered. Right, Milt?" Hallstead appealed to Dr. Cohen, holding his palms outstretched. "Don't you remember? We were in New York that night, for that conference? We even shared the same hotel room to save money."

"Oh, yes, right," Dr. Cohen answered, rattled, then he addressed Dr. Verbena. "Adam, your niece must be mistaken. I was with Grant at the conference that night. We both came back the next day on the train. We got the news about Gail then. It's an awful mistake to think that he killed her, or that he would kill anybody. He's a physician. We're all physicians."

Dink seemed stalled, and Amy went to her side, putting an arm around her. Christine felt shocked. Her theory was all wrong. Her lead was completely false. She didn't understand how she'd been so wrong. Hallstead might have been having an affair with Gail, but he hadn't killed her. He had a rock-solid explanation for where he was that night.

"Uncle Adam," Dink said, beginning to sob, "he had an affair with her. I know that for a fact! He *was* having an affair with her! He's just the worst, the worst!" Dink burst into tears, finally breaking down, and Amy wrapped her arms around her, giving her a hug, then looked over her shoulder at Christine.

"Who are you, anyway? How do you know Grant? What's your involvement here?"

"Nothing, I'm sorry," Christine said, backing away from the appalled crowd. She didn't want to give her name or any information.

"What did you tell her?" Amy called after her. "How do you know Grant? Who *are* you anyway?"

"I'm sorry, I have to go." Christine took off, mortified and upset. She hurried away from the dreadful scene and ran toward her car in the ER parking lot, which was after a pocket parking lot for doctors. She reached the car, chirped it unlocked, and jumped inside.

She started the engine and drove off, stricken.

Chapter Forty-nine

Christine felt her eyes brimming, joining the line of cars leaving the hospital. Traffic was moving swiftly, which was merciful because she had to flee the scene. So many emotions welled up inside her, she couldn't begin to parse them. She felt a wall of regret that she had gotten Dink so distraught, if not fired. She flashed on all of the nurses at the vigil, bereft. She remembered Gail's parents, in abject grief. She had disrespected the entire vigil.

Rain pelted the windshield, coming down in earnest. She flicked on the wipers. Christine turned onto Marshall Street, blaming herself for everything she had done, from the beginning. For going to Graterford, for working with Griff. For canvassing neighbors, visiting crime scenes, and playing detective. For thinking that she knew what she was doing. All of it had blown up in her face, now not only hers, but Dink's and Griff's. She had made a mess of everything, and worst of all, she had done it believing in Zachary's innocence. Now she knew she'd been a fool.

Christine turned onto High Street, wiping tears from her eyes. She was driving while crying again, but she couldn't hold it together. She had to accept the fact that Zachary had really killed Gail and the others. She couldn't be in denial anymore. He had lied about meeting Gail, about meeting the other nurses, and he even lied to her about who was paying his retainer. She had believed him because she'd wanted to, but she had been a fool. She had never felt worse than she did at this very moment, compounded with a wave of exhaustion and nausea. She was pregnant with the child of a serial killer, and now it couldn't be denied. Rain pounded on the windshield.

Christine headed down High Street, and just then her phone started ringing. She dug in her purse as she drove and checked the screen to see that it was Griff calling. She didn't know if she should pick up in her current state, but he had a right to know about the fiasco at the vigil.

"Griff?" she said, answering the phone.

"Christine? What's the matter?"

"It's a long story." Christine didn't know where to begin. "I'll give you the headline—"

"What's the matter? You sound funny."

"I'm trying to tell you, I was wrong. I was very wrong. I was wrong about everything."

"Christine? What's going on?"

"Gail had a married boyfriend, but he didn't do it."

"For goodness' sake, don't blubber about it. You're not driving, are you? You shouldn't be driving and yapping on the phone. All these devices, they'll lead to perdition."

"It was a terrible scene, a terrible scene."

"What was a terrible scene? You're not making any sense. Are you okay?"

"I'm fine," Christine said, blinking away tears, but she didn't know when she'd been worse. She drove down High Street in the downpour and passed her hotel, realizing that she was going the wrong way. She hadn't had a chance to put Griff's address into the GPS, she'd been too upset when she got in the car.

"Come back to the office. We'll talk about it."

"I will, I missed the turn. I think he did it, Griff. I think he's guilty. I think we've been working too hard and it's all for nothing, for nothing."

"Oh boy. What's the matter with you? What's come over you?"

"Everything is going to hell, Griff," Christine heard herself saying, her heart breaking. She thought of Marcus and how much she loved him, and how she didn't know if their marriage would survive this baby, Zachary's baby.

"Christine?" Griff said, his tone gentler, and just the sound of it in her ear reminded her so much of her father, who used to talk to her just that way, and she realized that she would never hear that tone from him again, that her father was already gone, that she was losing everything, that nothing was left.

"Christine? Answer me."

"I should go, I just want to hang up." Christine blinked her eyes clear to take the next right turn after the hotel, trying to get back to town, but she was stuck on a slick, two-lane road that curved around a park. She looked for a street to turn right, but all the streets were one-way, going the wrong way.

"Don't hang up. Now you have me worried about you."

"Don't worry."

"This is ridiculous. Come back now."

"I will," Christine said, following the road that seemed to be heading out of town.

"I have better things to do than to worry about you. This is why I work alone."

"I'm sorry, Griff. I'm sorry I screwed everything up."

"Stop feeling sorry for yourself. Where are you?"

"I don't know, I'm lost," Christine said, realizing the truth in the words.

"Help yourself then. Look for a sign."

"There's no sign." Christine drove ahead while the houses disappeared, replaced on both sides of the road by three-rail fences bordering pastures with herds of grazing horses, their backs dappled dark with rain.

"Of course there's a sign. Look for it."

"No, I don't see any." Christine rounded a curve and spotted a white route sign through the rain. "I'm on Route 842."

"Silly girl. You're headed out of town. Turn around and come back."

"Okay," Christine said, wiping her eyes as she cruised ahead. There was too much oncoming traffic to make a U-turn, so she kept driving, past bucolic scenery that she was crying too hard to appreciate.

"Did you turn around yet?"

"I will when I can."

"Stop blubbering. You're going the wrong way. It turns country fast. There's nothing out there but cornfields. Buck up."

"Okay," Christine said, but the tears kept coming, and her nose stopped up.

"I'll stay on the phone. I don't want you to kill yourself in a crash."

"I won't crash."

"I'll stay, nevertheless."

Christine felt touched. "No, that's okay, it's not safe, you're right. Let's hang up. Thanks."

"See you soon," Griff said, then hung up.

Christine hung up, wiping tears from her eyes, heaving a heavy sigh, and trying to compose herself. She dug in the console for a napkin to blow her nose with, but there was only one left. She blew her nose and wiped her eyes as she passed horses and cornfields along Route 842 and drove through a tiny town of Unionville, only three blocks long. Raindrops bounced off the windshield, coming down harder, and the road wound through even prettier country, with no houses or farms except for tall white silos far from the road. Cornfields surrounded her, their green swaying in the rainy gusts.

Christine's tears finally stopped, and she gave her nose a final blow with the soggy napkin, looking for a good place to make a

U-turn. There was still too much oncoming traffic. She glanced in her rearview mirror and noticed that a white Mercedes sedan was flashing its headlights at her. She accelerated, realizing she must have eased off the gas during her crying jag.

She drove ahead, looking for a street to turn into, but it was hard to see in the driving rain, and there were only cornfields. She glanced behind her again, and the white Mercedes was still flashing its headlights at her, which she didn't understand. There was no room to pass her, and Christine was going as fast as she could, so she put her right blinker on to signal that she would be turning soon.

She spotted a gravel road up ahead, slowed to get ready to turn right, then steered onto the gravel road. It was only one car wide, heading out of sight between the cornfields, and she braked to turn around, which would take some doing because it was so narrow. Reflexively, she checked the rearview mirror again. Oddly, the white Mercedes was still behind her.

She blinked her eyes clear, not understanding what she was seeing, but in the next moment, the driver of the white Mercedes lowered the window and stuck a hand outside, waving it frantically. The driver must have been a woman, and gold bangles lined her wrist.

And she started honking at Christine, trying to flag her down.

Chapter Fifty

Christine braked, startled to see the Mercedes driver get out of her car, slam the door behind her, and hustle toward her in tan heels, splashing through the watery gravel, heedless of the downpour. Rain flattened the woman's fancy salt-and-pepper coif and drenched the shoulders of her pink pastel suit.

"Can I help you?" Christine lowered her window, blinking against the rain just as the woman got there, her forehead buckled with pain and her mascara running, as if she had been crying, too.

"Who are you?" the woman demanded, distraught. She hooked her manicured fingernails over the top of Christine's window, her brown eyes desperate.

"What? Who are *you*?" Christine drew back from the window, and raindrops sprayed inside the car.

"What's your name? Do you work at the hospital? Are you another nurse?"

"Who are you? Why do you ask?" Christine said, bewildered.

"I'm Grant's wife Joan. I need to speak with you."

"Grant who?"

"Grant Hallstead, please don't pretend you don't know." Joan's bloodshot eyes filled with tears, and mascara dripped a black drop down her cheek. Rain poured down on her, drenching her suit, but she seemed not to care. "We're trying to work on our marriage, we're in counseling now, and he swore everything was going to be different now that Gail's gone. I'm asking you, I'm *begging* you to end your affair with my husband."

"*What?*" Christine asked, astounded. "I'm not having an affair with your husband!"

"I knew you were going to deny it, but please, I'm begging you, woman-to-woman, to leave him alone. We have three kids, still in high school, and I'm trying to keep my family together for them." Joan clung to the edge of the window in the pouring rain, and Christine felt terrible for her.

"Look, come inside the car, we can talk about this. You're getting soaked out there." Christine motioned her inside, and Joan scurried around the front of the car, and Christine slid the window up and unlocked the car doors as Joan jumped inside. "Joan, I'm not having an affair with your husband, I swear to you."

"Just hear me out, we can talk about this in a civilized way." Joan put up both palms, with slim fingers. "I don't want a fight or anything like that, I'm not going to make any trouble—"

"—no, really, I'm not having an affair with your husband—"

"—I just wanted to try to reason with you, and try to explain to you what's going on in our marriage, so that maybe you would respect it." Joan spoke fast, her words running together, powered by emotion, but Christine had to get a word in edgewise.

"Joan. I'm really not having an affair with your husband—"

"I see that you're married, too, and I hope that you can understand what it's like in a long-term marriage. I can see I'm older than you, he always picks younger nurses"—Joan's lower lip trembled, still bearing the traces of pink lipstick—"and I thought it would change after Gail, he swore to me it would, so I was so surprised to see you at the vigil with Dink—"

"—I'm not a nurse. I don't know your husband. I never met him before."

"You didn't?" Joan blinked a few times, then wiped a smudge of mascara from under her lower lashes.

"I'm not from here. I'm a teacher from Connecticut, and—"

"How did you meet Grant?" Joan frowned, bewildered, but she seemed to be slowing down, breathing more normally.

"I don't know Grant. Truly, I never even saw him before today at—"

"But why were you at Gail's vigil if you're not a nurse? Are you a friend of hers?"

"Joan, please, relax. I can explain." Christine dug in her purse, pulled out one of Griff's business cards, and handed it over. "My name is Christine Nilsson, and I'm working as a paralegal with Francis Griffith, a lawyer in town who's representing Zachary Jeffcoat. I've been investigating Gail's murder for the defense, and I should really apologize to you because I mistakenly thought that your husband could have been a suspect. I was wrong."

"Oh my." Joan looked up from the business card, and an astonished smile began to appear on her lovely face, which was heart-shaped and delicate, even fragile. She must've been in her late forties, but she barely looked thirty-five. "Are you serious?"

"Yes, completely. I really am sorry that I embarrassed your husband and you." Christine almost welcomed the opportunity to absolve herself. The rain picked up, thundering on the roof of the car and fogging the windows. "Were you part of that group after the vigil?"

"Yes, I was there with some of the administrators and the other wives. I was parked in the doctors' lot, and I saw you get into your car, so I followed you." Joan sighed happily and handed Christine back the business card. "I've never been so happy to find out that my husband was falsely accused of murder."

"Ha!" Christine liked Joan immediately. Any wife who could find the humor in the situation probably deserved a better husband, but Christine didn't say so.

"You have no reason to apologize." Joan met her eye, her crow's-feet wrinkling with irony. "Grant has a lot to answer for, God knows, but he wouldn't kill anybody."

"I'm sorry, though."

"Don't be, he deserved it." Joan's smile flattened. "I can't say that I mind that he got called out in front of his boss for the affair. That's the kind of thing that will make him think twice, too. He says he wants to save our marriage, so we'll see."

"Right." Christine was in no position to give marriage advice, so she kept her own counsel.

"You represent Jeffcoat?"

"The lawyer I work for does."

"You don't think that he killed Gail? You don't think he's the Nurse Murderer?"

"No, I don't," Christine answered, because she had to give the party line.

"Why did you think Grant did it?"

"I overheard Dink in the ladies' room, saying that Gail was having an affair, so I went to Dink, who said it was with Grant, but then she flew off the handle. Evidently, I'm not as good a detective as I thought." Christine felt uncomfortable talking about it so frankly, but Joan didn't seem to mind. With the pounding rain and the foggy windows, the conversation turned girlfriendy.

"You know, I did some snooping myself, when I started to suspect that Grant was fooling around with Gail." Joan pursed her lips, with a sheepish half smile. "I looked up where she lives and started to go by her house, to see if I could catch his car in the backyard."

"Really?" Christine shifted forward, interested.

"Yes, and I did catch him, and I confronted him and he admitted it."

"That must've been sad."

"It was, but it was also good in a way because it gave us a chance to turn it around. I think he deserves a second chance. I think everybody does."

"Right," Christine said, thinking of Marcus.

"You know, I saw Jeffcoat there one night, I think it was on a Thursday."

"Really?" Christine remembered that that was the same night that Jerri Choudhoury had seen him, too.

"Yes, it was late at night. I went to Gail's because Grant had told me that he had a meeting at the hospital and I didn't trust him. It's hard to break the habit when you find out someone's been unfaithful. You check receipts, you check his phone and email, things like that." Joan paused, her expression darkening. "I even checked Gail's house the night she was murdered."

"You did?" Christine asked, surprised. "Did you see anything?"

"I went there because Grant said he had a business trip with Milton Cohen, you heard him."

"Yes, I did."

"But I wasn't sure I believed him. I looked up online to see that the seminar was being held, which it was, but I didn't know if Grant was really going or if it was just his story. I worried that he could sneak back to see Gail, so I drove over to her house."

"Did you see Jeffcoat's car or did you see him going up the stairs?"

"No I didn't."

"Do you know what Jeffcoat looks like?"

"Yes, he's blond, but the man I saw wasn't blond."

"Oh my God. You saw a man there the night she was murdered?" Christine's juices started to flow. Joan could have seen Gail's murderer, and it evidently wasn't Zachary.

"Yes, but I left after I saw him because I got a call from Grant, and I knew he really was at the seminar in New York."

"Why didn't you go to the police?"

Joan met Christine's eye, newly defensive. "They said on the news that they caught the murderer red-handed, right at the scene, so I knew it couldn't be the man that I saw."

"Who did you see? Did you know him?" Christine had to contain her excitement.

"No, and I never saw him there before."

"Did you take any pictures of him?"

"No." Joan shook her head. "If it wasn't Grant, I didn't care who it was. I just wanted to make sure that he wasn't lying to me anymore."

"What did the man you saw look like?" Christine felt her heart start to pound.

"Let me think a minute. It was starting to get dark at that hour, too." Joan frowned in thought. "He was white, decent-looking. I forget what he had on. A sweatshirt and pants?"

Christine knew that could be anyone. "Tall or short?"

"Medium?"

"What kind of car did he drive?"

"He drove a—" Joan stopped abruptly. "Come to think of it, he didn't drive any car there. I just saw him on the steps going upstairs to Gail's, without pulling into the parking lot in the back."

"So he walked to her house?"

"I don't know." Joan shook her head. "All I know is, he didn't drive there."

"So he could have been anyone." Christine's mind raced through the possibilities. "A transient who parked somewhere else, maybe because he didn't want his car to be seen at Gail's house—"

"This man didn't seem like a transient. He walked with purpose, went right up the stairs. Like he knew where he was going, like he'd been there before."

"He could have been a man who lived within walking distance, even a neighbor." Christine felt appalled by the thought. "I interviewed the neighbors to see if they had seen anything that night. Most of them were women, but they all had husbands or boyfriends. Maybe it was one of the husbands? One who was cheating with Gail?"

"Well, we know that's possible." Joan sniffed.

"Sorry." Christine hadn't intended to be so tactless, but she was getting excited. She looked over, apologetically, then happened to see in the rearview mirror that a car was coming down the road behind Joan's Mercedes. "Oh, a car."

"Does it have room to pass? I can't see a thing for the fog and rain." Joan turned around in the seat, and Christine squinted at the rearview to see that the car had just enough room to get by.

"It's okay. We don't have to move."

"Good, I'm wet enough."

"It's also possible that the killer targeted Gail without their being in a relationship, because she was a nurse. They all knew she was a nurse. She gave block parties." Christine grabbed her phone from her purse and started scrolling through the pictures she'd taken when she canvassed to see if they yielded anything, though she hadn't been thinking of the neighbors as suspects.

"A neighbor killed her?"

"It's possible. The only male neighbors I met were Phil Dresher, a student at West Chester who lives a few doors down from Gail, and Dom Gagliardi, who lives with his wife around the block. They were both at Gail's vigil." Christine realized that the car hadn't passed yet, so she checked the rearview again. The car was parking behind Joan's Mercedes, which seemed strange. "The guy's pulling over, God knows why."

"Probably thinks we need help."

"In the rain?"

"That's how people are here. They help each other." Joan smiled.

"If he wanted to help, why not pull up beside us?"

"He couldn't see inside my car, maybe." Joan gestured at the phone. "So, you were saying."

"Right." Christine returned her attention to her phone and scrolled through her photos, which were all exterior shots of Warwick Street, but none of Phil. "Damn."

"No luck?"

"Not yet." Christine checked the rearview and saw that a man was getting out, hurrying toward them. She couldn't see his face because he had the hood on his parka up against the driving rain, but she'd deal with him when he got here. Instead she scrolled ahead to the photos she had taken at Linda Kent's, then pressed to enlarge one of Linda's backyard, and in the corner of the picture, almost out of the frame, was Dom's face.

"That's *him*." Joan pointed to the photo. "I recognize him. I saw him going up Gail's back steps that night she was killed."

"Oh my God. He told me he didn't know Gail, but if you saw him that night at her place, then he lied." Christine remembered with a jolt that Dom was the one who had found Linda Kent's body. What if he was the one who had put it there? He could have surprised Linda in her apartment. He knew that she smoked outside at night.

"Of course he's going to lie if he thinks he's getting away with cheating. Or murder."

"Joan, we have to go to the police with this." Christine's heart hammered. "Will you go with me?"

"Yes." Joan nodded, grave. "I couldn't live with myself if my silence caused a serial killer to go free."

"Or an innocent man to stay in jail." Christine looked at the rearview to see that the man had almost reached the car. The hood of the parka hid his eyes and nose, but he gave her a friendly wave and flashed a smile that she realized she had seen before. On Daley Street.

It was Dom.

Christine reached for the ignition and started the engine. "Joan—"

"What's going on?"

Suddenly Dom wrenched Christine's car door open, but she floored the gas pedal. The car lurched forward, but Dom clamped powerful hands down on her shoulders and lifted her bodily from the seat.

"No!" Christine screamed, terrified.

Dom yanked her from the moving car.

Joan yelled for help.

The car careened forward from momentum.

Christine felt an agonizing blow to the head.

And her world went black.

Chapter Fifty-one

Christine regained consciousness, crumpled on the gravel road. Rain pounded everywhere, pouring from a dark gray sky. Her cheek lay in a puddle; water filled her nostrils. Her clothes were soaked. A bolt of agonizing pain shot through her skull. She willed herself to wake up, remembering what had happened. She had been wrenched from the car, she heard Joan screaming.

Christine lifted herself up on her elbow. She whipped her head wildly around, blinking against the pouring rain. The car had rolled into the cornfield, askew. The engine was running. Her car door hung open. Dom was hurrying around the back fender to the passenger side. Joan was trying to get away, climbing over the console into the driver's seat.

Christine had to help Joan. She forced herself to move, to act. She staggered to her feet, but in the next moment, she saw Dom grab Joan's hair and yank her back into the passenger seat. Christine couldn't see what happened next. Horribly, Joan stopped screaming.

"No!" Christine cried out, horrified. Terror seized her heart. She couldn't save Joan. She had to save herself. She had to get away. Dom must have followed them from the vigil. He had to have been the serial killer.

She lurched off the road and threw herself into the cornfield. She ran away as fast as she could, whacking the stalks away. There was no clear path to run, she couldn't see any rows. The corn grew together like a thicket. Stalks sliced at her arms, and legs, razor-sharp. Bugs flew into her eyes. Crackling filled her ears, louder than the rain. She didn't know if she was running to the right or left. She had no sense of direction. Her head pounded from the blow. She ran ahead as straight as possible. Away.

"You bitch!" Dom yelled, raging. He didn't sound that far behind her.

Terror powered Christine forward. She couldn't let him get her. He would kill her. He would kill her baby. She powered through the corn, her legs churning. Rain filled her eyes. She could barely see. The leaves cut like knives. Cornstalks crunched under her feet. She tripped and almost fell.

She realized with horror that Dom could see her head as she ran. The corn only came up to her chest. She ducked her head and ran in a crouch. Her breath came raggedly. She got a stitch in her side. Her thighs burned, her feet ached. She suppressed the urge to scream. She couldn't waste the energy. There was no one around to hear.

Christine swung her arms like a machete, whacking away the cornstalks from her path. Rain set her shivering. Her teeth chattered uncontrollably. She stayed low so he wouldn't know where she was in the vast cornfield. Suddenly a flock of huge black crows flew from the corn, flapping their black wings beside her head, startling her.

"I'll kill you, you bitch!" Dom shouted, drowned out by the rain.

The crows gave away Christine's position. She couldn't stop now. She summoned every last ounce of strength, thinking of her baby. She had to save her baby. She was its mother. Her first duty was to protect her child. She thought of the butterfly heart on the ultrasound. The image powered her forward.

She could hear Dom breaking stalks behind her. He was a runner. He would make up for her head start. He was gaining on her. She put on the afterburners and ran even harder. She kept as low as she could, visualizing herself like a prizefighter, punching the cornstalks as she ran. Rain thundered in her ears.

Cornstalks crunched under her feet. Leaves sliced her hands and arms. The stems of the cornstalks were thick and strong. She whipped them aside with a backhand, cracking them in two.

Rain pounded in her ears. She heard the faint sound of traffic. Trucks rumbled ahead, and a horn honked. She angled her run to the left. Route 842 was there, and traffic. If she could reach the road, somebody would see her. Cars would stop. Dom couldn't slaughter her in full view.

Hope lifted her heart. She protected her belly with her left arm and whacked cornstalks with her right. Tears of pure fear streamed down her face. She tasted blood in her mouth.

"I'll cut your throat!" Dom raged, louder.

Christine felt a bolt of sheer terror. Dom sounded closer than before. She was losing ground. She panicked, tripping. She fell. She caught a faceful of cornstalks, filth, and bugs. Her hands plunged into mud and dirt. She could hear Dom's footsteps behind her, the crunching and rustling of the stalks as he ran.

She sprang up, lunging forward, trying to find ground with her feet. It was harder to run on an angle, against the grain of the rows. She threw herself at the cornstalks, desperate. Her breath sounded ragged. The rain poured. She whacked at the cornstalks with both arms. Some snapped back, others sliced her face. She winced in pain. Still the sound of the traffic got closer.

Christine's chest heaved. She didn't know how much longer she could keep running. She kept stumbling. Rain and bugs flew in her eyes. Her legs burned, her arms were heavy. She thought of the baby. She remembered she had moved her belt buckle this morning. She couldn't die. She had to save them both.

Suddenly she heard another sound, a mechanical one. Instinctively she looked up, but raindrops drenched her face. She almost lost her balance and fell again. The sound intensified. A rhythmic thwacking sound came from the sky behind the dense cloud cover. She recognized the noise. It was a helicopter.

"Help, help!" Christine screamed. She straightened up as she ran, waving her bloodied hands. She prayed the helicopter could see her cutting a swath through the cornfield. It sounded closer and closer, a mechanical thumping.

She glanced up, blinking rain from her eyes. The helicopter popped through the cloud cover, its big rotors turning. It was flying low and coming toward her. She waved her hands as she ran. It got closer, and she felt the turbulence from its rotors. Bugs and birds flew everywhere. The helicopter was the corporate green of Chesterbrook Hospital. It was a medevac.

Christine screamed for help, waving her hands in the turbulence. She was going to be rescued. Help was here. She didn't have to die here, not now, not today. She looked up again only to see the helicopter fly past her.

"No, no, help!" she screamed, running and running. The helicopter choppered to the gravel road. It must have been for Joan. Christine was on her own. She almost cried out with despair. No one was coming for her. She had to save herself and her baby. She didn't know if Dom was behind her, but he wasn't shouting anymore. He must've realized that he had to stay quiet and low or the helicopter would see him.

Her chest heaved, her lungs burned. She was almost out of breath. She didn't know if she could go another step, but she kept running, hacking away at the cornstalks, powering herself forward.

Suddenly she heard the faint sound of a police siren cutting through the rain. The police were on their way, coming toward her, but too far away. She had to keep going. Behind her she could hear the crackling getting closer, less than six feet, then five. Dom was closing the gap between them. He could reach out and grab her. He could kill her and get away.

The rushing sound of the traffic got louder and louder. She heard the honk of a car horn. She heard the louder rumbling of truck tires churning on the wet asphalt.

Christine screamed for her life, running and fighting her way through the corn. The rushing of traffic got closer and closer. She caught glimpses of the cars on the road through the stalks.

Suddenly she popped out of the cornfield, staggering to stay upright, her momentum carrying her forward into the road, where cars were rushing back and forth. She screamed as a pickup almost sideswiped her, skidding, but righted itself as she kept running across the road. She reached the other side, just as she heard a sickening *thud*.

"No!" Christine whirled around from the other side, just in time to see Dom struck by the massive chrome grille of a tractor-trailer that carried him forward before he vanished beneath its chassis.

Christine collapsed to her knees, in a flood of tears and rain. It could have been her, but it wasn't. She was alive.

And so was her baby.

Chapter Fifty-two

Christine experienced the next few hours as if they were a blur, after being collected at the scene by the Chester County Police, who arrived in force, taking statements from drivers who had witnessed what had happened, rerouting traffic around Route 842, establishing a perimeter with flares and yellow tape, and erecting a blue tent with screens around Dom's body, until the coroner came. Christine was taken to the hospital in an ambulance, sirens blaring, and she felt a sort of mute shock as she lay strapped into a gurney, while the EMT took her vital signs and phoned them in ahead.

Christine kept all of her emotions at bay, whisked to the emergency department at Chesterbrook Hospital, where she'd parked only hours before and caused the scene with Grant Hallstead. She never would've guessed that it would end with the gruesome death of Dom Gagliardi and the attack on Joan Hallstead, who was already in the OR. Dom had cut Joan's throat and left her for dead, but amazingly, she'd been able to reach her phone to call 911 in time. The hospital hadn't hesitated to send a medevac for the wife of one of its most prominent surgeons, and the word was that Joan had lost a lot of blood but was expected to recover.

Christine had been wheeled into the ER, changed out of her sopping wet clothes and into a hospital gown, then she'd been given a heated blanket and a saline-drip IV. Her cuts had been examined, irrigated, and covered with Neosporin. She'd asked the nurses to call Griff and Marcus, who was on his way. She figured he wouldn't arrive until the middle of the night, and she didn't want to think about how he had reacted to the news.

They checked her and the baby and both were given a clean bill of health. She got her discharge papers, but not before the nurses replaced her hospital gown with a fresh set of scrubs, as a parting gift. Scrubs were color-coded at Chesterbrook Hospital—navy scrubs were for nurses, maroon for radiologists, and teal for OR nurses—and Christine felt honored to don the navy scrubs that only nurses like Gail Robinbrecht were entitled to wear. But she tried not to think about that either, keeping tears inside.

Christine had been allowed to remain in the examining room to give a statement to the Chester County detectives, rather than go to the station house, and she waited for the detectives, muting the flat-screen TV in the corner, when CNN started running a video of the rainy scene on Route 842, above the banner, BREAKING NEWS—NURSE MURDERER DEAD IN TRUCK COLLISION. She glanced at the screen and flashed on her good-bye party, when she had first seen the video of Zachary's arrest. She knew she should feel happy that he would go free, but she kept even that emotion at a distance.

The first detective to enter the examining room was the one who had taken her through the crime scene, Detective Stuart Wallace, in his black logo polo shirt and khaki slacks. "Remember me?" Detective Wallace asked gently, crossing to the foot of her bed, his smile warmer.

"Yes, of course." Christine smiled back, though her face hurt from the cuts and scratches, as if her skin were too tight.

"How are you feeling?"

"Okay, good." Christine didn't elaborate. The truth was, she was trying not to feel.

"Griff says hi. He's out in the waiting room. He's been here since just a few minutes after you got here."

"Really?" Christine asked, touched.

"He called 911 on your behalf, even before Mrs. Hallstead did. He asked us to send a squad car after you to make sure you were okay. He asked us to look for you, just past Unionville."

Christine felt puzzled. "But how did he know I needed help?"

"He said he got a phone call from you, that you were upset or something?" Detective Wallace smiled sympathetically. "He was worried you were going to have an accident, driving distracted. We were already on our way when the 911 call came in from the doctor's wife." Detective Wallace pulled out a skinny notepad, and so did the two detectives behind him. "So, Christine, why don't you tell us exactly what happened, in your own words?"

Christine told him what had happened, starting with the vigil and ending with the hospital, and answered all of his questions. She managed to stay in emotional control, tearing up only when she remembered Joan's frantic attempt to get to the driver's seat and even Dom's getting hit by the truck, a horrific sight that would be seared into her brain for a long time. After Christine had finished her statement, Detective Wallace helped her to her feet and walked her to the waiting room, where he took his leave.

Griff rose unsteadily. "Good to see you're in one piece," he said, his lips parting in the beginnings of a relieved smile.

Christine entered the waiting room, crossed to him, and opened her arms. "I'm going to hug you, ready or not."

"No, no."

"Yes, yes." Christine gave him a big hug, and Griff emitted a soft little grunt. He felt soft, warm, and cuddly in his airplane-propeller bow tie and his rumpled seersucker suit, with a black umbrella hooked over his forearm. He smelled like cedar chips and pencil lead, and as she released him, his hooded eyes twinkled behind his smudgy tortoiseshell glasses.

"What was *that* for?"

"Thanks for waiting for me."

"What choice did I have?"

"Thanks for calling 911, too."

"What was I supposed to do? Who else will work for free?"

"Ha." Christine felt her smile widen. "What does this mean for Zachary? Do they let him out?"

"Not yet. It takes time. They just started their investigation of Gagliardi." Griff leaned closer, lowering his voice. "But the D.A. told me confidentially that Gagliardi is definitely the doer. They seized his computer and found photos of Robinbrecht, McLeane, and Allen-Bogen, taken postmortem."

"You mean, dead?" Christine asked, disgusted.

"Yes." Griff frowned. "It's not uncommon for serial killers to take pictures or trophies."

"What about his wife, did she know?"

"Evidently not. They have no kids."

"So why was he in the hospitals in the first place?"

"He brokers corporate insurance, mostly for health care systems. He calls on hospital administrators. That's how he finds his victims. If you hadn't stopped him, he'd still be killing." Griff's half smile returned, and Christine had to admit she was starting to feel satisfied, if not happy.

"I think somebody has to say 'good job,' don't you?"

"Good job." Griff's smile broadened, begrudgingly.

"Thanks." Christine warmed, knowing it was the best she'd get, and it was more than enough. She hadn't done it for Griff or even Zachary. She'd done it for herself and her baby. "So when does Zachary go free?"

"A day or two, after the government gets through with its red tape."

"So do we go tell him?"

"First, let's stop in at the office. I have someone you should meet."

"Who?" Christine took his arm, and Griff waddled beside her as they left the waiting room.

"You'll see. By the way, there are reporters outside. Should we tell them I bite?"

"They'll figure that out." Christine realized she'd have to come clean to Griff about who she was when they got back to the office. She wanted him to know the truth. "So are you going to make a statement?"

"No, I'll tell them 'no comment.'" Griff looked over at her. "Besides, I don't know if you caught the bad guy. Or the bad guy caught you."

"A little of both." Christine managed a smile as they made their way slowly down the hall. "You helped."

"No I didn't." Griff shook his head.

"Yes you did. You showed me I could do it." Christine had always said that teachers could do anything, and now she knew it was true.

"Let's take our time, going out. It's still raining. They'll get wet."

"Good idea." Christine smiled.

"You know, I made a decision. I'm not ready to retire."

"Good. Don't." Christine could see a throng of reporters through the glass exit doors, firing camera flashes in the rain.

"I'm going to get bunion surgery, then get back in business. I've got a lot of life left in me. That's what you showed *me.*"

"Good." Christine felt warmed. "But you need a new suit."

"Nah. All I need is a bulletin board." Griff laughed at his own joke.

Christine joined him, laughing, as they strolled out, arm in arm.

Chapter Fifty-three

Griff entered his office ahead of Christine, who was tired, hungry, achy, and not completely delighted to see a woman sitting in one of the chairs opposite his desk. The woman had chin-length red hair, and was slim and pretty in a white V-neck T-shirt and hip yoga pants. She had been scrolling through her phone, but she leapt to her feet with an excited smile when they came in.

"Tanya Spencer, meet Christine Nilsson." Griff eased into his desk chair with a tiny grunt. "And vice versa. From the Latin."

"Christine, my God, are you okay?" Tanya beamed at Christine, her admiration plain. "It's amazing, what you did today! You're a hero!"

"Oh, I don't know about that, but thanks." Christine crossed the room and extended a hand, then stopped herself because it was covered with Band-Aids. "Tanya, I'd shake, but maybe that's a bad idea."

"Totally, of course, you *are* a hero! You could have been killed!"

"Luckily, I wasn't." Christine sat down, realizing who Tanya was, because her red hair was the tip-off. Tanya must have been Zachary's new girlfriend, who had paid half of his retainer.

"Thank you so much for what you did for Zachary." Tanya retook her seat, perched on the edge, close to Christine. "You risked your life to help him. The news is on every channel. I saw the video on my phone."

"Well, it's not the way I wanted it." Christine and Griff exchanged looks since she had filled him in on the way over in the car. "But I'm glad that Zachary isn't going to have to stand trial for a crime he didn't commit."

"I agree, that would've been an awful injustice." Tanya's eyes flared, a light hazel color, set close together, with no makeup. She gave off a vaguely organic vibe in brown huaraches. "I can't stand that he's in prison right now. He doesn't belong in a disgusting place like that. He never did."

"No, he doesn't." Christine found herself curious about Tanya, especially after Hannah had thought that she was the only girlfriend. "Anyway, it's nice to finally get to talk to you."

"Finally? What do you mean by that?"

"I heard about you from Zachary and the woman at the prison. You're his girlfriend, aren't you?"

"No," Tanya answered, with a sheepish smile. "That's just a story we made up to tell the people at the prison."

Christine blinked. "So who are you?"

"I'm a single mom, and I conceived my son using donor sperm. Zachary was my donor."

Christine couldn't believe her ears. She didn't know what to say or do for a moment. Griff had fallen uncharacteristically silent, watching her and Tanya. Christine was going to tell him tonight, so she might as well. She turned to face him, but before she could say anything, he winked at her.

"Christine, you didn't really think I bought your reporter story, did you?"

"You didn't?" Christine asked, her face reddening, despite the tiny cuts.

"I had my doubts. Like I said, you're too nice." Griff smiled, his eyes wrinkling into his deep crow's-feet. "But I didn't know what you were up to until Tanya showed up. You're here for the same reason she is, aren't you?"

Christine swallowed hard, looking from Griff to Tanya and back again, then took a deep breath. "Yes, I am. Zachary is my donor, too. Donor 3319 at Homestead. I was going to tell you, tonight."

Tanya's smile turned sympathetic. "Sorry, I didn't mean to bust you. You didn't have to say if you didn't want to. I just don't think there's anything to hide."

Christine couldn't say she disagreed, but she did feel bad and turned back to Griff. "I'm sorry I lied to you. It just felt too strange to tell you why I was really here. I'm pregnant, is the thing."

Griff shrugged. "This is a brave new world, my dear. I would have lied to me, too."

Tanya interjected, "Right, Christine, everybody's different, so I totally get why you kept it to yourself."

"Thanks." Christine had never expected to meet another woman who had a child fathered by Zachary, so she was still trying to process the revelation.

"I used a donor because I hadn't met anybody that I wanted to marry yet, all the men I met were too immature, and I didn't want to miss out on having a child. I was going to freeze my eggs, but then I thought, why not just have a baby already?" Tanya's face lit up. "My mom and dad were all for it, they'd been dying for a grandchild. We all just adore him."

Christine understood completely. "So how did you find out about Zachary?"

"I'm a jewelry designer, and I have my studio at home. I keep cable news on in the background. I just happened to look up, and all of a sudden, there he was on TV. My donor. I recognized him from the adult photo he gave Homestead."

"Me too." Christine was actually happy to hear it, in a way. It made her feel less crazy.

"But it was *super* scary, thinking that the donor was a serial killer. Creee-py." Tanya shuddered in an exaggerated way.

"Exactly." Christine began to feel better, having the truth out in the open, even though it was awkward to have something so intimate in common with a perfect stranger.

"I freaked out and I called Homestead, but they wouldn't tell me anything. Neither would my doctor. She didn't even know."

"That's just what happened to us."

"I live in Baltimore and I thought, Philly's not that far. Let me go up and see what's going on."

"That's just what I thought." Christine felt her heart open up.

"So I went to Graterford, met Zachary, and I asked him, and he told me yes."

"So you told him the truth?" Christine asked, surprised.

"Yes, didn't you?"

"No, we haven't told anybody." Christine didn't want to explain. "So you already have a child?"

"Yes. Ranger." Tanya beamed. "He's great. My mom is baby-sitting him so I could come here, but I'm home with him, all the time. He's only eleven months old, but he's already pulling himself up on the coffee table, trying to walk. You want to see a picture?"

"Yes, please." Christine shifted over, her heart pounding.

"Here's my little monkey man." Tanya picked up her iPhone and displayed her customized phone case, which held an enlarged photo of an adorable strawberry-blonde toddler with bright blue eyes, patting a gray cat.

"He's so cute!" Christine felt a happiness that was hard to explain, as well as confusion. She realized that she was looking at the half-sibling of her own baby.

Suddenly, there was a knock on the doorjamb, and they all looked over. Marcus stood in the doorway, his suit rumpled, his tie off, and his face a mask of concern as his eyes met Christine's. "Honey, are you okay?" he said, hustling across the room.

"Marcus?" Christine said, confused, as he reached her side and enveloped her in a gentle embrace. She had no idea how he'd gotten here so fast, and it was hard to process that he was really here, even as she put her arms around his waist and laid her bruised cheek against his chest. She felt tears come to her eyes, but she didn't want to feel any feelings in front of anyone else. She just wanted to go home and pray that everything could be okay again.

"Honey, I'm sorry I let you come down here alone." Marcus released her, and his weary eyes scanned the cuts on her face. His lips parted, and he seemed appalled, but at himself. "Thank God you're okay."

"It's okay, I'm okay." Christine held back her tears, trying to compose herself. She gestured at Griff, stiffly. "Marcus, this is Griff, Zachary's defense lawyer."

"Nice to meet you," Marcus said, nodding in Griff's direction.

"Likewise. Your wife is an exceptional person." Griff smiled, almost proudly.

"Thank you." Marcus smiled back, his eyes glistening.

"And this—" Christine hesitated, not knowing how to introduce Tanya and too tired to keep lying, but she didn't want to upset Marcus more than she already had.

But Tanya jumped to her feet, reached for Marcus's hand, and pumped it with vigor. "I'm Tanya Spencer, and your wife is my hero! She risked her own life to prove that Zachary was innocent."

"I know, it's incredible." Marcus's face remained impassive, betraying none of the jealousy and resentment that Christine knew he must be feeling. "And Tanya, you are—"

"I'm a donor recipient of Zachary's, too. Just like you guys. I have a little boy, and Zachary is his biological father."

Marcus froze, then blinked.

Christine's mouth went dry. "Honey, I'm sorry, I just met Tanya five minutes ago, and I shared with her and Griff that Zachary is our donor."

Marcus's gaze shifted to Christine, and there was a new tension around his mouth.

"Marcus, I'm sorry, it just came out." Christine didn't know what else to say. She couldn't explain it anymore. She couldn't make the situation any better. She was tired of apologizing for nothing, of keeping a secret that couldn't be kept anymore. His ego was killing their marriage.

Griff had gone completely silent, and even the effervescent Tanya lowered herself into her chair, deflating like a birthday balloon.

Marcus inhaled visibly, turning to Christine. "Will you sit down, honey? We need to talk."

Chapter Fifty-four

M arcus, please." Christine sank into the chair, crestfallen. "You have to get this in perspective, you just have to. We can't keep it secret anymore and—"

"No, it's not that." Marcus reached down and caressed her shoulder. "Honey, I have news for you. Zachary Jeffcoat is not our donor. He's not Donor 3319."

"*What?*" Christine asked, dumbfounded.

"What did you say?" Tanya said, shocked.

Marcus looked down at Christine, his expression soft. "Gary got Homestead to tell us. He spoke with the parent company today. They offered to settle our lawsuit. They confirmed that Zachary Jeffcoat is *not* Donor 3319."

Christine felt confounded. "That's not possible. I mean, he told me he was. He matched the profile."

Tanya nodded, frowning in confusion. "Yes, and I asked him directly. He told me he was, too."

Marcus pursed his lips. "The truth is, he is not Donor 3319."

"Then who is?" Christine felt absolutely bewildered.

"Homestead wouldn't say." Marcus's expression remained gentle, his tone heavy. "That's not part of the settlement. They won't breach the real 3319's confidentiality. We agreed to settle if they would confirm or deny that Jeffcoat was 3319, and they confirmed that Jeffcoat is *not* 3319. He may look a lot like 3319, but that's a coincidence. In fact, Homestead took the real 3319 sample off the shelves because other patients were calling about the similarity. I left the office as soon as Gary told me, to bring you home. I was almost here when I got the call that you were in the hospital."

Christine shook her head, trying to process the information. A million thoughts raced through her brain. She felt herself slump, looking down. Her entire body ached. Her head thundered. She'd gone through hell and back, for no reason. Zachary wasn't her donor. She wasn't carrying Zachary's baby. She didn't know who their donor was, after all that. She looked up at Marcus. "So we're back at square one?"

"No, not at all." Marcus frowned slightly, buckling his lower lip.

"How so?"

Tanya interrupted, stricken, "I don't know how this could happen."

Griff raised his arthritic hand. "Let's go ask him."

"Now?" Christine looked over at Griff, and so did Marcus and Tanya.

"Yes. Lawyers have twenty-four-hour visiting privileges. I was going to go over, I was waiting for you, Christine." Griff rose, pressing himself up by a hand on his desk. "Let's go."

"Okay," Christine said, dazed.

Marcus took her hand and helped her to her feet.

Chapter Fifty-five

Christine, Griff, Marcus, and Tanya crowded into the inter-view booth, waiting wordlessly for Zachary to be brought in. Griff and Christine took the two chairs, with Marcus and Tanya standing behind them, and Christine tried to get her bearings. She couldn't wrap her mind around the fact that Zachary wasn't their donor, or the horrific events of the day.

The interview booth was the only bright spot in the visiting room, which was otherwise completely empty, with all the chairs vacant and the overhead lighting dim, having been turned on only because they were here. The entire floor was quiet, though Christine could hear shouts echoing hollowly elsewhere in the prison. The booth felt warm and damp, the air close and dusty. A corrections officer stood guard outside.

Christine straightened up when she saw Zachary through the Plexiglas of the door, approaching with a corrections guard. His face was still bruised and his eyes swollen, and Christine realized with a start that they had that much in common. Otherwise, she felt only confusion at the sight of him, not the connection she'd felt before, her emotions bollixed up. She didn't know what Marcus was thinking, standing behind her chair, and she was glad she couldn't see his face.

The corrections guard took the handcuffs off Zachary, opened the door on the secured side of the booth, and led Zachary inside, where he started talking before he sat down, his blue eyes shining with happiness despite the swelling in his right eye.

"Is it really true?" Zachary sat down in his chair, leaning forward, his hands on the counter. A huge grin animated his expression. "Am I getting out of here? Did they get who did it? One of the COs told me, he saw on the news! I'm in ad seg, I don't know anything! What happened? Griff, when am I getting out of here?"

Griff held up his hand. "I spoke with the D.A. He's not sure yet. These things take time. It might be tomorrow or the next day."

"What happened? How did they find out I didn't do it? How did they get the guy who did it?" Zachary looked at Christine, confused but still wildly happy. "What happened, Christine? Were you in some kind of accident? Why are you in scrubs? You look like a nurse!"

Griff kept his hand up. "Zachary, you need to thank Christine. She almost lost her life today, trying to prove your innocence. She is the reason you will be released."

"Christine, thank you so much." Zachary met her eye directly. "I don't know what you did, but I thank you from the bottom of my heart. I didn't kill Gail, I didn't kill anybody. I knew you believed in me. Thank you so much for whatever you did. For everything you did. I don't know how I can ever repay you."

"You're welcome," Christine said, on autopilot. She felt shaken to her very core. She thought she saw sincerity in his expression, but she didn't know whether to trust it. She didn't trust him anymore. She didn't trust herself, either.

Griff cleared his throat. "Zachary, I know how you can thank her. You can explain to her, and Tanya, why you lied."

Tanya interjected, standing behind Griff, "Zachary, are you 3319 or not? You told me you were, but Homestead says you're not. Christine's husband found out."

Zachary's smile vanished and his lips parted. His gaze went to Tanya, then to Marcus, and finally to Christine. He heaved a deep sigh in his orange jumpsuit, and his lower lip puckered with apparent regret. "Okay, Christine, Tanya, I did lie about that. I'm sorry, I truly am. I'm not Donor 3319. I never donated sperm, or blood, like I told you I did. I'm sorry, but I lied, I did."

Christine swallowed hard. The words had a visceral impact, and she absorbed them like a blow. She wasn't angry, she was confused. The fact that Zachary had been her donor had powered her every thought, and now that he wasn't, she felt as if the rug had been yanked from under her.

Tanya interjected, wounded, "Why did you lie to us? Why did you lie to me?"

"Tanya, I'm sorry to you, too." Zachary looked up at Tanya, his mouth forming a regretful line. "When you came to the prison that morning, you seemed so sure and so nice, and I thought if I told you yes, that you would help me, and you did. You did help me. You were there for me, you even gave me half of the retainer. I'm sorry that I lied to you, but if you want to know why I lied, I was desperate. I needed help. I didn't know what to do. You can imagine what it's like. I go to meet Gail for a date, and she's bloody, and she's dead, and I call 911, and the next thing I know, they arrest me for killing her. They think I'm a *serial killer*. I was desperate." Zachary lowered his gaze to Christine, leaning forward urgently. "Christine, I'm so sorry I lied to you, but that was why. You know how they say, 'desperate times call for desperate measures'? I was desperate. I had to get out of here. When I met you, and we started talking, I really did like you."

Christine felt a twinge. She wanted to believe him, but she didn't. Or she couldn't. Either way, it didn't matter now, and she didn't want to interrupt him, so she let him talk.

"I had seen the other reporters, but they were so tough and hard, and I thought there was something different about you, something nicer. Lauren, too." Zachary smiled warmly. "When you started to ask more personal questions, I started to think that you probably came to me because you saw me on TV, like Tanya had. You thought I was your donor."

Christine could see how it could happen. She hadn't known that Tanya was another donor recipient, but if she had, she would've suspected Zachary's admission that he was Donor 3319. Christine had thought that she had gotten to Zachary first, but she had been mistaken. Tanya had, and that made all the difference.

"Christine," Zachary continued, his voice gentler, "I was in the gen pop then, I went on the computer and looked up Homestead. Tanya had told me the name and the donor number. I read 3319's online bio, I got the details, and I used them when we talked. I'm a salesman, and I sold you. But I'm not proud of it and I'm not bragging, I hope you know that."

Christine did. She nodded.

"I'm sorry I lied, but I think you can understand it, can't you? You didn't tell me the truth, either. You lied for the same reason that I did, didn't you? You were desperate to know if I was your donor, and you didn't want to ask me, straight up, like Tanya did. I don't know why you didn't, but I don't blame you for that. You had reasons of your own, and I had reasons of my own. I had to get out of here. I saw my *entire life* being taken away. I was in the gen pop then, I saw TV. I was *convicted* by TV." Zachary's voice took on a new urgency, undergirded by fear. "I was being railroaded. Even after I saved the guard, it didn't make any difference. They say 'innocent until proven guilty,' but it isn't. As soon as you get arrested, you get treated like you're guilty. Christine, we both used desperate measures, didn't we?"

"Yes," Christine had to answer, hearing the truth in his words. She had lied to him, too. She had been desperate, too.

"But the thing is, it doesn't mean that I'm not grateful to you.

I'm not lying about that. I never thought that my lying to you would endanger you, in any way. I thought you would be there for me, and then, when you signed on to help Griff, I thought that was nice." Zachary frowned, his expression darkening. "But I never thought you would be jeopardized. I didn't think that you would try to catch a *serial killer.*"

Christine managed a smile. "I didn't mean to, but it turned out that way."

"Thank God you're safe, and I'm free! Almost." Zachary smiled, hunching over the counter. "Now, who's going to tell me what happened?"

Chapter Fifty-six

Christine, Marcus, Griff, and Tanya strolled together toward their cars, Marcus's Audi and Griff's Honda Fit, which they had parked in front of the prison because the lot was empty at this hour, except for a handful of official vehicles. Night had fallen, but the guard towers remained illuminated, and their ambient light glinted cruelly off the coiled razor-wire around the institution. The rain had stopped, but moisture saturated the air, making hazy clouds under the lights in the parking lot and bringing up the natural earthy scents of the surrounding countryside.

Christine breathed in a deep lungful of air, and though it smelled good, she suddenly missed home, where the mist off the ocean salted every breath. She stood in front of Marcus's car with him, turning to Griff and Tanya. "Well, I guess we should go," she said, her throat unexpectedly thick. "We'll stay at the hotel tonight but leave in the morning."

Tanya gave her a quick hug. "Take care, Christine. I'm driving back tonight. It's not that far and I want to see Ranger Rick. It was great meeting you, and you have my information if you want to get back in touch."

"I agree, it was great meeting you, too," Christine told her, meaning it. She really liked Tanya's free-and-easy attitude about her baby, and it had been fun to get to know another mom who had used a donor.

"Are you okay with the way it turned out with Zachary?"

"Yes, are you?"

"Totally." Tanya glanced at Marcus. "To me, it doesn't really matter how a baby comes into the world, only that it does. I just feel lucky in who my baby is. Best of luck with yours."

"You, too." Christine heard the wisdom in Tanya's words, though she wondered if Marcus did.

"You did a really great thing today." Tanya smiled, her grin bright even in the darkness. "You're going to be a great mother, I can tell."

"Thanks." Christine smiled, but she still felt shaky, especially when she turned to Griff. "I'm going to miss you, coach."

"I'm going to miss you, too." Griff smiled wryly. "Do we have to hug?"

"You know we do." Christine opened her arms and gave him a final hug, then let him go. "Take care of yourself, okay?"

"I will. You, too."

"And stay in touch, will you? I want to hear how your bunion operation goes."

"No problem. I'll email you." Griff chuckled at his own joke.

Christine smiled. "The laugh is going to be on you, Griff. The future is here."

"Don't threaten me." Griff chuckled and looked up at Marcus, extending a hand. "Take care of her, young man. You've got a keeper. I miss my wife every day."

Christine teared up at the unexpected tenderness in Griff's tone. It was too dark to see his expression in any detail, and she knew how his face would look, right at this moment. Still, she would never forget him, or the lesson he taught the teacher.

Marcus shook Griff's hand. "I will, sir. Stay well, and fight the good fight."

"Nah. I'd just rather be a lawyer." Griff laughed in earnest, and they all joined him.

Marcus turned to Christine, his mouth still tight. "Honey, ready to go?"

"Sure," Christine answered, waving good-bye to Griff and Tanya. "Good-bye now!"

"Drive safe!" Griff called back. "Stay off the damn phone!"

Christine laughed as she walked to the car, turning her back on the prison. It felt good to put the place behind her, maybe even to put Zachary behind her.

After all, she knew what she was leaving behind.

She just didn't know what she was going to.

Chapter Fifty-seven

Christine rode in the passenger seat while Marcus drove in silence, wending his way through the country roads that led back to West Chester. She knew him well enough to know that he was mulling over everything that had happened and formulating his thoughts. He would know what he wanted to say by the time they got to the hotel, where they would probably have it out. She hoped that they still had a marriage, by midnight.

"You hungry?" Marcus asked, as they steered around a curve.

"Yes, but I don't really want to eat anything right now. I'm mostly tired."

"I bet." Marcus fell silent, and Christine rested her head on the headrest, turning her face to the window, though she couldn't see much. There were no streetlights along the two-lane road, and dark clouds passed in front of the moon. She watched shadowy pastures whizz by and horses grazing in groups, their shadows indistinct. She realized she had seen enough horses for a lifetime. She wanted to see boats, again. And the beach.

"Are you in pain?"

"No," Christine answered, though the question was ambiguous. Even she didn't know the answer, anyway. She wasn't sure what she knew, anymore. She would know better after they had their fight at the hotel.

"Did they give you Advil or anything like that?"

"No, it's fine."

"Who held your hair when you threw up this morning?" Marcus's tone softened, and Christine smiled.

"I had to do it all by myself."

"That sucks. By the way, Lauren says hi. She was worried about you. I called your mom, too. I didn't want her to find out from TV. Luckily they had the game on."

"Thanks." Christine felt a guilty twinge.

"She's okay, but she wants us to call her tonight. We can call from the hotel."

"Thanks for calling her."

"No problem." Suddenly Marcus slowed the car, pulled over, and braked by the side of the road, their tires popping on the gravel.

"What are you doing?" Christine turned, puzzled.

"I want to talk to you, and I don't want to wait."

"Okay." Christine felt her chest tighten. She looked Marcus in the eye, and she could see that he was upset, the troubled curves of his handsome face illuminated by the bluish-green lights on the dashboard.

"I was wrong, and I'm so sorry about everything that happened, the way it all went down." Marcus hesitated, clenching his jaw. "I never should've let you come down here yourself. I've been a total jerk about everything, from the very beginning, even from my diagnosis. You were right that night in the backyard, I made it all about me. It was all about me."

Christine swallowed hard, in surprise.

"But when you left, after I saw what you were willing to do, how far you were willing to go for that baby, our baby"—Marcus's eyes began to glisten, but he blinked them clear—"it made me think. It made me understand. I married you for a reason, because

I love you and because I want to go through this life with you. I didn't want you to be alone ever, especially not during the tough times. We're in this together, no matter what, but it took your going away for me to realize that."

Christine couldn't believe what she was hearing. Marcus had never spoken this way before, or with so much emotion. She felt herself soften, letting her guard down.

"And that's when I realized that that's what being a parent really is. Being a parent, being a *father*, is putting somebody else first, but I never was a father before, and truly, I never put anybody first before, not even you." Marcus's eyes brimmed with tears. "But that's going to change, it already has, and that's why I left this morning, even before Gary called. I was coming down here to bring my wife and my baby home, where they belong."

Christine felt all of her love for him come rushing back, warming her from the inside and out, flowing through her veins like lifeblood, but she didn't interrupt him because she could see he wasn't finished.

"I want to be a better father than my father was, not let my pride and ego get in the way of everything in my life, ruin it all, and hurt the people I love most, like you. Honey, it took me awhile, and I'm slow on the uptake, but I finally figured out *exactly* who the father of that baby is. It's *me. I'm* the father."

"Oh, babe," Christine said, reaching for him, and Marcus reached for her at the same moment, and they clung to each other, husband and wife, bruised and battered, alone in the darkness, in the middle of the countryside. But for the first time, their embrace made a shelter for their baby.

And it was time to go home.

Epilogue

I t was a typical January in Connecticut, and the third winter storm of the season blew outside, hard enough to rattle the windows in the house. Snow buried main roads, covered rooftops and cars, and burdened tree branches and power lines, but Christine felt safe and warm, cocooned inside their bedroom. Marcus had insisted that they buy a generator, not wanting to take any chances with a power outage since the arrival of one Brian Paul Nilsson, currently nine pounds, two ounces, born two weeks ago with a smile on his face.

And everyone else's, too.

Christine's labor had gone as well as could be expected for the most excruciating pain any woman would ever have, but Marcus had cheered her on, telling her when to push and when not to and cutting the umbilical cord after baby Brian had made his entrance, so quietly that they both worried something had gone wrong. Brian had burst into lusty crying soon enough, and Christine got to be in the other scene she'd always dreamed about, the one with the new mom lying exhausted and sweaty after labor, holding an adorably weighty package of person, who had blue eyes, cute little lips, and enough brown hair on his head to qualify as a fright wig.

The memory lingered happily as she lay in bed, in the middle of the night, the bedroom dark except for the TV, where a bundled-up meteorologist stuck a yardstick into a massive snowdrift. She kept the TV tuned to the Weather Channel these days, sitting out the endless cycle of bad news on CNN and the like. She had seen enough violence for an entire lifetime, and she still couldn't get the images out of her mind, popping into her consciousness when she least expected it, like a mental ambush. She took comfort in knowing that the authorities had more than ample proof that Dom Gagliardi had murdered Gail Robinbrecht, Susan Allen-Bogen, and Lynn McLeane; there had been horrifyingly incriminating photos in his computer, and they'd found so-called "trophies" he kept from all three nurses, which the police did not reveal to her, and she didn't need to know more. Zachary had been set free, returning to his job at Brigham and saving for medical school with renewed determination.

Christine thought of him from time to time, even now, and though the entire episode had been awful, it had been a blessing in disguise. Marcus had been right that they weren't back at square one, because without what happened with Zachary in Pennsylvania, she and Marcus never would have gotten their marriage back on track, and Marcus would never have embraced the baby the way he had, from the moment Brian was born. A new father was born that very day, too, and the truth came out in the open, never to be denied again, even to Brian himself, when the time came.

Christine counted her blessings, lying there in the darkness, knowing even as she was living it that this was another scene from a movie she'd always wanted to be in, where the father was taking a nighttime feeding with the baby, using her pumped breast milk. He was trying to give her a break to sleep, but she couldn't and didn't even want to, savoring the sweetness of the moment. Through the baby monitor, she could hear Marcus humming his little Swedish folksong as he rocked the baby in the nursery. The very sound brought tears to her eyes, and Christine didn't know how she got so lucky, or so blessed.

She looked forward to the other scenes she'd always hoped she'd be in: the one with Brian's first steps, then when he went to kindergarten, when he read his first Dr. Seuss book, when he met his first girlfriend, then went to prom and college, and on and on and on, in the series of scenes that are the expectations every parent has, in the movies we make of our own lives. Christine knew that some of her expectations would be met, some maybe even surpassed, and still others would go very differently from the way she'd expected, but she was ready for everything that came their way.

What she had wanted the most was a child, perfect in all its imperfections, and she had gotten what she wished for.

In fact, she had gotten something even better.

A family.

Acknowledgments

I have been wanting to write about a teacher for a long time. I feel as if educators don't get the credit they deserve, and the more teachers I meet, the more amazed and impressed I am by their energy, dedication, and heart. I feel like they are true heroes, so it was natural for me to finally make a heroine out of one, the fictional Christine Nilsson, and I hope that by doing so, we can shine a spotlight on teachers everywhere.

The first thanks go to teachers, for all they do for all of us, and especially to Kellie Bean, a reading specialist in the Owen J. Roberts School District. Kellie took me to an elementary school, introduced me to all of her amazing colleagues, and answered every question I had about life as a teacher. I am so grateful to Kellie for the time she took and for her sharing all of her expertise with me. I like her so much and admire her even more, and she deserves major thanks here. And thanks to Malinda McKillip, principal of French Creek Elementary in the Owen J. Roberts School District.

On a different point, I loved writing this novel partly because I learned so much about the subject of infertility and its treatments, as well as the emotional difficulties that people who have fertility issues undergo. For that I turned to a number of experts, and I would like to acknowledge them. It should go without saying, but it never does, that all of the doctors, medical professionals, and medical clinics in the novel are entirely fictional, and also that any and all mistakes in the novel are mine.

Thank you to Dr. Michael Glassner, Dr. John Orris, and Dr. Sharon Anderson of Main Line Fertility Clinic, who spent so much time educating me about infertility and its treatments. They are simply the most dedicated and caring professionals you can ever imagine, and they perform miracles every day. I couldn't be more grateful or respect them more, and they deserve big thanks here. And thanks to Liz Verrecchio, andrologist, and Anne Yarrow Walters, insurance specialist, also at Main Line Fertility, for all of their help. Plus Raisinets!

Thank you to Dr. Andrea Boxer and to Dr. Judy Mechanic Braverman, both of whom are psychologists who specialize in treating couples dealing with infertility. Both of these incredible women shared their expertise and their kindness with me, helping me understand what it would be like to be in the position of the main characters in this novel. I am indebted to them, and thank them very much.

Thank you to Rose Jardine, an experienced genetics counselor, who helped me understand the genetics behind sperm and egg donation. Thank you to Dr. Allison Shirker of Women's Health Care Group of Pennsylvania.

Special thanks to John Bierkan—and Smartie Martie!

Finally, I'm a bookaholic, so I read a lot which I hoped informed this novel. (As the reading specialists say, first you learn to read, then you read to learn.) I heartily recommend the following books: *The Root Cause: Male Infertility and How to Get Past It* by Gabriel Leone, *Test Tubes and Testosterone: A Man's Journey into Infertility and IVF* by Michael Saunders, *How to Make Love to a Plastic Cup: A Guy's Guide to the World of Infertility* by Greg Wolfe, *What to Expect When You're Expecting* by Heidi Murkoff, *Finding Our Families* by Wendy Kramer and Naomi Cahn, *Taking Charge of Your Fertility* by Toni Weschler, and *The Serial Killer Files* by Harold Schechter.

I'm a lawyer, but criminal law wasn't my field. I needed help and I turned to my dear friend, as well as a brilliant and dedicated public servant, Nicholas Casenta, Esq., chief of the Chester County District Attorney's Office. Nick has helped me with every single book so far, and I wouldn't dream of writing without his advice and expertise. Special thanks as well to Jerry Dugan, Esq., one of the most experienced lawyers in Philadelphia, who helped me navigate the legal details in the book.

Thank you to Linda Vizi, a former Special Agent with the FBI in Philadelphia, and to Ray Carr, a former profiler with the FBI in Philadelphia, for their expertise and for the time they took to answer all of my questions.

For medical expertise, I turned to genius cardiologist Dr. John O'Hara at Paoli Hospital and to my favorite medical student, soon-to-be-doctor Nora Demchur. And thank you to Sklar Medical Instruments and Vince Gay, Ron Templeton, and Yajaira Reyes.

Special thanks to Keith and Rita Kaplan.

Thank you to my editor, Jennifer Enderlin, who improves every one of my manuscripts, and more important, inspires me every day. And big love and thanks to everyone at St. Martin's Press, the terrific John Sargent, Sally Richardson, Jeff Dodes, Paul Hochman, Jeff Capshew, Stephanie Davis, Brian Heller, Brant Janeway, Lisa Senz, John Karle, Tracey Guest, Dori Weintraub, Michael Storrings, Anne-Marie Tallberg, Nancy Trypuc, Kerry Nordling, Elizabeth Wildman, Elena Yip, Talia Sherer, Kim Ludlum, and all the wonderful sales reps. Big thanks to Michael Storrings, for outstanding cover design. Also hugs and kisses to Mary Beth Roche, Laura Wilson, Samantha Edelson, and the great people in audiobooks. I love and appreciate all of you!

Thanks and big love to Robert Gottlieb of Trident Media Group, whose dedication and wisdom has guided this novel into publication, and to Nicole Robson and her digital media team, who helped me get the word out about this book and my other ones as well. Nicole is so dedicated that she worked through her own pregnancy, for which I am forever grateful! (Welcome to the world, Elle!)

Thanks and another big hug to my dedicated assistant and best friend, Laura Leonard. She's invaluable in every way, and has been for more than twenty years. Thanks, too, to my pal and assistant Nan Daley, and to George Davidson, for doing everything else, so that I can be free to write!

Finally, thank you to my amazing daughter, Francesca, for all the support, laughter, and love she has given me.

Reading
Group
Gold

MOST WANTED

by Lisa Scottoline

In Her Own Words

- "An Idea Is Born":
  An Original Essay from the Author

Keep on Reading

- Ideas for Book Groups
- Reading Group Questions

Special Extra!

- An Excerpt from *One Perfect Lie*

Also available as an audiobook
from Macmillan Audio

For more reading group suggestions
visit www.readinggroupgold.com.

 ST. MARTIN'S GRIFFIN

*A
Reading
Group Gold
Selection*

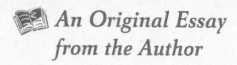

An Original Essay from the Author

"An Idea Is Born"

Readers always ask where I get my ideas, and it's an excellent question. The ideas for my novels always come from some emotional truth in my life, or a personal experience I've undergone, which resonates with me, long afterward. *Most Wanted* is no exception, and on the contrary, arises from the single greatest event of my entire life:

The birth of my only child, my daughter Francesca.

But to tell it true, her birth didn't come at a good time during my marriage. In fact, the marriage was falling apart and my divorce practically coincided with her arrival, almost simultaneously making me a mom and a single mom. (She would later ask me: "Mom, if I'm an only child, does that make you an only mom?" Answer: yes.) It felt as if it were the two of us against the world, but I'm not complaining. None of us knows where our lives will lead, and though our family wasn't a conventional family, we made it work.

My truest goal was to give her a happy home, even if it didn't contain two parents. And no matter what our familial configuration, I fell deeply and madly in love with my beautiful baby Francesca, and I felt lucky to be her mother. Amazingly, my desire to stay home and raise her was the reason I changed my entire life, gave up practicing law, and tried my hand at writing, which led to this wonderful career, thanks to all of you, my readers.

My relationship to my daughter has only grown stronger with time and, paradoxically, I think more often than I ever have before about how lucky and blessed I am to have her in my life. But whenever you count your blessings, you naturally think the opposite—you go to

> *"Whenever you count your blessings, you naturally...go to the what-if question."*

the what-if question. What if I hadn't been so lucky to have had her? What if I hadn't been able to conceive? What about all the marriages unable to produce a baby? And what happens when the vulnerability of a couple desperate to become parents meets the big business of fertility treatments?

From here, the idea for *Most Wanted* was born.

Lately, we are talking more about infertility and reproductive issues in public, and I think that's all to the good. The stigma of infertility has been lifted, as even celebrities are sharing their heart-wrenching stories, and the demand for fertility treatments is a growing business. Oftentimes, modern medicine can intervene and make the dream of a baby come true, but not always without complication. Like my own story, life doesn't always go according to script—and doesn't necessarily turn out the way we expect. However, as for Christine, and for me, the power of a mother's love can conquer all.

Ideas for Book Groups

A note from Lisa:

I am a huge fan of book clubs because it means people are reading and discussing books. Mix that with wine and carbs, and you can't keep me away. I'm deeply grateful to all who read me, and especially honored when my book is chosen by a book club. I wanted an opportunity to say thank you to those who read me, which gave me the idea of a contest. Every year I hold a book club contest, and the winning book club gets a visit from me and a night of fabulous food and good wine. To enter is easy: All you have to do is take a picture of your entire book club with each member holding a copy of my newest hardcover and send it to me by mail or e-mail. No book club is too small or too big. Don't belong to a book club? Start one. Just grab a loved one, a neighbor, or a friend, and send in your picture of you each holding my newest book. I look forward to coming to your town and wining and dining your group. For more details, just go to **www.scottoline.com**.

Tour time is my favorite time of year because I get to break out my fancy clothes and meet with interesting and fun readers around the country. The rest of the year, I am a homebody, writing every day, but thrilled to be able to connect with readers through e-mail. I read all my e-mail, and answer as much as I can. So, drop me a line about books, families, pets, love, or whatever is on your mind at **lisa@scottoline.com**. For my latest book and tour information, special promotions, and updates, you can sign up at **www.scottoline.com** for my newsletter.

Reading
Group
Gold

The Bunnies Book Club of Scottsdale, Arizona, submit
their photo for Lisa's book club contest.

*Keep on
Reading*

 *Reading Group Questions*

1. The struggle to have a child can strain a marriage. What is your overall impression of Christine and Marcus's marriage? How did it evolve over the course of the book? Do you think they would have had problems in their marriage even if they did not have to deal with infertility? If so, why?

2. A large percentage of couples face fertility problems for a variety of issues and turn to modern medicine in order to have a child. Was there anything that you learned about the process that surprised you? Had you ever heard of Marcus's condition? What are your feelings about the entire process? Some view helping infertile couples conceive as "playing God." Do you agree or not? Do you think this is generational? Faced with Christine and Marcus's situation, what option do you think you would have chosen?

3. Through Lisa's research for *Most Wanted*, she discovered that although there is extensive testing of egg donors, including psychological evaluations, the same was not true of sperm donors. Why do you think the standard practices and regulations are so lopsided? Do you think this is reflective of the double standard between men and women? What responsibility do you think the sperm banks should have to their customers? How much follow-up do you think they should be required to do with their donors? Do they owe it to their customers to report concerns, after the fact? Isn't it also true that there are costs associated with such monitoring? And do you think infertile women and men view their medical conditions differently?

4. Couples may be understandably vulnerable by the time they rely on medical intervention to have a baby. Do you think the industry is regulated

enough to protect these people from unscrupulous business practices? What should people do to protect themselves? With the legalization of same-sex marriage, the use of sperm and egg donors is sure to increase. Do you think the industry is prepared for the increase in demand?

5. What rights do you think the child has in this situation? Interestingly, the United States allows anonymous sperm donations, but the United Kingdom requires disclosure to the offspring. What do you think about that difference? Although the donor provides a detailed history, do you think that is enough information for the child? Would you want to meet your donor parent? If you used a donor, how would you feel about your child meeting the donor? At what age, if ever, would you tell your child? Some experts Lisa consulted said six years or even younger is the age at which to tell the child. Agree or disagree?

6. What do you think about nature vs. nurture? Do you think that a tendency toward violence is inherited through DNA or created by the environment to which a person is exposed? What are your thoughts about the warrior gene? Do you think it is a real genetic indicator? With the amount of violence in today's society, do you think children should be tested for it? If yes, under what circumstances; if no, why not? What would be the benefits of this and what would be the downside?

7. The competitive tension between Marcus and his father is palpable. In what ways do you think the competitiveness was positive for Marcus, and in what ways did it have a negative impact? Do you think it was a good idea or a bad idea for Marcus not to partner with his father in his firm? In what ways are Marcus and his father similar,

and in what ways are they different? Who did you like better, and why? Do you think mothers and daughters compete the same way that fathers and sons do? If not, do you think it's all about the testosterone?

8. Like most mothers, Christine will do anything for her child and won't take no for an answer. What is the craziest thing you have done for your child, or what is the craziest thing your parent has ever done for you?

9. Often the allure of committing a crime is the notoriety it brings. Christine poses as someone looking to write a book about the serial killer. Although there are laws in most states that regulate felons making money off book, movie, and TV deals, the attention is still appealing to the criminal. What can we do as a society to reduce the amount of fame that comes with committing a crime? Why do you think we often focus more on the criminal than the victims? How much of the responsibility lies with the media for the stories they report, and how much of it lies with the general public, which supports the sensationalization of these stories?

10. In the end, *Most Wanted* is the story of a family, although one in crisis. Every family faces challenges that can make them stronger, or divide them. What challenges has your family faced, and how did it change your family? In looking back, what would you have done differently, and what would you do the same?

Read on for a sneak peek at Lisa Scottoline's next novel

One Perfect Lie

Available April 2017

Chapter One

Chris Brennan was applying for a teaching job at Central Valley High School, but he was a fraud. His résumé was fake, and his identity completely phony. So far he'd fooled the personnel director, the assistant principal, and the chairperson of the social studies department. This morning was his final interview, with the principal, Dr. Wendy McElroy. It was make-or-break.

Chris waited in her office, shifting in his chair, though he wasn't nervous. He'd already passed the state and federal criminal background checks and filed a clear Sexual Misconduct/Abuse Disclosure form, Child Abuse History Clearance form, and Arrest/Conviction Report & Certification form. He knew what he was doing. He'd done it many times before. He knew he was perfect, on paper.

He'd scoped out the school and observed the male teachers, so he knew what to wear for the interview—a white oxford shirt, no tie, khaki Dockers, and Bass loafers, bought from the outlets in town. He was six-foot-two, 206 pounds, and his wide-set blue eyes, straight nose, broad cheekbones, and friendly smile were generic enough to blend in here, or mostly anywhere. His hair was sandy brown and he'd just gotten it cut at the local Supercuts. Everyone liked a clean-cut guy, and they tended to forget that appearances were deceiving.

His gaze took in Dr. McElroy's office. Sunlight spilled from a panel of windows behind the desk, which was shaped like an L of dark wood, its return stacked with forms, files, and binders labeled **Keystone Exams, Lit & Alg 1**. Stuffed bookshelves and black file cabinets lined the near wall, and on the far one hung framed diplomas from Penn State and West Chester University, a greaseboard calendar, and a poster that read DREAM MORE, COMPLAIN LESS. The desk held family photographs, pump bottles of Jergens and Purell, and unopened correspondence next to a letter opener.

Chris's gaze lingered on the letter opener, an old-fashioned one. Its pointed blade gleamed in the sunlight, and out of nowhere, he flashed to a memory. *No!* the man had cried, which had been his last word. After that had come agonized guttural noises, barely human. Chris had stabbed the man in the throat, then yanked out the knife. Instantly a gruesome fan of blood had sprayed onto him, from residual pressure in the carotid. The knife must have served as a tamponade until Chris had pulled it out, breaking the seal. It had been a rookie mistake, but he was so young, back then.

"Sorry I'm late," said a voice at the doorway, and Chris rose as Dr. McElroy entered the office on a knee scooter, which held up one of her legs bent at the knee, with a black orthopedic boot on her right foot. It was an odd entrance, but otherwise she looked like what he'd expected: a middle-aged professional with hooded blue eyes behind wire-rimmed bifocals, and a lean face framed by clipped gray hair and dangling silver earrings. She even had on a dress with a gray and pink print. Chris got why women with gray hair dressed in gray things. It looked cool.

"Hello, Dr. McElroy, I'm Chris Brennan. Need a hand?" Chris rose to help her, but she scooted forward, waving him off.

"No, thanks. Call me Wendy. I know this looks ridiculous. I had bunion surgery, and this is the way I have to get around."

"Does it hurt?"

"Only my dignity. Please sit down." Dr. McElroy rolled the scooter toward her desk with difficulty. The basket in front of the scooter held a heavy tote bag stuffed with a laptop, files, and a quilted floral purse.

Chris sat back down, watching her struggle. He sensed she was proving a point, that she didn't need help, when she clearly did. People were funny. He had researched Dr. McElroy on social media and her faculty webpage, which had a bio and some photos. She'd taught French for twelve years at CVHS before being promoted to school administration. She lived in nearby Vandenberg with her husband, David, and their Pembroke Welsh corgi, Bobo. Her hobby was agility training with Bobo, who had earned MACH11 points from the American Kennel Club. Dr. McElroy's photo on her teacher webpage was from her younger days, like a permanent Throwback Thursday. Bobo's photo was current.

"Now you know why I'm late. It takes forever to get anywhere. I was home recuperating during your other interviews; that's why we're doing this now. Apologies about the inconvenience." Dr. McElroy parked the scooter next to her chair, picked her purse and tote bag from the basket, and set them noisily on her desk.

"That's okay, it's not a problem."

Dr. McElroy left the scooter, hopped to her chair on one foot, then flopped into the seat. "Well done, me!"

"Agree," Chris said pleasantly.

"Bear with me another moment, please." Dr. McElroy pulled a smartphone from her purse and put it on her desk, then reached inside her tote bag and slid out a manila folder. She looked up at him with a flustered smile. "So. Chris. Welcome back to Central Valley. I hear you wowed them at your interviews. You have fans here, already."

"Great, it's mutual." Chris flashed a grin. The other teachers liked him, though everything they knew about him was a lie. They didn't even know his real name, which was Constantine Rogolyi. In a week, when he had gone, they'd wonder how he'd duped them.

There would be shock, anger, and resentment. Some would want closure; others would want blood.

"Chris, let's not be formal, let's just talk. Since we're running late, I have only a few questions for you." Dr. McElroy opened the manila folder, which contained a printout of Chris's job application, his fake résumé, and his other bogus papers.

"That's fine with me. Shoot."

"Chris, for starters, tell me about yourself. Where are you from?"

"Mostly the Midwest, Indiana, but we moved around a lot. My dad was a sales rep for a plumbing supply company, and his territory kept changing." Chris lied, excellently. In truth, he didn't remember his father or mother. He had grown up in Dayton, Ohio, in the foster-care system.

Dr. McElroy glanced at the fake résumé. "I see you went to the Northwest College in Wyoming."

"Yes."

"Got your certification there, too?"

"Yes."

"Hmmm." Dr. McElroy paused. "You know, most of us here went to local Pennsylvania schools. West Chester, Widener, Penn State."

"I understand." Chris had expected as much, which was why he'd picked the tiny Northwest College as his fraudulent alma mater. The odds of running into anyone here who had gone to college in Cody, Wyoming, were slim to none. People on the East Coast thought the West was flyover buffalo.

Dr. McElroy hesitated. "So, do you think you could fit in here?"

"Yes, of course. I fit in anywhere." Chris kept the irony from his tone. He'd already established his false identity online, with his neighbors, and in town at the local Dunkin' Donuts, Friendly's, and Wegmans, his persona as smoothly manufactured as the corporate brands with their bright logos, plastic key tags, and rewards programs.

"Where are you living?"

"I'm renting in a development nearby. Valley Oaks, do you know it?"

"Yes," Dr. McElroy answered, as he'd anticipated. Chris had picked Valley Oaks because there weren't many other decent choices. Central Valley was a small town in south-central Pennsylvania, known primarily for its outlet-shopping. The factory store of every American manufacturer filled strip mall after strip mall, and the bargain-priced sprawl was bisected by the main drag, Central Valley Road. Also on Central Valley Road were Central Valley Dry Cleaners, Central Valley Lockshop, and Central Valley High School, evidence that the town had no imagination, which Chris took as a good sign. Because nobody here could ever imagine what he was up to.

Dr. McElroy lifted a graying eyebrow. "What brings you to Central Valley?"

"I wanted a change of scenery. My parents passed away five years ago, in a crash. A drunk driver hit their car head-on." Chris kept self-pity from his tone. He had taught himself that the key to evoking the sympathy was to not act sorry for yourself.

"Oh no! How horrible." Dr. McElroy's expression softened. "My condolences. I'm so sorry for your loss."

"Thank you." Chris paused for dramatic effect.

"How about the rest of your family? Any brothers or sisters?"

"No, I was an only child. The silver lining is that I'm free to go anywhere I want. I came east because there are more teaching jobs and they're better-paying. Teachers here are rolling in dough, correct?"

Dr. McElroy chuckled, as Chris knew she would. His starting salary would be $55,282. Of course it was unfair that teachers earned less than crooks, but life wasn't fair. If it were, Chris wouldn't be here, pretending to be somebody else.

"Why did you become a teacher, Chris?"

"It know it sounds corny, but I love kids. You can really see the influence you have on them. My teachers shaped who I am, and I give them so much credit."

"I feel the same way." Dr. McElroy smiled briefly, then consulted the fake résumé again. "You've taught Government before?"

"Yes." Chris was applying to fill the opening in AP Government, as well as the non-AP course Government & Economics and an elective, Criminal Justice, which was ironic. He had fabricated his experience teaching AP Government, familiarized himself with an AP Government textbook, and copied a syllabus from one on-line, since the AP curriculum was nationally standardized. He wondered if the folks at Common Core ever imagined the use that people like Chris could make of that. But whatever, it worked for him if they wanted to turn the public schools into chain stores.

"I must warn you, you have big shoes to fill, in Mary Merriman. She taught here for twenty-two years and was one of our most beloved teachers. The students adore her."

"I'm sure, but I'm up to the task." Chris tried to sound gung-ho. Mary Merriman was the teacher he'd be replacing.

"Still it won't be easy for you, with the spring semester already in progress."

"Again, I can handle it. Don't worry."

"It couldn't be helped." Dr. McElroy sighed, frowning. "Of course, we all understood her need to take care of her father, after his fall. She's reachable by e-mail or phone and would be happy to help you in any way she can."

Whatever, Chris thought but didn't say. "That's great to know. How nice of her."

"Oh, she's a peach, Mary is. Even at her darkest hour, she's thinking of her students." Dr. McElroy smiled. "You'd have to start right away. If I expedite your paperwork, I can get you in class for Thursday, April 16, when the sub leaves. So, you enjoy teaching at the secondary level. Why?"

"The kids are so able, so communicative, and you see their personalities begin to form. Their identities, really, are shaping. They become adults." Chris heard the ring of truth in his own words, which helped his believability. He actually *was* interested in identity and the human psyche. Lately he'd been wondering who he was, when he wasn't impersonating someone.

"And why AP Government? What's interesting about AP Government to you?"

"Politics is fascinating, especially these days. It's something that kids see on TV and media, and they want to talk about it. The real issues engage them." Chris knew that *engagement* was a teacher buzzword, like *grit*. He'd picked up terms online, where there were so many teacher blogs, Facebook groups, and Twitter accounts that it seemed like the Internet was what *engaged* teachers.

"You know, Chris, I grew up in Central Valley. Ten years ago, this county was dairyland, but then the outlets came in and took over. They brought jobs, but we still have a mix of old and new, and you see that in town. There's been an Agway and a John Deere dealership for decades, but they're being squeezed out by a Starbucks."

"I see." Chris acted sad, but that worked for him, too. He was relying on the fact that people here would be friendly, open-hearted, and above all, trusting.

"There's an unfortunate line between the haves and the have-nots, and it becomes obvious in junior year, which you would be teaching." Dr. McElroy paused. "The kids from the well-to-do families take the SATs and apply to college. The farm kids stay behind unless they get an athletic scholarship."

"Good to know," Chris said, trying to look interested.

"Tell me, how do you communicate with students best?"

"Oh, one-on-one, definitely. Eye-to-eye, there's no substitute. I'm a friendly guy. I want to be accessible to them on e-mail, social media, and such, but I believe in personal contact and mutual respect. That's why I coach, too." Chris was also applying to fill their opening for an assistant baseball coach. He'd never coached before, but he was a naturally gifted athlete. He'd been going to indoor batting cages to get back in shape. His right shoulder was killing him.

"Oh, my, I forgot." Dr. McElroy frowned, then shifted through his file. "You're applying for assistant baseball coach. Varsity."

"Yes. I feel strongly that coaching is teaching and vice versa. In other words, I'm always teaching, whether it's in the classroom or on the ball field. The setting doesn't matter, that's only about location."

"An insightful way to put it." Dr. McElroy pursed her lips. "As assistant baseball coach, you would report to Coach Hardwick. I must tell you, he doesn't keep assistants very long. His last one, well, moved on. You haven't met the coach yet, but he can be a man of few words."

"I look forward to meeting him." Chris had researched Coach Hardwick, evidently a well-known jerk.

"The assistant coaching position has remained vacant because Coach Hardwick uses Francie, a retired alum of the school, as his assistant. They're contemporaries."

"I'm sure I can assist Coach Hardwick. Whatever he's doing, he's doing it right. He's an institution in regional high-school baseball, and the Central Valley Musketeers have one of the finest programs in the state."

"That's true." Dr. McElroy nodded, brightening. "Last year, several players were recruited for Division I and II."

"Yes, I know." Chris had already scouted the team online for his own purposes. He hoped there would be a few boys from the baseball team in his Government classes, which would double his chances to evaluate them and choose one. He needed to befriend a quiet, insecure boy, most likely a kid with a troubled relationship to his father. Or better yet, a dead father. It was the same profile that a pedophile would use, but Chris was no pervert. His intent was to manipulate the boy, who was only the means to an end.

"So where do you see yourself in five years?"

"Oh, here, in Central Valley," Chris lied. In truth, he only had a week. It gave new meaning to the word deadline.

"Why here, though? Why us?" Dr. McElroy tilted her head skeptically, and Chris sensed he had to deliver on this answer.

"I love it here, and the rolling hills of Pennsylvania are a real thing. It's straight-up beautiful. I love the quiet setting and the small-town vibe." Chris leaned over in a way as if he were about to open his heart, when he wasn't even sure he had one. "But the truth is, I'm hoping to settle down and raise a family. Central Valley feels just feels like *home*."

"Well, that sounds wonderful! I must say, you lived up to my expectations." Dr. McElroy smiled warmly and closed the file. "Congratulations, Chris, you've got the job! Let me be the first to welcome you to Central Valley High School."

"Terrific!" Chris extended his hand over the desk, flashing his most sincere grin.

It was time to set his plan in motion, commencing with step one.